Ferris Beach

Jill McCorkle

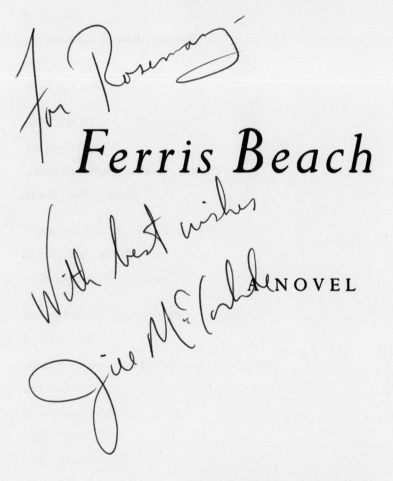

Ferris Beach

A NOVEL

For Rosemary —

With best wishes

Jill McCorkle

Algonquin Books of Chapel Hill

1990

10/11/90

Published by

Algonquin Books of Chapel Hill

Post Office Box 2225

Chapel Hill, North Carolina 27515-2225

a division of

Workman Publishing Company, Inc.

708 Broadway

New York, New York 10003

The author wishes to thank her parents
and parents-in-law for their constant
support and encouragement.

Library of Congress Cataloging-in-Publication Data

McCorkle, Jill

Ferris Beach : a novel / by Jill McCorkle. — 1st ed.

p.   cm.

ISBN 0-945575-39-4

I.   Title.

PS3563.C3444F4   1990

813'.54—dc20   90-37089   CIP

10   9   8   7   6   5   4   3   2   1

First Edition

In celebration of Claudia

For Dan, with love

Ferris Beach

One

Our neighborhood was never the same after Misty Rhodes and her family moved in across the street. While my mother and our neighbor, Mrs. Theresa Poole, mourned the loss of the farmland and the barns and sheds dating back to the 1800s, I rejoiced in finally having the chance of someone my own age close by. The days of blindfolding myself and wandering around my room in Helen Keller simulation, spelling words into my own hand as I acted out Annie Sullivan's role as well as Helen's, were drawing to a close. Instead I perched by the window, watching as moving van after moving van came down our street.

"The split-levels are coming! The split-levels are coming!" Mrs. Poole had announced at a meeting of the historical society at which she and my mother and several others attempted to prevent the sale of the stretch of land in front of us. Known for her do-gooding and her white Lincoln Continental, Mrs. Poole was soon known as well for that proclamation.

Our own house was built in the early 1800s, and my mother had gone to great lengths to learn its history. "There was a time when there was not another house within ten miles of this one," a state historian had told her when he came to photograph our house and list it on the state historical register. He gave her a lot of information which she carefully typed on heavy bond paper and filed away with all of her other historical information. My mother had grown up in Boston, and didn't live in the South until she was sent to a girls' school in Virginia. She had many papers, like pedigrees, that told of various ancestors. The sharp edges of her accent had been filed down over the years, slowed and softened; they appeared only occasionally when she talked about raking the *yard* or playing *cards* or how life was *hard*.

"You, Mary Katherine, have the best of both worlds," she told me the day we were pulling together all of the paperwork necessary for my joining the Children of the Confederacy. I was not thrilled over joining a club, but it was one of those times when it was just easier to go along with her. She had relatives who had served on both sides, so finding the name of the necessary ancestor was as easy as flipping open one of her books. I think her greatest ambition was that I, too, spend my summer mornings at little meetings where I had to dress as if it were Easter Sunday.

She fanned out brochures on historical organizations and showed me her collection of various pins and certificates, essays she had written in school, lectures she had given while teaching school, all the while ignoring my father's comments on *his* lineage, which he said was composed of Scotch, Irish, Polish, and whatever else *took root* down in South Carolina. He had grown up in a small town the other side of Ferris Beach.

"You're half Scotch and half soda," he said, and raised his glass. My mother didn't even glance up from her yellowed certificates, her broad bony shoulders bent slightly as she smoothed her fingers over some document or the Formica tabletop. Sometimes she ignored him completely, unclipping and retwisting her thick hair and humming over his voice. Once dark, her hair was almost completely gray and the severe pull of her bun made her look older than she was.

My parents never looked like they went together to me, even in the wedding photo that was permanently placed on our living room mantel. I expected the real spouses to step in from the wings on either side. My dad was a lean man, always with a cigarette between his thin fingers, his gestures quick and animated as he moved through the house, forever pacing. Though most of his time was spent teaching math at the local community college, he had great ambitions of writing the perfect murder mystery, one with a plot that had to be solved mathematically. It was not unusual for him to suddenly jump up and run to write down a series of numbers while my mother shook her head and looked up at the ceiling. My mother was tall and big-boned, usually the tallest woman in the room but never settling for flat shoes. For every animated move my father had, she had composure and reserve; the only time my mother lost her calm control were those times my cousin Angela showed up at our house and my father escaped behind the closed living-room door or out into the darkness of the porch to have talks with her, conversations that were not repeated or explained.

Really, all I knew of Angela was what he had told me, that his sister, unmarried and only seventeen, had a complicated delivery and died soon after, that his mother had raised the baby and as a result he felt Angela was more like his little sister or even his own child. I had no memories of my grandmother, but he spoke of her so often that I saw her in a magical sort of way, this little white-haired lady whose husband had run a shrimping boat, her face and hands a weathered brown from hot days spent surf fishing or shaking the sand from white sheets she hung on a line. When I imagined myself being lifted from the world like the Little Match

Girl, she was the one who came for me. My father said that she was a brilliant lady, a poet's soul buried in a tough little shell; my mother described her as a poor sad woman who lost her mind.

My father's name was Alfred Tennyson Burns, known to all as Fred. My grandmother had told him that he was named for a lord, a nobleman like the ones she'd spent her entire palmetto-spangled life dreaming of, a poetic lord or a knight to ride up and carry her off across the coastal plain, tide pools spraying and sand flying. She had originally wanted to name him for a knight, her first choice being Sir Arthur Conan Doyle, but at the last minute decided that she preferred Fred to Art.

"Why didn't she just name you Robert?" my mother once asked. "It would have been the easiest route to a poetic name. Robert Burns."

"Had to be a lord or a knight," he said. "You can call me 'my lord.'"

"This from such a brilliant lady," my mother said, and shook her head, giving me a *you see what I mean* look as she unclipped her bun. She held a gold bobby pin between her thin pink lips as she pulled her hair back more tightly.

Either way, my father had been affected by his given and almost-given names; he was forever quoting Tennyson or telling me in great detail a Sherlock Holmes plot. He was a Thomas Hardy fan, too, and at my birth had wanted to name me Arabella, which my mother said sounded like something you'd better hope not to get during pregnancy. I thought my life would have been so different if I had started off with another name, an inspirational name like Madame Marie Sklodowska Curie or Joan of Arc, Amelia Earhart. Arabella. I used to stand in front of the mirror in the entryhall of our house and run that name over my tongue in whispers. Just the movement of the mouth to sound the word was sexy, its open-mouthed ending coming with shallow, quickened breath. I would watch my plain face sound the word, and for a second it seemed like there was something else there. I could say "Angela," and my mouth would form the same shape, tongue pressed forward to shape the lull of the *l*, as when I said "bella." My mother's name, Cleva, was tight-lipped with teeth clenched on that long *e*, and my own, Katie or Kate, was like a short sharp bite.

I was five when I first met Angela. My father took me to Ferris Beach, making a big show when we crossed the South Carolina line. We stood for hours just listening to the roar of the surf and wedging our feet into the cool packed sand. Angela appeared at the top of a sand dune, her thick auburn hair blowing behind her. My father squeezed my hand and laughed out loud, as loud as the surf. "There she is," he screamed, and then once again, almost in a whisper, "There she is." She greeted me as if I were grown, her cool fingers gently cupping and covering my left cheek and neck where I had a birthmark the color of wine. ("It's not your fault, Cleva," I had recently overheard Mrs. Poole tell my mother. "I suspect God has his own reasons for painting her that way.") Angela pressed her lips to that same cheek, and then she draped her many strands of beads around and around my neck while we ate the fried chicken she had packed in a basket.

"What was I thinking, Fred?" she asked. "I forgot something for the child to drink." I sat there with her on the faded quilt while my father walked up the beach and through the dunes to the old bait shop to buy a carton of milk. She twisted the cork from a bottle and filled her glass with burgundy. The day was supposed to be a secret, but in the exhilaration of seeing the ocean for the first time, I let it all slip from my mouth into my mother's ear, where it fell solid, lodging in her chest.

Not long after that we were invited by Mrs. Poole and some of her church friends to a picnic at Cherry Grove Beach, which Mrs. Poole said was "light-years better than Ferris Beach." These women were quite a bit older than my mother, so I was the only *child* present. They didn't even wear bathing suits but sat fully clothed under big striped umbrellas, and the whole day was all planned as neatly as if bells went off in their heads to signal the next event. Keep your shoes on because the shells are sharp and will cut clean through to the bone. Set the places and we mustn't forget to set *His* place, we mustn't forget to thank *Him* for this cold fried chicken and the quart of milk. Don't you forget if you get the urge in that warm salty water to take off your bathing suit and pee, that *He* is watching you, and *He* will know what you did, and if you have a thought about how good it feels to be all naked and running your hands down your body, then rest assured *He* will know. And, oh, my Lord, don't even look to your left unless you want to see a suit that shows all that a woman has to show.

I spent much of the day digging in the sand by the edge of the water, burying my feet and then letting wave after wave wash them clean. The things those women talked about were things that could keep you awake for the rest of your life, death and illness and poverty and insurance policies and *he will get his due*. It was so easy to sin, as easy as telling a lie, or saying damn or saying that men come from monkeys, or kissing the glossy paper mouth of a movie star on a poster. And how could God keep it all sorted, all these *direct lines*, these prayers that were shot up to him like bullets, crisscrossing, ricocheting, contradicting, negating. *I just hope that she will live until young Owen graduates from college. Well, I just hope she dies quickly and quietly—at peace. How can you be wishing her dead like that? I for one pray that there will come a cure for cancer. I pray for the doctors in the laboratory. I have a cousin whose son-in-law is working at the NIH in D.C. I pray they don't get a divorce even though my cousin says she prays for what is best for the both of them.* If his eye had been just on those three striped umbrellas on the Cherry Grove strand, he could not have met their demands, not even to mention those of the rest of the world; this was prime time, a Sunday afternoon, and the thought of having to sort through all those requests made my head spin. It was that very day that I attached to Angela everything beautiful and lively and good; she was the easy flow of words and music, the waves crashing on Ferris Beach as I spun around and around because I couldn't take in enough of the air and sea gulls as they swooped and whined. Angela was energy, the eternal movement of the world, the blood in my veins and the wind in the bare winter branches that creaked and cried out in the night like tired ghosts in search of a home. She was the answer to a prayer and I thought about that day at Ferris Beach often, recreating every word and every movement before I fell asleep.

By the time I was eight, when her face was getting hard for me to remember, I imagined her holding my hand and spelling secret messages into them. By then I had read the biography of Helen Keller nine times, each time finding something new, each time working on the alphabet on the last page, each time conjuring what was left of my memory of Angela.

"You cannot check this out another time this year," the Pine-top librarian had said when I tried to check the book out for the tenth time; she was exasperated by all the noise a classroom of eight-years-olds can make just entering a room. "Somebody else might want to read about Helen Keller."

"What if I wait until the end and nobody's checked it out?"

"There are other classes, you know," she said, her lips pushed forward like all those cartoons of the North Wind getting ready to blow, and then she stomped off to yank Merle Hucks and R. W. Quincy by the arms and to tell them to stop rubbing their feet on the new indoor-outdoor carpet and then touching people to shock them. It was the only exciting thing going on in the library. "You're gonna rub this carpet bare," she said. There were perspiration circles under her plump arms even though it was wintertime. "Now find a chair." She turned to heave herself back to the desk while they ran around behind her acting surprised like they *had* found chairs. Nobody pronounced R. W. Quincy's name right, like the teacher begged us to do. "R Double U," she would say, and he'd tell her his name was "R Dubyah," that he was not a fancy talker and if his mama had meant for him to be named R Double U, then she would've called him that instead of R Dubyah. The librarian said it our way, which made our teacher give her a dirty look. R. W. was the tallest boy in the class because he had stayed back once in first grade and again in second; he wore a dirty piece of twine around his neck with a little blue ratfink hooked to it. Merle Hucks had a black ratfink with red eyes, which was supposed to be good luck since they were so rare.

"So can I read Helen Keller?" I whispered.

"Are you deaf?" she asked me, and R. W. Quincy, who was standing there wanting to check out a book on stockcar racing, said, "What? What, Miss Liberrian?"

"The split-levels are here," Mrs. Poole said the day Misty's family moved in, and waved her hand at the row of houses as if she could make them disappear. "That kind of house is not designed for country like this, now is it?"

I was nine that August, and for a month I had watched one big moving van after another bringing someone new to our street, always it seemed, a family with babies instead of someone close to my age. Misty's house was identical to the other six split-levels already occupied and the three which were springing up around the corner. "I'd need bread crumbs to find my way home," Mrs. Poole said, her pursed lips painted the same shade as the blooms on our fuchsia plant. "I hear somebody over on Maple," she paused, pointing her thin finger through the split-levels to the street parallel to ours, "is building a ranch out of some kind of board that just goes its own way in the weather."

Misty's house was my favorite of the whole bunch; it was white with blue shutters—*electric blue*, Mrs. Poole said in a hushed whisper later that same day while she stared at the big moving van with South Carolina tags. "I saw what looked like it might be a bar, you know to house liquor," she whispered. "I've heard of neighborhoods going down this way." Mrs. Poole kept talking but stared over at the Rhodeses' house. "It happens slowly in the beginning, one house here, another there, and then before you know it, the decent people stop coming, and more and more riffraff come in, prices drop and so others can afford to come in." She paused and then tilted her head toward the back of our property lines which ended in a tangled field of kudzu and a row of tiny pastel houses. "A colored family lives down there," she whispered. "It *can* happen."

"Peacock blue," Mrs. Rhodes said, smiling at Mr. Rhodes, a Sherwin-Williams paint sampler in her hand. Mr. Rhodes was up on a ladder putting the final touches on the trim of the porch awning. "Now nobody will mistake our house for another." I had been standing on the curb for about three minutes, though it seemed like hours. Mr. Rhodes wore an old baseball cap to shield his face from the sun, but already his cheeks were bright pink like the skin on Misty's sunburned nose. Misty looked just like him with that strawberry hair and doughy white skin, made even whiter in contrast with her mother's tan, a shade so deep you might wonder if she was from another place altogether. "Do you think she's foreign?" Mrs. Poole had asked and then turned back to her rose bushes, the nozzle of her hose tuned to a fine mist.

"Peacock blue just like my Misty's eyes," Mrs. Rhodes said, and hugged this plump pale girl, who seemed to be much more interested in the superball that her skinny older brother was bouncing against the brick wall of the carport than she was in meeting me. "My Misty is just your age, nine going on twenty," Mrs. Rhodes said to me and laughed, but Misty was still eyeing me suspiciously, and why wouldn't she? I had come bearing a paper plate of delicate little homemade ladyfingers and my mother's instructions to ask where they were from. If I had been in her shoes, I would not have trusted me either.

"Wouldn't you love to have peacocks in your yard?" Mrs. Rhodes asked, and turned to me. Her thick dark hair was pulled back in a ponytail as she stood there barefooted in cropped jeans, her toenails painted pale pink. It was her eyes that were peacock blue, and this Misty that she hugged up so close had just a washed-out version to go with her frizzy orange hair and freckled arms. I was about to nod that I'd love some peacocks, but before I could she was asking another question. "Fourth grade?" she said to me, which I came to learn quickly was her way of asking a question, all but the key words deleted—like hungry? tired? sad?, the way you might talk to an infant. "Yes," I said and tried to take in all the things scattered about in their carport because I knew I'd be quizzed: a black sewing mannequin dressed in a lime-green miniskirt and halter top, a stone statue of a fish with its mouth wide open, a little miniature pagoda, bags and bags of gravel, and lots of little lanterns and tiki torches. "Pinetop?" she asked me, which was the name of the elementary school nearby, and again I nodded yes. Misty was still just standing there staring at me. She was slapping a flyback paddle against her bare thigh.

"Let's eat these cookies you brought. I just can't wait." Mrs. Rhodes grabbed me by the hand and then pulled both of us through the coolness of the carport, past the mannequin and rocks, and into the box-cluttered kitchen, where she poured glasses of Coca-Cola and put on an Elvis Presley record. I was not allowed to drink soda on a regular basis, but I didn't say a word. Rather, I sat in complete awe of this woman whose purple wooden earrings swung back and forth as she talked. I envied the silent girl across from me.

Misty. On first meeting, I thought her name a cruel joke, as cruel as someone huge named Bitsy or Teeny. "What's your name again, hon?" Mrs. Rhodes asked. Her hips moved back and forth in rhythm with "Heartbreak Hotel." "Mary Katherine— but people call me Katie," I said and then without thinking added, "My dad sometimes calls me Kitty." It slipped, this nickname my mother despised. "Kitty," she said, and stared at me, smiling, while Misty gave me a dirty look. "I like that. I like the way it sounds, the same way I like Misty."

"Right." Misty finally spoke. Her voice was nasal and much deeper than I'd expected from someone with such pale skin. "I was named for a horse. And you were named for a cat." Her deadpan expression brought Mrs. Rhodes over to her chair.

"No, honey," she squealed in laughter and threw her arms around Misty's neck. "You know the story of how I thought of your name." She turned to me briefly. "Misty is named for Themista Rose Allen, a young woman I never knew but just heard about, sort of a local legend where I'm from." She pressed her cheek against Misty's. "You weren't named for the horse, even though I did think that was such a romantic sounding name, Misty of Chincoteague, only you were Misty of Ferris Beach." Misty just stared down at the vanilla wafers and ladyfingers on the paper plate in front of her, her mouth tightened into a straight line. "Johnny Mathis must think it's a romantic name, too; he named a song that."

"Yeah, yeah, yeah, and you're named for the Three Stooges," Misty of Ferris Beach said, and paused with a vanilla wafer in hand. "Hello? Hello? Hello? Hello!" she said, in perfect Three Stooges rhythm, and she was beginning to smile now, as if this was a routine the two of them had played through many times before.

And then her mom, hand gently placed on Misty's head, began singing, *Look at me, I'm as helpless . . .* "Oh yuk," Misty Rhodes said and bit into a ladyfinger, leaving a ring of powdered sugar on her lips. "These cookies are pretty good," she said. "They're almost as good as the store-bought kind." Then for the first time, I heard that laugh, shrill and hyena-like. I often thought it was like in the comma rule When in doubt do without; Misty's version was When in doubt, laugh, and the louder the better.

"So what's your brother's name," I asked. I could see him

through the window, there at the base of the ladder staring up at his father. He was a perfect blend of mother and father, dark hair and pale skin. He looked like he was probably two or three years older than us.

"Flicka," Misty said, and again laughed that laugh. "Do you think he's cute?" In the same way that Mrs. Rhodes asked her key-word questions, Misty asked the impossible-to-answer kind. If I said no, which was my impulse after having seen his thin pointed features and the blue veins visible in his cheek, then they would be insulted. If I said yes, then I was in for teasing or my own humiliation when they told him and he responded to whether or not he thought *I* was cute. I shrugged.

"Misty," Mrs. Rhodes said, and smiled. "If you aren't a card and a half. Don't embarrass Kitty." It sounded so odd for her to call me that, and I knew that I had made a terrible mistake in telling her about the nickname. "And I did not name the child Flicka even though I was tempted." She turned to me, her eyes briefly lingering on my birthmark. "His name is Dean. James Dean Rhodes."

"But we like to call him Flicka."

"Now, cut that out, you." Mrs. Rhodes swatted playfully at Misty. "Kitty's not going to want to come back if you act this way." She went to the kitchen window and rapped on the glass. "Dean? Dean?" she called until he ran over and pressed his face flat against the glass like a Pekingese. "Cookies?" I decided I'd leave while he was coming in, so I stood up.

"Is that a birthmark you have?" Misty asked, and leaned forward, her bare legs squeaking on the red linoleum seat of her chair.

"Misty!" Mrs. Rhodes stepped forward, hands on her hips, and I focused on the tiny gold chain around her ankle while I nodded, while James Dean Rhodes walked past us and opened the refrigerator.

"It's just a question," she said, more to her mother than to me, and then reluctantly she reached out and tugged on the back of my T-shirt. "I'm sorry."

"It's okay," I said, and quietly pushed my chair away from the table to stand. "I need to go home."

"Oh, I wish you'd stay," her mother said. "Why, you haven't even met Dean. Dean, this is Kitty from next door."

"You can call me Katie," I said, but he just shrugged and went back to drinking from a water jar that had his name stuck to the top with masking tape.

"I didn't mean to hurt your feelings," Misty continued, her face not showing any emotion at all. "I think it's kind of neat." She was trying way too hard by this time. "It's sort of shaped like Italy, you know, like an old granny boot."

"Misty." Mrs. Rhodes's face was as red as her husband's, but something in what Misty had to say, though not my favorite thing to hear, had struck me. It did sort of look like Italy; she was completely honest and I found I liked that.

"I have some granny glasses," she told me. "Want to go to my room and see?"

There was more in her room than I had ever seen, big paper flowers and fans and a stuffed bear that filled one whole corner. She had a chewing-gum-wrapper chain that reached all the way around her room, and it was made from only Clark's Teaberry and Clove, making her whole room smell like those wax lips and whistles that we all bought at Halloween.

After demonstrating the Teaberry shuffle several times, making her little ceramic-dog collection rock on the top of her dresser, she showed me how to make a chain. She played "Hold On" by Herman's Hermits on a record player she had right there in her room. Misty had also memorized every single word of "The Ballad of the Green Berets" and quoted it while I sat there on her bright orange-and-yellow swirled bedspread.

"I have a picture of Sgt. Barry Sadler," she said, and opened a drawer, pulling out a picture of the singer. His little green beret was cocked to one side. "My parents' friend Gene was in the 82nd Airborne Division." I wasn't sure *exactly* what that meant, but I just nodded in agreement, acted impressed because clearly she was. "Gene says if he ever meets Sgt. Barry Sadler that he'll get his autograph." She could also sing "Secret Agent Man" by Johnny Rivers and did so while she twirled her baton over and under her extended arm, doing *the pancake* she called it.

And she did have some granny glasses, dark-green glass in rectangular wire frames; "Like a hippie," she said, while rearranging her paper flowers in one of those melted and stretched-out Coke bottles. Like Annie Sullivan, I was thinking, wanting those glasses for my own.

"You can borrow them sometime," she told me as she put the glasses back in their little plastic case. She unwrapped her last stick of Teaberry gum, bit half, and handed me the rest. "You can borrow them right now if you want."

"It's peacock blue," I reported to my mother and Mrs. Poole, who sat in the kitchen waiting for my report, under the guise that they were planning the big Fourth of July celebration. They both looked so plain and somber compared to Mo Rhodes and her loud-colored pillows and sparkly wall hangings in Oriental designs. Our house looked so sparse and bare compared to the big paper fans and parasols that belonged to the Rhodes family, or to their ceramic table shaped like an elephant. "And they came from Ferris Beach." I tried to say the place as if it meant nothing at all to me, as if I hadn't spent thousands of hours thinking about that one time I had been there, but all it took was the set of my mother's chin to make my cheeks grow hot.

"I find that hard to believe," Mrs. Poole said. "I certainly don't visit the place but certainly I am familiar with most of the names dwelling there." I wanted to say that names don't dwell, people do. "Mr. Poole and I used to take the train and spend a long weekend there every fall. Of course, that was back before you moved here, back when Ferris Beach was a quaint little fishing village and not," she paused, looked at my mother and shook her head, "well, not like it is now." Mr. Poole had been dead for my whole life and all I knew of him was what I had overheard my father say that other people in the town had said: that he had a lot of money, was a powerful man politically, and no one knew why and how he had managed to marry and live with Theresa Poole all those years.

"Misty liked Ferris Beach," I said, watching my mama's back stiffen. "She's my age and has an older brother. Mrs. Rhodes grew up here in town. She moved to Ferris Beach when she married Mr. Rhodes, who was from around there."

"Hush," Mrs. Poole said. "Then you know I'll know who she is. What was her maiden name?" I shrugged, still thinking about all those boxes they had to unpack and trying to imagine what was in them. "What's her first name?"

"Mo," I said, tempted to do the hello hello hello, just as Misty had done, only my mama and Mrs. Poole wouldn't have gotten it, a waste of perfectly good breath. "I think her whole name's Ramona."

"Ramona." Mrs. Poole sat up straighter, her finger in the air like she was about to make an important announcement. "Oh, it's on the tip of my tongue. Her father kept the horse stable down near the river."

"I know she likes horses," I said.

"Oh, of course." Mrs. Poole raised one eyebrow, her face pokerlike. "I do indeed recall that family, the Wileys. Yes, Mo Wiley. She is much younger than us but I do remember her." I wondered why Mama let Mrs. Poole carry on with that "us" when Mrs. Poole must've been at least fifteen years older. Mama poured her another cup of coffee, no sugar no cream. "She was riding horses when she was just a teeny little thing. I used to see her over in the pasture where the highway is." Mrs. Poole pushed away the ashtray and sipped her coffee with her pinkie hooked;

that awful fuchsia lipstick of hers smeared on the cup. "But they were not *her* horses," she said with authority. "They belonged to the boarders, who did not really like a seven-year-old child exercising their horses." She looked at me when she said this, as if to say that nobody liked children—period. "The Wileys did not have a pot to——" She paused, still staring at me.

"Pee in," I added, to which my mother raised a stiff eyebrow.

"Nor a window out of which to throw it." Mrs. Poole sat back and relaxed by letting her hands rest on the table. She could not stand to end a sentence with a preposition.

"I wonder if Mrs. Rhodes knows Angela?" I asked boldly, the excitement of the time I had just spent at Misty's lingering with me. My mother looked up as if in slow motion. Mrs. Poole was leaning forward to hear my mother's response.

"I wouldn't know," Mama said. "She might."

"Now, who is Angela?" Mrs. Poole was still leaning forward. "Not your sister. No, you don't have a sister. Is Angela Fred's sister?" Mrs. Poole was rifling through her purse for a cigarette.

"Niece."

"She doesn't visit very often."

"Hardly ever," Mama said, her voice falling into its original sharpness, her pronunciation like a harsh honk of a goose. She turned to me then. "Kate, why don't you run tell the Rhodeses about the Fourth of July picnic and how the whole town comes. Tell Mrs. Rhodes if she has any questions I am happy to answer them."

"Find out what all those rocks are for," Mrs. Poole called after me, and then I heard her continue talking to my mother. "I just can't imagine what all those rocks are for. And that little wooden structure like something of the Orient. What could that be for? You know I don't think much of the Japanese, haven't since the war. Mr. Poole was in the Pacific, you know, purple heart and various other citations."

My mother's steady flow of yesses and uh huhs were like little commas punctuating all that Mrs. Poole had to say. Every now and then, my mother smoked a cigarette—Mrs. Poole's lengthy tales seemed to trigger the desire—though she would never have let my father know; it was her mission to monitor his heart, to get him to give up his three-pack-a-day habit. Her lectures would be meaningless if he caught her in the act. She breathed in and out heavily, emitting a stream of smoke, while nodding along with Mrs. Poole's words. "I have Mr. Poole's machete and you must've seen it." Yes. "Yes, hanging there by the fireplace. He wrote every day from the Pacific. He said, 'I killed a Jap yesterday.' Just like that: 'I killed a Jap.' You know Mr. Poole was quite the man's man." Uh huh "Yes, hunt, fish, win citations for bravery, you name it. He said, 'Theresa, don't you *ever* buy anything made in Japan, which of course I wouldn't have even thought of doing. Cheap. I don't go for cheap."

By the end of that first week, Mrs. Poole stood on her front porch and watched Mo Rhodes spread rocks all over the lawn, digging up what little bit of grass had begun to grow. She dug a little goldfish pond, in the middle of which stood her fish statue, a fat, friendly-looking fish in sandstone, and she planted a big clump of pussy willows out near the street. "Oh God, oh God," I heard Mrs. Poole mumbling, her head shaking from side to side. The little pagoda was the mailbox and in a perfect line from top to bottom said: Rhodes, 202 Wilkins Road. "Oh God, oh God," she said. "Do let a strong wind come and carry it all off, every pebble you might chance to find. Please just do that for me. Please just answer this one very small prayer and I'll never ask for anything else."

Two

Ferris Beach, just by its very name, had always made me imagine huge Ferris wheels and strings of blinking lights, and cotton candy whipped and spun around a paper cone like I had seen at the small carnivals that passed through town from time to time. My father had grown up just a few miles from there, and he talked about it often, the ocean, his father's boat, the sea gulls circling overhead. I was five the day he took me there, and what I remembered most was the excitement of it all, a surprise, a secret, my mother thinking that we had gone to Clemmonsville to look at new cars. My bathing suit was rolled up with his in a bath towel on the backseat.

"You're going to meet your cousin, too," he said, turning his head to grin at me. "She's gonna love you." He emphasized *love*, laughed as he twisted the radio knob up and down. All we could pick up was the faint static of the Clemmonsville station.

Ferris Beach was nothing as I had expected; there wasn't even an amusement park there, just a pier and lots of bait-and-tackle shops, no motel or tall buildings like in Clemmonsville, just a trailer park and rows of small pastel houses, much like that stretch behind our backyard. Still, I stopped asking to see amazing Ferris wheels when I began to smell the salt breeze and held my hand out the car window to feel the damp mist that seemed to hang in the air and sparkle like a spider web.

"You're about to see the ocean," he said as we crested the old wooden drawbridge, and sure enough, when we came down the hill, I saw green water, smooth as glass way out where it met with the sky, and rolling and cresting and breaking up near the sand. I could not take it all in fast enough, and when we finally got to where we could park and get out, I ran out onto the sand. I kept checking to make sure my father was still there and he was, squatted by a dune, rolling up his trousers. I waited and then the two of us, holding hands, stepped into the water, the waves breaking on our ankles and then on my legs. He lifted me each time a big wave threatened to hit me above the waist—and then I saw Angela. Watching her come down the dune was almost like seeing a movie in slow-motion, seeing every step of her long bare legs, her feet sinking into the hot loose sand. My dad's hand left my shoulder and flew up in a wave, back and forth, back and forth, like a flag heralding the beginning of a parade. She was beautiful there on top of the dune.

"Angela, Angela," he said over and over, his voice muffled in her thick hair. He pushed her back and looked at her, so young-looking and glamorous in her two-piece sparkly gold suit that hit right below her navel.

"And you"—Angela stepped back from my father and stared at me—"Mary Katherine Gates. I'm so glad to finally meet you." She squatted down, a rush of her scent coming to me with the ocean air, perfume or shampoo like gardenias. She studied me carefully, her eyes lingering on my cheek as I reached up to hold it. "Oh, don't hide your pretty little face," she whispered, and took my hand. Her lips were coated in a pale pink frost like cotton candy. "She looks like a Burns," Angela said, and twisted her hand round and round the brightly colored beads she wore, their turquoise blue a perfect match to the terry cloth coverup and the barefoot strapped sandals she carried. "See the copper in her hair?" Angela lifted a strand of my hair, and I strained to see it as well. "And those fine full lips." She pinched my cheeks in like a fish face and then lifted her fingers to her own mouth. "Perfect for doing this," she said, and played her lips up and down while humming like a funny musical instrument or underwater sounds. "And Freddie," she said, and looked up, my dad's shadow falling over her like a net, "you are a sight for sore eyes." She blinked hard several times. Her lashes, separated and painted black, had left small brush strokes just below her thin arched brows.

"Yes," he whispered, and reached out to touch the strand of hair which fell near her eye. "So are you."

"How's the general?" she asked and laughed, her question confusing me until my father said, "Cleva's fine. You know she really has missed you."

"Yeah, right." She waved a hand. "I'll fry like a french fry if I don't put on some lotion." She leaned in close to me, and again I got a deep breath of her gardenia smell, as rich and sweet as our backyard in the early summer.

We sat on her quilt while my dad walked up and over the dunes to go buy some milk for my lunch. She scooped the sand and uncovered a bed of coquinas, their polished, colorful shells seen briefly before they began to dig their way into hiding; she placed one, purple and white, into my palm, and then one by one curled my fingers down around it. "Don't say I never gave you anything," she said, and threw back her head laughing, her tongue stained deep red from the wine, her teeth as white as the shells that glistened with each wave. Her hand was cool, lightly touching my cheek as if it were a burn or a tear, something painful.

When we left Ferris Beach, she was still sitting there, her

hands stretched out behind her, knees bent, head thrown back like in a cover-girl photo. The sun was low in the sky, heavy orange light that made even the most run-down of the bait shops appear gold-flecked and misty, like in a dream.

"I'm meeting someone," she had said when we left her there.

"A man?" my father asked, and she turned her face toward the ocean, leaving us to stare at her profile, and at her beauty mark, a round dark mole just above her lip.

"Always the big uncle now, aren't you?" she asked, laughing softly, her own voice drowned out by a circling gull. "I'm a big girl now, Freddie. Cleva will tell you." She reached out and moved her hand like a crab on the sand to his foot. "I'm a lot older than I look."

"So am I," I said as a way to rejoin their twosome, perhaps to get her to crab her soft hand with those long, glazed nails my way, and they both laughed.

"I just turned twenty-two, remember?" she asked, twisting a strand of her hair round and round her fingers. "I'm legal, dear *uncle*, white, single, the works."

"Well," my father said as he stared out at the ocean, then took a deep breath. "I'm just about always at the college."

"Always?" she asked, laughed again, little lines gathering around the corners of her eyes.

"You know what I mean."

"Yeah, yeah." She waved her hand and then reached and took hold of his. "Monday through Friday. I'll be in touch." She nodded and then turned to me. "And I hope you will keep in touch, too." She pinched my nose lightly and then let her hand linger near my cheek.

"You can touch it again," I told her. "It doesn't hurt." But she just smiled and then let her hand drop to the sand, her glazed nails disappearing in the shiny white grains. "Leave, leave," she said, waving her hands again. "You two are going to be in big trouble with *you know who* if you're late for supper."

When we got to the top of the dunes, my father turned to

look back and she was still there, her arm raised and waving to
a man on the beach; I couldn't tell much about the man from
that distance, only that he looked very tan and wore a cap pulled
low on his forehead. He moved towards her like in those com-
mercials that switch to slow-motion. I walked backwards up the
huge dune, expecting her to turn and wave one last time. "Take
one more look at the ocean, Kitty," my father said, but he was
not watching the ocean. He was watching Angela, who by then
had her head leaned against that man's shoulder as he hugged her
close.

"Who was that man?" I asked.

"I guess a friend of hers." He pushed me towards the dunes
and the bathhouse where I had left my clothes, both of us turning
to wave once more but she wasn't looking. My father was silent
as he drove, smoking one cigarette after another, checking his
watch again and again. The sun was so low that I could stare right
at it without hurting my eyes, and we drove toward the orange
light, weaving along the small bumpy highway that cut through
an empty stretch of marshland.

When we got home Mama was out on the front porch, her
hands in the pocket of her gardening jacket. Her hair, pulled and
pinned and sprayed into place, was hidden under a multicolored
scarf tied at the back of her neck. "I was getting worried!" she
called out. Her cheeks were flushed with color. "Supper's about
ready." She rearranged the clay pots of geraniums on the porch
rail as we walked up. "I was beginning to think you'd left me."
She laughed a quick laugh, her eyes never leaving his face.

"We had a great time," he said. "I drove the new Buick they
had. Boy, is she a beaut."

"Must've been a convertible." She put her fingertip on my
nose and pressed lightly, then turned the collar of my blouse upright, slipping the neck to one side; her fingers felt cool to my hot
shoulder as she touched the line of white where my bathing suit

had been. "Yes, some convertible at that," she whispered, glanced at him once and then turned away. "C'mon, Katie, I think a nice lukewarm bath and some Jergen's lotion will feel real good to your sunburn."

"Well, sure, she got some sun. We pass right by the turn to Merriman Lake on the way to Clemmonsville. You know that. Went for a swim after we finished car shopping."

"At the lake?" Now she looked at me, her eyes steady, and I nodded just as he had done, and then in no time he had his arm around her and had coaxed her into a laugh by demonstrating the difference between a proper and an improper fraction. *Proper*, he said, and guided her onto the sofa, placed me up on her lap. *Improper*, he said and placed me on the center cushion, motioned for her to sit on me.

But later, when I was stretched out on a cool sheet, nearly asleep, and Mama's hand was rubbing lotion into my back, I mentioned the waves rolling and rolling and the little animals that dug their own secret hiding places. With my eyes closed, I could still feel the movement of the sea, the surge and pull as I stood at the edge while my father and Angela waved to me from the quilt where they sat side by side. Like the waves and the energy I had felt on that shore, I could not contain myself.

"You went to Ferris Beach, didn't you?" The movement of her hand never stopped and I just nodded. "Did you like it?"

I nodded, my eyes so heavy I found it difficult to focus on the roses of my wallpaper.

"Did you like . . ." Her voice slipped off like into a well and there was a long pause. I could hear her breath, a deep inhale. "Did you like your cousin?"

"Yes." I dozed then, flowing in and out as if I were riding a wave, her hand on my back, her lips brushing my cheek, the soft yellow glow of the ruffly pin-up lamp above my bed.

After that night, our trip was never mentioned again. The only time I heard Angela's name for a long time after was late at night when I lay in bed and climbed the roses on my wallpaper, up and down, as their voices carried through the vents. He said, *You aren't her mother, Cleva*, and she replied, *But I wanted to be.*

Maybe it was on one of those nights, when I heard their voices muffled and unintelligible, that I came up with the Helen Keller game, the prelude to all those afternoons I spent blindfolded in my room as I remembered Angela and that day at the beach. I would lock the bedroom door, blindfold myself, and then I would begin, pacing off the familiar spaces of my own room. It was amazing how quickly I became disoriented, my hands stretched out, expecting to find the chenille bedspread, to touch its rough nubby knots, and striking only air. It seemed the more I tried to find my way, the harder it became, the harder to breathe, like the panic that comes suddenly in deep water. I would end up ripping the blindfold from my face, blinking back the daylight, always surprised by the softness of my room, with its the pink floral wallpaper and the stuffed toys on the window seat. When I could comfortably make my way without panic, I added the earplugs I had found in my mother's medicine chest. "Katie? Katie, what are you doing up there?" my mother called with each bump and stumble, her voice faint like the distant buzzing of a fly. Helen could not have even heard that. Helen could not have answered had she wanted to. The frustration of it all was overwhelming and left me feeling dizzy and tired.

"Were you playing Helen Keller again?" Mama asked me at supper one night. My father turned his head to one side and coughed a laugh into his linen napkin. "I just don't think it's healthy," she continued. "I don't think it's good to close yourself up in a room and pretend to be blind. My goodness." She brushed a strand of hair, damp from the heat of the kitchen, back from her face. "For one thing, it's making light, making a game out of a horrible thing. What if *you* were blind. Imagine that."

"Sounds to me like that's what she's been doing," my father said, got up and walked over to the buffet where he kept his scotch in a cut-glass decanter. "Lots of response to my editorial the paper published about how we need a traffic light over near the junior high school." I knew he was trying to change the subject, to get me off the hook. I wanted to tell her that it was her very own words, her very own—"What if YOU were this way or that way or the other way, then YOU would realize that a little birthmark is NOT the end of the world"—that had gotten me imagining Helen's life in the first place.

Mama let him change the subject, praising his editorial, saying how everybody, even Mrs. Poole, said he was the best freelance writer that paper had ever seen. He continued talking through dinner about the history of the stoplight. "They cut this from the article," he said, wiping his mouth, his eyes focused on the checks in the tablecloth as if he were counting them. "I thought it was the best part, too. You see, the stoplight was invented by a man named Garret Morgan. Now think. Just *think* how many lives he has saved since the invention."

"Am I supposed to guess a number?" Mama asked, because nine times out of ten he *did* have an answer for what sounded like hypothetical questions.

"No, just want you to think," he said. "To get a feel for the importance of this man. He also invented the gas inhalator. Again, all those lives saved."

"And?" My mother leaned forward, waiting impatiently for him to loop back around to his story.

"Well, when people found out he was black, they cancelled their orders for the masks." His fingers traced the checked lines on either side of his plate. "He had to get a white man to sell his invention, but they cut that from the article. I said it was a terrible thing, right up there with what happened to Bessie Smith." I asked who she was, and then we were off and running on a brand new tangent. "What kind of father am I that you don't know Bessie Smith?" he asked repeatedly. "I'm a failure, a complete failure."

"Not complete," she said, and laughed, the conversation once again winding back to all the compliments she received about him, what a fine teacher he was, and so on.

I thought she had forgotten the whole Keller episode, but when I went to bed that night, she came into my room and read me a poem called "Lord Forgive Me When I Whine," which was about a person walking around and feeling sorry for himself until he passed a crippled person, a blind person, deaf and so on, which made him feel small and stupid and insignificant to have ever felt sorry for himself when he had legs and eyes and ears. Downstairs Bessie Smith sang "Nobody Knows You When You're Down and Out" full blast. I think what Mama really wanted to say was something like *Be careful what you wish or be careful what you say because things come true*. If you cross your eyes, they're liable to stick and stay that way forever.

Merle Hucks could flip his eyelids inside out, and that's what I thought about when Mama left the room. He would flip them inside out and then have blood-red eyelids like little caps where his eyes should've been. "What'll you do if they stick like that, mister?" our third-grade teacher had asked him, while R. W. Quincy was up and running circles around the classroom.

"Get a job at the fair." Merle turned and looked right at her with his eyes flipped that way. "Big money in eyelids. Buy all the liquor and women I want."

After my mother read "Lord Forgive Me When I Whine," I confined my Helen play to nighttime when I was certain she was in bed; I felt my way about the room until I stopped before the window that faced the cemetery. If I could guess the slant of the moon on those tall iron gates before looking, then I owed myself a quarter. I never told anyone else about the Helen Keller game, not even Misty. More and more, the game took place in my mind, like a thought or a silent prayer.

I kept a small transistor under my pillow and listened to a station in Fort Wayne, Indiana; it was as far as I could get from home without static, and I tried to imagine the invisible lines connecting me, millions of threads stretched over rooftops, crisscrossed with television antennae that rotated when the station was turned. Fort Wayne, Indiana, was far far away but Petula Clark sounded just the same.

By the time I was nine, it was getting harder and harder to recall Angela's face. Sometimes when we sat on that faded quilt, the waves crashing as she took my hand, it was right, the real face, but other times it was Miss Kitty from "Gunsmoke," or Anne Bancroft; sometimes it was Ann-Margret, who Misty and I had recently seen in an Elvis movie, because her hair was the right color, but more and more often it was Mo Rhodes. I loved to think of her, the way she breezed into Misty's room when I spent the night and in one swift moment tucked the covers around us and then stretched out at our feet to tell a story, sometimes real, sometimes made up, sometimes funny and sometimes sad. "Good night, Moon," she would whisper, and tiptoe from the room, her long purple kimono trailing behind her.

Three

Our house was built in the 1800s by a man named Luke Wilkins who had four sons. All four died in the Civil War and were buried in their small private churchyard, which was the beginning of what was later named Whispering Pines Cemetery. I could see the gates and some of the more recent tombstones from my bedroom window, *recent* being the turn of the century. There were no vacancies in Whispering Pines, though my father had once drawn up an elaborate plan of how he could skim a measley two yards off our side yard and sell something like twenty new plots. "Of course, the folks would have to be willing to stretch out north-south," he had said, still fiddling with a small metal ruler. "None of this facing the sunrise. Of course, if they're some real short people . . ." My mother said that she better *never* hear of this idea again, that he had had plenty of bad ones but this was the worst. It was when he was into composing limerick obituaries for people he didn't care for, so I never knew if his cemetery-expansion idea was serious or something crafted to irk my mother.

We had walked through the cemetery many times, my mother curious about dates and names, my father just curious, always making up stories of these long-ago dead people, how they died, whether or not they were murdered or committed suicide. *Really*, my mother was forever uttering, shaking her head in disgust, refusing to look up when he asked her to look at him and say that she did not find the possibility intriguing, refusing to discuss his ideas about what *they* should have written on *their* tombstones. The two times that we had gone to Boston to visit my mother's brother, we had spent most of the trip in cemeteries, looking for Hawthorne and the Alcotts and Mother Goose and Ben Franklin's parents, on and on, my mother marveling at those frightening skull and crossbones that were so popular in the 1700s. "How come you like everybody's tombstone but mine?" my father asked. "If Paul Revere had written a limerick, you'd think it was wonderful, poetic, inspirational. Admit it," he continued. "You have something against Southern tombstones."

The Wilkins family plot was the farthest from our house, a thick wooded area that in the summer was completely hidden from view. There was a short iron fence surrounding the graves, which were completely overgrown with tall grass and weeds; the markers were worn smooth, the name of the wife of the oldest son illegible. Not far from there was an old caretaker's cottage, a small closet-size building where at one time gardening tools had been kept. The yellow dirt paths were overgrown and went in crazy circular patterns, in and around the tombstones and markers. Misty and I had spent many afternoons scaring ourselves, seeing who would go the farthest, who would go closest to the caretaker's house, closest to the Wilkins plot. Our hearts pounded as we screamed with the rustle of a squirrel or a bird and pushed and shoved each other to get back to the clearing near the tall iron gates where we could see my house.

The opposite corner of the cemetery backed up to a dead end where teenagers met and parked on weekend nights. Sometimes when my window was open, I could hear their loud radios and gunning engines. Misty always wanted to sneak out and spy on them, and we spent a lot of time concocting elaborate plans that we never had the nerve to carry out. It was much easier in the sunlight as we sat on a limb of the large oak tree and imagined what these teenagers *did* out there.

"I'll show you," Misty had said one afternoon, when white winter light made everything look sharp and clear, a perfect focus. And she had jumped from a lower limb, kicked through the leaves until she found a long twig. She went over near the road where there were lots of balled-up paper bags and crunched-up beer cans, and I watched, swinging my legs, breathing in the cold air and smell of woodsmoke. She squatted down, the twig held out in front of her as if she were fishing, and in a few minutes held the stick out for me to see what looked like filmy plastic on the end. "Yep. Just as I thought," she said and strolled toward me, waving the stick.

"What is it?" I asked, refusing to climb down from my perch as she motioned.

"What is it?" She threw back her head and laughed. "What does it look like?" She waited for me to answer, but when I shrugged she grinned and stepped closer. "*This*," she said, holding the stick up towards me, "*this* is a *rubber*." I watched as she ran back to the street, the stick in her hand, as she kicked her feet through the weeds and trash. "Here's another one!" she yelled, and raced forward as if on some kind of wild scavenger hunt. "Man, oh man," she laughed. "And we were wondering what they *did* over here!" I could not help but think of the souped-up red GTO I had seen race around that corner so many times, a girl with long blond hair we had seen twirling a baton with the high school band now holding her hand out the passenger window, a cigarette between her fingers; I imagined a beer can held between those denim thighs and then the driver's hand reaching across the seat, his fingers crabbing towards her, imagined them kissing like what we'd seen when Mo Rhodes let us watch "Peyton Place" one Friday night. "Another one. Man, oh man. Let's see who can count the most."

The cemetery looked like a different place those afternoons as we ran up and down the paths, spoke to graves by name.

Sometimes it scared me to look out at night and see those tall iron gates, ivy covering the brick pillars on either side, and other times it was a comfort, this resting place for the Wilkins family. Sometimes I tried to picture faces to go with the names I had read there in the cemetery: Luke, Jr., Mark, John, and the youngest, Matthew, who was only sixteen when he died. I always wondered why they didn't name those boys in New Testament order.

I imagined the Wilkinses to look just like all the characters in *Shenandoah*, which Misty and I had watched three times in a row one Saturday at the Cape Fear theater, and sometimes as I lay in bed, I imagined where they all had slept. Mr. Wilkins, who looked just like Jimmy Stewart, slept down in my parents' room; the youngest boy slept in my room with his brother, John, the older two boys across the hall in the guest room until they took wives and built small houses of their own within sight of the main house. I imagined that the pastel houses just past the field at the edge of our lot were where Luke junior built. I had a clear sharp view of those houses from our sleeping porch, and in the summers I liked to sneak out there and sit on the narrow cot, my knees pulled up under a cotton nightgown.

Merle Hucks and his mean brother, both of whom had pale

skin and thin light hair like their mama, lived in the light blue house with the tar-paper roof. Their daddy was as dark and hairy as the mama was pale and washed-out. A baby girl was usually holding onto the mama's housecoat when she passed by the window of what must have been the kitchen, the room lit by a bare bulb swinging on a chain. Occasionally I'd see Merle come into the room and pass in front of the window like a flash of white. I never would have told anyone, not even Misty, that I sometimes watched the house. There was something wrong about my watching, and yet it was like I couldn't help myself.

"That is ridiculous," Mama said when I asked if their house had always been there. "Those old houses were thrown up right after the Depression; I'd be surprised if their walls are made of anything stronger than cardboard." She said that the Huckses' house and the others along that back stretch of land were an eyesore and she wished they'd move elsewhere. She complained often about Mr. Hucks, how he never cleaned his yard, how tools from when he worked at the old ice plant close by were strewn about like straw. Mr. Hucks was known to everyone in town as "Beef," a nickname he had earned in high school when he was the star athlete. "There's not enough kudzu to cover it," she said, and then went on and on about the rudeness, the horrible nature of Mr. Beef Hucks, hesitating in order to give herself ample time for proper enunciation of the name. She and Mrs. Poole often talked about all the families who lived back there and how ours was the last "nice" street before the town *fell*.

I was told from the time I could crawl that I was *never* to play back there, never to go beyond the thick hedge which marked our property. "There are snakes near that overgrowth," I was told, which was true, proof being the skins Merle Hucks once brought to second grade, grainy black snakeskin which he wore tied around his neck. Nobody, not even the teacher, said a word about it. When he saw me looking at him, he just grinned, one front tooth missing, and then licked dry Kool-Aid from his dirty palm. And when he was called on to read aloud, his face went red and his voice shook and sputtered on every single word, while the teacher stood there with her own mouth open as if she could draw the words from his mouth. If it had been anyone else in the class, people would've laughed, but even as second graders we had all heard of the Huckses; we had all heard about Merle's oldest brother, who was doing time in Raleigh for something so bad it was only whispered among adults, and we had all heard of his brother Dexter, who was two years ahead of us and always in the principal's office. The little sister, Maybelline, was born that December during second grade. "Say something about it," Merle had said as he held a little crumpled-up snapshot out to the class. "This is why I didn't come to school last week."

Merle was still using the old first-grade book, and when he finally got to the end of the line "See Spot run. Run, Spot, run," he closed his book and put his head on his desk. When the teacher questioned him he looked straight ahead, his chin shaking but his words as solid and sturdy as a rock. "Who gives a goddamn? If a dog's got legs it'll run." Then he pulled out his pack of cherry Kool-Aid, the same way he would in a few years pull out a pack of Marlboros, and poured the powder into his open palm.

"I once saw a dog without any legs." He grinned at me again when he saw me watching but I turned away from him before he could make the deep, gutteral cat sound that he made whenever he saw me. "My big brother, Dexter, he made the dog that way." Some boys in the back of the room laughed nervously, and the teacher ignored him as she usually did. She called on me to read, and I picked right back up where I had left off in an advanced reader. I could feel him watching me; I could almost hear his tongue licking the grainy bits of cherry Kool-Aid, and I knew that it was only a matter of time before he strained his thin neck out and screamed like an alley cat. I had made the foolish mistake one day of telling the teacher that I had a nickname, that at home my father sometimes called me Kitty or Kitten instead of Katie.

"Meeerrrrrrooooowwwwww," he called out and grinned. It was the one sound he could make clear as a bell without stammer or hesitation.

"That old crackerbox house of Beef," my mother paused for pronunciation time, "of the Huckses, well, there was no such blemish on the land during the plantation days of this house. This house was a marvel, the finest in this whole coastal region." She had stared off in the same way I imagined she must have done before I was born, when she taught school, her voice carrying up and down rows of desks. "This house was to this area what Beacon Hill is to Boston, Georgetown to Washington, Charleston to the whole state of South Carolina. . . ." She paused, probably expecting my father to call out *Snob* from some other room in the house, but he was teaching that day.

"The house then was nothing like it is now," she continued. "It was gutted by fire during the war. Only the structure remained, and that was just a small part of what's here, now. Your bedroom and the kitchen below it were all added on in the 1920s by a man named McCarthy." The McCarthys were also buried in Whispering Pines, but I never really fashioned a place for them in our house; I just clung to the Wilkins family, especially to Matthew, dead so young, too young to have lived really.

Misty's mama once told us that there was nothing so tragic as someone struck down in his prime. Long before people had begun asking, "Where were you on November 22, 1963?," Mo Rhodes had been doing it, keeping up with those who had died. She wasn't talking about Kennedy that day, but Buddy Holly, his record playing in the background while she layered marshmallows and Hershey bars and then let us sit in front of the oven waiting for s'mores as if it were an open campfire. It was pouring down rain that day, and she kept going over and looking out the window, glancing at the clock, then back to the window.

"I want to run out and get the newspaper before it gets

sopped," she said, and smiled at us, her face bright and clear. Her toenails shone pale pink as she stood there barefooted on the old green linoleum. She was the youngest mother I had ever known and the only one who ever would have let us eat all the s'mores we wanted. She leaned against the counter and waved, both hands over her head, to a car that passed on the street, a blue Galaxy 500 like a police car, a huge fan of water arcing into the yard, and then she watched until the car turned the corner and disappeared; it seemed she forgot about the paper and instead ate a s'more and started her record over with the song "Raining in My Heart" and then "Brown-Eyed Handsome Man."

"You know if I have another child, I'll name it after Buddy Holly," she said, once again staring out the window.

"What about a girl?" Misty asked. "I'm Misty of Chincoteague and she could be Trigger, or what about Mr. Ed for a boy?" She smirked, her pale blue eyes opening wide as she tried not to laugh. Then she leaned and caught her mother's arm, squeezed it.

"Holly for a girl and Buddy for a boy," she said. "And you, for the last time, are *not* named for a horse, though I love that book dearly, and it's one you should read if you haven't." She hitched up her little purple hot pants and pulled a box of macaroni from the cabinet. I had heard this routine of theirs so many times that I could just about predict what she'd say next. "You were named for a woman from Ferris Beach by the name of Themista Rose Allen, who drowned in 1900 at the age of sixteen."

"Well, that makes me feel a whole lot better!" Misty bit her s'more and then wiped the stringy marshmallow from around her mouth, her fingers held apart as she reached for a napkin.

"I heard the story of Themista Allen often when we lived there. It's sort of a local legend and people still leave flowers there on her grave." She wet a paper towel and then wiped Misty's hand like she was five instead of thirteen. "She was wading across the inlet at low tide to meet a young man and lost all track of time. She knew her daddy would kill her if he found out she had gone to meet this man, and so she had no choice but to cross back even though the tide had come in and the water was over her head." It seemed each time Mo Rhodes told the Themista story it got a little bit better, and every time she told it, Misty made an analogy to the Red Sea crashing down; she said that when she imagined Themista's young man, he always looked like Charlton Heston.

"No, I believe in giving a name another life," Mo said that day. "Especially the young. If you ever get up and turn on your radio and they are playing the best songs someone ever recorded back to back, then you know something has happened. I knew Buddy Holly had died before the announcer even said so. February of '59 and you, Misty, why you were barely a year old. Dean was just three and that was about the time that he knew every single word of 'Witch Doctor.'" Mo stared out at the rain as if she could see a three-year-old Dean standing there. "It was so cute to hear him do that." She turned back, a string of marshmallow clinging to her silky shorts. "No, when they played 'Peggy Sue' right after 'Maybe Baby,' I knew."

"My father's sister died when she was seventeen," I told them. My own voice sounded foreign telling this story I had only heard on a few rare occasions. "She died when she was having a baby." I couldn't picture Angela as a baby and instead got a picture of her stretched out on the beach, that man inching his way towards her, his hand crabbing across the faded quilt where she held the bottle of wine between her thighs.

"How awful," Mo said with a slight shake of her head, tears coming to her eyes. "How terribly sad." She went over to their stereo and turned up the volume for "True Love Ways," which was the song I liked best on the album. I wanted to tell more of the story, how my father's sister had never told them who the father was, how she was holding Angela within five minutes of her last breath, but it all seemed too sad to say aloud. Misty's mama usually enjoyed a good sad story but that day she seemed a little distant, a little jumpy. Besides, I wasn't even sure if I remembered it all or not; my father had told me the story in bits and pieces over the years, a little here, a little there, the same way Mo told the Themista story.

"Here's your favorite song, Kitty," Mo said. I sat there and listened, with the whole house smelling of chocolate and marshmallow, rain pelting the kitchen window to the beat of Buddy Holly, and Misty poring over the long lean girls on the cover of *Seventeen*, futilely conjuring ways for us to become more desirable than anyone else in the seventh grade. "Themista never looked like this," Misty said, and held up the magazine to show the flawless face of the young cover model. Mo came from the window and wrapped her arms around both of us, pulling us close so that we were all face to face. "No," she whispered. "Because Themista was the *most* beautiful and now you two are the most beautiful." I was waiting for one of Misty's sarcastic remarks, but instead she just giggled, pressed her sticky lips against Mo's cheek, and I imagined Angela saying Mo's words to me, imagined me kissing her that same way. It was April then and by the time school got out, Mo had announced that she *was* going to have a baby, a *Christmas* baby, Holly for a girl and Buddy for a boy.

Four

Mrs. Poole was forever having a tea of some kind or another, and there were many women in town, my mother included, who thought her teas were the greatest thing since God said Let there be light. If there was a reason to have a tea—wedding, baby, debut, retirement, charity drive—Mrs. Poole was ready to have it. In the wintertime, when the trees in the side yard were bare and spindly, I could just sit on our porch and watch the women come and go, but in the spring, I had to creep closer, or climb one of our trees. The teas were always elaborate and the women were expected to dress for the occasion, mohair or Ultrasuede, whatever happened to be the thing.

"What on earth do they *do* over there?" Mo Rhodes asked me one day. It was the fall of eighth grade and she was clearly pregnant, her woven poncho stretching over her stomach, as we sat in their Camaro and waited for Misty to come out the front door of Samuel T. Saxon Junior High. "Just this morning there has been a florist truck and the Coca-Cola man, and I swear I think I just saw the butcher from Winn-Dixie going in." She glanced up in the rearview mirror, looking first at me as I sat there in the small low backseat, and then at herself, rubbing a light fingertip over the edges of her dark lashes.

"I don't know what they do," I told her. "Talk, I guess."

"Don't you just know they *talk*." Mo laughed and cranked the car so she could turn on the heat. It was one of those drizzly days, leaves sticking to the windshield, headlights on; it looked much later than three o'clock. She turned on the radio and pressed the buttons, up, down, static coming and going until she finally turned it off. "That woman was known for all of her talking when *I* was a child." Somehow, it was not so difficult imagining Mo as a child; the picture that came to me was one of a child Liz Taylor, a young Velvet Brown racing Pie across an open field.

The rain was coming down harder, and I watched Merle Hucks and his brother, Dexter, and R.W. Quincy huddled up near the breezeway that led to the cafeteria, just beyond the rush of water that poured from the old rotted-out gutter. They had their hands cupped to hide the cigarettes they held, Merle's hair wet and stringy, pushed back from his eyes; I had once seen Merle hide a lit cigarette in his pocket when the principal walked by. Dexter Hucks, though two years older, was several inches shorter than Merle and the shape of his face and his features reminded me of a scrawny little bird. He rode a motorcycle and had all kinds of biker patches sewn to the back of his denim jacket. I couldn't help but wonder *who* had sewn them on. *Would* his mother do that, or had *he*, this tough guy who threatened to spit on you if you looked at him wrong, sat down one night with needle and thread and done it himself? Misty's brother, Dean, had told her that Dexter Hucks had "done the deed" too many times to count, that half of the condoms she had counted probably belonged to him. Dexter had once been suspended from school for asking a teacher to "step behind the bushes and see what a real man could do."

"Where is Misty?" Mo asked, revving the engine. "I have some people at our house. I told them I'd just be gone for a second." In over four years I had never seen Mo Rhodes getting impatient but lately she had been. Misty said it was the baby's fault, hormones out of control. Finally I saw Misty coming out the door, her arms wrapped around her notebook, bell-bottom jeans dragging the muddy schoolyard as she made a run for the car. Dexter Hucks had his hands up to his mouth and he yelled something, but I couldn't hear what because of the radio. Merle, his hands in his back pockets, turned and watched as Misty got in the car. Several times I had seen him working at Mrs. Poole's house during one of the teas; she had him carrying Coke crates or sweeping the porch, washing windows. I imagined that he was heading there now, head tucked down as he made a run across the yard, Converse hightops drenched as water sprayed with each step. Dexter and R.W. were still standing under the breezeway, smoking; Dexter flipped up the skirt of a black girl who walked by them just as we pulled away.

"Should I give that child a ride?" Mo asked, and motioned to Merle who was already a block closer to home than we were.

"No!" Misty screamed and began wiping her composition notebooks on the car seat. "I'm sorry I'm late but old Mr. Billings made our science class go back to the cafeteria and one by one apologize to the woman who collects the dishes." She looked at me, laughed. "Like our class was the first to ever splash her." It was common practice in the junior high to slam silverware into the little bucket of water rather than place it there. If the woman was standing beside it collecting trays and wiping them off, she got sprayed with water. I knew Mo was preoccupied when she didn't even ask Misty what that meant, *splashing* the woman. Usually she had to know everything; Mr. Rhodes, Dean, and Misty often called her Curious George and joked about her incessant why why why.

"Well, I just wish I had known," she said. "Our new carpet came today and Betty came to help me rearrange everything."

"Today? It's already in?" It didn't take much to make Misty happy; she had been talking for weeks about how her mother had always wanted and was finally getting purple shag, the long pile, for her bedroom. "Is Betty still there?" I had met Betty several times; she was a close friend of Mo's who had waist-length frosted blond hair and had once lived in California.

"Yes," Mo said. "That's why I'm in such a hurry. Betty came and brought Gene with her so we could move the furniture around. It's the man's day off and I'm sure he doesn't want to spend it raking purple carpet." I had met Gene before, too; he was the man who had once promised Misty that if he ever met Sgt. Barry Sadler he'd get his autograph. Of course he hadn't met *him*, but what he had done was get Misty and Dean free tickets to go see the *real* shot-up car of Bonnie and Clyde, which was on display in a big trailer in front of J.C. Penney. The ticket sales went to buy new automobiles for the highway patrol. Misty had so many free tickets that we went three different times, each time in awe that those were the *real* bloodstains and *real* bullet holes. Misty could quote every single word of "The Ballad of Bonnie and Clyde," and it seemed the tune stayed in my head for weeks after.

When Mo stopped in front of my house, Merle was just a tiny speck rounding the corner six blocks down Wilkins Road, and the local radio station van was in Mrs. Poole's driveway. "Now what has that woman got going on?" Mo laughed, and then waved to Gene, who was standing alone in the Rhodeses' living room and looking out the picture window. "Come over and see the carpet," Misty said when I got out. "Or just call me." Misty and I talked on the phone every single night for at least an hour. Sometimes we didn't even talk, but just laid the receiver down and tuned to WFRO NightBeat, which was the local radio show, and went on with whatever we were doing, homework or looking at a magazine, and occasionally yelled for the other to pick up.

Mama met me at the front door, her high heels clicking as she walked over to stand in front of the hall tree, where she started toying with her hair. I knew that she had just had it fixed that morning, a smooth perfect French twist, teased and sprayed, and now she had to get from our house to Mrs. Poole's without it getting ruined. "We should build an underground tunnel," my dad had said on another such occasion.

"My goodness, I was getting worried." Mama opened one of those little plastic hats that will fold to the size of a quarter and carefully placed it on her hair. "Your father will be home before too long. I should be back well before six, but just in case, the roast is in the refrigerator and all the instructions are on the table."

"Why is the radio station there?" I asked, and followed her onto the porch, waited while she opened her umbrella and surveyed the puddles along the sidewalk. She waved to a carload of women who passed slowly and then parked right near the edge of our yard.

"Mrs. Poole is heading up UNICEF and she's going to advertise for the Halloween carnival." The rain was coming down harder now, and I could hear the streetlights prematurely buzzing on. Merle Hucks ran through Whispering Pines, hurdling the lower tombstones as if he were on a track. Mama didn't notice him there or she would have said something. Instead she thrust the umbrella in front of her as if it were a shield and she were leading the battle. "Back soon," I heard her call as she lumbered forward, bits of mud flipping up on her hose. I was convinced that part of Mama's allegiance to Mrs. Poole was the fact that they were the two tallest women in town; they could be friends without making the other feel huge.

The light came on in Mr. and Mrs. Rhodes' bedroom and then

I could see them all passing back and forth, and furniture being moved. I caught an occasional glimpse of Misty's orange hair.

The cars kept parking at Mrs. Poole's, the rain coming down harder all the while. Everything I ever read or saw at the movies or on TV had a part for Mrs. Poole; I might have to take away her long Salem cigarettes, fuchsia lipstick, and color-coordinated pantsuits, but there was always a part for her. She was the busybody neighbor, the wicked witch, and the teacher with the ruler in her hand. She was that misplaced woman who attempted to maintain aristocracy in a primarily blue-collar town. Having teas was just one way to go about it. She could see no merit in *any* changes, whether it was the Coca-Cola bottle getting taller or Mo Rhodes turning the yard of her split-level into a Japanese garden, or black children walking the halls of Samuel T. Saxon Junior High. She was the pillar of the community because she could afford to be; Mr. Robert Manchester Poole, known to the town as Bo, had left her in fine shape financially.

When the children's home down around Ferris Beach was burned to the ground by one of the children, who on local TV said he was tired of living in the hellhole, Mrs. Poole rented out Brown's Econo Lodge on Old 301, which had gone bust with the building of I-95, and they all moved in until a new home was built. In 1968 when Santa Claus, also known as Mr. Beef Hucks, was stumbling drunk down in front of the Goodyear Tractor and Tire store where Misty's daddy was manager, Mrs. Poole stepped from her white Lincoln and proceeded to make her way over to him, finger shaking all the way. Mr. Landell, the black man whose job was to drive her around all day while his wife cleaned her house, just stood by the car and shook his head from side to side.

"This, children, is NOT, I repeat, NOT really Santa Claus, but a man who took on the role as a means to make money. Those who offer to help Santa, just as those who offer to help the Lord, must have their hearts in the right place. If they don't, well then"—she gasped for breath—"well, not only have they not done GOOD work, but they have done BAD work. You are dismissed on behalf of the town of Fulton, Mr. Hucks." Her hand was down and rummaging through her purse, looking for a cigarette I was sure, though I was also sure she would not smoke one right that minute. She always followed the rule about a Southern lady smoking only while seated, with a roof over her head; the Lincoln counted as a roof and she was just getting ready.

"That ain't what your old man said when I ran eighty yards against Clemmonsville." Mr. Hucks pulled off his white beard and threw it onto a big tractor tire. He started unbuttoning the front of the red suit, revealing a dingy white undershirt. "Ain't what he said when I pitched a no-hitter against Sandy Bluff." A small boy stared in horror at the stripped-down Santa before releasing a shrill scream and burying his face in his mother's coat. "No sir, me and Mr. Bo had a fine time that night. Yeah, Mr. Bo was quite the baseball fan."

"You are not in high school, Mr. Hucks," she said. "You are not playing ball but serving the public and you are dismissed. If Mr. Poole were here he'd tell you the same."

"If Mr. Bo were here, he'd say, 'Well, Beef' "—he paused and spat off to the side—" 'let's us ride out into the county and see what we can find to drink.' " People laughed nervously and then things got even quieter than before.

"You are a filthy, lying man who cannot even support his family." Everyone waited, expecting him to hit her or to pull up all those poinsettias, tell all those sniffling children to shut up, something, but he just stood and watched her walk away. When she got to the car, she turned back to the crowd; by then Misty and I had crept up near the office of Goodyear so we'd be near Mr. Rhodes in case a fight broke out. I saw a flash of green and knew she had a pack of Salems in her hand.

Old Merle was red in the face like at school when he got

called on, and mothers were dragging their children away so they wouldn't see Santa Claus weave off to his old beat-up Chevrolet without taking their Christmas orders. He beckoned for Merle to follow but it was like Merle hadn't even noticed, just stood there kicking the side of that tire and making the poinsettias shake. His hair was just as slick and dirty-looking as it had been at school the day before, when he won the fifty-yard dash, and he was wearing those same black jeans, way too short, that he wore nearly every day of the fifth grade. It was like he didn't even see his daddy there waving to him, and we knew Merle was just waiting and hoping that somebody would say something so he could beat that person up.

"Now, dear people of Fulton," Mrs. Poole announced, her mouth like a tight fuchsia line. "I am going to get the REAL Santa Claus. Mr. Landell?" He opened her door and off they went. Within two hours, she was back with a big fat Santa Claus from the Clemmonsville mall, who spent the next week taking orders and giving away candy and reminding everyone that Christmas was to celebrate Jesus' birth and not to get all carried away with a Big Wheel or Barbie or such. If he forgot to say all of that, Mrs. Poole was there often enough to remind him. Misty's daddy said he couldn't wait for Christmas to come and go, he was so tired of dealing with her.

Nobody in fifth grade mentioned Merle's daddy getting fired, but who would've? Merle said he kept a switchblade in his scratched-up mock-leather boot, and since he was a Hucks, no-body had a reason to doubt it. "My old man should've punched the shit out of that bitch," he finally said, and all the boys in class nodded in agreement. They knew better than to disagree. Merle had been caught drinking a beer up in a tree on the school yard the year before, and we had heard many times how Dexter Hucks had put a firecracker up a cat's butt and blown it to bits. I used to go to great pains to keep my own cat from roaming out of the yard, fearful of what would happen if he wound up on the wrong side of the kudzu.

It was still pouring down rain when I went out on the upstairs sleeping porch and tuned my radio to the local station so that I could hear Mrs. Poole's advertisement. The rain misted through the screen mesh as I sat on the glider, my knees pulled up to my chest. There was one streetlight at the back end of the cemetery, but other than that slight glow, our yard was dark. The windows of the pastel houses were black. People were not even home from work yet, but the sky was like night, and leaves were blowing everywhere, sticking to the screens. A shirt was hanging on the Huckses' clothesline, and I watched it whip back and forth like a banner of surrender. *The night they drove old Dixie down.* The D.J. was singing along with Joan Baez, in an obnoxious off-key way. Up and down the back street, lights began to come on, and headlights were turning into driveways. "I am Mrs. Theresa Poole and I am speaking to you live from my living room, where I am hosting a number of our community's finest citizens in a little tea, where we are planning our annual Halloween carnival, which will be held October 31st, which is Halloween, down at the Pinetop Elementary School cafeteria." Mrs. Poole talked on and on, and I could tell that by the end she was being hurried to finish. Finally in the last second, she managed to say, "All the funds go to UNICEF." Prior to that she went on and on about what would be served at the carnival, how apples donated by Mr. Thomas Clayton would be bobbed for, and finally how there was more to Halloween than dressing up like little goblins and begging door to door. The obnoxious D.J. was a welcome relief after Mrs. Poole finally finished.

I went downstairs to put the roast in the oven—my father was still not home from work—and when I returned, a blanket around my shoulders, there was a light on at the Huckses' and I could see the mother passing back and forth, maybe from stove to sink or sink to refrigerator. Again, I wondered about Dexter Hucks's patches and who had sewn them, especially that nasty skull and crossbones on the seat of his worn-out pants. Dexter Hucks was in a gang, or so Merle had told people, a biker gang where he was much younger than all the others. When Todd Bridger asked about the gang, what they called themselves, Merle said it was none of his business. Todd Bridger was one of the most popular guys in school and had been since kindergarten. He was squeaky clean, with short hair, and was always elected president of *something*, a club, the class. He was always the teacher's right-hand man, and for years he had been the ultimate dream of a boyfriend. I was not alone in the fantasy of having Todd Bridger's heavy silver ID bracelet around my wrist. He was the catch of our class, though it seemed during that year he was trying very hard to impress Merle Hucks, who was not easily impressed.

I caught a glimpse of white at the top of Mrs. Poole's fence, and then there was Merle, swinging his leg over and then dropping with a splash into my yard. Mrs. Poole would've fired him just like she fired his daddy if she had seen. It seemed he paused there a minute, and then he walked quickly through my yard to the edge, where he disappeared momentarily in the overgrowth. When he came up on the other side, he turned and stared over our yard. The rain was just a fine mist by then, but I still felt certain it was too dark for him to see me sitting there. Still, I held my breath, waiting for the search to end. I half expected to hear him scream like an alley cat, though it had been years since he'd done that to me, and then my father's headlights turned into our drive and blinded him, one frozen moment like a frightened animal before he bolted.

"Meerrroooowwwww!" Merle had yelled. It was three years before, a springlike day. I was stretched out in the sun, thinking about Angela and Ferris Beach. The memory was harder and harder to grasp those days, Angela's face coming and going, distant and then near, much like the shapes and colors on my eyelids as I faced the sun, my schoolbooks tossed to one side, my old tabby cat, Oliver, rubbing his nose against my cheek with a strong wheeze of a purr. We were both alarmed by the loud catcall. I sat up suddenly, and poor Oliver clawed my chest and then took off under the house where it was safe. I knew it was Merle's voice, but all I saw at the far end of my yard was the thick hedge of abelia, the small white blossoms already appearing with the approach of spring, and then the tangled overgrowth, strawlike weeds and briars that tumbled around old discarded boards and pieces of chicken wire which did not belong to us. I felt my heart beating faster and faster as I waited, almost holding my breath, and then slowly I got to my knees, began gathering my books.

"Yeah! I see London, I see France!" I looked that time to see a flash of bright yellow-white hair and pale skin. Once a boy at school said that the Huckses were albinos, and when Merle got wind of that, he beat the boy in the stomach until the principal came to break it up and sent Merle home for the day. I had never had the nerve to speak to Merle, tried not to look at him, and if I felt I had to look at him, made certain I did it while he wasn't looking. And there were times when I felt that I did have to look; there was no good reason except that I had to. It was like I imagined poor Lot's wife must have felt when she had to get just one more glimpse of Sodom; she had no good reason for looking back except that she was able to swing her head around and do it. I felt sometimes I had to look just to make sure he didn't have pink eyes as a real albino would have.

"Yeah! I see London, I see France, I see old puss face's underpants." His hair was unusually clean that day as if he had just taken a shower or gone swimming; instead of being slicked back, it looked like pale thistles, like a fluffy baby duck's down. There was no shaking to Merle's voice by then. He still got called out of class once a week to go out to the little mobile classroom where the speech teacher stayed, and we all assumed that it was *because* of these visits that his voice was so clear. It was rumored that he also met with the guidance counselor every single week, but nobody had seen him come out of the counselor's trailer and nobody dared to ask.

"Meeerrroooowwww." I heard a laugh and leaves shredding from branches as he slid from his perch and landed just within vision on the other side of the hedge. "What's your problem?" he yelled, but I ignored him and went quietly up the back steps. I prayed that Oliver would stay put, up in the cool shadiness beneath the house. I had such a clear picture in my mind of the cat that was supposedly destroyed by a firecracker that it made me jerk to think of it, my hand automatically reaching and covering my cheek.

"Why you hiding your face?" Now he had disappeared behind the bushes, and I could only hear the faint rustle of his feet and and knees in the brambles. "Trying to hold in the ugly?"

"Go away!" I yelled, my voice high and foreign-sounding as I crawled up under the house where the cat had gone. Then I just sat there for the longest time, leaning against the high brick pillar, that damp musty smell comforting in that it reminded me of all those rainy afternoons or hot summer days when Misty and I had played under there, drawing Barbie-house floor plans in the dirt. I had one day taken a red Magic Marker and very carefully colored in my Twist-n-Turn Barbie's left cheek, thinking it would make me feel better, but when I looked at her, I hated her. I knew she would never be touched again. I pulled her head off and threw it out into the kudzu.

"Buttermilk might make your place go away," Misty had offered. She was sincere and yet her choice of words—*your place*, like a scab or some unfortunate accident—stayed with me. "I bet it'll be gone by the time we're in high school," she told me, her eyes the palest blue I'd ever seen, her skin china-white without a trace of the freckles like on her legs and arms. "And I'm going to be thin and glamorous." Her plumpness and thin fuzzy hair were only reminders of my own imperfections and still I clung to Misty every step of the way. She didn't seem bothered by her own appearance; if she ever did cry about the way she looked, she did it behind a closed door at 202 Wilkins Road, where no one could see or hear her. I sat under the house feeling trapped, wishing that Misty would come over, that I'd hear her familiar steps on our long gravel drive.

"Just make me," Merle yelled, and I spied pale yellow hair as he crawled up closer to our hedge, but I didn't move from my spot under the house. I scooped Oliver up in my arms and held him there, my breath warm in his fur. "I know you're under there! Hey!" He stood then, just his eyes and the top of his head showing over the bushes. He waited for what seemed like forever. "Hey girl, I know you can hear me!" His words were slow and deliberate. If Misty had been there she would have asked him if that's what he learned in the mobile speech trailer. "Do you hear me?"

"I don't know if she does." It was my father. I could hear his footsteps just over my head as he crossed the back porch and stepped out onto the steps, the screendoor whining and held open. "But I sure do hear you and I can't hear myself think." I saw Merle's head disappear and then there was that same scrambling sound as when he'd crept up to the hedge. "I think he's gone now, Kitty," he said. "Where are you? Under the house?" I heard him shuffling there, waiting, and I knew exactly what he looked like: coarse hair disheveled, pants baggy and wrinkled, faded bedroom shoes, but his white dress shirt with sleeves rolled three-quarter would look like it had just been starched and pressed. Even my mother pondered this phenomenon, this perfectly clean creased shirt like the eye of a storm, still and untouched. "Under the house," I heard him say and the door creaked shut over my head. "Of course, the body is under the house. It came in a roll of insulation the day after the murder. Kitty? Kitty, are you down there?"

"Yes."

"Well, come on out, honey. I think there was a boy over here to see you." By then he had let the door slam shut, and he had gone through the side porch mumbling his nutty plot. I got to the top step just in time to see the back of his perfect shirt and to hear him trying to decide how many yards of insulation should have come on the roll.

"MMMMeeeeoooowwwwwww." The leaves rustled again but I didn't turn around. I ran inside, ignoring my father's request that I roll him up in our living room rug and see if I could drag it.

That was three years ago. Now, I saw Merle run from the glare of the headlights and into the darkness of his yard and I knew the tea was over. I knew that within minutes Mama would be home and calling for me to come downstairs to set the table. I twisted the knob of my transistor, but it was still too early to pick up anything far from Fulton. The rain was pouring again, making my clothes and hair damp from the mist. Across the field, through the lighted window of the Huckses' house, I glimpsed Merle's pale yellow hair. He stood with his back to the window, and then his mother was there, placing her hand on the top of his head. I still caught myself thinking, from time to time, about when he called me ugly and trapped me under my own house. I was somehow surprised by the fact that he had spent so much time just trying to bother me. I had been afraid to go to school the next day but it turned out he just looked at me and grinned, handed me a piece of candy, an old hard-as-a-brick Mary Jane, all flat from being in his nasty back pocket. When he was safely out of view, I promptly threw that candy to the ground, and hoped that no one, not even Misty, had seen.

The phone rang, breaking the quiet rhythm of the rain hitting the roof, and I watched Merle move away from his mother and the window and disappear beyond my view. "Katie?" My mother's voice carried from where I knew she was standing at the head of the stairs. "Misty is on the phone, and then you need to come set the table." Now the window was empty, just the stark white of the wall showing through. Misty was calling to say that she couldn't talk on the phone that night, that her family and Betty and Gene Files were going to see *Airport* over in Clemmonsville. "I would've invited you," she said. "But there's not room enough in the car. That brat kid of theirs is going, too. They *say* he'll sleep in a dark theater. Oh brother. Well, I gotta go. Listen to NightBeat and see if they play a song for anybody we know." She paused, and I could hear lots of voices in the background, Mo's laughter. And then she whispered, "You are not going to believe how purple this carpet is. Oh man, it is *purple*."

At the Halloween carnival that fall, Misty draped herself in the carpet remnants and went as the One-Eyed Purple People Eater, and I painted my face red and went as the devil. R.W. Quincy and Dexter Hucks came as themselves, which everyone agreed was the *worst* they could be. Todd Bridger, who came as Ironside, won first prize; if he had not borrowed his grandmother's wheelchair he wouldn't have stood a chance. "Originality is nine-tenths of the prize," Mrs. Poole said and grinned at Todd, handing him a five-dollar gift certificate to The Record Bar in the Clemmonsville mall. "And though you look *nothing* like Raymond Burr, you *are* original."

"And I'm not?" Misty whispered to me, just as Merle Hucks, dressed in white coat with a round piece of aluminum foil stuck to his forehead, passed. We weren't sure if he was supposed to be Marcus Welby or a spaceman and no one asked. After the judging, he took the circle and coat off anyway and spent the rest of the night keeping apples in the bobbing tubs and loading empty Coca-Cola crates in the corner of the cafeteria. He seemed oblivious to everything going on around him, even when R.W. Quincy stole Todd's wheelchair and pushed Dexter around and around before running him into the wall. Todd was standing there laughing nervously, acting like he wasn't worried about anything, though it was clear that he was. Without his wheelchair, he was just a little guy in a suit, and in that moment as fear and lack of courage drained his face, he looked as insignificant as I always felt at these functions. I looked for Misty so I could tell her about this realization and spotted orange hair and purple shag at the other end of the cafeteria, where she was cheering and clapping for more stunts from R.W. and Dexter. Mrs. Poole's hand was moving like crazy in her purse, and it was just a matter of minutes before she ran to the teachers' lounge where she could sit primly like a lady and suck on a Salem, leaving my mother in a state of bewilderment as she attempted to oversee the carnival and explain to R.W. Quincy why he had to stop doing wheelies in the wheelchair.

Five

"It's a birthmark," my mother said over and over. "Lots of people have birthmarks." She had said it so many times that by the time I was in the eighth grade, those words made me sick. I always wanted to say that if it was a *birthmark* it must be *her* fault, in the same way she was to blame for my legs getting so long that I was a head taller than almost every boy in my class. I wanted to tell her that I'd rather take my chances drawing a mother out of a hat, that I wished Mo Rhodes would adopt me, wished I was an orphan like Angela.

"Think of the birthmarks some people have," she said, holding my shoulders so that I had no choice but to look at her. "Some people are born without limbs. Some people are born without brains." I hated her right then. I hated her for not simply saying, "I'm sorry. I am truly sorry that this bothers you." But no, instead she wanted me to think of everything in the world which was worse, famine and earthquakes, the young black woman recently murdered in the county, her last breath choked and broken by a man's sock twisted around her neck. There are some children who cannot dress or feed themselves; there are people who have no homes and wrap their legs in Saran Wrap to keep warm. There was no end to the heartache and sadness of the world, and again I wanted to drag up Angela, young girl without a mother, shunned by her only living relatives.

"Well, let's make her feel real good," my father said and stepped into the kitchen. "Let me go get the paper and we'll read the police report aloud to one another. Even better, let's watch the local news." I stepped away from my mother, hand on my face, and watched her spine go more and more rigid with every word he said. There had been something going on anyway, something to do with one of his trips to Ferris Beach, something about him loaning *her* money *again*, and this was the outlet they had been looking for, a channel for this anger that hung in the air like fog. If I asked *why* or *what's wrong*, they pretended not to hear, immediately becoming civil to one another and discussing their days as if they were Ward and June Cleaver.

"And after dinner how about this?" He clinked the ice cubes around and around in his glass. "Let's ride down to the hospital emergency room and sit there in the lobby for awhile, you know." He chuckled and pinched her hip softly, but she pulled away, dishtowel raised as if she meant to swat his face. "Yeah, let's see the sights." I laughed with him, relieved momentarily by his playful pinch of her hip. Things could go either way; we were straddling the wire, there in the kitchen, where my mother's cornucopia spilled colorful fruit and vegetables onto the table. In less than a week we would be sitting there, the three of us plus those without relatives like Mrs. Poole, naming what we were thankful for. I would be thankful if the conversation at hand just passed overhead like a cloud, but I knew it would only take a few more exchanges before she would go silent and he would return to his study and leather recliner, which she had ordered for a birthday surprise and he had thanked her by absentmindedly sticking the tip of his cartridge pen in and out of the arm. He would play his scratched-up old Al Jolson and Judy Garland albums that bumped and gristled under the hard prehistoric needle of the ancient hi-fi. He would play their Swanees back to back as if it were a contest or that he HAD to decide which version he preferred. It became difficult not to fall into the rhythm if I was walking or washing dishes or just swinging my leg. Sometimes "Swanee" lingered in my head as I tried to sleep, gradually fading like the gray glow around a TV turned off in a dark room. I couldn't help but wonder why he loved that song so, what in the world he thought about as it played over and over.

A birthmark. I was at an age when, instead of getting easier, it was getting harder to deal with. It was my weak spot, like a bruise, and it seemed people knew that was the place to seek. Misty and I had been on a church retreat just the weekend before and had had a horrible time. I don't know why we went to begin with except maybe for lack of something better to do. It was at Lake Merriman, and we hadn't even gotten to walk along and throw rocks in the water because of all the activities, like making big felt banners that said PAX or had big white doves carrying olive branches, or thinking of rock songs that could be sung in the sanctuary with the accompaniment of an electric guitar; it was a time when controversy was *in* and so the more old people like Mrs. Poole you could distress during a service, the better. *Jesus Christ Superstar* wasn't good enough; these people were set on writing their own opera that weekend. The climax came when Jesus went up to the Woman at the Well and sang "Hello, I Love You"; somehow it didn't seem to be what either Jesus or Jim Morrison had intended.

"Agape" I had been renamed, because we all had to give each other *new* names for the retreat. The girl, newly named Charity, had studied me a long time before coming up with it, ignoring a whispered suggestion that I be named Cain. Cain, with his face marked like a cow branded for slaughter. The suggestion came from R.W. Quincy, who had read to page three of the Old Testament and had retained this bit of information since it had just filtered in that very morning. "She's a marked woman," he said and elbowed Merle Hucks, laughing.

"That means God's love," Charity said. She was real plain and quiet until she took her role as the Woman at the Well and then she was in with the best of them, clapping and singing, responding to "Hello, I Love You" with "Bend Me, Shape Me," which she said was a modern version of "Have Thine Own Way." You were supposed to wear your new "reborn" name on a tag all weekend; I'd hear "Agape" and I wouldn't even turn around until tapped on the shoulder. For one thing instead of putting that accent on the end, I simply heard the word as *a-gape*, like my mouth was most of the time, and that was because of the frightening proclamations I heard around me: "Jesus is coming. He is coming soon."

"To which theater?" R.W. Quincy asked. "The Cape Fear or the Clemmonsville?" Misty and I laughed, until we realized that it was just as bad to be on R.W.'s side as that of the girl who had given me my name and the others who spoke in scripture all day long. The retreat cost fifteen dollars for the weekend, and everybody knew that R.W. and Merle Hucks were there on donation gifts from Mrs. Poole's Sunday school class. Dexter was not there because he was with his biker club, which R.W. said he was going to be joining soon. R.W. said that the only reason he and Merle had come in the first place was because it was free, free food, and free women who were in need of a man in the worst way.

Much to my horror, I was instructed to rename Merle, and it took most of the weekend to do it. I'd watch him creep up into the woods to smoke a cigarette, and rack my brain for something appropriate. I kept thinking "Whitey" because of his pale straight hair, but there was nothing in the Bible that matched. I thought of Samson because his hair was long and scraggly and because he was one of the strongest boys in eighth grade, but I was afraid that he'd think I liked him. It was *after* Misty and I had laughed along with R.W. that she suggested names for both of them.

"It's easy," she said when she had gotten everyone's attention. "You are Frankincense," she said, pointing to R.W. "And Merle is Myrrh." She threw back her head and laughed, her hair frizzing all around her face, her hands on the hips of those red-white-and-blue spangled jeans she had had a fit to buy; she had lost five pounds and had squeezed into a size thirteen to prove it.

"You mean he's Frankenstein," Merle said, and held his arms up in monster position.

"Frankincense," I repeated. "That's the perfect name for R.W. Quincy." I surprised myself and Misty by speaking out. Charity had given Misty the new name Bathsheba, because they had had a little disagreement over the *exact* words of "Bend Me, Shape Me."

"Why is Frankincense such a good name, Agape?" Charity asked, the feigned sweetness with which she had named me diminishing as fast as you could say "Day by Day" or *Godspell*. Charity and her friend, Brotherly Love, were saints until you crossed them.

"Because he has a very distinct smell," I said, and braced myself for bolts of lightning and rolls of thunder or, worse, those who were now going to say that they would pray for me. Merle grinned at me, I think more impressed than anything, and R.W. was not fazed. He just started saying that I had "leopardsy" just like in the Bible. Merle slapped R.W. and called him "Franko," looked at me again and grinned.

My greatest fear was that my name would be the next to appear under his on some graffiti board. All over the school Merle wrote his name great big, Merle Hucks, and no one, not the teach-

ers or principals could figure out when he did it. Then, within
a day where Merle wrote his name, someone with a different-
color ink, would change the *h* to an *f* and then write a girl's
name below. Misty's name had appeared once but mine never
had. Merle himself had marked through her name, but she didn't
see it as an insult at all; she said he was calling more attention
to her name than all the others that had appeared. Though no
one would ever admit it, it was kind of a status symbol to have
your name appear there; it was a status symbol in the same way
as making out was. At that time I had neither experience. *Lord
Forgive Me When I Whine.*

That last night we had to list our sins and it seemed Misty
and I could have filled a book. We lay in a narrow bottom bunk
and whispered back and forth long after lights were out and
the Woman at the Well had asked us numerous times to shut
up. "Bathsheba? Agape? Can you hear me?" she called from the
other side of our cabin, but we ignored her, our bodies quivering
with laughter, the November chill, the excitement of breaking
the rules. "I've got to tell you who all I like," Misty whispered,
her breath like Teaberry gum. "I like Dean's friend, Ronald, you
know the tall one?" She squeezed my arm and I nodded. "I still
kind of like Todd Bridger, but who doesn't." I nodded again.
"And"—she twisted my arm, which was our abbreviated way of
saying *don't you ever as long as you live repeat a word of this it is graveyard talk*—"R.W. Quincy." She started laughing and I did, too,
though I knew that a part of her was *serious.* "And I like Merle,"
I said sarcastically, and laughed in the same way. We lay there
shaking, our noses cold as we huddled under our sleeping bags.

"Agape? Bathsheba? I mean it now!"

Oh Lord, forgive me when I whine; it was so easy to sin.

"It's a birthmark," Mama said again, all the while rearranging
her cornucopia so that it looked like a *natural* tumbling-forth.
"And I don't think that makeup Mo Rhodes gave her does one bit

of good other than to get on her clothes." Mama looked at Daddy as if they were the only two people in the room. "I just want her to see that she can't let this ruin her life; there are things we just have to *accept*." She said the word as if it carried some special message to him. Accept. I wanted him to ask her why she did not *accept* Angela. "Why, poor Misty's weight problem and that orange hair is ten times worse."

"Think of it as a beauty mark," my father said, and turned towards me, his warm type-stained hand cupping my cheek, thumb rubbing firmly as if he could erase the mark. "You see, I recently read how there are people these days who have no wisdom teeth at all, none under the gums even when they x-ray."

"And how much is tea in China?" Mama asked, and broke the spaghetti strands not once, but two, three, four times before dropping them into the boiling water.

"You could'a just fixed rice, Cleva," he said, and grinned. Then he pulled out a kitchen chair and motioned for me to sit. "Anyway, these folks without their wisdom teeth, well, it's evolution in action. What happens when people do cut their wisdom teeth?"

"They get wiser." Mama started chopping the salad lettuce as if she were making slaw.

"They get them pulled," I said.

"Damn right. Evolution." My father raised his glass, toasted it softly against my cheek. "One day, wisdom teeth will be extinct and one day everybody will have a beauty mark. You're just ahead of things."

"Fred." Mama stopped her chopping and turned to stare at him, the long kitchen knife held firmly, her knuckles white with the grip. I knew what she wanted to say, things about false hope and false pride, truth, reality and justice and God's own way.

"She pulled a knife on me," he said. "It was a dark and steamy night and it all took place there in the kitchen, mayhem and murder." She just shook her head and turned back to the boiling pot. Steam clouded the kitchen window, erasing the view of the yard and the row of pastel houses, the new Stuckey's being built in the distance.

"Anyway, some people have beauty marks and some people don't. Now, take my niece, Angela," he said, glanced at Mama's stiff back and then turned back to me. "You remember Angela?" I nodded, anticipating an explosion of some kind. "Well, she has a mole, a little raised mole even, right above her lip." He pointed with his little finger. "I'm not talking a little tiny mole either. Big, a big mole, except nobody calls it a big mole. No, no, no, it's known as a beauty mark. Some women draw one on, I'll tell you, that's how anxious they are to evolve. Take your mama, for instance." She didn't turn but I watched her reflection in the window, shoulders limp as if the steam had taken all of the starch from her body. She just stared at the back of his head, her mouth quivering slightly, cheeks flushed. "Your mama painted herself a great great big mole there on her face. I didn't know until after we were married that she could wash it off at night." I knew from the look on her face that there was no truth in that story. She never even glanced at me though I know she was aware that I was watching her. She turned back to the stove and lifted the pot lid to release a thick cloud of steam.

"No, sir, Angela is fully evolved, beauty mark and all."

"Isn't it a shame we aren't all so evolved?" Mama asked, and found her way over to my chair, placing a cold damp hand on my shoulder.

"And I was talking about wisdom teeth." My dad reached over and put his hand on top of hers and squeezed until she looked up and met him eye to eye. It seemed that they stared at each other forever, their hands heavy on my shoulder. "I didn't mean to rile you up, Cleva," he whispered, and then waited for her smile—a weak one but a smile nonetheless. "Anyway, I was in the service with this old boy who had a couple of wisdom teeth pulled, got a hemorrhoidectomy and got circumcised all on the same day."

"Fred," Mama said, her face flushed, but with a lingering look of amazement. "I do not believe that." I didn't understand the full logistics behind circumcision, only that it involved the penis, which was enough to make me look down at the linoleum.

"He was not feeling real good, I'll tell you," he said, and shook his head, stood and grabbed Mama by the waist when she passed his chair. They were almost the same height, and in every way she was broad and rounded, he was lean and angular. As a child I had felt terribly guilty for always thinking of them when I heard the rhyme about Jack Sprat and his wife, so I confessed it to my Sunday school teacher, who unfortunately at the time was Mrs. Poole. For years after, people at church would sometimes refer to us as the Sprats. "Why did you tell *her*?" Mama had asked, but I hadn't really known. Now, her hands were up against his chest, her body stiff as he tried to whirl her around. "Anyway, I was talking about evolution." He paused and laughed. "That old guy with the wisdom teeth? Well, clearly he was not there yet."

I was never certain which of my dad's stories were true and which had been embellished; I'm not even sure that he himself knew. He always had a joke to tell and for years he was asking things like "Why did Little Moron throw the clock out the window?," only what I heard was "Little Mo Ryan," all the while picturing this round little Irishman with red hair and face. Somehow the knowledge of an idiot, a moron, was such a letdown after picturing this whimsical leprechaun, that my father had to find a new target. Pollack jokes were out, due to respect for Madame Marie Sklodowska Curie, and Helen Keller jokes were certainly out of the question. It was then that I realized your best jokes are at someone else's expense. But whose? We finally agreed, much to my mother's distaste, that we would tell Theresa Poole jokes. How many Theresa Pooles does it take to screw in a light bulb, and so on.

My favorite one he did that very night while Mama was rearranging her tumbled-forth vegetables. He filled a bowl with water and set it on the table. "This is the public swimming pool of Fulton. It's the first day and here come all the white people." He took the salt shaker and shook it over the bowl. "And here come all the black people. This is an integrated pool." And he shook the pepper all over the bowl. "Everyone was swimming and having a great time when all of a sudden who came to the pool but Mrs. Theresa Poole and, oh, my God, she was in a *bathing suit*." He ran around the table with his hands up to the ceiling, then clutched his head, up and down, up and down, while Mama rubbed a cucumber with Crisco to make it shine, all the while shaking her head back and forth. He stopped by the sink and put a little bit of dishwashing liquid on his finger. "She dove in the pool and . . ." He dipped that same finger in the bowl and when he did, all the little grains of pepper flew to the side. Mama turned away so that we wouldn't see her laugh.

For years he had cut the obituaries from several different newspapers. He kept them in a cigar box, sorting them statistically by age and cause of death and geographical region. He subscribed to the Sunday edition of all the major papers, which arrived in Fulton on about the following Thursday, so it was a routine thing for him to do his cutting on Friday nights during "Gunsmoke." "Pass me those scissors, Miss Kitty," he said in Matt Dillon simulation. The only thing that irritated my mother more than this voice was when he imitated Jimmy Durante.

"Please," Mama said. "I can't stand when you call her that. Kitty sounds like, well, just like what you see there, like Miss Kitty." She stood there and shooed a hand at Amanda Blake. "Miss Kitty with too much makeup and a spot drawn on her face. She's the only woman on the whole show so you know what we're to think." I couldn't help but laugh, all those jokes Misty had told me about Matt Dillon and Miss Kitty while we sat way up in the tree hoping to see some afternoon parkers.

"Matt Dillon sure seems to like her," he laughed, and went back to his cutting and sorting. "Lots of people draw on their faces, Marilyn Monroe did, for example."

"Well, she's a good one to admire." Mama sat down and opened her mouth as if she were about to comment on all those newspapers, and then stopped herself.

"Most men think so." He put down his scissors and lit a cigarette. "It seems to me there's a lot of cancer in California."

"Well, there are a lot of people." She stared at his cigarette, eyebrows raised as if to complete her thought, though I knew if he weren't around and it were Theresa Poole sitting there, she would gladly smoke one herself.

"Little Angela has a beauty mark," he said, and just that easily I saw it all starting again.

Mama drew in a long breath and let her copy of *Fondue Cookery* fall to the floor. "What *little* Angela has is a mole, a dark mole that sticks out just above her lip. And . . ." She stared at the glossy picture of little fondue forks there near her foot. "Smoking is hazardous to your health."

"It's a beauty mark," he dragged out, in an attempt to mimic Festus, who my mama also could not stand, exhaling a stream of smoke aimed right for her. "You could paint one on, Miss Cleva," he continued. "Why don't you paint one on?"

She retrieved the book, which had recently prompted her to dip everything imaginable into melted chocolate, and held it in one hand, the fingers of her other hand spread flat, smoothing the material of her skirt. I went into the kitchen to call Misty, but the line was busy so I kept redialing over and over. I could have walked over there, but I really didn't want to visit as much as I just wanted to get away from Miss Kitty and Festus. In between dialing I could still hear them, those harsh whispers they always used when they were angry but didn't want me to know. If I walked in there that second, the room would become silent and my dad would tell a joke or she would say, "What about a kiwi in chocolate?" She was all into exotic fruits which the Winn-Dixie of Fulton did not carry.

"Angela has a mole," she whispered. "A mole. A dark spot. It could be cancerous there beneath her skin. God knows, you come from a long line of strokes and heart attacks, might as well throw in cancer since that's what you're so interested in."

"A beauty mark," he sang back. "And my mother died of pneumonia."

I stood listening to Misty's busy signal and looked through the doorway, where I saw Mama stand, turning her hands over and over as if she didn't know what to do with them until she found the deep pockets of her robe. "*Angela* should move to California. Maybe she could get a job of some kind." I could see the glassiness of her eyes, though she never once turned and looked at me, and when she finally left the room, I gave up calling Misty and went upstairs.

I sat out on the sleeping porch, an afghan pulled around me and watched the lights in the Huckses' house, bare bulbs casting a glare on curtainless windows and cracked plaster walls. I tried to imagine the life in that house, what it must feel like to be a member of that family, and I realized again I was using my mother's old trick on myself, imagining the very worst scenario so my own life looked better. I wanted to run over to Misty's and lie there beside her in the big iron bed, her plump white skin carrying the scent of Intimate, which she had started wearing just that month when she turned fourteen. I wanted to hear her laugh and wipe the little tears that always gathered in the corners of her eyes. I wanted Mo to come in and sit on the end of the bed to tell us good night, the whole house smelling of chocolate and marshmallows just as it had that rainy day last spring when she first talked about having another baby. I wanted to whisper secrets back and forth, the bed shaking with our giggles. I'd tell her everything I knew about Angela and see if she could help me piece it all together.

I sat on the sleeping porch until I finally heard the dull scrape-scraping of the old phonograph needle after about the fiftieth straight run of Bessie Smith's "Empty Bed Blues."

"I think you need to get to bed." My mother was standing in the shadows of the doorway, and though I jumped with the sound of her voice, I didn't turn. "Let's get some sleep." I nodded and it seemed she wanted more from me though I couldn't imagine what. Finally she turned and I listened as she made her way back down the stairs. I imagined her pulling her cotton gown close around her as she slid under the thick spread; she would lie there as still as death, eyes on the ceiling, hands on her chest, and she would not move once while waiting for my father, who tossed and turned and doodled, writhed and coughed and dreamed in his ink-stained leather chair.

As I sat there, I couldn't help but feel like someone was watching me right back, someone, God, the Wilkins boys, Merle Hucks or maybe even Angela, crouched and hidden in the darkness, needing to talk to my father about whatever secret they shared. I liked to think there was a guardian angel, someone to look up to, someone I could imagine in a lofty protected part of the sky, who could on a whim simply look down and see me sitting out on the sleeping porch and somehow make sense of my placement in the world.

Having exhausted the Keller biography, I had begun anew, reading and rereading Anne Frank's diary, hearing her "Dear Kitty" as an endearment of myself. I read the letters so often, so snared by her "Dearest Darling Kitty" that sometimes I almost believed that I *was* her Kitty, and that she was still very much alive and writing her letters, and sometimes I caught myself suddenly filled with hope for her salvation and future. Just as I had imagined the Wilkinses and Annie Sullivan and even Angela, I could close my eyes and see her there in her pinafore, thick dark hair clipped on one side; I could stare at the picture I had seen so many times until it was colored, until her deep blue eyes narrowed with a laugh. Maybe she would describe the changes in herself now that she was getting older, the way she saw Peter in a different light, the way her mother did not understand her at all, the way she would like to hoist the dirty children off the street and in through her window so that she could bathe them and mend their clothes. Her voice came to me with a Southern lilt similar to my own. I had also managed to lift any rough edges and hesitations from the voice of Helen Kellar, which I heard in a rich Southern baritone, a voice very similar to the one I had assigned to Angela, since I could no longer remember how she sounded.

I wanted to cling to the sensation that there was someone out there for me, someone simply out there, hovering, loving. I wanted to believe that I, too, would one day be there, uplifted and held by the truth of it all, that there would be someone out on a sleeping porch crouched and shivering while the world spun back around to day, someone who would wonder what purpose there could be to it all, and I could, with the breath of a weeping willow, with the honesty I felt when I looked into Misty's clear blue eyes, lean down and whisper an answer as soft as ducks down.

Six

It was during Christmas vacation, a late afternoon, when Angela came to our house and waited on the front porch until my father got home. She looked so different from the way I remembered, and yet I knew immediately it was her. She was wearing low-slung bell-bottom jeans with a chain belt and a fuzzy fringed vest made out of what looked like pinto pony. Her dark red hair was parted down the middle and clipped back from her face; she wore large gold hoop earrings and a suede choker with a peace sign sewn in Indian beads.

"Kitty? Little Kitty?" she called, and rose from the swing when I came up the steps. "Look at you." Her voice was higher, flatter than I recalled. She hugged me close, her gauzy Indian-print shirt smelling of incense and cigarette smoke. She kissed my right cheek then pushed back, holding me at arms' length. "You've grown so. You're what, thirteen?"

"Yes." I stood while she returned to her seat in the swing and took a little beaded cigarette case from her suede fringed purse. "I'll be fourteen the first of August."

"Of course," she said, and lit her cigarette, took a deep draw and pushed off the porch floor with the toe of her black crushed patent-leather boot. "I remember that day well."

"You do?" I waited for her to say more but she just smiled, pulled a tube of lip gloss from her little bag and applied it. Across the street Mo Rhodes pulled up in the driveway and began unloading groceries from the trunk of her Camaro. The baby was due in only two weeks and she looked like it could come any minute as she stood there, hands pressing in the small of her back. Reaching one hand in the driver's side, she beeped the horn several times for someone, Mr. Rhodes or Dean, to come and help her. I yelled hello and she turned and waved a bunch of carrots.

"Are you going to spend the night with us tonight?" she called, and I nodded. "Are you going to eat dinner?" She looked both ways and came across the street while she motioned for Dean, who was in his sock feet, ankle weights on those thin ankles, to take the groceries inside. She came up our walk, hands in the pockets of her gray pea jacket, which did not stand a chance of buttoning, her dark curly hair pulled up in a twisted knot on top of her head.

"I think Mama expects me to eat here but I can go ask," I said. Angela stood up to look over the hedges and then the two of them just looked at one another, then smiled slightly. "I'll just eat here."

"No," Mo said, and came up our steps, hands clasped on her stomach. "You go ask your mother if you can eat with us. I think we're just going to go to Hardee's, and then I thought we could ride around and look at decorations. There's not much else I can do these days." Then she turned slightly and nodded to Angela, who was lighting another cigarette. "Hello."

"Hello." Angela leaned her head against the chain and blew out a thin curl of smoke. "Looks like you don't have much of a wait." She laughed and Mo nodded. The late afternoon light made Angela's hair brighter, the coppery glow of a new penny. "If I were you," she said, her attention on me, "I'd go out to eat. It's always nice to go out to eat."

"This is Angela, Angela Burns," I said, stumbling to think of what I should call her, my father's niece, my cousin, the relative I haven't seen since I was five. "And this is our neighbor, Mo Rhodes." Again they smiled at each other. "Mrs. Rhodes used to live at Ferris Beach."

"Of course," Angela said, eyes squinted as if she were giving Mo a careful study. "Yes. I knew I had seen you before."

"Yes," Mo said quickly, and then turned her attention to the open trunk across the street, Dean standing there with two bags and trying to lift a third. "I better go help him," she said. "Kate, just give us a call. Nice to see you, too." She nodded quickly in Angela's direction and then headed back, her boots making a grainy click on our sidewalk. When she got to the Camaro, Mr. Rhodes wrapped his arm around her, his other hand rubbing her stomach. Angela stood against a post, cigarette held up near her cheek as she watched them. "Is that Mr. Rhodes?" she asked and I nodded. "Hmmm." She shifted her weight and turned towards me, blowing a short puff of smoke off to the side. "He's not the type I'd imagine her with."

"Why?" I asked, still feeling awkward under her gaze.

"Oh, I don't know." She laughed. "Don't you ever look at people and ask that?" She waited for me to nod, while taking a deep drag on her cigarette. "I thought it when I first met Cleva," she whispered. "Cleva was not what I expected for Fred."

"How long have you been here?" Now I was wondering if she had even knocked on the door or rung the bell. Did my mother even know that she was out here? I could smell the faint traces of onions, garlic, and peppers browning, the beginnings of spaghetti sauce, and I knew my mother was just on the other side of that door and down the hall. Already the light was on in the foyer, and any second she would turn on the one over the front door.

"Not long," Angela said, and pushed off again, thumped her cigarette over the banister. "I didn't see Freddie's car so I figured he wasn't here." Though different from my memory, she was still very pretty. I tried to imagine her meeting my mother for the first time; I had no idea when that even would have been, whether it was before or after they were married.

"Kate?" I jumped at the sound of Mama's voice and turned quickly. "Misty just called to see if you want to go to Hardee's with them. I told her that I'm cooking spaghetti but that if . . ." She stopped when she saw Angela and just stood there with the door held open. She was wearing the size nine-and-a-half fluffy purple slippers I'd given to her for her birthday; I had known when I bought them, little satin heels and feathery wisps like from a boa on the toe, that they were way out of character for her; in this picture with her gray tweed skirt, long gray sweater vest, face frozen in dismay, the contrast was grotesque.

"Why, *Aunt* Cleva." Angela thumped her cigarette into the yard and stepped forward, hand outstretched. "It's been such a long long time."

"Yes, it has." Mama turned to me then and began speaking in high gear. Why didn't I go pack my things to go to Misty's and wasn't it nice of them to invite me to go to Hardee's but she insisted on paying for mine and just to go right in her bedroom and get the money from her purse. It was so sweet of Mo to even have me when that baby could come any day now especially since it's the third child. I felt her pulling me, a quick hug and then she pushed me into the foyer and shooed me upstairs. There was a lilt in her voice and laugh that I'd never heard before; it was as unnatural as those strange yellow lights they had put up near the interstate to make you think it was daylight. My mother was not herself; it was as if Angela had some strange power that had reduced her to a nervous babbling stranger.

I quickly grabbed my gown and toothbrush, a couple of dollars from my parents' room, and then waited quietly at the foot of the stairs, hoping that I could hear what they were saying. "I don't understand why you do this to us," my mother said, and I leaned up against the dark wall as she walked past, the front door closing behind her, cutting off Angela's words, what sounded like a laugh. I could hear Mama in the kitchen so I carried my overnight bag out onto the porch, carefully easing the door so Mama wouldn't hear. Angela was still just sitting there with a cigarette, one leg pulled up under the other while she leaned her head against the chain. I spoke to her again and hopped up on the porch rail, my feet locked behind the spindles. It was getting colder and I pulled the neck of my coat up closer. It was not even five o'clock and already it was dark. Soon the streetlights would come on and slowly the neighborhood would light up, Christmas trees and all the adornments that Mrs. Poole had called sheer tackiness. "And to think they do all this bulb-blinking and snow-spraying and so forth in the Lord's name," she had said.

"Kate?" Again Mama was at the door, and this time her face was serious as if I had committed a crime by coming back out on the porch without telling her. "Can you come help me just a minute?" She smiled and gave Angela a quick nod before closing the front door behind us. "Now, before you go over to Misty's I want you to help me do one thing." I followed her into the kitchen, where she had a little bag of garden peas which she wanted me to shell. I mentioned that they were having spaghetti and surely weren't going to have peas with it, and she said she needed these for a casserole she was making to send to a woman whose husband was in intensive care and would I *please* just shell them. Her face was red as she stressed each syllable while buttering more garlic toast than the two of them would ever eat. I knew that she was nervous and that she had gone to great lengths to *find* something for me to do.

"Why is Angela here?" I asked and she just shrugged, shoulders sloping as she leaned forward to wash the dishes in the sink. After having looked at Angela, I thought she looked so large; her broad back moved up and down as she rinsed each piece of flatware, turning it over and over in her hand, the steam making her hair damp and still flatter than before. "Is she here to visit or what?"

"I have no idea."

"Well, how did she get here?"

"I don't know." I could see her vague outline in the window, but shifted my gaze instead to take in the houses on the other side of the field, several of them lined in brightly colored bulbs that had already begun the nightly blinking. "I guess your father will know why she's here."

"Shouldn't we ask her in, though?" I threw the hulls into the trash and stood there waiting for her to acknowledge me, and instead she watched those blinking lights that just the night before she had called a fire trap.

"Hello. Hello." The front door slammed, and my father kept calling out his greetings of hello, good evening, happy holidays, seasons greetings, bon appétit, and peace be with you until he found us in the kitchen. "Why the long faces? Ho, ho, ho." He grabbed her around the waist and nuzzled her thick neck. It was one of those moments when I couldn't help but wonder what the Sprats had ever seen in each other. He kissed her cheek, peck peck peck like a starving chicken after some corn, and finally she turned and looked him in the eye, her shoulders dropping as she sighed.

"Where's your niece?"

"Gone." He waved his hand. "You know Angela, breeze in and breeze out. Here today and gone tomorrow."

"Yes." Mama sat down at the table and just left the spaghetti sauce lid jumping and spitting and the sink half full of dishes. He went and readjusted the eye of the stove, then stood behind her chair, his fingers stroking her cheeks. "Anyway, what are we doing tonight?" he asked, his voice light as he playfully shook her shoulders.

"I'm spending the night at Misty's," I told him, at the same time showing Mama the bowl of little green peas. "How did Angela leave?"

"A friend picked her up," he said, while Mama traced her finger up and down the little squares on the oilcloth. I pictured the man from the beach, cap pulled low on his forehead as the two of them loved up in the cab of a truck.

"I bet Misty is waiting on you, honey," she finally said. I kissed them both, then lingered in the hallway waiting to see what I could hear. They must have known I was waiting, listening, because there was a pause and then my father told her a joke about Round John Virgin. He told her what the weather forecast was for the weekend, who was number one in the NBA, how many people made a C on his exam. She said, My and Isn't that something and Well.

As I walked out, I heard my father go to his study and within moments Jolson's voice burst through loud and clear with "Mammy." I stood on the porch and the cold air felt good as I took a deep breath and tried to reconjure the picture of Angela there in the swing; already her voice was leaving me again.

Misty's yard was all lit up, little red and green blinking lights in the azalea bushes and up and down the pagoda mailbox. There was a plastic reindeer up on the roof, his nose blinking red; and in the picture window, which was edged in spray-on snow, I could see their tree, a silver tinsel one with pink and blue ornaments, a silver star on top. It was not my taste in decorations either but I loved seeing them; I loved the nerve behind doing something so elaborately. "I don't believe in killing trees," Mo had said when she refused Misty's begs to buy a real one.

We were supposed to get our tree the next day, and I couldn't wait. My dad didn't believe in killing a tree either, so we always got one with the roots bound in burlap and then set it out in the backyard down close to the property line. Our Moravian star, simple and white, was my favorite of all decorations, but we had not even gotten it out yet; that night I welcomed the loud and lively lights up and down Misty's side of the street. I needed something dancing busily in my mind. I stepped into the middle of the road and just stood there, the streetlights stretching in either direction, glowing in the damp chilly air. I could see my breath, could feel my own warmth as it formed there in front of me. Behind me, our house looked dark, faint lingerings of *I'd walk a million miles*, and I wasn't even sure if it was really playing or if I was imagining the familiar, the same way a bright light will remain when you close your eyelids, the way I imagine the sight of an eclipse would burn its image into your eyes forever.

The street was completely still, empty; it was one of those times when I told myself that I would remember this moment forever and needed to do something that would later remind me. I had picked up a piece of coal on my last day at Pine Top Elementary School and still had it in my jewelry box. It was just that important. I saw Misty run through their living room and put a package under the tree. Then she was getting her coat from the closet. They would be outside within five minutes; they would be looking for me, blowing the horn to go. I looked around, walked quickly back up our driveway where it was dark, the slight glow of the kitchen light coming off the side porch. My own room was dark, the sleeping porch faintly lit by the upstairs hallway. I turned quickly towards the tall stone gates of Whispering Pines and felt a sudden chill, a sudden dare issued to myself. "Come on already." Dean Rhodes was standing in their carport and leaning in the side door. "Kate isn't even here yet." It was in that split second that I took a deep breath and ran in, eyes straight ahead as I went midway up the first small path to the large monument that said McCarthy, and then on, farther, until the bare branches of the large oak creaked and whined over my head. I reached and felt in the darkness, there around the large gnarled roots, looking for something, a rock, plastic flower, lost marble or penny. I could feel the thick damp clay on my hands, the dead grass brushing against the legs of my jeans. "Kate? Katie?" Misty's voice was like she had a megaphone, and I could imagine my mother's ears perking with the sound of my name in spite of Al Jolson and cars on the interstate and spaghetti sauce gurgling and spitting.

I felt something cool and hard and lifted it to see in the haze of the distant streetlight a petal from a hard plastic flower. It was a pink fake rose petal, caked in clay, and as I held it there, I would have sworn that I heard something move just on the other side of the path. I froze, waiting, knowing that I'd see Oliver playing there, but then it got quiet just as suddenly as I'd heard the rustle. Mr. and Mrs. Rhodes were coming out of the house now, and I had no time to linger. I heard the rustle again, this time caught a glimpse of something white, and in a sudden rush, I turned and ran as fast as I could, down the path and through the gates. "Coming!" I yelled in response to Misty's calls, and grabbed my bag where I had left it at the corner of the house. My heart was beating so fast it felt like it was in my neck and my ears. The petal was in my coat pocket, and I squeezed it until it hurt my palm.

"Where were you?" Misty was standing there with her hands on her hips. She had her eyes all made up and was wearing her new crushed-velvet pants and jacket. "Your mama said you were waiting on the porch."

"I was looking for Oliver." I slowed down, released my grip on the petal. "Why are you so dressed up?"

Misty nudged me and glanced over at Dean, meaning she didn't want him to hear what she had to say. He just glared at me the way he always did. When he climbed in the backseat, she grabbed me and whispered that his friend, Ronald, *you know the tall guy*, was going to come over later to spend the night. Misty was always in hopes that one of these nights one of Dean's friends would fall madly in love with her. We got in the backseat and, as Misty usually planned it, I was sitting right beside Dean, rigid for fear that my leg would accidentally touch his. Mr. Rhodes backed out of the driveway too fast, and it threw me in that direction; I tried to sit up but when I did, I felt Dean's hand on my forearm, holding me off balance. I turned suddenly, to look as we passed the cemetery, to see if there *was* someone out there, to see if I could see the exact spot where I had been, but when I turned, Dean was there looking at me, his dark-blue eyes almost black. His face softened as he pushed me back into my spot in the center and then with his arms crossed, fingers safely hidden, I felt him squeezing my upper arm. I wasn't sure what to do so I just sat there, Mr. Rhodes and Mo in the front seat pointing out these or those decorations, Misty talking about how the *four* of us *kids* could sit up late and watch "Shock Theatre," how we could fix popcorn and milkshakes and so on.

Misty's favorite song of the week was playing on the radio, "Have You Seen Her," and she rocked back and forth while she sang along with The Chi-Lites. Misty had a good voice and was the only white kid in school who could get away with singing Jackson Five or Supremes or Chi-Lites songs without *sounding* like she was *trying* to sound black. As a result she had befriended several black girls that other people were scared of and spent a lot of her time in front of the warped bathroom mirrors singing backup to Lily Hadley, who had an Afro that would've put Jimi Hendrix to shame.

"We'll see about the sitting up late," Mo said, but not once did Dean say no and that was so unlike him. Before we got to Hardee's, he had worked his hand over to find mine and held it against the cold vinyl of the seat, carefully hidden by his fur-lined denim jacket. I began thinking that Misty and Dean had *planned* this and that she had conveniently forgotten to tell me; I wasn't sure how I felt about Dean. He was not and never would have been my choice for a boyfriend, and yet, I had never really had one so what did I know. I sort of liked the way his hand felt, fingers curled around mine, our hands probably the same size, but I couldn't help but wonder if I would feel this same way in the daylight, face to face with him. Misty kept singing along with the radio, never even elbowing me, so I knew that she had no idea what her brother was doing. Don McLean was singing my favorite song of the month, "American Pie": *Did you write the book of love. . . .*

"Okay. Here we are." Mr. Rhodes pulled into the bright parking lot and just as discreetly as it had found me, Dean's hand disappeared. I clutched the plastic petal in my pocket and tried to think of some topic to start with Misty that could get and keep her talking. "Do you remember the name of that real sad movie we watched where the black girl who had been pretending to be white was chasing after her mama's funeral at the end?"

"*Imitation of Life*," she said, eyes eager as always when she talked about movies. Her favorites were the tear-jerkers, anything from *Stella Dallas* to *Old Yeller* to *Splendor in the Grass*; she read *T.V. Guide* faithfully. *Stella Dallas* was my favorite, and if I ever felt like working up a good cry, all I needed do was picture Barbara Stanwyck in those old clunky shoes as she hung on the iron fence and peered in the window at the daughter she'd let go. It sent a sudden chill through me to imagine myself as the daughter, Angela coming to our house to see *me*. And you're finally going to meet your cousin, my dad had said that day we went to Ferris Beach; she's going to *love* you. *I remember that day well*, she had just said about my birthday.

"*Madame X* is a good one. So is *Backstreet*," Mo said, and pushed open the door. "Misty, get me a Huskee Junior, some fries, and a chocolate shake," she said. "Thomas, what do you want?" Mr. Rhodes gave us his order too, and then the two of them went to sit and wait at a table. They picked a big one in the corner of the room, so we had windows on both sides and could see all the cars that circled the building. *Madame X* was the one when the mother was forced by the evil mother-in-law to leave home, never to see her child again, but to be thought of as dead. Suddenly there were so many possibilities and I wanted to pull Misty home and into the solitude of her room that very minute and start slowly at the very beginning, telling her everything I knew, and then the two of us would sit there and put it all together.

Dean sat across from me, and two times I felt his foot press down on the toe of my boot, and I wasn't sure if it was intentional or not. In the fluorescent light, he looked very pale, his long dark lashes making him look fragile, almost feminine like some kind of little foreign doll. His eyes were the shade of Mo's, that deep blue that almost looked violet in the right light, Liz Taylor eyes, my father had once remarked, to which Mrs. Poole had huffed and puffed and looked around in disbelief. My eyes were dark like my father's; my hair looked auburn in certain lights.

"Kate?" Mo was looking at me with those dark-blue eyes. I felt the pressure letting up on my toe as Dean leaned back in his chair and waved a french fry back and forth through ketchup. "Does your cousin visit often?" She was sitting with her legs apart, hands on top of her thighs, while Mr. Rhodes' arm rested on her shoulder; he toyed with the material of her collar. "I've never seen her visiting y'all before."

"No, she doesn't come often." At the risk of making Dean mad, I pulled my feet up close under my chair. I could not concentrate on him touching me and Mo talking about Angela at the same time. "But you do know her?"

"Well, I've seen her," Mo said. "I don't really *know* her."

"What's her name?" Mr. Rhodes asked and toyed with the chain around his neck. It was one of those broken charms that tells how you'll be reunited with one another one day. Misty had told me that her mother had the other half in her jewelry box, that they had given those to each other when they got married. Mo's stomach moved and Mr. Rhodes' attention went there instead.

"Angela," I said. "Angela Burns."

"Angela." He stared down at Mo's stomach and then shook his head. "I don't know. How do *you* know her?"

"I don't really," Mo said, and gently lifted Mr. Rhodes' hand from her stomach. "I've just seen her around, talked in the grocery-store line or something. I always assumed she was married?" She looked at me for an answer, and I shrugged, said that I had never heard if she was; I was embarrassed by my ignorance of my own relative. It seemed to me that Mo was relieved when I said that Angela had already left, but I couldn't tell for sure because she quickly changed the subject. I told her that if she or Mr. Rhodes *did* remember knowing Angela to tell me, and she said oh yes, she sure would. We had only ridden about three blocks when she said she wasn't feeling very well and thought we better get home. Peter, Paul, and Mary were singing "Leaving on a Jet Plane," and all I could think about was Angela; I could see her singing that song, leaving someone behind. Maybe on this very night that's what she had done; maybe she had come to tell my dad that she was leaving. Maybe she had left me. Maybe that's why my mother and I weren't close like Mo and Misty. Maybe she wasn't really my mother; the thought made me feel both guilty and exhilarated. I felt Dean's hand groping around my right side, thumping my ribcage like I might be a melon. *Hold me like you'll never let me go.*

Before midnight the Rhodeses went to the hospital. The last thing Mo said before leaving was that we should not sit up all night. She didn't say that Misty and I should go over to my house rather than stay there unchaperoned; she just said to think of her, they'd call soon with a Buddy or a Holly, and then she went into her old joking of Maybe Baby, That'll Be the Day, Well Allright. "Unplug the tree lights and the reindeer before you go to bed!" she called, and they were gone. Misty and I stood in the picture window and watched them drive off, Mr. Rhodes not even stopping at the stop sign at the corner there by the cemetery.

"Hot damn," Misty whispered, her eyelids still all glittery

green to match her crushed-velvet outfit. She had lately read that redheads should wear lots of green, and though I hadn't told her yet, I'd already heard at least one person in school refer to her as the Leprechaun of Samuel T. Saxon. "Now we can go watch movies. Ronald has been giving me the eye." I didn't tell her that Dean had been giving me the foot, the hand, and the eye. Instead I started talking about Angela, trying to work my way up to this new thought I'd had, this whole theory of my birth and adoption, but Misty kept interrupting, turning on the radio, then off, TV on and then off; she was so excited that she couldn't even look at me for more than a couple of seconds before she was up and moving all around.

"We're going out," Dean called, and Misty ran into the other room. They were going out the side door.

"Where? Where are you going?" She stood there, hands on her hips. "What if Mama calls? What if they need us?"

"She ain't gonna have it right this second." Dean looked at me, then looked down. "We don't want to hang out with y'all anyway. What're you gonna do, play on the telephone?" He made his voice high and girly sounding, one hand held limply in front of him. I was relieved. I had tried to imagine sitting in the dark living room with the glow of the Christmas lights, holding hands with Dean while Misty and Ronald watched TV in the other room.

"We might go with you," Misty said, but finally just shooed them away, locked the side door and turned back to me. "What do you think?" she asked. "Does he like me or what?" I shrugged, shook my head. I had not heard Ronald utter one word other than a quick "bye." "Well, let's think of what we'll do when they get back. I know." She clasped her hands and laughed that hyena laugh. "Let's short-sheet their beds." It was clear that with all the excitement, Misty was not going to be in the mood for any graveyard talk.

By the time we had done every old practical joke in the book, popped popcorn, and *not* gotten scared when we heard Dean and Ronald outside scratching on the window screens, Mr. Rhodes had called to say that Misty had a brother. Buddy Jefferson Rhodes, seven pounds and two ounces. We went outside and stood in the carport until Ronald and Dean saw us and came over from near the parking side of the cemetery.

"It's a girl!" Misty shouted and danced around, her arms lifted as she twirled, now wearing a heavy flannel gown and thick chenille robe. I was still in my clothes as I sat on the step and watched her leaping over the oil spot in her quilted bedroom shoes, her hair pulled back with a pink hairband. The excitement of the baby, combined with sitting up until the wee hours, had made her no longer care what Ronald thought about her appearance. "Her name is Cassandra Melissa Clarissa Patricia Inez Iona Rhodes and she weighed"—Misty slung her arms around Dean's neck and squeezed—"fifteen pounds and four ounces."

"Wow." Ronald stood there staring and shaking his head. "You don't believe that, do you?" Misty asked, her blue eyes wide and clear as she stepped right in front of the boy and threw her arms around his neck and kissed him on the mouth. "Well, if you believe that I have a sister with that name and weight, then you should believe that I did not kiss you just now." Ronald was standing there moving his head up and down as if he was having to think back through everything she had just said. Misty had said he liked to smoke pot, and it seemed maybe that was part of his problem. I was watching them and didn't even notice Dean standing right beside me until I felt his hand on my waist.

"You have a baby brother," I said without looking up. "Buddy Jefferson Rhodes."

"Thanks," he said, and reached inside to flip off the yellow light. I heard Misty blurt, "What," and then stop, maybe deciding that she wanted to be in the dark with Ronald. Again, Dean found my hand and held it while we watched Misty dancing circles around Ronald. He was laughing and just trying to keep up

with where she was. "Now, what's the baby's name?" he asked
again. I hoped Misty would not venture out into the street where
Mrs. Poole or my mother might look out and see her dancing in
her long pink bathrobe, which did *not* go with her hair.

I could feel Dean leaning in closer to me, and I knew that if
I turned my head to the side he would kiss me. It was just that
easy and yet, it was like my neck went rigid, like I could not
bend. I reminded myself of my mother when she did not give in
to those obnoxious peck peck pecks my father gave her. I let my
hand go completely limp, maybe the worst thing you could do
to a fifteen-year-old boy who had gotten up the nerve to make a
move, especially if you are a thirteen-year-old girl who has never
been approached by anyone who might even kind of like you.

I thought of Angela, her head leaned against the chain of the
swing, her eyes distant and dreamy without a care in the world. I
imagined her riding away, her friend at the wheel, his cap pulled
low, the windshield coated in the thick salty dampness as they
sang along with the radio, wind rushing past open windows.

Dean tried to pull me into him, but I froze and stayed that
way until he went inside and slammed the door. It was after three
in the morning, the moon at an angle I rarely saw. I pulled the
pink plastic petal from my pocket and held it in my open palm.
It would remind me of the street so empty and quiet, how I
crouched there in the darkness of the cemetery, the sudden fear
that came over me like a chill; it would remind me of Dean holding my hand and pressing my foot, of Misty deliriously dancing
about in her bathrobe. It would remind me of the birth of Buddy
Jefferson Rhodes, and it would remind me of Angela waiting in
the porch swing, how maybe her heart quickened as she saw me
from a distance, how she stood as I made my way down the sidewalk and then up the steps, how she reached out her arms and
hugged me to her.

Seven

It was New Year's Day when Angela called, her voice frantic when I lifted the receiver. "Fred?" she called. "Fred, is that you?" I could hear noise in the background, music and voices, as I held my hand over the mouthpiece and called for my father. He was stretched out on the sofa watching football, the volume of the set turned completely down so that he could hear his album of wildlife sounds. One minute he was at a bowl game, the next he was in a jungle with loud bird sounds, like chekaw chekaw. My mother sat at the end of the sofa, with my father's feet propped on her lap as she worked on a needlepoint piece that she would soon sew into yet another pillow to decorate the wicker settee on the sunporch. She had quite a collection, all Victorian floral designs on a black background. When my father got up to answer the phone, she stopped her work to watch and listen, motioned for me to turn down the long-winded blast of an elephant and the rapid chatter of a band of monkeys.

His back was to us as he stood there twisting the phone cord. "Who was it?" my mother asked, and stretched her legs out on the coffee table, an unusual pose for her, a *vacation* pose. There were about three times during the year, New Year's Day being one of them, when my mother declared she was on vacation and was not going to do anything except cook, which she did not consider work, but hobby. It was on these rare days that she announced she'd like to have a drink, more specifically a beer, and then proceeded to have one; now she sat watching my father, a can of Schlitz neatly bound in a Christmas napkin lifted to her mouth. I shrugged but she kept looking at me, waiting for more.

"It was real loud," I said, "like maybe there was a party or something, or maybe it was a pay phone."

"I see," she said. "Well, dramatic things always seem to happen around the holidays."

"Like what?" I was tired of the cryptic messages that she so often delivered; messages that seemed not meant for me but instead simply her thoughts escaping.

"Like what? Well, let's see." She took another sip and leaned her head back against the couch. "Well, someone could do something dramatic like run away and get married, or maybe drink too much and drive into a parked car." She laughed sarcastically, eyes on my father as he stepped back into the room, his face flushed as he nervously raked the fingers of his right hand through his hair. I was still standing by the stereo, which was now emitting only faint growls and chatters, as I waited to hear more, the answers to the riddles.

"If only Theresa Poole could see you now," he said and laughed, though it was easy to see through his attempt at lightening the mood. "She'd at least suggest that you have some sherry or perhaps a bit of port." He crooked his finger, another attempt at being funny but it was clear that he was falling flat.

"And what if she could see me?" Mama asked, and drained the can. I knew as well as she did that Mrs. Poole was out of town and there was no chance that she'd *drop by* as she so often did. It occurred to me then that *that* was the system to timing my mother's beer and needlepoint vacations; she took a vacation when Mrs. Poole was out of town. "So, who was on the phone?"

"Angela." He said her name while staring out the window, watching the bare limbs of a tree moving back and forth, two squirrels collecting twigs to jungle sounds. "She's in a bit of trouble."

"Told you." Mama looked at me and nodded, then raised her eyes to his sudden look of surprise. "Yes, that's right. I was telling Katie how the holidays always have a really dramatic effect on some people. You know, it's the suicide season; wreck your car, run away and get married."

"And all those are one and the same?" He sat down beside her, his arm reaching behind her head, finger stroking her cheek. "Suicide and marriage?"

"She tried to kill herself?" I asked, having not yet had time to absorb the fact that apparantly she *had* gotten married, that she *had* run into a parked car.

"Of course not," my father said; for the first time I'd ever seen, there was a huge ink spot on the pocket of his crisp white shirt. "And she barely bumped her car that time, Cleva."

"It was *our* car," she said and then turned to me, her elbow propped such that it looked as if she were toasting with that Christmas-wrapped Schlitz can, like some kind of Statue of Liberty parody. "And she thinks far too much of herself to ever commit suicide."

"And thank God for that," he said, motioning for me to lift the needle which had reached the end of the safari sounds. "Just turn it off," he said when he saw me flip over the album to read what was on the other side, "Swamp Sounds." "She wants to move out. She has no place to go."

"And so you said, 'Why don't you stay here with us for awhile.' Right?" She put the can on the table beside her and stood up, smoothed back her hair and began straightening the room. Mauve and violet wool threads lay in a jumble where she had been sitting. "Happy New Year."

"I told her I'd ask you." He stood and grabbed her by the wrists, waited for her to look at him. I kept waiting for one of them to ask me to leave, to send me on some scavenger hunt of an errand, but they didn't. "Look, the guy has threatened her." He lowered his voice, leaned in until their foreheads were touching. "Physically threatened her."

"What guy? Her husband?" Again, I pictured the man on Ferris Beach. A bright summer day, but he was dressed in long pants and a long-sleeved blue shirt, hat pulled low on his forehead, a flash of silver like a chain or a belt buckle.

"Yes, her husband," my father said quietly. "I think this marriage is over. It was a big mistake and Angela knows that now."

"Why didn't anybody ever tell me . . ." Before I could finish my thought, my mother was going on and on in an exaggerated way. *Why and who ever would've thought that this marriage, this union crafted in heaven and founded on the floor of a bar and grill and/or bowling alley would come to an end?*

"Can I bring her home?" He spoke in a slow deliberate voice. "Just until she can find something else." He lifted her chin and they locked stares; I was holding my breath, "Swamp Sounds" still in my hands. When she nodded, gave into his embraces, I reached for the paper sleeve and put the album away. "It'll be okay this time, honey," he said and then was gone, reaching under the sofa for his shoes, grabbing his coat from the hall closet. "I don't know when we'll get here," he yelled. "I'll call you if it looks like it's going to be real late." We both stood quietly, listening to the distant sound of his engine turning over. She watched the silent football game on TV for a few seconds. "You better punt," she said, and then waited, nodding as she saw her advice put into action.

"When did Angela drive our car?" I finally asked, the silence unbearably awkward. I began straightening pillows and magazines to avoid looking at her.

"Off sides." She pointed to the screen and then sighed and turned it off; under normal circumstances, I would have marveled at her knowledge of football. "When she was a teenager. We were still living in South Carolina."

"Was I born?" I asked, and she shook her head. "Is that when she was living with you?"

"Yes." She went and lifted her needlepoint, sat back down in her corner of the sofa, the imprint of my father's head still on the pillow at the other end. "It was right before you were born. We didn't need that kind of worry." *We* didn't, the two of them, the three of them? I imagined my mother standing on an unfamiliar sidewalk as she examined the dented car, Angela in tears, her long hair swept up in a high ponytail.

"There's a lot that you don't know, Katie," she began. "We took Angela in even before your grandmother died and I treated her like she was my daughter, which wasn't easy given that she was a teenager and I had never had a child." She paused, lips pressed together as she shook her head. "I wasn't exactly *old*, you know. Thirty-five may *sound* old to you, but it's not at all." She sat there, wisps of hair slipping from her bun. "It hurt me when she left so abruptly. All that time I had spent helping her, sewing her clothes and cooking her meals and paying her way to the movies or wherever she needed to go; I had just finished writing to junior colleges in hopes that she could get in somewhere and then she was just gone, a three-line note pinned to her pillow." She paused, as if trying to picture the words. " 'Thank you for what you have done for me. But I have got to leave right now. I'll tell you more later.' " She spoke the words mechanically. "I mean that's all she said."

"Was I born then?"

"Yes," she nodded, her poised needle threaded in violet. "You were born two weeks before she left. So finally when I really *needed* her, she was gone."

"Why?"

She shrugged, breathed out. "Fred had already taken his job here, and we were all set to move. She said that she didn't want to leave South Carolina, so she went to Dillon and got married."

"She's been married all this time?" I sat in my father's corner of the sofa and propped my feet on the coffee table, where there was a mixed stack of his *National Geographic*s and her *Better Homes and Gardens*. I thought of Mo Rhodes in Hardee's the night Buddy was born. *I always assumed she was married*, she had said.

"Oh, no." My mother shook her head, stared at the empty TV screen. "That lasted a very brief while." She pulled out a strand of black wool and held it up to the light to thread the needle. "This is the *second* husband she's leaving today."

I was too stunned to ask anything else for awhile, and so just sat and also stared into the blank green screen. The blue sky was already darkening, and I realized that I had not gone over to Misty's house as I had promised that I'd do. *I remember that day*, Angela had said about my birthday. What if it was all true, everything that I had imagined, Madame X or Stella Dallas. I needed to tell Misty, to add these new facts to all that I had outlined for her on Christmas Day as we sat on a high branch of the tree and waited for parkers. "Wow," Misty had said. "Just think. You may be a real live *love child*. And somewhere you may have this young, really cool Dad." She grinned and tossed an acorn out into the cemetery, snapped her fingers and in her best Diana Ross mode, began singing "Love Child." It was what we called *graveyard talk* both literally and figuratively, words never to be spoken to another living soul.

"Can I go to Misty's?" I asked. She jumped with the suddenness of my question, dropping her needle. "I promised her that I would."

"Sure." She sat up straight, smoothed back the wisps of her hair as if my going out the front door and stepping across Wilkins Road was like opening our home to the world. "Please don't say anything about where your father has gone." She bit her lip in hesitation. "It's the kind of thing Theresa Poole would enjoy hearing and spreading. Now . . ." She raised her finger as if to erase any thought that I might be preparing to have. "I am not saying that to be unkind because Mrs. Poole is a *good* woman and she *is* a friend of mine. Still . . ." Another wave of her finger. "I can't always trust her on things like this. I mean it's just too tempting. *I* would be tempted by such gossip." She stood, once again placing her needlepoint in her seat. "*St. Peter* would be tempted by such gossip." She laughed and then waited for me to assure her that I wouldn't tell where my father had gone. I was almost out the front door when she called me back, and I feared she was going to make me *cross my heart and hope to die* that I wouldn't say anything at all and then I'd be torn between confiding my feelings to Misty and living without the invited threat of death.

She was in the middle of the kitchen, a big pot in her hands. I stood in the doorway, waiting, one hand hidden in the pocket of my jacket in case I needed to cross my fingers. She was wearing her purple bedroom shoes, and she had untwisted her hair and let it fall down her back, another *vacation* thing to do, and I felt a pang of emptiness as I watched her there, the holiday having come to a quick ending.

"Mary Katherine," she said, her voice slow and controlled. "I have something very important to say."

"Okay." I stepped closer, wondering if I should sit or stand, if I should laugh or cry.

"I never grew up eating a *special* meal on New Year's Day." She sucked in a sharp breath. "I don't even know that I consider black-eyed peas and cabbage to be *special* foods." She turned to me then, tilted the pot to show black-eyed peas cooked down to mush, a big piece of fatback covering the top. "I personally don't think it has one damn thing to do with luck and I am right now thinking that I'd just as soon have manicotti or ratatouille; I wouldn't mind having macaroni and cheese."

"Okay."

"You're not superstitious?" she asked, and I shook my head. "Good." She turned and dumped the pot into the trashcan. "Because I've eaten this mess of a meal since I left home years ago and I've had my fill, hoppin' John, hog fat surprise. I say, bring on the chowder, baked beans, lobster." She scraped the pot with a fork. "And I wouldn't say that it's made such a difference in my luck. If it has, then heaven help me." I stood there waiting, and when she finished her scraping and turned towards me, her face was flushed and her eyes were watering. "Don't be late," she said, and I hurried outside and across the street where Misty was in the carport twirling her baton. She had gotten a new one for Christmas, a *real* one, she had said over and over, *not one those little kid dimestore jobs*. I recognized the car in their driveway, an old Galaxy 500 that belonged to Betty and Gene Files.

"I was wondering where you were," she said, lifting her knees in marching simulation as she did the figure eight. "I had to get outside. That Files kid is so horrible, he's getting on my nerves bad." She began marching forward and then flipped the baton over one shoulder and caught it behind her back. "Pretty neat, huh? Betty taught me how to do it." Misty stopped twirling so she could talk. "She used to be a majorette in high school, and I didn't even know it."

"Misty?" Dean was leaning out the side door. "Dad said to come in and get your picture made. He's got the camera all set up." He glanced at me and then went back inside, the door slamming shut on all the laughter and talk.

"I can't wait to tell you something," I whispered when she motioned for me to come with her. She asked *what*, but there was no way I could tell her under such rushed circumstances. This was one of those stories that, if we couldn't get to the cemetery, required the perfect setting, everything in order, use the bathroom, get your drink of water, get all distractions out of the way before the story begins. I followed her inside where Mr. Rhodes was fiddling with a camera up on a tripod; it was set up like some kind of tall insect in the center of the room, and then all the people were squeezed in on the big Indian-print floor cushions opposite the silver tree.

"Hi, Kitty," Mo said, and patted the floor to her left. "You and Misty come sit right here." Buddy was all wrapped up in a blue blanket and asleep on her lap; it was amazing that he could sleep through it all, the chatter louder than any band of monkeys in any jungle.

"I thought it was a *family* picture," Dean said. "The two families."

"Kitty is family," Mo said. "Aren't you, honey?"

"I'll just watch," I said, and waved my hand, "really." Mo and Misty were the only two begging my participation; Mr. Rhodes would have, I was certain, but he was too busy fiddling with the camera. Jeffrey Files was three and had a gun that made a loud, whirring sound. "Like father, like son," Betty Files laughed, and patted her husband's hip where he had a holster and gun. Misty had once told me that a highway patrolman is always on duty; *It's the law,* she said.

I stood in the doorway watching: Betty Files with her arm around Gene, who was leaned back on his elbows, the handle of that large black gun right near his hand, Jeffrey sprawled out on top of him. On his other side was Mo, dark wavy hair hanging to her shoulders, her face still plump from her pregnancy, but beautiful as ever as she sat there in a shiny emerald-green shirt and a pair of black knit pants, barefooted as always, toenails painted. Dean and Misty knelt behind her, Misty's hands on her mother's shoulders; there was just enough room beside Mo for Mr. Rhodes to run over and sit before the flash. They took this same pose five times, Mr. Rhodes perspiring and out of breath when he finally decided to stop, the rest of them getting sillier and giddier with each shot.

"Please get in the picture," Mo called to me, and this time patted the tiny bit of space to her left, which now was primarily occupied by Gene Files's leg and handcuffs. "Please." She turned and patted Mr. Rhodes on the leg. "One more picture, Thomas," she said, and again motioned to me. "Come on now. You know we want you in the picture." I felt like an Amazon as I crossed the living room, all the blood rushing to my face as I sensed Dean's stare. Mr. Files flashed me a big grin. His wife managed a weak smile as she tried to release Jeffrey's hold on her neck.

"Make room," Mo said, and swatted Mr. Files's leg. "I will thank you to move those handcuffs." She laughed. "They're in Kitty's seat."

"And where should I *put* them?" he asked, momentarily toying with the silver circles before clinking them into his pocket.

"Don't be so difficult," Betty Files said. "Isn't he the most difficult?"

"Okay now, say mozzarella," Mr. Rhodes said, and dashed to his seat. He was all out of breath, his face pale, and I made the mistake of turning to watch him, the flash catching me in profile.

Before I ever got the chance to talk to Misty, it was decided that she and Dean would stay home with the kids while the four adults went to a movie. "I'll make it up to you, guys," Mo had told Dean and Misty. "Your dad and I need a little night out every now and then, don't you think?" By the time it was over, Dean had wiggled out of the deal and gone out with his friend Ronald, and Misty had accepted the job, provided she got paid for it. I followed Misty and Mo back into Buddy's room, where nursery rhyme characters decorated the walls. "Here are his p.j.s," Mo said, and nuzzled Buddy's little face. "Make the girls behave," she said. "Try to keep them from calling boys and hanging up when they answer." She didn't even look at us when she said this, even though Misty had been caught doing that very thing only days before. "Tell them sleep tight and goodnight and don't let the bedbugs bite. Tell them happy New Year." Mo kissed all three of us and then went back out into the living room with Betty and Gene.

"We won't be late," Mr. Rhodes said, and kissed the top of

Misty's head. "Hey, I'm driving this time," he said as they stepped out into the carport. "Somebody's got to be responsible, and we know from last time that the patrolman isn't." They were all laughing as the car doors slammed, and I imagined my mother standing on the front porch observing it all, observing laughter, observing life. Once again I thought of Angela. I was ready to talk to Misty but I knew that it was a hopeless night; I could never get the stage set and all the distractions cleared, as they needed to be for this particular story. "So what did you have to tell me?" Misty asked, matronly in an absurd way as she stood there in her tight bell-bottom jeans and tested baby formula on her wrist, all the while watching Jeffrey Files, who was in a rather precarious position as he stood on a chair and reached for Mr. Rhodes's Goodyear salesmanship plaque.

"My mother drank a beer today," I said, gaining momentum as I went along, Misty amazed and laughing, Jeffrey sliding the plaque back and forth, Buddy crying until his face turned blood red. "She did. A Schlitz. In the can. She wrapped it up in a little Christmas napkin." Misty struck a pose, lips pursed, nose in the air, and then laughed again.

"A *Schlitz*? So how many did she have?" Misty asked, finally getting Buddy to take the bottle.

"Just one, I think." The story was dwindling.

"That's what you were going to tell me?" she asked. She probably would have seen right through me had Dean and Ronald not walked in and stolen her attention. They went straight and turned on the TV, football and football and football. "Men," Misty said loudly, elbowing me, and then leaned close to whisper, "Don't you just *love* them?"

When I got home, my mother was back in her corner of the sofa with her needlepoint, Mozart on the stereo, a little night music, and I watched her feet point and flex with each beat, her slippers under the coffee table, what I assumed to be a new Schlitz all wrapped up beside her. Though she looked relaxed, the house smelled of Lysol and lemon oil and I knew she had done a quick cleaning. "Have fun?" she asked, without even looking up, and I told her it was okay. "We can eat whenever you're ready," she said. "I don't think we should wait for Fred." I sat down on the other end of the sofa and thumbed through a magazine until the needle reached the end of the album and she stood to say that we should eat.

"Happy New Year," she said when I got to the table and beside my plate of manicotti, she placed a little bowl with a spoonful of black-eyed peas and one little flimsy piece of steamed cabbage. "Why take any chances, right?" she asked and sat down, leaned forward with elbows on the table, face cupped in her large square hands. "We could use a little luck, couldn't we?" she asked and something in her face, her tone, her very presence, made me want to cry.

I stayed awake until long past midnight, WOWO Fort Wayne, Indiana, playing beneath my pillow as I waited to hear a car door. Around eleven-thirty, I heard Mo and Mr. Rhodes get home, calls of good night, and a car driving away. I heard water in the pipes, my mother still up and walking through the house, moving like a shadow from room to room as she looked for something to do now that her vacation was over. It was only ten forty-seven in Indiana as they once again played the year's top twenty songs. The night before I had listened to the new year roll in twice, once in Fulton and once in Indiana, a whole hour spent tossing back and forth between 1971 and 1972, and if I could have picked up stations all the way to the Pacific, I would have continued the pattern. Now I lay there, trying to stay awake, trying to imagine where my father was, what he was doing. Carole King was singing "It's Too Late," and though I tried to force myself awake, I fell asleep before they reached number one, Three Dog Night once again singing "Joy to the World."

Angela's stay was as brief as my father had said it would be, and no one discussed any of the circumstances surrounding her separation or the bruise on my father's face. I was in school the two days she was there, and in the evenings my mother *insisted* on helping me with my homework while my father and Angela watched television downstairs. I wanted to ask my mother questions, but there was something, the set of her jaw, something in the air, that kept me from doing it. The day Angela left, her old blue Impala backfiring as she backed down our drive, my mother proclaimed it a vacation day and proceeded to drink another Schlitz; this time she wrapped the can in a little ruffled Coke-bottle skirt, one of a set that Mrs. Poole had brought from her trip to Atlanta. It was four in the afternoon, and she drank it sitting right out on our front porch. When she was finished, my father and I both watching in silence, she stood and said, "*Now* I can make my resolutions," and she went inside to strip the sheets from the bed in the guest room. My father *immediately* handed me a piece of paper and pen. "Hey, you'll like this one," he said. "Multiply your age by seven and multiply that by 1443." He sat looking over my shoulder as I scribbled along, finally getting an answer of 131313. "Works every time," he said as I stared at the repetition of the bad-luck age. "You can count on this to work every year of your life."

It was a month or so after, when Misty and I had had plenty of time to muse over my situation, plenty of time to create numerous plots, all of them possible, that I took Misty's advice and told my mother that I needed my birth certificate for a report I was doing at school. "It's a report on *my* family history," I told her. "I'm supposed to tell all about *my* birth."

"What a wonderful idea that is," she said, and went straight to the small top drawer of her secretary, flipped through several papers, and surfaced with a white envelope, my full name written on the front. "Here. Now don't lose it." She closed the drawer. "You know I can help you with this. I can tell you so much about that day. From the moment I opened my eyes until the moment you were born." *I remember that day well.*

"Maybe she had it all planned," Misty offered later as we walked home from school. "I mean, she knew that sooner or later you'd ask questions, right? So you see she had this *fake* birth certificate all printed up and waiting in that drawer."

"I don't know."

"But it's possible," Misty said. "It really is possible."

Eight

Mo Rhodes left home on the fourth of July, taking Buddy, who was just over six months old, with her. I had seen them, the whole town had, just earlier that evening when we all went to the old air field to watch the fireworks. Most of the women brought big pieces of oilcloth and beach towels to spread, and then here came Mo with two quilts and nice plump bed pillows for them to lounge on. Misty and Dean carried the big laundry basket that Mo had filled to the brim with wonderful food. She was famous around town for her cooking and what surprised other women the most was that she was glad to give you a recipe. "I have no secrets," she once told Mama, who repeated this to Mrs. Poole, and then the two sat there staring at one another and shaking their heads in disbelief. Her recipes would say things like "Beat the hell out of it" or "Mash those lumps" or "Boil that rascal till the bones fall out." Even Mrs. Poole had to smile over some of those recipes.

By and large Mo had won over most of the women; they still said that her house with her little mock Japanese yard was taste-less and garish, and that she really should wear her skirts longer and her hair shorter, and that she should use more discipline on Dean and Misty, both of whom were known for their outspoken sarcasm, and yet all of these things were said in amusement as if some part of them truly envied her differences. She wasn't *one* of them, by any means, and I think that was probably what the other women simultaneously admired and despised the most. "You'd think she'd be honored that we asked her to join a club," Mrs. Poole had sat in our kitchen and said countless times.

Mo Rhodes looked like a movie star, and that's what I was thinking from our piece of yellow check oilcloth as I watched her there, her hair swept up into a huge tortoise clip, wisps falling around her neck and forehead in a Gibson Girl look. It seemed Mr. Rhodes could not take his eyes off her as she sat there cud-dling Buddy, who was all dressed up in a little red, white, and blue sleeper. I was about to ask Mama if I could go over there and sit, when Misty came walking over. The high school band, a sea of little white caps with orange and black tassles, was playing an off-key version of "Que Sera Sera." It was Misty's greatest goal now to be a high school majorette and so she carefully studied the Fulton Marching Band, so that later she could hum their off-key songs as she practiced marching in front of her mother's full-length mirror, while I lay on the purple simulated-fur bedspread and told her what did and did not look good.

"Well, hello, Misty Rhodes," my father said, the earplug of his transistor firmly wedged in his right ear. "Or is it Misty Highways? Misty Avenues?" She didn't laugh as she usually did, just smirked and flopped down. He readjusted the volume of his radio, a baseball commentary coming through loud and clear, and went back to scribbling in his little notebook.

"Have you eaten already?" I asked, and she shook her head. It was dusk by then, people moving like shadows, their voices mur-muring hums from blanket to blanket, matches flaring to light cigarettes and oil lamps, children waving flashlights like beacons. Soon the fireworks would begin. My father stretched out, hands behind his head and closed his eyes. "Bottom of the fifth," he said to my mother, and she nodded absentmindedly and patted his leg as you would an obedient dog. "No runs. Raining in St. Louis. Picking up some static."

"Fine, honey," Mama said, and patted him again; she was talking with Mrs. Poole, who always brought a chair from home. It was not even a webbed aluminum like most people brought but a folding adirondack with matching footstool. If she said *adirondack* once she said it a thousand times, while poor old Mr. Landell worked up a sweat just to lift it from the trunk of the Lincoln and get it all set up for her. Mr. Landell had left her with us and gone over to the other side of the field where some black families were gathered. "Lucky Mr. Landell," Daddy whispered when Mr. Landell walked off, with Mrs. Poole still calling out for him to be sure and come load her up just before it all ended so they could miss the crowd.

"Now, I do recall a time when Gracie Oliver made a Key lime pie for a party, or so she *said* it was a Key lime pie," Mrs. Poole was saying. "I don't think she had used limes at all, to be honest."

"Let's go over to your family," I whispered to Misty. She was staring in the direction of where they were all set up, two glowing tiki torches marking the spot.

"No way." Misty reached into our basket and got a drumstick and then just sat there holding it. Now people were like silhouettes against the darkening sky. Mr. Rhodes was no longer on their blanket, just Mo and Buddy. She was leaning back on her elbows, ankles crossed as she stared up at the empty sky. Buddy was lying beside her, asleep with his arms and legs spread-eagle.

"Where's Dean?" I asked, still watching Mo.

"He went to watch a fight." Misty glanced at my mother, Mrs. Poole, and Mrs. Edith Turner, whose hair seemed to have taken on a pinkish hue since the last time we'd seen her, and then flapped her hand, fingers to thumb, to indicate ceaseless chatter. "Dexter Hucks is going to fight a boy from the beach. Dean says there's a whole gang of them looking for a fight."

"Now, are you the little Rhodes girl?" Mrs. Turner asked, emphasizing "little," which I knew would make Misty furious. When Misty gave a slight nod, Edith Turner, who was wearing a long yellow tunic vest, went right back to her whispering. "I remember that Key lime pie," she said.

"Something's not right," Misty said to me then, the drumstick still in her hand. My father's radio was buzzing, the voices going up and down like a hive of bees, so I knew he had it turned up as loud as it could go to tune out some people from across the way who were singing "Tennessee Waltz" with the slow rambling bleats of the Fulton High School Band.

There were yells and screams from the far edge of the field, revved-up motorcycle engines, a row of blue-jeaned adolescents, black and white arms raised and waving, cheering the fight. There was a single sky rocket to indicate the show was about to begin, and I watched it soar well above the statue in front of City Hall, a little stone soldier erected to honor the dead. There was a breeze high in the limbs of those summer green trees, the smell of clover and onion grass, chicken and watermelon, and when I looked back over at Mo Rhodes, she and Buddy were gone, the tiki torches casting a yellow glow on the empty quilt. I turned to Misty, ready to ask her why her parents had left, but she was sitting there hugging her knees with her head dropped back as she stared up at the sky. A clover chain she had made earlier by threading flowers through fine slits in the stems hung around her neck as she leaned her head to one side, clover against her cheek. There was something in her silence that made me hold my question, and instead I inched over closer to her, hugged my knees, and stared up just as she was doing. My knee was right next to hers, and when the first boom and spray of lights hit the sky, I felt her knee press against mine, harder and harder. The fight was being broken up by some adults, and the yelling voices grew fainter as the cheering boys and packs of motorcycles were sent in different directions. "Bottom of the sixth," my father said, and my mother patted his foot and then held onto it in an affectionate way. I pressed back against Misty's knee just as a Roman candle burst into brilliant red flames, and as I turned to watch the falling sparks, I saw her jaw clenched and quivering as if she were about to cry. "I got my adirondack from the only place you *can* get an adirondack, and that's there in the mountains of New York State. The Adirondacks," Mrs. Poole was saying, and then there was a burst of light, bathing Misty's face for an instant in the glow and then giving way to darkness.

Mr. Landell came and packed up Mrs. Poole's adirondack chair and footstool just before the *grand finale*, which consisted of three sky rockets bursting simultaneously while the high school majorettes twirled fire batons to "Yankee Doodle." Misty did not even react to the fire twirling as she normally would have. Instead, she kept looking over at that empty quilt square, those tiki torches with their little native faces carved there near the top. "Won't you be scared to twirl fire?" I whispered to her, and I knew from her blank stare that somehow that bit of optimism, the assumption that she would one day *be* a majorette, had failed. I was not good at pretending and assuming that everything was all right, *stating* that everything was perfect; that was Misty's role, and there she sat, drained of all of her promises of how *anything is possible*.

My father had fallen asleep, and my mother had to sit there and shake his leg until he woke, sat up, and looked all around in a puzzled way that made us laugh. We gathered our things and began walking with the crowd over to where our station wagon was parked on the street. "Misty, are you going to ride with us?" Mama asked just before we got to the Rhodeses' things, and could see the muddy footprints on the light fabrics of the quilt where people had tramped. "Your mama forgot her things."

"Maybe I should just wait here," Misty said, and stacked those plump bed pillows, put the plastic red plates and tumblers back in the laundry hamper they had brought. "I mean they wouldn't have just left me." She emphasized *left*, her voice straining to laugh in that all-is-well way. I heard Dean before I saw him, his thin wavery voice rising above those of the boys he walked with. "See ya," he called, and then he was there in the light of the tiki torches, where my parents stood with their arms full of our leftovers and oilcloth. "Where are Mom and Dad?" he asked, and stopped right in front of Misty. She was on her knees, hair falling over her eyes as she began folding the quilt the way you might a flag, one long piece that she then began folding over in triangles.

"I don't know." She sat back in the grass and sighed. "You all can go on now, Dean's here."

"Well, where are your parents?" Mama stepped closer and I knew she was studying the face on that tiki torch; I could imagine her telling Mrs. Poole what it looked like up close. She reached and lightly ran her finger over the savage face. "You know, I bet they went to the store or something. The fireworks usually go on so much later, and they'll be here any second." Mama was smiling now, nodding, looping her arm through my father's. "So we'll just take you and Dean and your things home, and your parents will know that's what happened. They know we wouldn't just leave you here."

"But they would," Misty said and looked at Dean, her chin quivering. "They've left us."

"Bull—" Dean caught himself and stopped, kicked his toe into the grass. "Let's go." He picked up the laundry basket and we all piled into the car. It was so quiet while we rode the several blocks that I could hear Dean breathing, the air going in and out of his flared nostrils in short little puffs. "Wichita Lineman" came on the radio and my father turned it up. It was not until we parked at my house that I realized I had sat rigid all the way, afraid that my leg or arm might brush against Dean and he would get the wrong idea. It seemed like it was so easy to give somebody the *wrong* idea and so hard to give the *right* idea. I was thinking about all of that when I noticed that Misty was not even moving to get out of our car, but was turned with head on arm to look out the back window and down the tunnel of large oaks marking our drive, across the street to her own dark house. The only lights were those of the little iron lanterns on either side of Mo's Japanese footbridge that led to the front steps, and then the dull yellow of the carport bulb.

"I know," Mama was saying. "I'll fix us some popcorn." The way she kept coming up with ideas and the way she kept trying to touch Misty, to smooth her hair or pat her arm, made me uneasy. I knew my mother also felt that something was not right; I knew she was not one to *over*react and so if she was reacting at all, then chances were there was definite reason.

"I'm not hungry," Misty said, and then suddenly jumped out of the car and ran to where Dean stood in the center of our driveway, his back to the gates of Whispering Pines.

It was close to midnight when we saw Mr. Rhodes's car turn onto our street. Misty and I were out on the porch in the swing, Dean across the street in their carport, where he had taken apart an old lawnmower and was starting to put it back together. My parents had gone inside, but I knew my mother was still awake. Misty held onto my arm when the car stopped, her breath held as we waited to see if she was with him. Dean didn't move from his spot on the concrete, even when Mr. Rhodes stopped, looked down, his hand on Dean's shoulder, and then went through the back door, a slow trail of lights marking the way from kitchen to bedroom. Misty swallowed hard and then went limp against the back of the swing, the chains creaking with the sudden change in weight. "She left us," she whispered, and then as if in slow motion, she was up and moving down the steps, through the yard, and across the street, where Dean was waiting at the end of the drive. I sat, watching until the two disappeared in the house. It was warm and there was practically no breeze, the tendrils of ivy on the cemetery gate barely moving; I could hear the cars passing on the interstate, the whoosh of their passing, rising and falling like ocean waves. *Where* was Mo? *How* could she do this? I thought of her there on the quilt, and I thought of Angela; I tried to imagine them both, where they were, what they would be doing at this very moment. As I watched Misty's house go dark, I felt a chill all the way through. Suddenly I was afraid to be there on the porch without the protection of the walls of my room or the screens and height of the sleeping porch. I felt vulnerable, exposed, as if someone was out there hidden in the darkness, hidden and waiting.

Nine

Mo Rhodes was gone almost twenty hours before she called home. Misty and I were playing Chinese checkers and Dean was working on a model of a '59 Thunderbird when the phone rang. The TV was on, "I Love Lucy," the episode where Lucy has gotten a loving cup stuck on her head and has to get it off so it can be presented down at the Tropicana. "No!" Mr. Rhodes yelled when Misty ran toward the phone. "I'll get it." He had been sitting on the couch, staring at the same page of the newspaper for over an hour. It seemed the phone rang forever, Dean sitting there with the tube of cement glue and little spare tire lifted and frozen, Misty standing in the wildly patched-up cutoffs and green poor-boy shirt with the wide-toothed zipper that she always wore around home.

"Hello?" Mr. Rhodes voice was loud and deep as he stared at the speckled linoleum of the kitchen, flicked the cover of a book of matches open and closed. "Yes, I'm here." He glanced over at us, but it was like he could see through, as if we were made of glass or not even there. "You should have called sooner. You should have . . ." He stopped, again looking at us, his eyes dull. Then it seemed an eternity that he listened, tears rolling down his thin bony face and him not even bothering to wipe them away, not even turning his head so that we wouldn't see. Dean dropped the tiny wheel, and it rolled off the card table and was lost in the thick shag carpet. I reached out and began feeling for it, but he just sat there, like Misty, staring at Mr. Rhodes, who now was holding the receiver so tightly that his knuckles were white.

"Chainsaw?" Lucy Ricardo asked to an explosion of laughter.

"You're not thinking, Mo," he whispered. "It's not worth it. What about . . ." Again he listened, cleared his throat. "Look, you do what you want." He sighed, pulled a cigarette from his shirt pocket and lit it. "But you bring the baby home. The baby stays with us."

"Oh, great." Dean jumped up from the table, his fold-up chair falling behind him, crashing against the bricks of the fireplace. "She's really left us. She's gone." He was looking at Misty now, his face contorted as he tried not to cry, a smaller darker version of his father. "That son of a bitch." His high boyish voice sounded so foolish uttering the big manly words, and yet he still gained our attention and respect. Ethel was on the telephone asking, "Do you think you can get a loving cup off of a woman's head?"

"That's just your oldest son voicing his opinion," Mr. Rhodes said, his voice made stronger by Dean's words, threatening. "Yes, she's here. Kate is over here with her." Misty sat staring at the mention of her name, a look of hope on her face, as Dean pushed the table up and over, hundreds of tiny black and silver parts disappearing into the carpet.

"You cannot have Buddy." His voice was loud now, forceful and angry. "I don't give a damn about you." He paused and in that second Misty was up and running to him, reaching for the phone, crying, begging, but he held her away with one hand against her chest. "But Buddy's place is here. You're not fit to have him. And hey"—he laughed loud and sarcastically—"how about asking the son of a bitch to give Betty a call. She still doesn't believe it's true, doesn't believe you would do this to her." He cradled the receiver under his neck and with his other hand pressed down to break the connection. Misty slapped his hand away and sat on the floor, face in her hands.

"It's all your fault," she screamed when he tried to lift her. "I hate you. You let her leave. You let her." He knelt there, his hand suspended above her back as if he were afraid to touch. "It's going to be all right, baby," he said. "Maybe she'll change her mind. Maybe she'll decide to come home."

"Will she?" She spat the question and then stopped cold as she crawled towards him.

"She's bringing Buddy home. She'll be here tonight," Mr. Rhodes said. "She promised."

"But will she stay?" She looked up at her father, and he looked away, over at the sink where Mo's wildly colored apron hung.

"I don't know," he said.

Neither of them looked up as I put all of the Chinese checker marbles in their right color and then closed the box. Lucy still had not gotten the trophy off her head and was sitting there crying, Ethel by her side. Neither Misty nor her father looked up as I tiptoed past and out the side door into the carport, where Dean was throwing a rubber ball up against the brick wall. He held his throw while I started to walk past and then right when I got in front of him, threw it hard into my side. I stopped and stared at him, his teeth bared like a bony-faced camel as he stepped up to me. "Why don't you get the hell out of here?" he said, his breath like soured milk, but when I took a step forward, he threw his arm out and caught me under the neck. "You are the ugliest girl I know," he said, and pressed in closer, pinning me to the wall of the carport where his superball had left perfect little circles of dirt. I stared down, at the grease stains on the concrete, at the bright yard beyond the shade of the carport, seeing clover patches and a huge bumblebee, the sway of the oaks lining our driveway, taking in the smell of cut grass and the sound of a distant mower droning like the window units and the traffic of the interstate. "Why are you always hanging around here? Huh?" He pressed in closer, his soured mouth open on my neck, on the right side, as I pushed against him, surprised by the strength in that thin chest and wiry arms.

"Let go," I said, feeling my voice finally surfacing. "Let go." I was on the verge of screaming when he looked up, his eyes tracing a line from my left cheek to my neck and back again; he let go and stepped away. I walked as fast as I could, and when I hit the bright sunlight, he began throwing the ball again, the dull thud rhythmically finding its way into my steps as I crossed the street to my own house. The shade of the porch was a relief, but I didn't feel that I could really breathe until I got inside, the hardwood of our foyer cool against my feet, gardenia blossoms floating in a silver bowl on the table by the door, my face and neck flushed a deep splotchy red when I looked at myself there in the hall tree. I waited until my legs felt sturdy again before going to the kitchen, where my mother was washing mint leaves for the iced tea and putting up tomatoes while Mrs. Poole sat at our kitchen table talking about the upcoming Country Day Fair hosted by the Junior League. I knew she was *really* there in hopes of learning a little bit of news.

"Well?" Mrs. Poole asked, her lipstick marking all but one of the cigarette butts in the crystal ashtray. I opened the refrigerator and looked in, feeling the cool air on my face and legs. "Is she with that highway patrolman who is *supposed* to be a friend of theirs?"

"I don't know." I stood with the water pitcher in my hand, still unable to believe that Mo Rhodes had left, unable to believe what Dean had just done to me. Mo's face was in my mind, her laugh; but more than that, I couldn't help but try and imagine what the scene looked like at her end of the phone. Was she with Gene Files? Was she sitting in some strange hotel on a strange bedspread in some familiar outfit that smelled like her house, the honeysuckle sachets that she kept in her bedroom drawers? Was she wearing the gauzy embroidered blouse she had worn to the fireworks, or had she slipped off with her brightly striped terry cloth caftan that she wore every morning while drinking coffee and listening to the radio? Had she packed her clothes and hidden them somewhere, behind a bush, in the laundry hamper under the quilts and fried chicken? My mind raced as I stared into the refrigerator, the cool air feeling so good to my face where Dean had pressed his sticky mouth and pulled in on my skin like he meant to hurt me.

"Honey, close the door now," Mama said, and she looked older to me, wearing a starched white apron like you might see on a maid in a swanky restaurant. Overnight she seemed so much older, while Mrs. Theresa Poole was ancient-looking, ringed in her own cigarette smoke.

"What kind of woman leaves her family?" Mrs. Poole asked, and looked at my mother.

"She's coming back." I blurted the words without thinking, leaving out all the parts I knew to be true, that she was coming to bring Buddy home, that she had in fact left her family for her best friend's husband, a man with great big hairy arms and a gun strapped to his waist.

I spent most of the afternoon in the upstairs hallway, sitting on the little window seat there in the dormer and watching Misty's house, waiting for Mo to get home. I watched the approach of a summer storm, the brisk wind, and then suddenly the sky was black, and tree limbs thrashed about. I saw Misty standing barefooted in their carport, lightning in the distance, dark clouds growing and swirling as she leaned against one of the wrought-iron posts. Her hair was blowing wildly, orange against the dark sky, while her dad stood leaning from the door and motioning her to come in. "Mother!" she screamed. "Mother!" Mrs. Poole was coming from her car, umbrella opened to the beginning drops of rain, and she also turned to watch Misty. "Mother!" I heard her scream over and over. We were all waiting, behind our doors or from windows above, watching and waiting.

Now it was night, and the rain had slowed to a steady drizzle, the roads still steaming. I wanted to call Misty but was afraid of Dean answering the phone; I still could not shake the odd feeling that came to me when I thought of his damp sour mouth on my face, his wiry body pressed against me, so close I could smell the detergent in his cotton T-shirt. She finally called me, but after two minutes her dad told her to get off; he was afraid Mo might try to call him again. "I saw you sitting in your window," she said hurriedly, and laughed. "Man, oh man, did I put Mrs. Poole in a jerk."

"I'm sorry," I said. "I didn't mean to spy like that." I waited but she made no response. "Misty?"

"I don't care," she said hurriedly. "What do I care?"

It had been over an hour since a car had turned onto our street, so I finally gave up and went to my room. I stood in the doorway with my eyes closed and felt my way slowly, step by step over to the window where I could feel dampness and a fine whistle of air around the old panes of glass. My mother took great pride in the distortion of some of our windows; it meant they were the originals with all their impurities, the waves and tiny pinhead bubbles signs of imperfection. "Of course this is nothing like what I showed you in Boston," she had said numerous times.

Besides visiting cemeteries, we had spent a lot of time walking
Beacon Hill, up Chestnut Street to see the amethyst window
panes, the "treasured accident" of too much manganese in the
glass shipped from London. It puzzled me, the differences made
in the perfect and the imperfect, how a flawed coin or piece of
glass becomes more valuable. I felt the window with my fingertips, still intrigued by my dad's explanation of how glass is a liquid
and how over the years it runs, slowly, a movement hidden from
sight or touch. It was possible that the glass in my window had
been running, oozing that slow race, since the 1920s. There were
windows downstairs that had been sliding downwards since the
Wilkinses were in this house. Thinking of them, as I stood before
the window that overlooked their resting place, made me shudder, so I turned and felt my way to the bed. My eyes were still
closed as I settled under the sheet and spread. Even in the summer, I had to have the spread; the sheet did not weigh enough to
make me feel protected.

I fell asleep fighting the impulse to imagine Mo in the burly
arms of Gene Files, to think of Dean as he pinned me against the
wall of their carport. I did not want to know what I looked like
at that moment; I did not want to see my own look of horror and
fear, my impurity. And yet those are the photos that win prizes,
those moments of torture and pain, those moments when human
faces, like Mr. Rhodes', split to reveal the deepest, darkest fears.

I didn't want to think of my own impurities; I didn't want
to think of Mo Rhodes kissing that man, with all that hardware
swinging from his belt. I concentrated on the street noise as a
means of escape; with my eyes closed I tried to measure the distance of the coming and going of the cars on the interstate. I kept
expecting to hear a car door slam, and that would be my cue to
wake and run to the window. The cars were coming and going,
rounding the turn there at the city limits, under the overpass
bridge, where a billboard boasted the cheapest cigarettes in a

hundred-mile radius, past the Texaco station and the new riding stables, the Stuckey's restaurant which Mrs. Poole said was way overpriced for the service. I imagined myself in a car driving it all, around and around, every square inch until I felt I could have done it blindfolded.

I woke to the rhythmic creak of our front porch swing, and when I opened my eyes it was gray out the window. A slight breeze lifted the white curtains like a tired ghost. I ran into the hall and down the stairs, certain it was Misty there. The boards of the porch were cool and damp beneath my bare feet, and before I even turned to answer her hushed whisper of my name, I glanced across the street at her house. All the lights were on inside, illuminating her dad, who stood, bare chested and in his pajama pants, in front of the picture window, with a cigarette in one hand and a coffee cup in the other. Dean was in the carport, the yellow light framing his body as he sat there waving a golf club back and forth.

I knew before even looking over at our swing that something was not right. Misty was in her yellow seersucker pajamas, bare-footed, her hair pulled straight back and held down with a pink barrette. She was holding Oliver on her lap and stroking his back rhythmically, as he arched and stretched against her hand.

"Misty?" I asked, and stepped toward her. "What are you doing?" A car I didn't recognize pulled up and stopped in front of their house, and after a few minutes a man and a woman got out.

"My mother is dead," she whispered, and my whole body went cold like ice water rushing over me. "And Buddy." I just stood and watched her, unable to move, every creak and pull of the swing chains causing my chest to tighten and ache. "They wrecked." Her whisper was a monotone like you might use to tell a ghost story or a joke, leading up to a "boo" or a punchline, but instead her words just stopped and lingered there. I hadn't noticed Dean coming over, and I jumped with the sudden sound of his voice.

"Aunt Edith and Uncle Ray are here," he said, not looking at me at all. "Daddy said to come home right now."

Misty got up without saying another word and followed him across the street and up to their front door, where now in the picture window I could see this woman, Aunt Edith, Mr. Rhodes's sister, with her arms wrapped around his waist, her cheek pressed against his thin stark chest. They stood there as I went to sit where Misty had been, her seat still warm, Oliver still waiting, in hopes of another rub. I could barely see over the tips of the lagustrum bushes and into their picture window, where Uncle Ray stood with his arm around Misty. She looked so pale, so much smaller as she stood there beside him. The whole lot froze like the end of a play, and then Aunt Edith pulled the drapes, leaving me to only imagine what was going on behind them. It had not registered with me yet. I could not believe that Misty had just been here, this very seat; it was as if I had dreamed it all until our phone rang and then I knew it was truth. It was as if I could sit and watch the whole town wake and respond to the news—cake pans pulled from the pantry, chickens frying, florist trucks up and down our street. By noon the wreath on their door was already drooping in the heat, and everyone knew the whole story.

Ten

When Mo died I felt she took with her some knowledge of my own life. There was a look of recognition the time Angela met her face to face in the front yard; there was a moment when the two stood there, mouths about to drop open in an "Oh, it's *you*" but then a change of heart, a thought that it's better not to speak. I imagined that Mo knew the whole story, knew all about Angela's young marriage. I imagined that Mo had been wanting to sit down and tell me the whole story, that she had been waiting for just the right time.

I thought of it all, only to feel guilty for thinking of myself while Misty lay beside me, her eyes red and swollen, her breath restless as she turned from side to side, periodically getting up to look from my front window to her own house. "He's gone to bed now," she had reported with her last look, sighing as if relieved. The hands on my clock glowed ten after two.

It had not fully registered with any of us, and still didn't the next day when Misty was rummaging through her mother's drawers in search of a handkerchief to take to the funeral. I was over there, but the impulse to turn and run was almost more than I could stand. Mr. Rhodes was in Buddy's room, just sitting in the rocking chair with a stuffed turtle on his lap. He stared at the turtle and passed it gingerly from hand to hand as if it were made of glass. I was in the hall, waiting for something to happen, knowing that something had to happen. The only saving grace was that Misty's Aunt Edith was there to tell everyone what to do.

"What do you think?" Misty called out, and when I walked into her mother's room, where the bed was carefully made, she was standing in front of the full-length mirror with a multicolor scarf tied around her forehead. "Do I look like Rhoda on 'Mary Tyler Moore'?" she asked, and when I shook my head no, she began crying again.

"Stop it." Dean burst into the room, pushing me to the side and yanking Misty by the arm, twisting until her skin turned pink under his grip. "I'm sick of you acting this way. Daddy is like a zombie, and you're a basket case. Just stop. Stop!" He screamed and slapped her face with his open palm. Then he stood there and waited while she held her cheek and slowly sat up, eyes wide and empty. "It's time to go. See if you can get him to come out now." He nodded his head toward the nursery and then headed for the door. I stepped to the side to let him pass, but he stopped right in front of me. "What are you looking at?" he asked, getting right in my face. "You're in the way over here." He looked me up and down and then stepped back. "I ought to slap your face, too. It'd be good to make your cheeks match for a change." Instinctively my hand went back to its old position of covering, and had it not been for the sight of Misty leading her dad like a blind puppy from the room, I probably would have left and never come back.

It seemed the whole town was in the church, where it was standing room only. In just a few hours there would be a crowd in the small neighboring town where Gene and Betty Files lived. For the thirty-odd hours that Mo Rhodes was out on the highway with her lover, both running away, deserting homes, spouses, children, for those hours, they were the talk at every table, on every phone—cheap and dirty and hussy and whore, low and lousy and thoughtless and cruel, stupid and hellbound and not worth the breath in their bodies. And then forty-eight hours later it was as if nothing had happened: Mo Rhodes had made a mistake and was on her way home. *She was coming home.* All the people who just one day earlier had voiced shock and disgust were now talking about the last time they saw her, about which recipes they had in her energetic scrawl with which humorous instruction. And didn't she look just like a young Liz Taylor? Wasn't she such a beautiful woman? Wasn't it the most tragic loss this town had seen? A woman and her baby? And there was no mention of *Uncle* Gene except to say "all" died, "both" cars. There was no mention of the receipt from the Motor Lodge, where only one room was rented, no mention of the letters neatly tucked away in the zippered part of her purse. It was almost as if the town had killed her; hatred and accusations and condemnations had riddled her name like bullets just the day before, and yet, now that she was no longer alive, no one would voice an opinion, no one would say that what she had done was *right* or *wrong*. There was such a difference in condemning the dead and condemning the living, though I failed to grasp what it was.

I was at the front of the church, in a pew behind Misty and her family. I concentrated on the stained-glass window so that I would not picture Mo sitting alone on that same quilt we had sunbathed on just the week before when she sprawled out beside us and told story after story of her own adolescence—the time she slapped a boy's face for trying to kiss her, the time she won a dance contest down at Myrtle Beach, the time she won a blue ribbon in a horse show just because the judges, all male, liked the outfit she was wearing. I had waited that day for my story to be told next, all the secrets that she knew about my family, but instead she talked about the Fourth of July and how she knew a boy while growing up who was blinded by a faulty Roman candle, talked about how fireworks were dangerous and that we should always be very, very careful.

She was alone that night as the Roman candles lit up the sky, alone on the quilt just like Angela was years before as my father and I walked over the sand dune and left her there on Ferris Beach. Like Mo, Angela had been waiting for a man to come for her. Was a man so important that she would sacrifice her children—her life? Was she even thinking of what would happen in a day or week or year? Was she really coming home to stay like everyone now believed—a belief designed to preserve whatever self-respect Mr. Rhodes might have left? And why wasn't *she* very, very careful, why didn't she tell *him* to be very, very careful. I stared at the colored glass, at Jesus with his pure solemn face, hands outstretched to the flock of lambs, always ready to take them in while the afternoon light came through the reds and blues and yellows. I could not bear to look at Buddy's coffin, no bigger than a little foot locker. *Suffer the little children to come unto me.* But please don't let them suffer.

It seemed the service took forever and the strained silence remained long after the last amen, long after the chords of organ music ended; then finally we were out the door and heading for the final ride to the cemetery, the new one outside the city limits. "A blessing," my mother had said, "that there weren't spaces left in Whispering Pines, that Thomas would not have to pass by her grave every day."

It was when I was getting into the car that I thought I saw Angela, a flash of auburn hair and a black silky dress, a man I did not recognize, a car I'd never seen. I looked around throughout the graveside service but I didn't see her or that car again. The more I thought about it, the more certain I was that it was her, and the more it reminded me that the one person who could have revealed any truth to me, or *would*, rather, was there in front of me, her life ended for the sake of one lousy man. And here she was in the family plot, and one day Mr. Rhodes would be beside her and any passerby would look at them there side by side— husband and wife—when the truth was that had she lived, she would have been far, far away from here; she would have been in Atlanta just as they had planned.

Misty knew it. She was the one who told me about the letters zipped up in her mother's purse, letters that proved that Mo and Gene Files had had something going on before the Rhodeses even moved from Ferris Beach. *They were friends*, I had offered, a part of me also wanting to believe the best, but she shook her head back and forth. "I read them," she whispered. "My dad has no idea that I snuck them and read them." She closed her eyes, jerked her head and shoulders as if to shake the thought away. I waited for her to tell me what she had read but she didn't. "Dad burned them," she said.

That night she told me how she had prayed that her mother would come home and stay home. "And look at how it was answered," she sobbed. "She's home for good, isn't she?" I felt her fingers wrap around my arm, nails squeezing into me as she lay there shaking, breath shallow.

Misty was determined to take the blame, to absorb it all like a sponge. More than ever she wanted to watch the old movies; she seemed to take comfort in the ones where it was the *child* who had left the mother. During *Madame X* she kept saying over and over again how the mother-in-law *made* Lana Turner leave her family, and wasn't it so horrible that she couldn't get a message through, wouldn't it be so wonderful if somewhere there was a message. *Yes, yes*, I was thinking, wanting so much to tell Misty how I was searching for my own message, how I was sure that I had seen Angela that very day, but the time had passed for that. My own speculations were trite in comparison.

I knew Misty had turned their split-level upside down looking for her answer, and still had found nothing. She seemed desperate in those months to follow, looking, searching. One day I saw her from my upstairs window just standing in her carport. She was wearing one of Mo's loud scarves around her waist, holding a coffee cup in her hand, with Buddy Holly's "Everyday" turned up full blast as she collected the little pebbles that had rolled onto the driveway, tossing them one by one out into the yard. I still couldn't shake the image of her as she was that day, after Mo left home, screaming for her mother again and again, arms outstretched to the black swirling clouds.

Soon, enough time passed that she stopped spending her days around the house, and we were able to get back to normal. We talked about the approaching first day of ninth grade and what we were going to wear; I talked about my fears of algebra and having to dress out in one of those gray gym suits, and she talked about what boys she liked and what songs were her favorites. Misty had discovered the notion of predestination, the belief that her mother's life had no other course than the one taken, and she was clinging to it. I nodded in agreement. "It's possible," I said, offering her the same hope she had always offered me, though I could not stop thinking about her prayer, the prayer that her mother would come home and stay forever. I could not stop thinking about all the prayers, flying upwards, crisscrossing like the airwaves, one request put on hold while another is answered.

Eleven

Misty was subject to blimp jokes every year on the first day of school when she had to announce in her little self-introduction that her father worked at Goodyear. On the first day of ninth grade there was a whole new audience for these jokes, since our school system had enlarged to include a whole new population of kids from the county. Now our system was fully integrated and until the new school buildings were completed, we would all cram into the musty, creaking halls of Samuel T. Saxon. Misty and I were relieved on the first day to find that we had the same homeroom teacher; we had feared that they would divide us up alphabetically, which would have placed us at opposite ends of the school.

"Blimp," a boy in the back row murmured, and Misty paused, sucked in her cheeks as she stared at him a long hard second before continuing. He was a complete stranger to us. "And my mother is dead," she said, and turned to the teacher, smiled. "She died this summer in a car crash where she was thrown thirty feet from the car. My baby brother, Buddy, was with her and he also died. He was named after the late great Buddy Holly because my mother believed in naming after the dead, particularly the young dead. My mother never knew what hit her, they say. They say she was hit with the impact of a couple of tons."

Misty continued staring at the back of the room, though the boy who had uttered "Blimp" had his eyes cast downward on his desk. I didn't want to watch her either; it was too painful to see her there in a purple T-shirt that had belonged to her mother, the arm bands cutting into her skin. My desk was angled such that I could see into the hall, and I stared out there, at pencil scribbles on the cracked plaster and at the old water fountain where I knew someone had stuck a wad of bright green gum at the place the water should come out. I had given up on school water fountains by that time; if it wasn't a wad of gum, then it was the chance that someone would creep up behind and push your head down into the spout. R.W. Quincy had done that to a girl and chipped her front tooth the year before.

I could see into the classroom across the hall, where a sign on the door read "Davis Homeroom," and I could see Merle Hucks, or half of the back of his head, could see his wispy white hair as he sat crouched over a piece of notebook paper, a ball-point pen gripped firmly in the visible hand, the left one. His left foot was turned to reveal the worn sole of a Converse hightop and what looked like brown dress socks as he swung his knee back and forth.

"Thank you, Misty," the teacher said. "That's fine."

"I have her scarf at home," Misty said. "It still has slivers of glass in it."

"Let's see who's next." Miss McIntyre, a very young black woman perhaps teaching for the first time, ran her finger down the roster, probably afraid to give another student the floor as she had given Misty. Merle turned to say something to the girl across from him and, in turning back, looked over his shoulder and out into the hall as if he felt my stare. I knew he saw me looking; I knew there was that moment just before I looked down when he saw me and I was thinking about all of this, my face flaming red, when Miss McIntyre called my name, my hand flying instinctively to my cheek as I prepared to stand.

"Come on, Kitty," Misty said, and whirled to look at the back of the room. "Only her good, good friends call her Kitty. Others call her Kate. Only people who have shared things like death with her can call her Kitty." Misty, regardless of her motivation, if there *was* one aside from bitterness and the need to attract attention, had given me enough time to breathe steadily, time for my face to be less warm, my knees less rubbery before standing. I stared at Miss McIntyre while I spoke, ignoring her smile and her gesture for me to move my hand so that I didn't cover my mouth. I gave my name and told how my father taught math at the community college and how my mother had once taught high school history, American history, but now was a housewife; I said it all as quickly as I could, and when I sat back in my desk I would have sworn that Merle Hucks had heard it all, that he was looking out the door right up until the moment the teacher of his homeroom walked over and closed it, leaving only a chart of the periodic table, taped to the door, for me to see.

The story of Mo's death seemed to surface time and time again that fall, each time taking on new shapes and new explanations. Probably the most curious person about it all was Sally Jean Holmes, who had suddenly appeared and become a fixture in the Rhodeses' life. She was a thin, freckled woman who had met Mr. Rhodes only a month after Mo's death, when she went into Goodyear to get a new set of radials for her Rambler. She later told my mother it was when he said, "Your tires'll be worth more than your car," that she recognized something in him not often found in a man—*honesty*. They had just been dating a month when Mr. Rhodes got his hair permed and began dressing in what Misty called "Brady Bunch" fashion, leisure suits and such.

They had only dated four months when Mr. Rhodes got Misty and Dean all dressed up and in the car with him with the story that they were going to a *relative's* wedding. Misty came home furious and spoke only to me for several weeks after that. "My dad must have been hard up horny to marry such a drip," she said time and time again. "Next to my mother, she's ugly, REAL UGLY. And she's making our house just as ugly with her little cross-stitched signs that tell you how to do everything. She was going to give away my mother's things." Misty's mouth was set stubbornly, her face the thinnest it had ever been and she hadn't even been trying. "Imagine that. Just who died and left her queen?" Her eyes watered with the mistake of her own words, but instead of crying, she laughed and draped her arm around my shoulder. "She's not throwing away one stick of my mother's things. Not one damn stick." Then Misty pulled me inside, where she tiptoed around and showed me all of the little needle-crafted signs hung about.

It was true that Sally Jean did have a thing about cross-stitching little sayings, and this is what she did most of the time when she was not at the hospital where she worked as a nurse in the geriatric unit. Proverbs, that's what she had in common with my mother; but even my mother, who *loved* proverbs, found Sally Jean's to be a bit much, particularly the one Sally Jean framed and hung in their little guest bathroom which said, "We aim to please. You aim, too, please." She had already finished one for my mother that said "A Recipe For Friendship" and then had all sorts of things like "a dash of kindness" or "a sprinkle of tenderness."

"Friendship," Mrs. Poole had said, and flipped the picture over to examine Sally Jean's needlework *from the back*, where *neatness counts*. There was something kind of sad in all of that to me, like maybe Sally Jean was trying too hard, though I never would have voiced this bit of sympathy to Misty, who was doing everything she could to make the woman miserable.

My mother was friendly to Sally Jean, though I could tell it wasn't always easy. Sally had once seen Liberace in an airport, and she used this as a way to mark all of the events of her life. "Well, now, let's see, that was *before* I saw Liberace" or "That was just about the time I saw Liberace." I had already heard what he was wearing twice, so I was sure my mother had heard it at least five beyond that. Sally Jean was a nervous talker, just could not stop for two seconds. Sometimes her narrow, birdlike face turned pink before she could suck in a breath. "I like to have died when I saw him there, you can imagine, now can't you? Can't you just imagine?" She pushed my mother's arm for a response. "Sequins. I've never seen the likes of so many sequins, and I thought to myself how long did it take to sew them all? He made Elvis look *plain*, that's how flashy it was to see Liberace. It was dazzling. It was absolutely *extraneous*." Those were the times my mother bit her lips the hardest; Sally Jean's dictionary was nothing like anyone else's.

"Really."

"Yes. The whole airport went akimbo with excitement."

My mother was too kind to just come right out and correct her, but Theresa Poole was not. One day when the three of them were sitting in the kitchen drinking coffee and Sally Jean had already referred at least twice to seeing Liberace in the airport, she hung her head and laughed, clicked her tongue several times to create suspense. It was clear from my mother's and Mrs. Poole's expressions that she did not have them hanging on the edge of a cliff, but she didn't even notice. "Here's an antidote for you."

"What, have I been poisoned?" Mrs. Poole asked, and looked at my mother. "I said, have I been poisoned that I need an antidote?" She laughed but my mother was staring at the salt shaker, pretending she had not noticed the error. "I said . . ."

"I heard you," Sally Jean said, and leaned forward. "But just wait until I tell you mine and then we'll hear all about yours." That's when my mother laughed and then Sally Jean, pleased to have the floor, continued.

Sally had lived her whole life in Flat Pine, which is a small town right between Fulton and Ferris Beach; she continued living there even after her first husband had left her for their next door neighbor. It was when this story broke the surface that I was able to begin to understand what had drawn her and Mr. Rhodes together; they had both been left behind.

"She never even returned my meat thermometer that she had borrowed," Sally Jean told my mother, shaking her head sadly as if that thermometer carried the same weight as a husband. My mother, equally big on little proverbs, often said, *Oh, what a tangled web we weave*, a little lie will lead to a big one; a child who cheats in school will grow up to steal. Right then I imagined her saying, A woman who will borrow your meat thermometer and not return it will grow up to borrow your husband and not return him. I often looked at Sally Jean, which is what I called her since the title "Mrs. Rhodes" did not in any way fit her gangly, speckled ways, and wondered if she and Mr. Rhodes talked about their losses, spoke about how they were both losers, their love lost to another. I also couldn't help but wonder where Sally Jean would one day be buried, on the *other* side of Mr. Rhodes or back in Flat Pine all alone, the way she had spent much of her life? Cemeteries for Swinging Singles. It seemed to be the only *singles* institution not yet conceived of.

My mother described Mo's leaving to Sally Jean many times upon request, each time softening it all. I could not understand WHY Sally asked for it over and over, unless it was like the way Misty and I might watch *Shenandoah* or *Imitation of Life* or *Stella Dallas* to get a good cry, to somehow purify all that was unspoken inside us. Or maybe it was like pressing on a bruised patch of skin or hammering a tight sore muscle to see if it still hurt, as if applying pain to pain can somehow cancel out or negate the first. Sally had to hear it often, like a shot of medicine, to rid herself of the memories that probably filled that split-level, in spite of the fact that the house had been completely redone in Early American furnishings with embroidered samplers, wall-to-wall carpet in a tasteful avocado, and all accessories falling into the FALL category: upholstery fabric in rust and *avocado*; eagles, flags and liberty bells on the kitchen wallpaper; appliances in *avocado*; new linoleum in *avocado*; counter tops in *avocado*.

"I'll die if she says 'avocado' one more time," Misty told me, and led me into her room, where she had all of the previous adornments, Japanese fans and little lanterns, ginger jars in loud orange-and-navy swirls, like a shrine. Within a month of marriage, Sally had the pebbles removed from the yard, and she planted grass; she planted mums in *fall colors* for the fall and jonquils and daylilies for *fall colors* in the spring and summer. She painted the peacock-blue shutters a deep forest green. "Thank God," my mother and Mrs. Poole and everyone in the garden club said.

"I wish there were no fall colors," Misty told me, as she stood in driveway wearing the purple kimono Mo had worn throughout her pregnancy. Misty had by then taken to wearing only red and purple and chartreuse, sometimes all together; sometimes when she raised her arms or moved hurriedly, I would catch a brief scent of Mo, her cologne, the sachets she kept in her drawers.

To look at Sally Jean, you would not have thought she'd have the nerve to cross Misty and make all those changes around the house. It seemed she would not *want* to hear that story over and over again, that she would not want to hear the words, the *lovely* the *beautiful* the *vibrant*, that always seeped into a description of Mo Rhodes, especially when it was turned over to Mrs. Poole and her cronies, who seemed to enjoy talking about Mo just to see Sally's reaction.

It was almost as if Sally were waiting, hoping that one time the story would be told and there, rusty and open, would be the weak link, the reason to believe that Thomas Rhodes had not *really* loved Mo, much like when Laurence Olivier tells Joan Fontaine that he *never* loved the beautiful Rebecca, no, he *despised* her. But Sally's wait was a futile one unless she could in her own way concoct some belief.

"She left them with no warning," my mother said. "It was Fourth of July and we were all at the picnic. Why, Misty was right there with us as usual."

"I guess she didn't have much time for Misty," Sally said, a half-hearted question, as she rubbed her finger along the checked pattern of the placemat.

"Oh, no, the girls were just always back and forth from house to house, always together, I mean like they are . . ." My mother's voice trailed off, her "now" to end the sentence a low murmur as if she realized the truth, that though Misty and I were still always together, it was rarely over at their house.

"Oh, yes," Sally said, and nodded her head, the skin of her face as white as the nurse's dress she wore. "They are inseparable, aren't they?"

"Anyway, Thomas went looking for her. Misty stayed here with us until he got home late that night, but they didn't hear from her at all until the following day. I think she left a note that she'd be in touch, but nothing else."

"That would've been the fifth of July that she called," Sally said. It was as if she were etching it into stone. I imagined her sitting some evening when she was all alone with a calendar on her lap as she wrote out the timetable: 6:00 P.M.–people gather for the picnic. 8:30 P.M.–the fireworks begin.

"Yes, they always have a big sale down at Goodyear Tire, much like they do everywhere, but Thomas didn't go in that day. I remember because I kept expecting to hear his car crank."

"Yes, they still do have that sale," Sally whispered.

"Anyway, Mo left the picnic with the baby." Just the sound

of her name, on my mother's tongue, in Sally's ear, seemed to conjure an image that left both of them quieter. "She didn't stop by home or anything. Didn't talk to Misty or Dean."

"And she left with *him*."

"Yes." Mama stood and went to the stove. "More coffee, Sally?"

"No, I don't want my hands to be shaky at work." She laughed, her voice already shaky. "It's not good to be giving a shot or drawing blood with a shaky hand."

"No, I'd think not." Mama poured herself another cup and sat down again.

"It was so terrible for her to leave them that way," Sally said, her cheeks flushed. "She must have been an *awful* person." It was clear then that that was what she needed to hear, *she was awful*, but my mother, whether intentional or not, *never* gave a person exactly what he or she wanted, she always held out just a little, enough to get a beg, or maybe just enough to maintain control over a situation, or maybe it just never occurred to her.

"Well, I suppose what she *did* was awful," my mother said. This was her favorite way of qualifying, in the same vein as "we love people and like things." What she *did* was awful. It seemed the qualifying phrase worked on all who lived and breathed or did not live and breathe, with the one slight exception of Angela.

"We all suspected she might be with Gene Files, who was a highway patrolman. He had been a friend of their family, you know the children called him uncle and such. He and his wife, Betty, were over there all the time."

"Um hmmm, it's the same as that woman borrowing my meat thermometer."

"Well, I don't know about that." Again, my mother had pushed poor pale Sally Jean into the corner. "I mean, no one will ever know. It's clear that Mo was not thinking, but it could be that Gene Files was taking her to visit a friend in Atlanta. I mean there is no way of *knowing*." Sally Jean's face, solemn and defeated, was indication enough that she had not heard what she wanted to hear. "A lot of people do believe that Mo was coming home to *stay*. We'll just never know."

"No, not when they're all dead."

"And it was a terrible car crash," my mother whispered as she leaned forward, while Sally sat there like a bird charmed by the salivating quiver of a cat's mouth, charmed and paralyzed with fear and not really knowing how to distinguish the two. *Cats have the power to charm*, Mrs. Poole's housekeeper, Mrs. Landell, had once told me as she took her break on a kitchen stool. *It's all in the eyes. All of life is there in the eyes. When it's time to die I can read it like a printed word, there in the eyes.*

Sally's eyes were open and waiting, ready for the dull ache of truth to fill them. "Gene Files and the baby were crushed. They were on the side that got hit, the baby there asleep on the backseat." Sally Jean stared into her empty coffee cup, probably able to recite in her head what came next. "Mo was thrown. It took them hours to find her. They searched in those wee hours with flashlights and lanterns, expecting the worst."

"Thomas talked to her that afternoon. She called him at about midafternoon."

"She called from somewhere in South Carolina," Mama said in a normal speaking voice, and then lowered herself to a whisper again as if they had just taken a break from a ghost story. "Anyway, when they found her, they couldn't believe that she was lying there as if asleep, not a mark on her face. Her neck was broken but there was not a trace of blood." Sally was charmed to silence, paralyzed as she sat and stared at my mother. "Lord, forgive me," Mama said, her voice returning. "I don't need to be telling you all of this. My goodness, we should think on happy things, Christmas and the bazaar and such."

"I asked to hear it," Sally said. "I don't know why, but I felt I needed to hear it." I wondered then how it must feel to step into someone else's life as she had done, into a town where everyone knew your husband and his family and their past better than you did. You could change the furniture and the wallpaper in the bedroom and the shrubbery and the car you drove, but still she would be there, with every change in weather, with every date on a calendar. Time and time again I had heard Sally Jean tell my mother that Mr. Rhodes was the answer to all her prayers, and I could only wonder if she, in exchange, was an answer to his. I felt it was more likely that hers had been answered because his, the desire to have another chance, Mo Rhodes back in his arms and his life, were unanswered.

Mo Rhodes had been uplifted by death, as if the abandonment of her family were fully erased in the events of that moment— headlights around a curve blinding Gene Files, a hand reaching for Buddy, that last breath drawn in anticipation of the impact which had hurled her into the damp, mossy undergrowth. Her death had saved Misty and her family the embarrassment of abandonment. With the exception of that one night when Misty talked about it all, whenever the topic arose, she addressed only the wreck, only the death, as if her mother had been returning from purchasing their Santa Claus or the food she would prepare for Sunday dinner.

There was a change in Misty, a coarseness that showed her bitterness, the anger she would have felt if her mother had still been living, alive and well in some little apartment in Atlanta. Maybe Misty would have been invited to visit, would have received an occasional postcard. Maybe there would have been a plan to have one more child, a Files child to fully consummate this love, just in case Buddy had been a product of Thomas Rhodes. I knew Misty had imagined it all for herself; I knew she had a firm grasp of the truth no matter how many times she refused to look at it.

When conversations got bandied about in school, turning to the grotesque, Misty could charm the whole room with her coarseness. "Yeah, well, my mama got thrown thirty feet from a car; there were pieces of glass in her hair. The man she was with lost his head. When they pulled him from the car, his head fell off and rolled into the road." She could make the whole class go silent, and then she'd laugh that laugh, her skin turning a faint pink. That's how Misty spent much of the ninth grade, our last year at Samuel T. Saxon Junior High. She was the pale orange-haired girl whose mother had died a tragic death, and I was her tall birthmarked companion. I saw us as a pair to be pitied, though, *Lord forgive me when I whine,* Misty had convinced herself that we were a pair to be reckoned with and envied, and I clung to her hopes every step of the way.

Twelve

From my ninth grade English class, I could see the statue in front of the courthouse, a little stone man, his gun hoisted over one shoulder as if frozen in midmarch, a constant reminder of our Confederate dead. I saw the statue as a unique symbol of a unique town of which I was a part. I sat in the splintered, carved-up desk and imagined that the stone man could see me, the same way I had once imagined the Wilkins crew with all of their New Testament names could rise above the graves in Whispering Pines and look into my bedroom window. I sat there, my mind on everything except the vocabulary words on the old blackboard. The play of "The Miracle Worker" was in our textbook, and I couldn't wait until we had grammar out of the way so that we could read it. I knew all of Annie Sullivan's lines, and while I copied my vocabulary words, I imagined myself in Misty's old granny glasses—if she could dig them up in that room of hers—playing the part.

The first day I sat there, the same day that Misty told the homeroom about Mo's death, I had not even been able to see the statue because the trees shading the old cracked sidewalks in front of the school were still full and green. Mr. Tom Clayton, who for years cut my father's hair and who sounded just like that cartoon chicken, Foghorn Leghorn, once told me that the little stone man came down once a year to pee. I had believed him for years, no matter how many times my mother and Mrs. Poole said it was *pure* T foolishness. It still made me laugh to think about it.

"Yessir, comes down," Mr. Clayton said, arms crossed over his thin bowed ribs, a splat of tobacco juice off to his right, "pees, looks about the town of Fulton, says to hisself, 'Yep, everything's copacetic,' then gets hisself a drink of water from the fountain there and heads back up till the next year when he has to pee again." Mr. Clayton was the only person I ever knew who used the word *copacetic*, an old-timey-sounding word that seemed to fit that part of Fulton, the old part well divided from the area where the new junior high and high schools were under construction, and the new neighborhoods where homes seemed to appear overnight.

Copacetic. I thought of the stone man a lot that fall while I sat day by day and watched him come into better view as the tall oaks and elms shed their leaves onto the school ground. I wrote Todd Bridger's initials on my desk in pencil and then wiped them away, more out of habit than anything else. He didn't seem like such a big deal to me anymore, though I probably still would have gone with him if he'd asked me; it seemed like Misty and I were the only two girls who hadn't been with somebody. If the union only lasted twenty-four hours, like many of Ruthie Sands's going-steadies, it was better than nothing.

"Dean says that boys our age sometimes act opposite of what

they mean," Misty told me. Since Mo's death, Dean had become very serious and grown-up acting; he always rubbed his smooth hairless chin and stared off in a philosophical trance when offering advice. He was very polite to me, sometimes too polite, calling me Mary Katherine or patting my arm as he spoke.

"He says that if a boy acts like he's *not* interested in you, then probably he is." I did not have the heart to tell Misty that if this was true, then most of the boys in school loved us and hated Ruthie Sands, whose name was inked on their notebooks and the rubber toes of their sneakers as she cheered their various teams to victory, or hated Perry Loomis, a quiet, beautiful girl from out in the county.

Still, wishful thinking or useless hoping or whatever, Misty and I were hanging in there. We wore crocheted sweater vests, gauchos, fringed boots, and macramé bracelets; every morning before walking to school, we went behind the Presbyterian church and carefully applied makeup, mostly just cover-up, her to the acne she had begun getting, me to my mark. Some days we wore eye shadow and mascara, too, but it hardly made a dent of a reaction in the general student body.

It amazed me how much faith Misty had that it would all get better, that we would wake up one day and the world would have simply flipped to our side. In spite of her toughness, or maybe because of it, Misty's optimism was stronger than ever; she was determined that she was going to win, believed that she *had* to win. Sometimes I felt Mo was standing there, her fingers smoothing cover-up on my face, encouraging me to believe, to try, to hope. I was amazed that such faith could survive, and I was even more amazed that it could grow and strengthen.

Copacetic. Mr. Clayton died that very fall, alone in his shop, a copy of the local paper, turned to my father's article about naming the new high school, there on his lap. My mother had headed up the committee to name the school, and Mr. Clayton along with Mrs. Poole and several others had been members. My mother's suggestion of Edgar Allan Poe was one that brought quite a bit of controversy. *Why on earth would you name a school for him? A drunkard who married a child and wrote horror stories.* My mother, though she didn't confess this at the meeting, wanted to name the school after someone who shared her history, and he was the only famous person she could think of who was born in Boston and lived in the South.

"I say we go for Thomas Jefferson," Edith Turner had said, hands deep in the pockets of her long tunic, a fashion she always wore, people forever saying how she looked *just* like Bea Arthur of the TV show "Maude." "It's a good name. Always has been. Always will be. Stonewall Jackson is also a good one."

"I'd like to suggest that it be named for my husband," Mrs. Poole had said, and looked around, indignant that no one else had made this suggestion.

"Let's see now," Mr. Thomas Clayton had said. "The Bo Poole School. No, I just don't think so. Nevermore. Nevermore." He laughed and sat back down, and my mother in describing the meeting to us later that night said she felt that Mr. Clayton's comment had convinced the rest of the committee just to give up and go along with her.

"Well, please, God," Mrs. Poole had mumbled at the end. "Let's abbreviate. E. A. Poe will sound much better."

"I second it," Mrs. Turner said. "If there's no Thomas Jefferson then I say E. A. Poe is my second choice." She turned and held a hand to her mouth, laughed. "Bo Poole School."

Guns were fired at Mr. Clayton's funeral, and the few men who were left from the First World War wore their uniforms. Mrs. Poole stood there with Mr. Poole's old machete and motioned for blanks to be fired from a gun as if it were a cannon. A farmer from out in the county used his crop-duster plane to come into town and spiral and twist and leave trails of smoke like a dogfight. That was all people talked about for months, but I thought of Mr. Clayton's old-timey word most on glorious fall days when it seemed the whole dingy classroom turned to bronze, as the leaves sailed and twisted across the dirt school-yard, some flapping and clinging to the crumbling brick and thick wavy windows. The glass in the windows of Samuel T. Saxon had been oozing for a long, long time, a slow-motioned journey that would soon end with a wrecking ball.

Copacetic—the word seemed to fit, bringing to my mind *cornucopia* and *harvest*, an abundance of life and color. It made me think of Mo just the year before as she stood in her front yard and arranged decorations of huge corn stalks and bales of hay, her poncho stretched over her rounded stomach, cheeks flushed as she called us to see her creation. It made me think of Angela, hair like copper, as she leaned her head against the porch swing.

It was peaceful there in class, peaceful when our English teacher assigned us to just sit and read silently until the bell rang. Very few people read; some passed notes or talked, others drew little doodles, names, or initials on their notebooks. One day I looked up to see Perry Loomis take a note from the boy behind her. She read it, then turned and looked at Todd Bridger, smiled and nodded. Right before my eyes she was going through all the motions I had so carefully choreographed and played over in my head so many times. I clutched the little paper ball in my pocket where I had written several sets of initials earlier that day, all the people I kind of liked, which is what Misty always insisted on doing, and rubbed it together until my fingers were silver-gray with pencil lead, and all evidence that I had ever included Todd Bridger or anyone else on such a list was destroyed.

Since the first day that year I hadn't been able to help look-ing at Perry Loomis, to study her the same way I caught myself studying Merle Hucks and his slicked-back hair. Perry had thick blond hair that hung past her shoulders and dark brown eyes, made darker by the paleness of her face. Perry Loomis was beautiful and all the boys were talking about it, though it seemed they focused more on her body than her face. I had noticed that Todd Bridger seemed to stop to pull up his socks or to readjust a notebook whenever she was near.

After class I told Misty about the note I had seen passed to Perry Loomis, and she just shrugged. "Todd is such a jerk," she said, and then grinned as she watched R. W. Quincy stick out his big foot and trip a skinny little studious-looking girl from the seventh grade. "Hey, come on over to my house and we'll watch 'General Hospital.' We were walking down the sidewalk towards our neighborhood. All around us leaves whirled in the air, lifted and blown with each passing car. She turned several times, casting quick glances over her shoulder. I knew she was looking for R. W. Quincy. "Wait until you see what I did to my room last night. I got a black light and now all the posters look great, the way they're supposed to. Jimi Hendrix and Jim Morrison have got the whitest teeth." She kicked a rock and I watched it skip ahead of us.

As the weather got colder and the old radiators of Samuel T. Saxon hissed and clanged, I was often reminded of Mr. Clayton's story about the stone man. It was on those days when the phantom struck, which is to say that either R. W. Quincy or Merle Hucks had peed on the radiator in the boys' bathroom, leaving the whole school and the rusty old heating system to reek of urine for days. We all knew one of them was doing it, but no one was about to tell. Nobody wanted to tangle with either of them or both, rather, since they were always together; every morning they came to school smelling of bowling-alley food, the hot-dog relish and onion rings they had had for breakfast. For me the worst part was when we had a class picture taken for the yearbook and I had to stand in the back right beside them because I was so tall.

Tall. Now that was a problem. I used to lie in bed at night and will my legs not to grow another inch. I contemplated binding my feet off like the Japanese women so that they would never grow beyond their present size seven. I was only three inches shy of being as tall as my mother, and I was fearing the worst, that I was also going to be five feet eleven and wear a size nine-and-a-half shoe. "Tall and thin like a fashion model," all the salesladies said when I went to buy a new coat, all of them careful *not* to look too long at my left cheek. The coat was beautiful, white simulated-fur, which was what everyone was wearing. It felt wonderful, once I was safe behind my bedroom door, to hold out my arms and spin around, head thrown back as if I were taking in the skyscrapers of New York City like Marlo Thomas in "That Girl"; though one look in my full-length mirror shouted back that I looked like a big naked Amazon hiding under a bear rug. I needed only a bone in my nose to get my picture in *National Geographic.*

As I sat in my desk at Samuel T. Saxon, I willed the little stone man to smile at me. I willed my legs to stop growing and I willed my face a pure flawless white and I willed *someone* other than Dean Rhodes to think of me. Of course these had been my regular requests for several years; the one request that I had been able to drop from the list was the one I uttered constantly prior to integration, *that I not get hit over the head with a Pepsi bottle, my throat slit with the glass.* The stories had come to us again and again, riots and fires and fights and names called out in hatred. Integration had come and black, white, city, county, we were all scared. We were all *waiting* for whatever was supposed to happen, to happen. Now two years after the fact, we had stopped waiting and, instead, gray winter recesses were spent leaning on the radiator in the girls' bathroom, Misty and Lily Hadley dancing in front of the warped mirrors over the row of ancient sinks, their voices sweet and pure, as they belted out "I'll Be There" by the Jackson Five. With integration fears put to rest, I had more time to will my body to stop growing, to will that I would suddenly look more like my father's family, that I would look just like Angela. *We must bring salvation back.*

The only good thing to come out of getting so tall was the new coat, to be able to *finally* throw away the old blue nylon carcoat with the babyish gingham lining that I had worn for several years. I wanted to take all the clothes that I had outgrown, pile them up in the backyard, and strike a match, burn the bits of gingham and bows that look so ridiculous on tall people; I wanted to squat by the fire like a native woman, a bone in my nose and a skull around my neck, snakeskins wrapped around my throat like what Merle wore way back in the second grade. From the billowing black smoke I would cast a spell; I would carry us back to the day at Ferris Beach, when Angela, my face cupped in her smooth warm hands would say, *I'm going to take you home now, Kitty. You know you belong to me don't you?*, and my father would nod as I turned to him, though he would have to look away, unable to face losing me. I would carry us back to that rainy day at Misty's house when we cooked s'mores, when Mo was there, able to pick up the phone and call Gene Files, *Look Gene, this isn't right. I can't do this. I love my family too much to leave them. I want to live too much to leave them.*

My mother took the wadded-up clothes and carcoat and neatly folded each piece. "Someone will be thrilled to get these," she said. "Why they're all so nice and like new. Like this Villager." She held out a cotton blouse decorated with little tucks and covered buttons—like new but way out of style. "It may be the nicest thing that person owns."

The whining radiators of Samuel T. Saxon did not put out nearly enough heat and the large windows shook with every wind. Most of us wore our coats throughout the day, making the classroom a jungle of fake fur. About the only girl in our class who didn't wear a fur coat was Perry Loomis, who always wore the jacket of whatever boy she was going steady with that week; she wore his jacket and often a thick-linked ID bracelet with his name or initials. She had already gone with Todd Bridger twice, and in between those times she had gone with a boy who was three years older and lived down the street from the Huckses, a boy who, so Misty had heard, smoked a lot of dope and also had "done the deed" too many times to count. That's who Perry was with when we left for Christmas vacation, a boy named Walter; I had seen his name written on the front of her geography notebook. It didn't seem to stop the other boys from fawning and waiting, hoping their numbers would come up in a week or two; even Dean Rhodes had asked us about that *little blond girl* in our class. Most of the girls in our class despised Perry Loomis, but I couldn't help but envy her; it was almost like having a crush, so taken with this person's appearance, so much wishing I could claim it as my own. I saw her in the same way I saw Angela, the way I had seen Mo, glittering and shining, rare like a jewel.

Thirteen

The Christmas parade of Fulton did not physically amount to much, usually just a few flatbed tobacco trailers that had been decorated by local service clubs with cotton-snow and elves; sometimes high-school girls stood poised, waving the stiff formal wave of beauty queens while the tobacco beds rocked and swayed beneath them. There were usually a few Shriners scattered about on mopeds, their horns and whistles blowing, and of course the high school band was in full force, the majorettes drawing wolf-whistles from the high school boys who sat on parked cars and smoked cigarettes.

All of this took place year after year, the band and majorettes and floats all wedged between a police car with siren going and Santa bringing up the rear. Santa was usually perched on the back of a Volkswagon convertible made to look like a sleigh, cardboard reindeer strapped to the hood. The parade of 1972 was the same.

Mama and I stood in front of a store called Foxy Mama which specialized in Afro wigs. Misty was supposed to meet me there, and I kept scanning the crowd for her orange hair while the band approached. I liked the way the steady beat of the drums seemed to make my heart beat louder and faster. As the parade got closer, I was torn between wanting to grip my mother's arm in excitement and wanting to walk three blocks down so as not to be identified with her.

Across the street, I saw a souped-up red GTO, its owner stretched out on the hood with some other boys as he waited for her, his girl, that blond majorette, to march his way. If I turned to the side, I could see my reflection in the window of Foxy Mama, my hair much too curly for the shag haircut I had gotten. I willed my hair to look like Perry Loomis's, all one length and with flaxen waves like a princess. "What's so great about Perry anyway?" one of the girls in my class had asked in the bathroom one day. She was one of Ruthie Sands's friends, one of the few in that group who had not gone to private school when we integrated. "I just don't see why all the boys like *her*." She looked around, her light hair filling with electricity as she brushed. Six of us stood there in front of the dark wavy mirrors, the old bathroom cold and smelling of rusty radiator heat and various mixtures of cologne. The graffiti on the walls dated back at least twenty years.

"I know why," Misty said, winking at me. Lately, she had been trying her best to attract interest in the two of us and what she called our "knowledge of the world."

"Because she's new," I said, giving my contribution to the conversation in a way that seemed too well rehearsed yet still carried no impact at all.

"Nope." Misty slung her arm around my shoulder and squeezed. "It's because she puts out." I felt my face redden as the other girls stepped closer. Misty had them, these Ruthie Sands groupies, right where she wanted them. "Todd Bridger has all but *done the deed* with her." I knew Misty was quoting what Dean,

Mister Maturity, had told her; she was nodding, mouth stretched in a knowing grimace. The words left me feeling odd as if my insides had been twisted, and I forced the same nervous laughter that came from the other girls, so as not to show my embarrassment; or was it envy? I felt as if they had all seen right into my head—seen the way I had strutted across my mind in that fake-fur coat, like maybe I was Ann-Margret on my way to meet Elvis, seen the way I had kissed Todd Bridger or some faceless, nameless boyfriend in the back of the Cape Fear theater, and then taken his hand and pressed it to my chest. I had imagined I was there in the red GTO as that high school senior inched his hand over to the majorette's thigh; imagined that I looked just like Perry, that I *was* Perry Loomis.

"Well, what did he do exactly?" Lisa Burke asked in her high little-girl voice.

"Use your brain now," Misty said and crooked her finger to give a hint. "Kate knows." She patted me on the shoulder and again gave me the look which meant *lift your chin*. "Kate and I know a lot."

When Misty finally got to the parade, she whispered that she was late because she had stopped by Lisa Burke's house to loan her a copy of *Valley of the Dolls*. She assured me that I could read it next, and then she launched into her latest discovery, which was that Perry Loomis had to wear turtlenecks a couple of weeks ago because that older boyfriend of hers gave hickeys like mosquito bites. My mother and Mrs. Edith Turner turned and stared at Misty, Mrs. Turner giving Misty the pitying look they had all given her since Mo's death. Misty smiled sweetly, and then when Mrs. Turner wasn't looking, shot her the bird. The band was in front of us, and I felt my heart quicken as I watched the majorette and the boy on the GTO exchange looks, then a wink, lips puckered.

"The downtown has gone to pot," Mrs. Turner screamed, and

pulled her mauve tunic close around her. "I don't know how on earth they stay in business." She pointed to the Afro wigs on display, her head shaking back and forth. She had the habit of constantly removing her glasses and letting them swing on the rhinestone-flecked chain around her neck while she cleaned the lenses again and again with a little wadded-up piece of tissue, a nervous habit, I suspected, for she had already confessed to being "scared of the coloreds," her fear being that "they are taking over the town; give them an inch and they'll take a mile." My father called Edith Turner *the paranoid image of Theresa Poole*. Fortunately, the parade was too crowded for Mrs. Poole's adirondack, and instead she sat up in the manager's office in Woolworth and looked to the street below.

"What's it like at the schoolhouse? Hmmmm? Problems with them?" I realized that she was talking to me. "I said I bet they cause trouble there at the schoolhouse, taking over, using double negatives." I just stared at her not knowing what to say. "I do declare if your face hasn't improved. I would swear that place has gotten smaller or paler or something." She looked at my mother and nodded and then continued without even taking a breath. "And those children from out in the county"—she cleaned her lenses, peeked through and then cleaned them again—"bad. I hear they are so bad. The filthy language. Filth."

"It's bad, the language is awful, just awful," Misty said, and nudged me right as Todd Bridger and some of the other boys from our class stepped into the crowd on the other side of the street. I kept losing sight of him while Mrs. Turner and my mother discussed how important it was to line a commode seat with toilet paper before sitting on it. Mrs. Turner said it was especially important at places like the movie theaters where they no longer had a separate bathroom for the *coloreds*.

"Is she stupid or what?" Misty asked, and then she was waving and calling out to Dean, who was on the other side of the street. I just stared straight ahead, concentrating on the huge bare tree limbs and the bright blue sky, and the little stone man down at the end of the block where the parade would circle onto the next street. The crisp wind stung my face and gave me a good excuse to put my gloves against my cheeks. "The language is *filthy,*" Misty whispered in mimic. "What a stupid old bitch."

I saw Perry Loomis like a flash over on the other side of the street, and it was like she was looking right at me. One day I had said hello to her in the hall, and she had looked surprised, as if to ask who did I think I was speaking to her. She had quickly nodded and then hurried past, her books up to her chest. Now I saw her face in and out of the crowd, the boys from my class not far from where she was. I looked past the float with what was *supposed* to look like the nativity but instead looked like some hippies in a barnyard; I had decided that I *would* speak to Perry again if I got the chance, even with Misty right there beside me. The high-school drama students who were manning the float had *live* animals, and now Joseph had thrown down his walking stick and was wrestling a sheep who was butting the chicken wire that enclosed the flatbed trailer.

Once the animals were under control, and Santa finally passed, the crowd thinned. Children ran through an alley to catch the parade going back the other way. Again I saw Perry, now turning away from the curb and walking toward the corner. She was wearing a light-blue carcoat that for the world looked like the one I had outgrown, and she had a little baby propped up on her hip like a grocery bag. I had once overheard Todd Bridger say that Perry's mama was never at home and they could do as they pleased as long as Perry cooked supper and changed her little brother's diaper. I lifted my hand when I thought she was looking but instead I got the same blank stare she had given me in the hall that day. Todd and some of the other boys were standing around her, but she seemed uninterested as she shifted the child from hip to hip, turning to smile as if she were paying attention to what they were saying, though she looked as if her thoughts were miles and miles away. It hardly seemed fair that anyone should be so pretty, with such thick wavy hair and large dark eyes.

It was a relief for Christmas to come and go. Misty spent most of the days comparing that year to the one before, remembering the night Buddy was born, what her mother had baked and bought and said and sung. "Don't you remember that night Buddy was born?" she said so many times. "The way we danced around in the street? in the middle of the night? You remember how Mama said, 'Maybe Baby Well Allright That'll Be the Day'?" And then nine times out of ten, she would start to cry, shoulders shaking as she leaned towards me. It was warmer than usual that Christmas and rained so much that the families who usually went all out with lights and decorations confined their efforts to the insides of their houses. "Thank God, they're not stringing their lights this year," Mama said, and pointed to the neighborhood behind us, Merle Hucks's house dark. "There would be an electrical fire for sure." And though Angela had said that she *might* make it for the holidays, she never did.

Not long after we returned to school, I got my chance to talk to Perry. I had gotten permission to leave gym class to go to the bathroom, and there she was, sitting up on the old radiator with her hands cupping her chin as she rested against the large window sill. The light-blue carcoat was draped over her legs. She turned when she heard me come in and then quickly looked back to the schoolyard where a group of guys were shooting marbles under one of the tall elms.

"Hi," I said, pausing in front of the mirror to brush my hair. I saw her then turn and study my reflection, her lips in a full pout. She nodded. I hesitated, trying to think of something, *anything* to say. "You're not sick, are you?" She shook her head, dabbed one eye with the sleeve of her coat, and then turned back to the window.

"I used to have a coat like that," I offered, hoping for a bit more conversation. I turned from the mirror and waited to see if she would respond.

"You mean you used to have this one." She shook the sleeve all bunched up in her tiny hand. Somehow I was not prepared for the twang of her voice, the rusty flatness that went against every smooth line of her face. The sound was coarse and grainy. "I don't care," she persisted, her eyes as hard and cold as creek pebbles. "You can have it back if you want it. It's got a rip in the lining. The pockets hadn't even been cleaned out; I found all kinds of little notes." She paused and then laughed a forced laugh. "Take it if you want it." She hopped down and stepped closer to me, the coat held out in front of her. I felt like I was in the bottom of a well, like when I used to wear my earplugs. The image of myself in the white fake fur was ugly and garish; I was ugly and garish, and I was prepared to hear her say it.

"I don't want it," I whispered. If Misty had been there, she would have been forcing my head up. "I'm sorry, really." I wanted to tell her that I didn't know, didn't think, but I knew if I said another word I'd start crying. I looked back at her, tried to show in my expression that I hadn't meant to hurt her. She returned my stare, her eyes lingering just a second longer on my left cheek, and I waited for what was bound to come, waited for the lengthy, flattened insult.

"Who needs a stupid new coat?" she said and turned away. "All of y'all come in here like a fashion show." She flipped one hand out to the side and twisted her small body in mocked exaggeration of a model pose. "And I've heard the things that fat friend of yours has said about me. I ain't deaf, you know, but it seems I can't do nothing about it." I froze, waiting for more, still stunned that she had concocted her *y'all* to include me. I was one of *them*; I was one of the enemy and she had not even taken her best shot at me. She sighed and went back to the radiator, hopped up and pulled her short corduroy skirt down as far as she could.

"I'm sorry," I said. She shrugged without looking from the window, and I backed out of the bathroom as quietly as I could. I was back in the gym, feeling the vibrations of the basketballs bouncing up and down the old scuffed-up floor, when I realized that I had not even used the bathroom. And when the bell rang, I lingered, looking out the gymnasium door to where Perry stood on the curb in front of the school until she climbed into an old beat-up van and rode away. The van, blue with all kinds of spray-painted graffiti, was easily recognized; I had seen it parked at the Huckses' house from time to time. The gym was almost empty when I heard Misty's loud, boisterous voice calling for me to come on, we were going to be late for English. *I ain't deaf you know.* We were doing the first act of *The Miracle Worker*, and I had Misty's old granny glasses safely tucked away in my locker.

Slowly the leaves returned, green buds that soon opened like fans to camouflage the stone man so well that only those familiar with him would be able to trace his figure there against the sky. With spring, we received news that E. A. Poe High was close enough to completion that we would definitely go there in the fall; as a result, Samuel T. Saxon would finally be torn down. They would begin as soon as school got out, slowly dismantling the ancient mortar and brick, the thick wavy windows and stone sidewalks. They would bulldoze the yard, turning up lost erasers and marbles and pennies and burying them beneath the yellow dust.

Fourteen

L ate that spring I went to a tea at Mrs. Poole's house. Misty and I were still members of Children of the Confederacy, and so several times a year we had to go sit and eat cookies with seven other girls who also had at least one ancestor who had fought for the Confederacy. My mother didn't see much merit to this club, favoring of course the Revolutionary War, but still she liked the *idea* of me participating. Several years before, Mo Rhodes who thought the *idea* of it all was stupid, had asked Misty, "Are you *sure* you want to be in this kind of club?" I had wished that just once my mother would give me the option. But now there was no one to question our membership, and Misty's countdown was nearing its end; *in only two months it will be a year since Mama left home.* Sally Jean was trying her best to mark everything by the Liberace sighting or by her wedding day, but until that first year ended, there was no other way for Misty to mark time.

Mrs. Poole had volunteered to have a joint meeting of the United Daughters of the Confederacy, of which she was the long-running president, and the Children of the Confederacy. At her insistence, each *child* was supposed to present a project which in some way or another reflected respect and honor of the Confederacy. Certainly none of us took this club as seriously as Mrs. Poole did. I knew when she clinked a long sterling spoon on her iced tea goblet that we were in for an afternoon which could only be equaled by a church retreat or a tour of the local funeral home.

Sterling against crystal and the room went silent. All the women, my mother included, were used to this; you could tell by the way they stared into the swirled pattern of Mrs. Poole's hospital green wall-to-wall carpet. "She was the first in town to have wall-to-wall," I had heard my mother say several times. Now the green nubs were worn down by herd after herd of tea-takers.

"Let's begin," she said, and smiled a thin tight-lipped smile, "by introducing ourselves and giving the name or names of our ancestors who so bravely served." She looked around the room, smiling, just as she did when she taught Sunday school; she searched the crowd of us like a hungry eagle poring from the cliff top. Swoop, snag, claw. "Now, I'll go first. I am Mrs. Theresa Poole," she said, and laughed as if there *could* be someone in the town of Fulton who did *not* know her. "The men in my family served in the the Revolutionary War and the Civil War, World War I and World War II."

"They must have been real old by then," I whispered to Misty, and she stifled a giggle, then whispered that old joke to me, "Her people couldn't get along with *anybody*."

"My Mr. Robert Manchester Poole"—she pointed to his portrait hanging above the mantel and then to the famous machete she always made reference to, which was propped against the fireplace—"was in the Pacific during WWII." Mrs. Poole said double-u double-u, and Misty's elbow dug into my ribs. I knew that when she could without laughing she would whisper *dubya dubya*.

"We'll socialize a little later." She was staring right at us—we felt like bunnies in her fierce talons—and my mother was giving me the eye that said she'd just as soon put me on restriction as breathe.

"Now, I could go on and on with the names of my relatives, but perhaps I'll focus on the two names you'll recognize, General Robert E. Lee and Mr. Stonewall Jackson." She grinned again and even the other women began twitching on their chairs. How could you follow that? "We'll go around the room now." I prayed that she would begin the circle so that my mother went first and I could once again hear the *public version* of her relative who was considered the black sheep of his New England family. Randolph H. Anders was a physician in the Civil War, a convert to the Confederacy who died of pneumonia. My mother had told Mrs. Poole that the man was considered a black sheep for leaving the North and that he was a physician, but had failed to say that he died of pneumonia nowhere near a battle site and was a black sheep because he had become involved with his brother's wife. It irked Mrs. Poole that she did not have first-hand knowledge of my mother's family as she did everyone else's in Fulton. If my mother *really* wanted to get under Mrs. Poole's skin, she casually mentioned the *Underground Railroad* as if it had just been built and she herself had tunneled her way beneath the streets of Boston. Mrs. Poole could not stand to be left out.

"I am Cleva O'Conner Burns," my mother finally said. "And my great-great-uncle Randolph Anders, a *well known* New England physician, came to the South and served and died in the Civil War." She looked around and smiled, then smoothed her hair; she was wearing a long brown tunic, finally swayed to join the fashion trend set by Bea Arthur. Misty leaned in to me and whispered, "Beware of The Maude Squad," and I had to hold my little tiny napkin that came with that little tiny glass of grape juice up to my mouth to hide a laugh.

"Anyway," Mama continued, always confident when in a setting of historical discussion, "Randolph Anders was considered a black sheep by all of his family members. I mean you can imagine. His very own brother, Lucas Anders, worked on the *Underground Railroad*, there beneath the streets of *Beacon Hill*, helping those *poor* people to *freedom*." Mama's hands shook a little but she looked confident, her voice ringing with the same force and clarity it had when we had walked the Freedom Trail and she had narrated every little stone path and building along the way. She had shown me the statue erected to commemorate the *Union* dead; she had shown me the apartment building where she was born, a five-floor brick building with bay windows and a view of the Charles River.

My mother was telling of Randolph Anders's long work hours as a physician even while he was ill with pneumonia. Mrs. Edith Turner was twitching on her seat, heaving her weight from thigh to thigh; Mrs. Poole lit a Salem and blew a stream of smoke through her pursed fuchsia lips. My father referred to Randolph Anders as *that oversexed Southbound New Englander*. "They sent their bad blood to the South," he had said, pencil in hand as he doodled a picture of the East Coast. "States always think they're one better than the one just below. New York frowns on New Jersey. Virginia frowns on the Carolinas. Everybody frowns on Miami." He was now filling in the shapes of the states so closely that at first I thought he was tracing a map. "Used to if you were on the outs with the law, you went to Texas and were never heard from again. Then after Texas, Alaska became the place to go and disappear." He went to the upper left-hand corner of his paper and drew Alaska. "But way back when that oversexed Southbound relative of your mothers had to leave town . . ."

"So you have a lot of different lines, Cleva," Mrs. Poole said, and stood, then realized she had lit a cigarette and had to sit back down. "Now like me, I have pure, solid Southern lines, but you and your family are more in keeping with what we in America call 'the melting pot.' " She turned and looked at all of us C of C's as if we were in her Sunday school class for five-year-olds. "The Melting Pot. You can get the picture from that I guess. I mean, can't you see what is meant by a melting pot?"

"No," Misty said, eyebrows furrowed in a confused fashion. "Please explain just what *is* meant by the melting pot." Sally Jean sat up straight in her chair; it was obvious that she felt totally responsible for anything Misty said.

"Let me," Sally Jean offered, and smiled at Misty, attempting the *mother/daughter* bond that she had told my mother she was trying to achieve. "We call America the melting pot because"— her face was flushed bright pink—"well, because,'*It's a small world after all.*' " She never sang the words, just spoke them, her head nodding in rhythm. " '*It's a small world after all.*' " She looked at Mrs. Poole, who stubbed out her Salem and stood, hands pressed on either side of her head.

"Well, we will just have to finish this over our refreshments because we have *got* to keep going. Now, Sally Jean, you just *after all* yourself back to your chair if you please." Mrs. Poole flipped her hand like she might be shooing a dog while Sally Jean sank back into the big padded wing chair.

Mrs. Poole's husband, Bo, stared out at us from his portrait above the mantel, his dark beady eyes moving to wherever you stood in the room. "He died of consumption," I once heard my mother say, and my father laughed until he got red in the face.

"He did!" she insisted. "Anybody will tell you."

"I don't doubt that at all," he said. "I believe he died of consumption." He paused while she relaxed and then started up again. "I know lots of men who were with him while he was consuming. He consumed a lot. He consumed so much that his nickname was Hooch."

"Impossible," Mama said, and he just shook his head and hummed "The Impossible Dream," followed by "Impossible."

"Why do you have to always try and find something bad?" she asked. "Why can't you accept that we all have our *good* points as well as our *weaknesses*? Why can't you say something *nice* about somebody?"

"Et tu, Clevé?" he asked, eyebrows raised sharply.

I kept staring at Mr. Bo "Hooch" Poole the whole time we went around the circle. It was hard to imagine this man with his silver hair and Teddy Roosevelt moustache, this man who had once run for lieutenant governor, out in the county getting soused.

Mrs. Poole's house was like a museum with all of her bric-a-brac, little crystal and pewter and silver birds and figurines which my mother ordinarily would have called "dust collectors." The minutes from the last UDC meeting were boring, the topic meandering from side to side to discuss who had died and who was in the hospital and who had retired. We C of C's were supposed to just sit and grin and wait until talent time.

Except for Ruthie Sands, Misty and I didn't really know the other members, for they were several years older. Ruthie was going to be going away to a private high school in the fall, and you could tell by the somber set of her thin flawless face that she would rather have been anywhere except there. She sat with the older girls and other than saying hello, ignored us until talent time when she asked that we hold up her big flannel board while she arranged little blue and gray felt men and conducted one battle after another right up to the surrender at Appomattox.

I sang "Swanee" down on one knee like Al Jolson, my voice as deep and husky as I could make it. Misty had encouraged me to sing, and I had practiced in her cluttered bedroom the whole week before. Misty and Lily Hadley and some other girls were thinking of starting a singing group, and she had said that if I practiced more I'd have no trouble joining. She said they really needed another white girl since they had plans to stand black, white, black, white and do lots of neat designs with their arms and legs like the June Taylor dancers used to do on Jackie Gleason.

I noticed that while I was singing, my mother was staring off, through Mrs. Poole's large picture window which overlooked her side yard; if the hedge had been trimmed you could have seen our yard with the little white gazebo my mother had ordered in a kit and built herself. Ivy grew up the posts, loose tendrils hanging like threads. My mother's rose garden was beautiful, too, more beautiful than Mrs. Poole's but Mrs. Poole had never complimented her on it. I had listened one day as Mrs. Poole complimented everything from the peonies to the hydrangeas, obviously ignoring both the gazebo and the roses. "You could do a lot with this yard if you took a notion, Cleva," Mrs. Poole had said, my mother standing there large and lifeless, gardening scissors in the pocket of her dress.

People clapped when I finished singing but, instead of looking at me, looked at Mama, who had no choice but to look back and smile. I had told her I was going to tell about our trip to Boston and what it had meant to me to glimpse the history of the *other* side of the war; I had completely forgotten to tell her of my change in plans. And though she liked to hear me sing and though she often, during a *Lord Forgive Me When I Whine* session, reminded me of the God-given grace of a singing voice, she was not at all prepared for the deep jazzy Judy Garland style that Misty had encouraged.

When Misty stood up and began her talk on cotton, I felt like I was going to burst out laughing. Other than the relief at having my turn over and having received a few compliments from the older girls, there was no good reason to laugh, but still it came over me like a wave, making my face go red and my whole body quiver. I had to excuse myself and rush into Mrs. Poole's kitchen; when I got behind the swinging door, I made myself cough again and again so they would think I'd had an attack. I knew Misty knew this old trick because we had both used it at Sunday school and I listened, expecting her to lose her control but she was as composed and dry as ever. I waited there, peeping through the crack of the door to see Misty modeling her new peasant blouse with the lace and embroidery. "Cotton," she said. "This is 100 percent cotton."

I felt another wave coming over me but coughed instead. Whenever my mother allowed me to sit with Misty in church, we played a game where we'd close our eyes, open the hymnal, and then read the two titles with an ending of "in the bed," such as "Just As I Am *in the bed*" or "How Great Thou Art *in the bed*." It was Misty's game, recently learned from the *so very mature* Dean, and though it seemed a little sacrilegious, I couldn't help but shake with suppressed laughter, so desperate for the freedom to let it all out.

Misty bent the label from her skirt waistband and said, "Cotton." The older girls were trying hard not to laugh, while Ruthie Sands sat there with her cute little nose wrinkled in disgust. "Blends are inferior," Misty continued, still straight-faced. "Let the ladies feel your blouse, Ruthie," she said. "Let us now compare cotton to polyester." I had to put my hand over my mouth and slip back into the kitchen where I couldn't see or hear. Even my mother had looked as if she were about to lose control.

"You got the giggles, I suspect?" Maralee Landell was standing right behind me. I nodded, my hand still over my mouth. "You haven't visited over here in a long time, have you?" she asked, and I shook my head, peeked back out into the living room, where a red-faced, jaw-clenched Ruthie stood while people fingered her blouse. "I still see your mama over here right often. I guess you're old enough to go your own way, have for awhile now." She began running water in the sink, her tennis shoes squeaking on the spotless linoleum, while she arranged some little sandwiches on a tray. "You want a sandwich?" she asked, and when I said no, turned off the water and went and opened the back door. I saw her waving her right arm in a big loop while she held the door open. As I watched, I couldn't help but wonder where Mr. and Mrs. Landell went when another day of running Mrs. Poole's house had come to an end; I imagined them walking out the back door and down to where the pastel houses stood.

"Come on, honey," I heard her say. "You've worked up an appetite I know, and I've set aside some goodies for you." Mama glimpsed me in the doorway and gave me a look that said, *Come back in here and sit down*, so I faked another cough, all the while expecting to see Mr. Landell come in from the yard and take off the little cap he wore while driving Mrs. Poole around town.

"Yes, it's getting mighty warm these days. You need to wear some lotion so you don't burn, got a nose like Rudolph." I turned just in time to see Mrs. Landell throw her arms around Merle Hucks and give him a quick hug. "What's this nasty thing you got around your neck, baby?"

"Rawhide," he said, and pulled away. He still hadn't seen me. "It's what people wear these days."

"Well, looks like a shoe string to me."

"Yeah, I guess." He grinned at her and she patted his shoulder again. "I finished edging around the roses," he said. "Now I'm gonna mow."

"Well, come cool off a second," she said. "Is your mama doing any better?" He shook his head and followed her over near the counter, waited for her to hand him a sandwich. "I sure am sorry to hear it." She retied her apron, the ends barely reaching when she crossed them in the back and pulled them around to the front. "Yes sir, your mama sure has had a time." She turned and then stopped as if she'd forgotten I was standing there. "Why, I forgot you were here," she said, and Merle looked over at me. "You two must know one another. Merle lives right behind you." She motioned with her thumb to the back window. I nodded and looked away. "Kate's here for a meeting," Mrs. Landell said, lowering her voice. "Got tickled and had to leave the room."

Merle nodded, still staring at me. He had grass stains on the knees of his jeans. "Do you want some refreshments, too?" she asked, and I shook my head. She fixed a big glass of iced tea and handed it to Merle. "Has your mama been back to the doctor?" she asked but he shrugged, then glanced at me.

"I see," she said. "We can talk over all that later. You two just help yourselves to those sandwiches over there. Not these though." She pointed to the silver trays she had finished arranging. "Lord knows, not these. I got to run speak to Mr. Landell and I'll be right back." She wiped her hands on a dish towel, patted Merle's shoulder, squeezed it as if to send him some secret message, and then was gone, out the side door and around past the window. Merle sat down at the kitchen table, and I felt like I was frozen with no place to go.

"What are you looking at?" he finally asked, and I shook my head. "Well, what are you doing here then?"

"A meeting."

He laughed a loud forced laugh and then rearranged the salt and pepper shakers. They were cut glass with silver tops, and when he held them up, the light from the window hit and bounced in little circles. "I mean in the kitchen." He shook his head, and I kept waiting to hear him meow but he didn't. "The meeting's in there." He pointed to the door as if to tell me to go on.

"Where's Frankincense?" I asked, suddenly realizing what a ridiculous thing that was to say; it had been well over a year since the church retreat. When I looked back up, he was grinning, his front tooth that used to be gray, loosened, and chipped long before, was as white and straight as the others.

"Aw, he's off somewhere with my brother, Dexter." He reached for another sandwich. "They have club meetings, too."

"You're not a member?" I was slowly moving towards the table, wishing I could not hear the voices from the other room. Misty was now singing, her voice huskier than mine could ever

be, *in them old cotton fields back home*. I was close enough to read
the scribbles on the rubber sole of his tennis shoe, his initials,
a peace sign, New York Jets, heavy lines marked to scribble out
something else. Then I heard Sally Jean say, "A house is made of
brick and stone, but a home is made of love alone."

"I'm not much on clubs," he said, giving his head a jerk toward
Mrs. Poole's living room. "Don't like meetings." I nodded, and
pulled out the chair across from him, lifting carefully so it didn't
squeak against the linoleum. His eyes must have lingered on my
cheek longer than he had intended, because he suddenly started
and glanced away, raked his fingers through his damp hair.

"What's wrong with your mother?" I asked, my voice awkward and strained.

"Hysterectomy."

"Oh." I felt my face and neck get warm.

"No big deal."

"That's good," I said. Another long heavy pause. "What are
you doing here?"

"Working." He got up and went to get one of the sandwiches,
started to put it in his mouth, and then waited. "I do yard work
mostly," he said. "Do your parents need somebody to mow?" Of
course he *knew* where I lived, but somehow it surprised me to
hear him acknowledge that he knew. "You can let me know it
they do, at school or something."

"Yeah, okay." I watched him come back over to the table,
this time pulling out the chair closer to mine, across the corner, and when he sat, his knee brushed against mine. "I'll ask
my dad." I waited for him to say something else, but he just
nodded and smiled at me, his hands clasped on the table, dirt
from Mrs. Poole's roses still under his nails, a fine scratch across
the base of his thumb. I was about to ask him what happened
when he spoke again.

"Yeah, well, you can let me know anytime," he said again.
"If you miss me at school you can always call me at home. You

could . . ." He stopped midsentence when Misty pushed through the swinging door looking for me, her eyebrows going up in surprise to see Merle there. *I could what*, I wanted to say, but Merle had already leaned back in his chair, moving his knee so there was no risk of brushing against me again.

"I'm always looking for other yards to mow," he said, turning to Misty. "Both of you can let me know if you need somebody."

"My brother does most of the yards around here," Misty said. "We don't really have any grass, you know, but he's done Kate's yard for a long time."

Merle just smirked and shrugged, put that whole little sandwich in his mouth. "So maybe he's tired of doing it."

I called for Misty to come on but she ignored me. "Katie wouldn't want you mowing her yard anyway. You'd probably run over her cat with your mower, spray him all over the place."

"Right," he said. "You keep believing that."

"Maybe we will." She nudged me with her elbow. "Where's R. W.?" she asked, her voice softening with the question. She flashed him a flirty little smile I had seen her practice in the mirror of her medicine cabinet a million and one times.

"What's it to you?" he asked, and then they grinned at each other.

"Just curious." She picked up a little sandwich, pulled the sliced olive off the top. "Oh, Kate, I forgot to tell you. I think Dean might ask you to go to the senior prom." I didn't say anything, just stood there with my face burning, eyes on that crystal salt shaker. She had told me again and again that we would be much more desirable to guys if they thought *other* guys were after us. "What do you think, Merle? Don't you think Kate and Dean will look *so cute* together?"

"I don't," I began, about to say that I knew nothing about any of this and that Misty was way out of line to be discussing it when Merle's "Who cares who goes anywhere with her?" hit my ears loud and clear. Merle crammed another sandwich in his mouth. This time he didn't pick up one of the little party napkins as he had before but wiped his hands on his pants. "See ya," he mumbled as he passed Mrs. Landell in the doorway.

It was like everything had sped up, and I followed Misty back into the living room, where she wanted to know what I was doing in the kitchen with Merle Hucks to begin with. Did I *like* Merle Hucks? Did he act like he liked me? No, I told her, no, a thousand times no. He had given me no reason to think that he liked me; his knee had brushed mine but it was an accident, and yes, he had talked to me, but what else could he do when we were the only two people in the room. *Who cares who goes anywhere with her?* he had said. Over by the refreshment table, Mrs. Poole was smoking rapidly while Sally Jean told her that her house was anesthetically pleasing. "What?" Mrs. Poole barely got the word out of her mouth before Sally Jean launched into a newly learned proverb: *There are two special gifts we give our children; one is roots, the other is wings.*

I kept hearing Merle say "hysterectomy," and it seemed so out of character, Merle Hucks saying hysterectomy without laughing, without hesitation. "You could call me," he had said and I couldn't help but wonder what else he might have said if Misty hadn't come in. He seemed like a different person there in Mrs. Poole's kitchen when it was just the two of us, so different from the boy who came to school smelling of grease and onion rings. Even though he'd been out working in the yard, he looked cleaner there in her kitchen as he held the salt shaker up to the light and tilted it to catch the colors.

"Thanks a lot for laughing during my report," Misty said later when we were sitting on my front porch. "Did you see Ruthie Sands when I said her shirt was polyester?" Misty laughed her loud hyena laugh and then went silent. "I hate Ruthie Sands." She pushed off the floor to move the swing back and forth while I sat on the step and threw twigs out in the yard for Oliver to pounce on. "And Merle Hucks. Are you *positive* you don't like him? You know I won't tell." I threw another twig but Oliver just sat and watched it; he was not nearly as frisky as he'd once been.

"Shhh," I said, thinking that at any minute Merle would step from Mrs. Poole's house and start walking this way. He could go home the back way, scaling our fence as I'd seen him do before, but I really didn't think Mrs. Poole would allow that. "Someone might hear you."

"So what do you care?" Misty pushed off again, the swing chains creaking. "Or do you? Just say one way or the other."

"Well, I sure don't want him getting hold of Oliver," I said, and forced a loud, Misty-style laugh.

"Oh, he wouldn't really hurt your cat," she said and grinned. "I was just teasing around with him. But I really do think Dean might be thinking about asking you to the prom."

"Yeah, right." I went to the bottom step and rubbed Oliver's back as he arched and stretched under my hand. "And of course I laughed at your report. You *wanted* people to laugh."

"Who, me?" Misty batted her eyes, took a long drag from an imaginary cigarette as she mimicked Mrs. Poole. "Hey, your song sounded really good, too. I didn't get to tell you because you were in the kitchen with Merle." She paused, waiting for a reaction, but I didn't look up. "Anyway, I'm gonna tell Lily and the others that I want you to sing for them in the bathroom next week. It'll be like an audition. Lily has the idea that we'll call ourselves Lily and the Holidays and enter the school talent show on the last day."

I heard Mrs. Poole's front door close and then within seconds, he was there, coming down the sidewalk. "Won't that be fun?" Misty was asking; she still hadn't seen Merle coming. "My mother would love that name, wouldn't she? You get it, don't you, like after Billie Holiday. Lily and the Holidays."

"So what are you, Halloween?" Merle stopped right in front of my sidewalk and stood there, hands on hips, a toothpick in his mouth. Misty had to stand up from the swing to be able to see him over the tall lagustrums at that end of the porch.

"Yeah, right," she said and came to the edge of the steps, held onto the porch rail with one hand and swung around in a mimic of some kind of model pose she had seen and studied.

"Or Ground Hog?" Then he turned and looked at me. "So where's the prom date? Thought he'd be over here mowing the yard."

"He will be soon," Misty said. "And for your information, I'm more like Christmas; I'm Thanksgiving. I'm the Fourth of July. You know last Fourth of July my mother . . ."

"I was kidding," Merle said, before she could tell the story he'd already heard at least once at school. "You know. A joke. Just kidding." His voice got soft, almost like a whisper. I wanted him to look at me the way he had in Mrs. Poole's kitchen, to finish what he had planned to say about me calling him at home, but he turned and started walking, intentionally stepping on every single crack in the sidewalk until he made a right turn and disappeared through the gates of Whispering Pines.

"Did you see that?" Misty asked. "He was so *nice* to me; he was flirting, don't you think?" She turned and waited for my response, her eyes carefully lined in moss green. "He was flirting with *one* of us I'm sure."

I stood and walked to the other end of the porch, where Oliver had moved and was sitting on the banister, his tail going back and forth like a pendulum. I rubbed his back, slowly glancing to the side just in time to see Merle disappear behind a grove of trees.

"You know." Misty was beside me then and looking in the same direction. "One of us could go for Merle and the other for R. W." That time she said double-u, and it made us both laugh. She was still staring into Whispering Pines when she started talking about Mo, about how she didn't understand what her mother saw in Gene to begin with.

"You know," she said, staring at her hands there on the banister, at the bright red polish on her gnawed-up nails, "some mornings I wake up and I say, oh, thank God, because it seems like a nightmare, just a dream." Her chin began to quiver and she bit her lower lip, paused until she had control and had blinked back the tears. "Sometimes it's as long as a minute before I remember. Once I even called for her. I screamed, 'Mama,' and when I opened my eyes, Sally Jean was there in the doorway in that old ugly flannel housecoat of hers." She wiped her nose with the back of her hand and laughed. "Why did it happen? Of all the people in all the cars on all the roads, why did it have to be my mother?" She turned and looked at me. "And of all the women in all the towns who drive cars that need new tires, why, *why* did my dad have to pick the Queen of Proverbs?" She reached for me then, her arm tightening around my neck as she squeezed and pressed her face into my shoulder. She opened her mouth, gasping like I hadn't heard her do since that night before Mo's funeral, and I couldn't tell if she was laughing or crying. "Make new friends but keep the old," she finally whispered, voice cracking. "Some are silver, some are gold." She pushed me back and looked me in the eye, shook her head and then collapsed in laughter. She lay back on the floor of the porch, her tennis shoes propped up on the railing and moving back and forth with her laughing like windshield wipers. "So maybe I'll go for R. Dubya," she cackled, holding her stomach. "You know what they say." She paused, wiped the little tear from the corner of her eye, breathed deeply and then sputtered. "One girl's R. Double-U is another girl's R. Dubya."

"Anyone can be an R. Double-U," I added, by then down beside her, my long feet right next to hers. "But it takes someone *special* to be an R. Dubya."

"Bless this mess," she said and sighed, stretched like a big cat and then relaxed, eyes closed, while my mother's hanging planter turned in the wind, fuchsia blossoms drooping and scattering their petals.

Fifteen

Not long after school got out, Misty and I were out on the porch painting our toenails a color called Raspberry Dazzle when Merle walked by and Misty whistled. My impulse was to jump down into the shrubbery, but my toenails were all wet, and I had cotton wedged between my toes the way Mo had taught us to do. Instead I grabbed one of our fashion magazines and held it over my face. Merle stopped right there on the sidewalk like he might walk up on the porch but he didn't. "Who's that whistling?" he asked.

"Well, it certainly wasn't me." Misty got up and stood on the top step, hands on her hips. She had lost quite a bit of weight, and though she still had a way to go before she fit into all of Mo's old shorts, she was very confident about the change in herself, confident enough to wear short shorts. The imprint of the webbing of the lawn chair where she had been sitting was firmly mashed and molded into her white thighs. "What makes you think a girl would whistle at you?"

He just shook his head, squinted off in the distance of the warehouse. "I didn't say I thought a *girl* would. I was talking about *you*." I stayed seated and just listened to the two of them; there was a friendliness there beneath the surface.

"So what am I then?" she asked, and moved her hips. "A woman?" Misty threw back her head and laughed; she had told me that my project for the summer was to learn how to flirt, and that she was going to teach me.

"I thought an *albino*," he said and looked up and down her freckled white legs, bent down to pick up a pebble.

"Aw, go to hell," she said, swinging one leg back and forth, toe pointed. "You're just upset cause you haven't been getting anything off of Perry Loomis or whoever you're after."

"Shhhh." Impulsively, I jumped up and grabbed Misty by the arm, the cotton still between my toes. "My mother is going to hear you."

"Don't want you to get in trouble," he said and looked up, those pale green eyes squinted against the sun, but he barely glanced at me before turning back to Misty. He tossed the pebble onto my sidewalk, and I watched it roll up to the bottom step. "There's a cat," he said, and pointed to Oliver. "Why don't you dogs chase it?" His voice was the same tone as when the two of them had swapped insults earlier. He looked at Misty then and grinned.

"Cause we see a bigger pussy," she hissed in a low voice but loud enough for him to hear.

"Stop, will you stop?" I twisted her arm until it went pink under my fingers. "Please?" I looked at him, too, and he grinned.

"Oh, I'm just kidding," Misty said, and patted my shoulder, winked at Merle. "Katie takes everything so seriously."

"Yeah, I've noticed." He started backing down the sidewalk, hands in his back pockets. "So don't be so serious." He smiled and then turned and walked away. When he got to the edge of the cemetery, he stopped and looked back. "And you," he pointed to Misty, "you stop chasing cats. Kate used to think she *was* one." And then he made that sound, that high pitched meeeoooowww that I hadn't heard in years.

Misty looked at me with raised eyebrows. "You're getting the hang of it," she said. "Now next time you start flirting, well, do it without that." She pointed to the wads of cotton between my toes. Later that day, long after Misty had gone home and most people were inside eating supper or watching TV, I looked out my bedroom window and caught a glimpse of Merle out in Whispering Pines. He was just sitting on one of the large tombstones, as motionless as if he were a statue himself; he turned once, face into the wind so that his bangs were lifted from his forehead, and it seemed like he looked right at my window. There was a split second when I was sure of it, so I just stood back and watched him. All around him the sky was dark and swirling with the rush that comes just before a summer storm.

It was the following week that Angela arrived at our house without any warning at all, or, as my mother chose to believe, only with warning to my father, who, it seemed, had forgotten to tell us. I had decided to make a serious appraisal of myself based on a beauty scale in *Glamour* magazine, and I was doing just that, sitting in the swing and trying to determine the shape of my face and eyes, when the rusty blue Impala pulled up and stopped.

I hadn't even heard my father come out onto the porch, but he was there, standing on the top step, wearing a white shirt with the sleeves pushed up, waving his arm just as he had done that day years before on Ferris Beach. It all seemed to be in slow motion, the creak of the swing, my father moving down the sidewalk, Angela lifting the trunk and leaning in, the swish swish of Mrs. Poole's sprinkler as it fanned a misty arc over the top of the hedge.

My mother was there, too, a scarf covering her hair and tied loosely at the back of her neck. She had come out to shake the dust mop, and now she stood like a soldier at attention with the mop over her shoulder, in her faded knit pedal pushers and slip-on sandals, her legs alabaster white next to mine, which were already tan. Tanning was a beauty element in my favor, but I was too stunned to add this to the *Glamour* checklist. My mother looked at my father, eyes wide, mouth open, a look more of shock than anger, but he wasn't even looking. I watched her shoulders sink, saw the head of the mop fall loosely to the floor. "Fred," she whispered, her hand immediately reaching to remove the scarf and then dropping to the neck of her sleeveless top, but he didn't even hear her as he reached into the trunk and came out with two small suitcases. "Oh God." Mama glanced at me and then turned and dashed back into the house.

I felt torn, back and forth like the swing or the swish of the sprinkler, back and forth like the sound of a lawnmower down at the end of the block. The two of them hugged, standing beside the bags on the sidewalk, while I concentrated on the distant humming sound. Angela's hair was longer than before, parted down the middle, a small section on each side braided and pinned back. She wore short shorts made of fabric that looked like newsprint and a halter top to match. Even in her wedged platform sandals, she was still a good six inches shorter than my father, her calves shapely muscular. As they came up the walk side by side, I heard a sudden movement and knew that my mother had been standing there behind the dark mesh of the screen.

"Kitty?" Angela said. "How are you?" She pulled me up from the swing and took me in from head to foot; I was barefooted and still taller than she was. "You look wonderful," she squealed, and gave me a quick hug.

I followed them inside, where the foyer was cool and dark compared to the brightness of our yard. "Cleva?" my father called, and walked towards the kitchen. I knew she would act as if she had never seen a thing. "Cleva, we have company." Angela was still laughing about how her old car had barely made the forty-mile drive when my mother came out into the hall, her hair hanging loosely down her back; she had a fondue fork in her hand and a look of surprise on her face. It was planned spontaneity, right down to her bare feet, something she *never* did.

"Well, what a surprise," she said. "I'm just doing my same old little housewife things, just whipping up a little chicken Kiev, baking some bread, chocolate cherries and mandarin oranges for dessert." She smiled the same way she did when she had to reprimand me in public. "Honey, could you go see if Sally Jean has a stick of butter." She nodded and smiled as my father led Angela upstairs to our guest room and then turned quickly, eyes anxious as she grabbed my arm. "Tell Sally Jean that I need all the butter she has and some of those mandarin oranges that she is forever talking about." She twisted my arm harder. "Tell her if she doesn't have them to please go to the store and bring them to me, that I'll pay her back and owe her one."

Poor Sally Jean's cabinets were overturned as she searched out two cans of oranges, thrilled to be able to serve and please my mother; she gave me five sticks of butter with promises of how she would gladly go to the store if my mother needed more. I repeated all of this as I placed the butter and the cans in my mother's desperate hands, and then I went and stood at the screen door and stared out at the rusty blue car. Mrs. Poole's sprinkler was still going and there was a faint rainbow mist over the hedge.

Merle was walking by, and though he couldn't see me there behind the screen, I instinctively stepped back. He seemed to walk more slowly as he passed. His hands were in the front pockets of his jeans—new jeans they looked like—and he wore a plain white T-shirt. His hair was as blond as corn silks, and his face and arms were already tan. I had seen him pass back and forth just about every day as he went to and from work at the Cape Fear Warehouse, where he was loading tobacco.

He paused in front of our walk, and I imagined that he was looking for the pebble he had tossed the other day, a smooth pink pebble that I had picked up and placed up on the porch right after Misty went home. He bent down and held his hand out, made a clicking noise with his tongue. In a minute, Oliver was there, tail straight up as he nuzzled Merle's knee and then flopped over on his back, twisted from side to side on the walk. Merle rubbed his hand up and down the cat's stomach.

"Kitty? Oh Kitty?" Angela's voice echoed through the hallway, and Merle looked up quickly. I backed into the darkness of the hall so that he couldn't see me. "There you are. What are you doing just standing here?" Before I could duck into the living room, she had pushed open the screen door and was motioning for me to go out on the porch. My father was right behind her. Merle stood as soon as he heard the door, and I lifted my hand involuntarily in a nervous wave. He nodded quickly and was gone without a word, poor Oliver alarmed by the quick motions and staring after him.

"Did we interrupt something?" Angela asked, and ran her hands under my hair, twisting and lifting it off my neck. She bent forward to look at me and then glanced down the street where Merle was just turning the corner there at Whispering Pines. "Were you courting?"

"No way." I pulled away from her, shook my hair out.

"How about I put your hair up for you?" she asked. "Or better yet, we'll do a whole make-over." She cupped her hand under my chin and turned my face from side to side. "I took a course in beauty school once."

"She was so beautiful they told her not to come back." My father sat in the swing and propped his feet on the lawn chair, lit a cigarette. "You know, I wonder if there's some kind of solution you could put on a person's hair and poison him through the scalp."

"Probably," Angela said, and laughed, then glanced across the street, where Sally Jean was throwing grass seed. "Who is *that?*" she whispered, still staring as Sally Jean bent down to pick something up, probably another left-over pebble.

"That's who Thomas Rhodes married." My father thumped his cigarette out into the yard as Angela continued to stare, head shaking in disbelief. "I wonder where I can find out about scalp poisoning. What do you think?" Angela turned quickly, rubbed her hands all over her head as if lathering, and then gripped her chest and began staggering towards my father; he was trying to light another cigarette but was laughing too hard to succeed.

"Mary Katherine?" My mother's voice from behind the screen brought silence. "Come here one minute, please." I went inside and then followed her through the house and out onto the sunporch. Her cologne was like an invisible thread leading me, and along the way I noticed how the whole house smelled wonderfully clean, and I knew she had used her old trick of filling all the sinks with Spic 'n' Span and Lysol, swishing the cleansers around. She probably had apples and cloves boiling on the stove and had sprayed the curtains in the guest room with cologne. I could still hear Angela and my father laughing.

"What is it?" I asked when she finally turned to face me, lush green ferns hanging behind her like a jungle. Again I felt torn as I watched her fiddle with the sash of her silky aqua blouse. Not only had she thrown the house into shipshape, but she had also been working on herself. She had put on the cream-colored skirt she normally wore to church, hose and matching cream pumps, a thin gold bracelet on her wrist. She was wearing lipstick and a touch of color on her cheeks.

"How do I look?" she asked, and held her hands out to the side. Something in her behavior, a vulnerability that I had never seen, made something inside me snap.

"That's why you called me back here?" I glanced out the kitchen window just in time to see Merle make his way through the overgrowth to his house. I wanted to say, *Pretty is as pretty does*, but I resisted. "You look fine," I said. "What do you want me to say?"

"I don't know, Katie." She sat down on the edge of a chair, hands folded in her lap, ankles crossed. She was in her own house, her own clothes, with her own family, and yet she looked like a stranger, like Sally Jean in Mo Rhodes's kitchen.

The first thing Angela did when she and my father came inside was to go on and on about how wonderful my mother looked, what a lovely blouse, a nice hairdo, what cute *little* pumps, all words that seemed to make my mother look even larger and more awkward than she was. Though the tension during the chicken Kiev was so thick I felt I'd choke, it began to lift, slowly, quietly. Angela said that she had never tasted anything more delicious, that she didn't know how my mother kept our home looking so beautiful, that she loved mandarin oranges dipped in fondue chocolate, and how did my mother ever know? It was working and my father kept talking about the women in his life, *all three of you*.

When dinner was over and we were sitting out on the porch, Angela presented my mother with a present, the giftwrap a piece of aluminum foil; it was a silver pin, a crescent moon with a star at the bottom. *A fairy tale moon*, she said, *a token of my appreciation for you having me visit a few days*. I recognized the pin; my father had bought it at a craft fair at the community college and had been saving it for my mother's birthday. He winked at me when I turned to look at him. "How thoughtful," my mother said, and pinned it on her blouse; Angela laughed and said it was no big deal.

"I love you, Cleva," I heard my father say later as I stood in the doorway of their room; I was about to ask if I could run over to

Misty's but changed my mind when I saw them hug tightly. My mother was wearing her slip and those lavender bedroom shoes; the moon pin was carefully placed in the center of a doily on her dresser.

"I can't believe she brought me that," my mother said. "Maybe all your good intentions and beliefs are finally paying off." I stepped back so that they wouldn't see me there as he nuzzled her neck, gave her those peck peck peck kisses that usually irritated her.

"Didn't I tell you, honey?" he whispered, pushed back and cupped her chin in his hand. "It just took time. She's a different person now. She's older, wiser." He kissed her again, and then at what looked like the most romantic of all moments, asked if she would call her beautician in the morning to find out a few things for his research.

Sixteen

No one knew how long Angela planned to stay. My mother asked questions trying to find out, such as would she be going with us to the town picnic on the Fourth of July, but the answer was never there. Every time the Fourth was mentioned, she turned the topic back around to Mo Rhodes leaving home the year before and what a terrible tragedy it all was. I would have guessed from seeing those two little bags, one just for make-up, that she had come for the night. However, as she unpacked I saw that the weekend-size piece of Samsonite was filled with little short T-shirt dresses all rolled up, a week's worth of underwear, one very brief bikini, a pair of faded jeans, and a couple of halter tops. It seemed that she had come with every intention of staying awhile.

By the end of the first week and many trips to the shopping center, she had twice as many clothes as when she arrived. One afternoon she took me shopping and insisted that I try on very grown-up and glamorous evening dresses. She got a long frosted fall from the wig department and convinced me that I needed to grow my hair waist-length. Then she got some sexy spike heels from the shoe department and convinced me that being tall was sophisticated. She had me believing that I *was* beautiful. Then she bought one plastic bangle bracelet, and we left while the irritated saleslady rehung the pile of formals that Angela had tossed on a chair. "Wasn't that fun?" she asked when we stepped from the air-conditioning of the department store into the broiling sun. She laughed and held the red bangle out to me. "A gift," she said.

Angela was like the Pied Piper, and I felt important just walking along beside her, going to the movies or shopping or just lying on a blanket in the backyard to sun. I had never done that before, always afraid that Merle would be out in the field or up on his roof to yell something. With Angela I felt brave. Even my mother, at Angela's invitation, had begun pulling up a yard chair and stretching her legs out in the sun, a sight I had never thought I'd see.

"I feel like I have two daughters," Mama said one day when she came outside with a pitcher of lemonade. She was talking to Sally Jean, who was following, needlework in hand. I had never imagined that my mother could have such a smooth dark tan but there she was, living proof. Sally Jean was also wearing shorts, and her legs were stained orange with QT. It had been Angela's suggestion after Sally Jean told us how she sometimes had an allergic reaction to the sun. "You can't lay out with us, but you can still get a tan," Angela had said, and my mother had not even corrected her for saying "lay," rather had encouraged Sally Jean to take Angela's advice.

"I am way too old to be your daughter and you know it now, Cleva." Angela laughed and took a glass of lemonade. "We found that out years ago. I mean, I could be Katie's mama as easily as you." Again, I felt that old pang of wishing. "I mean, I would have

had to *have had* her at age seventeen, but it does happen." I felt
Misty pressing my leg with her foot. My mother looked down
at the lemonade pitcher; I knew she was hoping to avoid the
story that was coming. "My mother was only seventeen," Angela
said, and Misty rolled over on her side, shielded her eyes against
the sun. "Really," she nodded, knowing that she had Misty's full
attention. "She never told who my daddy was." She laughed and
looked at my mother, who was studying the seed catalog she
had brought out with her. "Imagine. She was ahead of her time,
wasn't she?"

"My mom was only eighteen when Dean was born," Misty
said. "But my parents were married."

"Well, of course they were," Sally Jean said, and drank a big
swallow of lemonade. "Of course Thomas married her."

"Don't say it like that." Misty sat up, the shoulder strap of
her suit falling to one side to reveal a stark-white band of skin.
"You make it sound like they *had* to get married." Sally Jean
looked away but Misty continued. "They were in love, so much
in love that my daddy couldn't stand being away from her." Misty
breathed in, all the while staring at Sally Jean.

"Well, I didn't mean it to sound that way." Sally Jean sat forward on her chair. "Really, Misty. Now, honey, I didn't mean
that. Sometimes what I say comes out, well, it comes out . . ."

"Bass ackwards," Angela said, and pulled down her big white
sunglasses.

"And I was talking about *Misty* seeming like a second daughter
to me," Mama said, and pulled her chair closer to Sally Jean's,
the seed catalog in her lap opened to a page with hollyhocks and
snapdragons.

"Hey, I see you used the QT." Angela turned from my mother
and pointed to Sally Jean's legs. "It looks good, too, doesn't it?"
She looked around at all of us, with Sally Jean waiting for us all to
nod. Her legs were orange and we all knew it but nodded just the
same. "Delicious lemonade," Angela said, and though it seemed

tarter than usual, I nodded again. Things were going too well to spoil it. "If life gives you lemons," Sally Jean said, and smiled, her arms orange, too, "make lemonade!"

"You know, Cleva," Angela said. "I think you should try your hair differently, maybe a short shag that curls on its own." My mother's hand immediately went up to smooth her bun. Sally Jean nodded in agreement while staring at her embroidery; *hang in there*, it said, and there was a kitten hanging by one paw from what looked like a swing set.

"I've always had long hair," Mama said, with a puzzled expression. "And Fred likes it this way."

"Fred? Fred?" Angela asked, pushed those big sunglasses up on top of her head. "Since when does he tell you how to *look*? Do you tell him how to wear his hair?" She paused. "You see. He has *nothing* to do with your hair." Angela pulled her sunglasses back down. "It's a woman's world."

"That's what they say," Sally Jean said, and nodded firmly. "I saw a cute little picture right here that says it all." She began flipping through her stitchery book, and when she got to the right page, cleared her throat. "A woman needs a man like a fish needs a bicycle." She nodded and passed the book to my mother, who glanced at it, one eyebrow raised, and passed it right back.

"Well, I disagree about that," Angela said. "I mean, we do *need* those men. Right? Now, don't you *need* Tommy, Sally Jean?"

"Well, of course I do." Sally Jean's face was bright red as she tried to follow where Angela was leading. "I love the man. We *love* each other." She looked over at Misty, who was stretched out on her back, one knee bent up and moving back and forth. "Thomas and I can't stand to be away from one another."

"I can fix my hair any way that I choose," Mama said. "I just like for Fred to like how I look."

"I think a man likes a woman who looks the way she wants to look," Angela said. "A woman who is confident enough to do what *she* thinks is the best." Misty stopped humming and sat up, nodded knowingly at Angela, and then turned over, her back snow white against the bright blue suit.

"You are absolutely right," Misty mumbled. "I'm that kind of woman."

"Misty," Sally Jean said, looking as if she were on the verge of spouting some proverb when my mother burst out laughing.

"Misty is sure a card," Mama said as she slowly pulled the pins from her hair and uncoiled it. "I don't know what we'd do without her."

"Be boring," Misty mumbled, which made Angela laugh louder and harder than ever.

For the whole next day my mother toyed with her hair. I saw her several times just standing in front of the halltree mirror, pulling her hair this way and that, turning her head from side to side the way I had done so many times in an attempt to see what other people *saw* when I passed by. She even borrowed one of my *Glamour* magazines, the pages folded back to a make-over section, and Angela was right there egging her on. "You could *surprise* Fred." Angela smiled knowingly, stepped closer. "He'll love it."

By the end of the next day, my mother's hair looked like it had been cut with pinking shears. It kinked and curled all around her face and was rinsed dark and free of the gray. Her bangs stood out from her forehead in a Cleopatra look. She kept looking in the mirror, a worried expression on her face. Even Mrs. Poole had walked into our house and not said a word, acting as if she didn't notice anything new, and all the while studying my mother furiously when she could steal a glance.

"Your mama looks like she just joined the Egyptian Marines, and Sally Jean looks like a damn carrot," Misty said two days later when we were back out in the sun with Angela. "Damn it all to hell and back if she ain't orange and if your mama's hair doesn't look like a frizzy pyramid."

"Oh, now," Angela said. "I was *trying* to help the two of them."

Angela smiled, lips together, eyes filled with concern and pity. It was the same look she had given my father when he asked us what had ever made my mother think of doing such a thing to herself. "What do you *really* think, Fred?" Mama kept asking, and he replied, "One in a million."

Angela told Misty she shouldn't talk about my mother and Sally Jean, but nonetheless she laughed every time the two were mentioned. My mother, on that very day, had her navy shorts rolled up three inches higher than she normally wore them. Clearly Angela had started something. Sally Jean was daily coating herself in orange, and Mrs. Poole had even been spotted in a pair of chartreuse polyester shorts.

"You are so lucky," Misty had said over and over. "Angela is so neat. Maybe she'll take us to the beach and let us stay at her place. Maybe we'll meet some boys." Now she turned and looked at Angela, lifting her sunglasses up the way Angela always did before speaking. "You knew my mother, didn't you?"

"I knew who she was." Angela nodded. "And of course I saw her Christmas a year ago." She looked at me to confirm the meeting. "What a beautiful woman she was." Misty nodded and smiled. "I knew I had seen her before because how could you forget someone so pretty, right?" Misty nodded again. "The truth is"—Angela lowered her voice—"I wasn't going to bring this up because I didn't want to upset you, but I was at your mother's funeral." She sat back, looked first at Misty and then at me. "My boyfriend knew Mo, said he had for years, that she was a wonderful, wonderful person." Angela leaned forward and brushed a piece of grass from the beach towel. "He said the same about your father, of course. He said he had never seen two people so much in love."

"You had a boyfriend?" I asked, quickly counting the short months between her visit to our house and Mo's death. She was barely separated.

"Yes." She reached over and patted me. "I wasn't divorced but

I was separated and if you're wondering, I met him *after* I left my husband, okay?" She waited for me to say something. "You are your mother's daughter, aren't you, honey?" I looked up and she laughed. "Friends?"

"Oh, she doesn't care if you had an old boyfriend," Misty said. "Of course you had a boyfriend. I mean look at you. Why *wouldn't* you have a boyfriend? That would be like my mother not having a boyfriend." She stopped suddenly.

"This boyfriend of mine," Angela continued, "he said he remembered when Mo had a little toddler and was pregnant, how radiant she looked and how your dad was always right there beside her."

"That would've been when she was pregnant with me," Misty said, and rubbed more lotion on her freckled pink legs.

"Well, you should be proud to have had such a beautiful mother. You have her eyes," Angela said, and Misty beamed, her hair pulled up and wrapped in a little knot like Angela had suggested, loose tendrils falling onto her neck and around her forehead. Her beauty advice had not done much for my mother and Sally Jean, but she had worked wonders on Misty; I had high hopes that the same sort of transformation would come to me.

"Thanks," Misty whispered. "I wish I could look *just* like my mother."

"You're getting there," Angela said. "Your hair will never be as dark as hers, but your features are *identical*." She said the word with such authority that I believed her, too. "I *love* this hair of yours," she continued. "You know, I'll bet with a little Sun-In you can be blond, like a pretty strawberry blond."

"Yeah?" Misty looked to me for my opinion and then turned back to Angela, playfully punching her arm. "But if it turns out like Kate's mama's hair or Sally Jean's legs, we're gonna run you out of town. Right?"

"Right," I said, and watched my mother as she worked in the gazebo, wearing those rolled-up shorts, her hair hanging in wild angles. She was clipping roses from the vines that grew up and down the trellis sides, and she had an armful, pale pink petals against her tan arms. I tried to imagine her pregnant, tried to imagine my father catering to her, helping her in and out of chairs, stroking her full abdomen.

"Did you have a boyfriend when you were our age?" I asked Angela. In answer she quickly cut off her "yes" and softened it with a *but*: "But people seemed to get together so much younger, got married so much younger, you know? So many people *married* their high school sweeties."

"Who was your high school sweetie?" Misty asked. "Some real stud, I bet."

"He wasn't bad." Angela stared out at the field and shook her head, laughed. "And yeah, he was pretty cute."

"How long did you date him?" I asked, and she shrugged, waved her hand. "A year? Two?"

"I can't remember."

"Was he the *only* one?" I asked, conjuring my own picture, a seventeen-year-old Angela, her auburn hair swinging shoulder length; I imagined white socks and saddle shoes as she raced out onto an empty football field to meet *him*, tall and thin with pale green eyes, and all the while she was trying to decide how she was going to break the news to him, this *accident* that had happened, this accident of a child who she would have to get rid of in some way or another if he didn't marry her.

"What is this, Twenty Questions?" she asked. "We'll call *you* Curious George." Misty smiled a drowsy smile and pulled a magazine up over her face, the smooth flawless face of Cheryl Tiegs staring up into the bright blue sky. The Huckses' back door slammed shut, and within seconds, I glimpsed Merle as he cut through the cemetery; he was wearing a white T-shirt and I could see him in and out through the trees as he made his way to the street. I felt Angela nudge me with her toe, and when I looked up, she nodded her head in the direction Merle had gone, and winked at me. "Maybe I should ask you guys some questions," she said.

"Fire away," Misty said, her voice muffled by the slick pages. "I have no secrets."

My mother was humming "Strangers on the Shore," as she moved out into the yard and over to the bed of hybrid roses. Despite the hair and rolled-up shorts, she was attractive in her own way, with her high cheekbones and full lips. Her steps quickened as she walked around the yard, ending her repertoire with "Tie a Yellow Ribbon Round the Old Oak Tree," which had been playing on the radio incessantly for a couple of months.

"Your mama ain't half bad," Misty said, and lifted the magazine. She wrinkled her nose, mouth screwed up to one side in what was *supposed* to be the look of a learned critic. "Her singing, I mean." Under Misty's supervision of song choice and Temptations-style stepping, Lily and the Holidays had come in second in the school talent show. I was still amazed that I had been up on the stage with them, my arm entwined with that of Roslyn Page, while we did several *Yes, I will*s in the background of "I'm Gonna Make You Love Me" as Misty and Lily alternated parts, Misty sounding as much like Diana Ross as Diana Ross.

"Maybe your mama wants to be a Holiday," Misty said, and laughed, nudged me with her elbow, and then whispered, "Halloween," which made Angela laugh a drowsy laugh as she lay stretched out on her towel, all of my secrets in the palm of her hand.

Seventeen

ngela told me that she had come to visit us because she needed to get away from the beach for awhile, to take a break, get the salt out of her joints. "I had a failed romance," she said one night as she sat on the foot of my bed in the slat of light from the corner streetlight, her legs pulled up under her thin cotton gown. "He was so handsome," she said, and paused, thinking. "He kind of looked like the guy who played Maverick."

"James Garner," I said, sitting forward and waiting for the rest of her story. I was already in bed, the covers over my legs. These late-night talks, what Angela called our "heart to hearts," had happened every night of the two weeks she'd been there. I'd hear her creep into my room and stand ghostlike beside my bed. "Kitty? Kitty?" she would call. "Are you asleep?" Sometimes she sat at the foot of my bed, and other times she crawled in beside me to whisper her stories.

That same night she told me about her first marriage. "It only lasted a couple of months," she said. "I was so dumb to have done it." She sighed. "Old Cleva has never let me forget it either." Once again I imagined the teenage Angela with her long ponytail swaying from side to side as she slow-danced around a jukebox, "Young Love" or "True Love Ways" playing softly.

"We couldn't wait," she said, "and then as soon as it was all done, as soon as we came away from that justice of the peace, I knew in the pit of my stomach that we'd never last." She laughed. "It's amazing what being sixteen and in the backseat of a car can do to your head."

I lay there beside her, lulled by her voice.

"Then of course I went and married a man who wanted to keep me locked up like a little doll," she continued. "He got insanely jealous if I even spoke to another person. Fred and I were always so close that I just naturally talked about him a lot and Ken, that was his name, Ken just couldn't stand it." She rolled towards me, head propped in her hand, the streetlight catching and lighting only one side of her face like a Harlequin doll. "I was waitressing at the time and I knew all the regulars so you know I was always chatting, not flirting, mind you, just talking." She paused and I strained to open my eyes wider, to stay awake so as not to miss any of her story. "Ken just jumped to the wrong conclusion is all." She paused, breathed deeply. "One thing led to another and Ken ended up slapping me one night, in the face. I got scared and I called Fred. He came to help me, and I was almost through with my packing when Ken walked in and slugged Fred right in the stomach. I was scared to death he'd broken a rib. I said, 'I hate you, you big son of a bitch,' and now, Kitty, you for one know that I don't normally talk that way." I nodded and sat up a little. "And of course you remember how Fred brought me here and let me get myself pulled back together while I got the separation all legalized." I nodded. "Cleva was fit to be tied. You remember, don't you?" I didn't respond. "Well, she *was*, whether you knew it or not."

"Why?" My question was simple, but it left Angela completely silent, the glowing clock by my bed ticking off the long quiet pause.

"Why not?" she finally asked, and then quickly continued. "You remember the day that I came over here before that, the day I saw Mo Rhodes? Well, I came to tell Fred that I was afraid, and I really was. I really feared for my own safety." She sighed. "I mean maybe Cleva felt I shouldn't have involved Fred, but I didn't have anybody else to help me. You know she is real insecure; I mean it's not like she was *ever* the belle of the ball." She leaned closer, her head touching mine as she whispered. "Good grief, she was over thirty when they got married. I mean, people are doing that more and more these days, but when she was coming along, she was considered *old*, an *old maid*." She laughed. "Okay, now it's your turn to tell me something."

"I don't know what to tell." I lay staring at the ceiling, the streetlight casting a distorted image of the window. Just the night before I had looked out and would have sworn I saw Merle sitting on the tombstone, the glow of a cigarette near his face.

"Well, you can think of *something*," she said. "I'm not going to tell anybody."

"Well." I paused, trying to think of something to tell her. "I'd like to have a boyfriend." I waited for her to respond.

"And?"

"Well, that's it. That's a wish that I have." I waited and then felt her side of the bed shake as she muffled a laugh in her pillow.

"Oh, Kitty," she said. "You don't ask for much, do you?"

"It's a lot," I told her. "I mean, I've never really had one before and sometimes I wonder if I will. Maybe I'll be an old maid. Maybe it's hereditary."

"What on earth are you talking about?" She sat up and leaned over me, and I held my breath as I imagined the dream come true: *Why, it can't be hereditary because you are not your mother's daughter, you are my daughter, Kitty, mine.* "Why, there will be hundreds who'll like you, who'll *love* you," she said instead. "Why, poor old Fred will have to beat them off with a stick. He has said so himself. He's told me so many times that he plans to deal with your dates the same way he dealt with mine." She paused. "You know Fred was like my daddy. He'd sit a boy down and ask him what his intentions were, where were we going and when would we be back and what is a logarithm."

"He did?"

"I'm exaggerating but he did give those poor guys a hard hard time." She laughed quietly and then stopped, rubbed her hand over my head. "But, Kitty, there will be plenty of boyfriends for you, just mark my words. You've got to believe in yourself." She rubbed her hand over my cheek and then just held it there, pressing in. "What about that cute little blond-haired fella who was on the sidewalk the other day?"

"Merle Hucks?" It sounded funny to hear his name whispered in my room as if by the very sound I had invited him in.

"Yeah, I think he's kind of cute." She shook me. "He walks by here all the time, too. I've seen him pass every day."

"He has to walk by here," I said. "It's on his way to work."

"Oh," she said, paused. "I know what." Again her hand brushed my face. "Tomorrow I'm going to give you a complete make-over, what do you think?" I told her I'd like that, and from then on I let my comments get further and further apart, feigning sleep to her final whisper of good night when she got up and tiptoed back across the hall. It seemed I could feel every creak of the house as it settled; every sound was harshly magnified. I thought of Anne Frank tiptoeing through darkness, fearful of loose floorboards or a simple sneeze as she waited for those brief moments when she could stand in front of the attic window, with bells chiming in the distance, sea gulls circling overhead. I thought how spatially *she* could have been my mother, the years just right, and yet confined to the pages of her diary, she was my own age. I tried to imagine all of them at my age, my mother and

Angela, Mo, and Sally Jean. I got up once to look out the window; the ivy hung ghostlike on the columns of Whispering Pines, the huge granite tombstone smooth and pale in the moonlight. I think I half expected to see Merle sitting there, blond hair blown back from his forehead as he stared at my window, and I got back in bed with that picture in mind.

It was late afternoon the following day when Angela finally sat me down in front of my vanity, spread out all of her cosmetics and gave me the make-over she had promised since her arrival. She wanted me to close my eyes so that it would all be a surprise, and so I sat for what seemed like hours while she rubbed her lotions around my eyes, over my cheeks and neck. As usual she talked about all of the places she had been and the things she had seen, Disney World and the big hotel at Myrtle Beach with the rotating restaurant. It had been in that very restaurant where the James Garner-man had told her that he was going back to his wife; if only he'd met Angela two years earlier, their lives would have been so different.

"He was married?" I asked incredulously, only to have her swat me playfully and say, *How was I to know?* "It's not like his wife was my best friend or anything. You know, like Mo Rhodes." Then she brushed my hair, lifting it up from my neck, back from my face.

"Where were you all day?" I finally asked, the question my mother and I had exchanged since early that morning, when my mother *thought* she was giving Angela a bread-baking lesson.

"Can you keep a secret?" She leaned in close, her cheek next to mine as I nodded. "I had a date."

"Who?" Without thinking I started to open my eyes and she held her hand in front of them.

"Here, face away from the mirror and you can open them." She pulled me around on the bench. "There."

"Who did you meet?" I asked again.

"Well"—she brushed over my eyelids with a little sponge brush—"really I already knew him." Her brows arched as she said "him," laugh lines stretching from her eyes. "The truth is that last night after you fell asleep, I called this restaurant where I sometimes used to fill in at Ferris Beach; you know, I thought it might be good for somebody to know where I am, check on my apartment, my mail and so on." She pulled my hair back on the left side and clipped it; I didn't say anything but I knew I'd never wear the left side clipped back. "Anyway, who answered the phone but Greg. I hadn't seen him in over a year. Actually I was still with Ken the last time I saw him." She lowered her voice and giggled. "Real, real good-looking." When I thought of Angela's loves, I saw the intersecting circles my father always doodled to pass the time, no circle isolated, no failed romance without another in the wings, hidden spouses within the shaded areas.

"Good-looking like who?" I asked.

"Ummm, let's see." She started braiding a thin strip of hair. "James Caan, that type, you know blue eyes, curly hair." I nodded my approval and closed my eyes again as she braided. When I thought of James Caan, I saw him as Sonny in *The Godfather*, and I thought of the vivid death scene where his body is peppered and thrown by gunfire, but even more so, I thought of the scene at the wedding where he sneaks into the bedroom with the bridesmaid. That scene was on about page twenty-nine of the book; it had gotten passed all over the ninth grade, that one page dog-eared and worn smooth.

"Anyway, Greg is such a sweetheart, volunteered to check on my apartment and then said he was going to be passing through Fulton and would I meet him for a quick lunch over at the Holiday Inn."

"But why didn't you tell us?" I opened my eyes and she was staring right back at me, her head tilted to one side.

"I was afraid, Kitty," she whispered, eyes cast downward. "You see, I so want your mother to be my friend. I really want all of us to be a family."

"I think she wants that, too," I said. "I think she'd be happy that you like somebody nice. He's not married, is he?"

"No, Miss Morality." She sat back on the floor, her small tan legs crossed Indian style. "But I told you last night, I have to be so careful around Cleva. Have you ever felt like you had to prove something to somebody?" She waited for me to nod. Surely she had known that answer just from all the times Misty and I had talked about wanting to be popular. "Well, your mama has seen me go through a couple of bad relationships, and I just don't want her thinking that I'm in another. I'd rather be sure about how I feel about Greg before I say anything. Like I'm going to see him again late tonight, and I'm going to ask him lots of questions about himself and just what he has in mind."

"But where will you say you're going?" I asked, trying to imagine myself in a position where I'd need to ask someone what his intentions were, what did he want from a relationship?

"I'm going to tell them I am meeting an old girlfriend of mine who works at the Presbyterian church in Clemmonsville, that she is recently divorced and having such a hard time and I'm going to take her to the movies and try to perk her up. Now you can keep a secret, can't you?" She turned me towards the mirror, waiting for my response, but I was too shocked by my own face; she had applied a fine coat of make-up that almost covered my birthmark and my eyes were outlined in charcoal gray, making them look larger, but not really *made up*. "What do you think?" she asked, and bent down close so that her face was right beside mine.

"I like it." I still couldn't believe what a difference a little bit of make-up could make.

"And about my secret?" Her eyebrows were raised as she waited, another of her expressions that Misty had already copied and put into practice. I nodded and in that second her arms looped around my neck, her lips pressed against my cheek as she squeezed. "I knew I could count on you, Kitty." She squeezed again and then pulled away. "You know," she whispered, and lifted my hair up from my neck, "it's amazing how much you look like Fred." I just laughed, turning my head from side to side to see how I looked from another angle. I had been thinking the exact same thing about her.

Angela went out three nights in a row, and each time she went on and on about poor, poor Sue and what kind of woman allows herself to be so controlled, so beaten down by a man; *honestly*, she'd rather live her life as a nun. And each morning she raved about my mother's bread and said how she had to get that baking lesson. My mother told her how wonderful it was that she was taking such an interest in another person's problems, that Sue should certainly be grateful for such a loyal friend, that maybe soon Sue would understand that just having a man, any man, does not make for happiness in the same way that money cannot buy love and that moving into a house does not mean that it will prove to be a home. Angela just smiled and nodded, agreed with every word. When I asked her later if there even *was* a person named Sue, since I had also caught myself briefly believing the lies, she laughed and slung her arm around my shoulder, her hair sprayed with the musk cologne she carried in her Indian-print bag.

I had avoided discussing the upcoming fireworks with Misty and was relieved when Mr. Rhodes and Sally Jean announced that they were going to spend the Fourth at Myrtle Beach with some of Sally's relatives. They left town the morning of the third and that night I could not sleep for thinking about Mo. Every time I closed my eyes she was there, smiling, in those little purple shorts, marshmallow stringing from her hand as her hips swayed back and forth to Buddy Holly's "Raining in My Heart," rain pelting her kitchen window. It was after one when I heard Angela come in and stand in my doorway. It seemed she stood there a long time without saying anything, without coming any closer.

"Angela?" I called, and she came in.

"I didn't want to wake you," she whispered, then kicked off her sandals and stretched out on the end of the bed.

"I can't sleep." I started to reach up and turn on the light but opted instead for the darkness. "I want to ask you something."

"Okay," she whispered. "And then I'll tell you all about tonight. What is it?"

"You said that you went to Mo's funeral with your boyfriend."

"Yeah?"

"Was that the James Garner guy?"

"Yeah."

"And he knew the Rhodes?"

"Well, he knew *her*, I don't know if he knew her husband or not. He certainly knew old Gene. We went to his funeral, too." She raised up, weight propped on her elbow. "We went out of curiosity more than anything."

"Why were you curious?"

"Oh, Kitty." She slapped my arm as if to dismiss it all. "You don't want to hear that."

"Yes, I do," I whispered, though I wasn't sure at all that I did.

She waited, maybe expecting me to tell her to just forget it, but I told her to go on.

"Well, Mo was no stranger around Ferris Beach, if you know what I mean." There was a toughness in Angela's voice that I had never heard before, and it made my stomach tighten. "She and Gene Files had been screwing around for years. Everybody but that poor fool husband of hers and that simple-brained Betty Files knew it, too." She waved her hand in the air. "Or hell, forget the wife. Gene had *another* girlfriend before Mo and was trying his best to keep her, too." *Fool. Simple-brained. Mo was no stranger.*

"But you two acted like you hardly knew each other."

"Well, I didn't *really* know her. She certainly wasn't a friend of mine. What was I going to say, 'Hey Mo, how's Gene doing?' I had never even seen her *with* her husband until that day I was out on the porch." Again with the mention of that day, Mo's face came to me so vividly, her stomach round with Buddy while Mr. Rhodes wrapped his arm around her waist and Dean carried the groceries inside where her artificial tree glittered.

"You told Misty what a good mother she had." I rolled away from her and faced out where I could see the glow of the street-light.

"What was I going to say?" She was sitting up then, her hand firmly on my shoulder. "That poor kid's got enough strikes against her without being told her mother was easy. That orange hair to name one thing." *Orange*, she said, after all of her talk about Misty's *strawberry blond* hair. "Kitty? Hey"—she shook my shoulder—"listen to this." Suddenly her voice was lifted into false enthusiasm. "The good news is that Misty's step-mother is *not* running around." She put her head down and laughed. "I'll guarantee that no man is going after old Sally Jean anytime in this century. Kitty? Kitty?" She nudged me with her foot. "C'mon, I'm kidding. Please laugh. I didn't want to tell you all of that. You asked me."

I closed my eyes, trying not to cry but I couldn't keep it in any longer. When she shook me again, I let out a sob, and then she was there, her arm wrapped around my head and pulling me in close to her. "Oh, Katie, I'm so so sorry," she whispered. "Please forgive me. I shouldn't have said anything. I shouldn't have told you." I just shrugged and lay there as she rubbed her hand up and down my arm. I faked sleep when she finally stood and leaned over me, whispered good night.

The next morning Angela was gone, no note, nothing. "I so hoped she had changed," Mama said, and put away all the things she had gotten out the night before for the bread-baking lesson that was to take place that morning. "Of course, maybe Sue needed her to come right away and Angela just didn't have time to write a note. That Sue sounds like one who'd go to drastic means." She turned to me, a stick of butter in her hand. "But I didn't hear the phone ring, and I *always* wake when the phone rings. Did she say anything to you?" She looked at me and I hesitated too long, that extra second that gave me away, though I knew I would never repeat what she had said about Mo.

"She met somebody." I said. "A man."

"You mean *while* she was going out with Sue." Mama felt her way into a chair, never for a second glancing away from my face. She shook her head, laughed sarcastically. "There's no Sue," she said with finality, tossed the butter onto the lazy susan and gave it a spin. "Well, then for sure she hasn't changed." She looked at my father, who was in the doorway, and he just raised his hands, then let them fall and slap his sides. She walked over and took a cigarette from his pack, lit it, breathed in and then out with a heavy sigh. "It's just like the other times."

"Cleva, you don't smoke," he said, a look of shock on his face, more shocked by her smoking than by Angela leaving.

"Nice to know where your loyalties lie," she said to me and then went and stood by the window, her hand quivering as she held the cigarette up near her cheek. "And no, I don't smoke"— she turned to my father—"at least not very often, but you're not going to quit no matter how many times the doctor tells you to, so I might as well do as I please. And you eat too much pork, too," she said. He looked like he was about to laugh but caught himself.

"Did she say anything?" She was looking at me again, her face pale. "Like, did she tell you she'd come back or never again or thanks for letting me eat and sleep here free of charge, kiss my foot or anything?" Her face was red, her voice shaky. "Did she tell you how many times we've gone through this? Way back in the beginning with husband number one, who was barely old enough to drive?" She took a deep drag from the cigarette and held it, the smoke slipping out as she began talking again. "Did she tell you what a terrible substitute mother I was? What a witch to try and keep her from running away with any Tom, Dick, or Harry who passed by?"

"Cleva," my father said and was there, his hand on her waist. "Come on now."

"No." I shook my head. "She didn't say anything about you."

Right before time for us to go to the fireworks, Angela called to say how sorry she was to take off like that, that she decided on the spur of the moment to take Greg up on his offer to give her a lift back to Ferris Beach. She had realized suddenly, in the wee hours of morning, that she was on the threshhold of a new life, that she saw a whole new future for herself.

"She said to tell you thank you, Cleva," my father reported as we drove to the Army Reserve field. "That she hopes you can forgive her this once. She said to tell Kitty how much she enjoyed all the fun times, sunbathing and talking." Mama sighed and shook her head.

Mr. Landell was just pulling Mrs. Poole's Lincoln into the parking lot of the old A&P as we crossed the street to the field. Mama said that she was not looking forward to Mrs. Poole's explanation of where she got her *adirondack* chair, that she hoped to God she didn't say adirondack once or she thought she might just ignite and head for the moon. Again my father looked like he might laugh but thought better of it and lit a cigarette instead. Fortunately, Mrs. Poole had brought a canvas director's chair. "Easier on Mr. Landell's back," she said, as she hooked a little umbrella onto the back of the chair and pulled it around and over her head to serve as a roof so she could legitimately smoke her pack of Salem 100s. I felt Misty's absence stronger than ever, and I kept thinking of things I needed to tell her, how Mrs. Poole had spent thirty stupid minutes talking about *little* Ruthie Sands going to prep school so as not to have to *participate* in integration, how I had heard the DJ on the radio say that they were going to open a new dedication line, how sometimes the thought of walking into that brand new high school made me feel so scared I felt sick, and how she was the best friend I had ever had and ever would have, and how I would give anything in the world if her mother had not left home. The band played a jazzed-up version of "Never My Love" as the tall leggy blond twirled her fire baton, the orange pom-poms on her boots shaking with every step. She was now the chief majorette and I knew that somewhere in the darkness of the trees and shrubs was her boyfriend, a cigarette in the corner of his mouth as he looked forward to when all this ended and he had her in that red GTO, parked on the other side of Whispering Pines. *It's amazing what being sixteen and in the backseat of a car can do to your head.*

By the end of the summer, things were back to normal and I stopped wondering when we would hear from Angela. There had been many nights when I awoke, thinking I heard her tiptoe into my room; somehow I allowed myself the luxury of overlooking that last night when she had talked about Mo, and I focused instead on all the nights before it. I missed her being there, on the foot of my bed or under the covers beside me, as she told story after story about the various loves of her life, as she laughed like a teenager into her pillow.

Mama stopped rolling up her shorts, and began mourning the long hair she had had her whole life. "What on earth was I thinking?" she asked repeatedly. Oftentimes she wore long scarves, which she knotted at the back of her neck like a simulated bun. Mrs. Poole denied that she had ever worn chartreuse shorts when someone else referred to the outfit, and Sally Jean stopped dying her legs orange. Ruthie Sands moved to her girls' school in Virginia and R. W. Quincy was caught spray-painting "We Surrender" on the base of the Confederate statue, which prompted a new circulation of memories and little stories about Mr. Thomas Clayton, his tale of the statue needing to pee, and his announcement that all was copacetic. And finally, Misty began measuring time by the approaching first day of tenth grade at E. A. Poe High, rather than by Mo's leaving home. Finally that first year was over.

Eighteen

Many of the boys in the tenth grade spent a lot of time talking about Harleys. Boys who would one day drive Volvos and BMWs and sip martinis on decks, boys who *knew* the closest they would get to a motorcycle was breathing fumes on the interstate, talked about Harleys. Some even imitated Harleys, their lips pressed together and sputtering air like some engine at the starting gate. They fantasized themselves as free-flying bikers leaning to and fro on black leather seats, Steppenwolf lyrics blasting in their heads.

"My brother just bought a Harley," Merle announced one day, looking at the class in a way that called for silence. He was leaned back in his seat, the collar of his denim jacket pulled up on his neck so that his hair fell over it. He had his feet propped up on the back of Misty's chair, and she didn't even shove them away.

E. A. Poe had brought to us—along with its spic and span

linoleum floors, gum-free water fountains and graffiti-free walls —rows of new desks with pastel plastic seats and backs, the aluminum legs splayed like some kind of insect. You couldn't even hide anything in your desk anymore, for there was just a wire basket beneath you, any balled-up paper or trash fell right to the floor. The school also had huge ultra-modern windows that didn't open except for a tiny transom at the top, making the school like a greenhouse from August to mid-October.

But now it was late fall and there was Merle's sockless foot propped up on Misty's light blue plastic seat back. It was cold that day, the sky gray beyond the glass wall, the brand new crystal-clear glass. Mr. Grange, the gym teacher and baseball coach, had told Merle if he couldn't come to gym with clean socks and gym shorts then not to come at all.

And so, even though he was the fastest runner in the whole school and one of the most feared on the basis of his last name, he had spent every gym period of football season sitting in the school auditorium and staring up at the slick new stage, where the chorus people sat in straight metal chairs and sang the same song over and over. Misty had been telling me of his presence since the second week of school, told me how he sat there and laughed every time they sang the song, which at that particular time happened to be "Spinning Wheels," a favorite (though several years old) of Mr. Radley, who led the songs. Mr. Radley had thin greasy hair and looked like a little lost toothpick beneath the large colorful dashikis he wore. He liked to use the latest jargon, or what he *thought* was the latest, *ten four good buddy, groovy, light my fire, yeah, I can't believe I ate the whole thing, and the devil made me do it*; he did a high five to every black student he saw, lifting his puny little fist symbolically. Misty was one of only three white students in chorus; she had tried to talk me into joining, but I joined Homemakers of America because I really enjoyed just sitting in front of a sewing machine for an hour without a lot of talking going on.

Even in late November when the chorus worked on Christmas carols for the upcoming assembly program, he had them end by singing "Spinning Wheels." All that semester, people were dropping out of chorus like flies, much to the surprise of Mr. Radley, who had told the principal that he feared the *kids* were in need of a *hipper beat* and though they had "Spinning Wheels" fine tuned, he thought he might also try "Proud Mary"; *yeah, let it all hang out. Big wheels keep on turning.*

By early December, just a couple of weeks before Christmas vacation, the chorus was *still* singing "Spinning Wheels," and Merle was still going sockless, still spending his gym time in the auditorium. The skin of his ankle was not as white as you might think it would be from looking at him, and he had hairs there on his lower leg that were much darker than any on his head.

He was in my geometry class, and I couldn't help but look at him as he sat there staring out the window, a pencil over his right ear, a hole in the knee of his jeans. Someone had just asked him about his brother Dexter, where was he and what did he do now that he had dropped out of school?

"He's around," Merle said, and glanced over at Perry Loomis, who was methodically drawing and then penciling in little tiny squares on a piece of notebook paper. "He's got a girl, for one thing." Perry looked up and the way the two of them looked back and forth at one another made me feel queasy. Perry Loomis was even more beautiful than the year before, her wavy hair longer and clipped back on just one side, the other side loose and tumbling near her eye; it was the same way Angela had wanted me to wear my hair. I hadn't really talked to Perry since that day in the bathroom, just said hello when I passed her in the hall. We never really looked each other in the eye, and I always considered myself lucky when she spoke back.

"Does he still have a Harley?" Todd Bridger asked. "Does he ever let you ride it?"

"Do we know this girl?" another boy interrupted.

"I doubt it," he said, and tossed his head to one side to get his bangs out of his eyes. "I really don't know her myself." He was looking out the window again, at the gray sky, treeless schoolyard stretching towards the new track and baseball field.

"Hey, I bet your brother . . ." Todd Bridger leaned in close to Merle, his hand cupped to hide whatever indecent thing he had to say, all the other boys looking on and nodding with authority. It was not hard to imagine where they would all be in ten years, twenty, thirty. Even at that age, even as they acted interested in Harleys and mimicked Merle's toss of his head, they were as predictable as the Fulton Christmas parade. Merle just shrugged his shoulders, no reaction at all.

"I heard that," Misty said, and then looked over at me. "I'll tell you what they said later." I just nodded and opened my math book to last night's assignment. I could feel their eyes on me like so many woodburners going through my skin. I hated when Misty did that to me, pulled me into a conversation where I clearly did not belong.

"How would you know the first thing about it?" Todd asked, and that face we had all loved for so many years reshaped and focused into that of a cowardly little jerk.

"I know *plenty*," Misty said, and looked at Merle but did not look so long that she'd be in another staring battle with him. "I do."

"Yeah? How could you?" Tony Bracy, a sour-faced little know-it-all, puffed up his cheeks at Misty and held his arms out to the side like he was waddling. He had just moved to Fulton over the summer and had already experienced the rising and falling of the new-person syndrome. He prefaced everything with "Nobody in *Greensboro* would do *that*," or wear that, or say that; he called Fulton "Gritville" and said he couldn't wait to go off to prep school the next year.

"Who'd touch *you*?" he continued, having collected a little audience for himself. "God, nobody would want that!" It was Napoleon's complex, Hitler's fever, little man's disease, and there was an epidemic that year, some of the guys standing eight inches taller than they had the year before, shadows of beards and deep voices, and others like Todd Bridger and his sidekick from Greensboro, little and hairless and taking it out on the world.

"You're a pig," Tony said after Misty told him to go to hell by way of Greensboro and Virginia. He made a snort sound in the back of his throat. "You're just a big fat pig." He knew the soft spot; he had looked her over and found what would hurt the most, even though she wasn't *really* fat at all. By then she had lost quite a bit of weight, but the pressure spot was still there. Now she sat, cheeks flaming and pale eyes watering in anger.

Our math teacher, a young pretty woman right out of college, was in the doorway talking to Mr. Radley, listening to him humming, "No, no, no, no, I don't smoke it no more." She was nodding hurriedly, the same way my mother did when trying to get Sally Jean or Mrs. Poole off the phone. I willed her to come in and begin our geometry class. I willed her to come in so the teasing could stop. Misty's face was still flaming as she sat quietly, quieter than I'd ever seen her. I needed to do something, say something, but I was afraid to speak out.

"Leave me alone, you stupid son of a bitch," she finally hissed, leaning forward on Merle's desktop, the fringe of her purple sweater vest falling onto his open book.

"Yeah, your mama," Tony said, and thrust his hips, legs apart in a suggestive way. "Right," he said, but Todd was no longer right behind him. "Her mama." He pointed at Misty and everyone got quiet. Todd Bridger's face was the one that was red now.

"My mother is dead," Misty said through clenched teeth, tears standing in her eyes, ready to roll with the least flutter of a lash. "And for your information—" The whole class was listening now, our geometry teacher shifting her weight back and forth as Mr. Radley scratched his thin hair and continued to talk full blast, his hands all over the place like frenzied birds let loose. It was clear that if Mr. Radley was the last human on earth our teacher would, if at all possible, go to another planet; he was so pitiful that you didn't even want to laugh.

"For your information, Mr. Clearasil," Misty was saying, "I have done more with a boy than even you know to think about!" My stomach rose with that one and I really thought I'd be sick. They were going to ask for proof and Misty had none. We shared that same boat of no experience. Her brother had kissed me, and her brother's friend, Ronald, had kissed her. That was our sum total.

"Who?" Tony hissed, still not ready to quit. Threatened pride on top of Napoleon's complex was like gasoline on a campfire. Misty sat there tossing her hair from side to side. "For me to know and you to find out, Little Zit."

"Liar." Tony was leaning over Merle now so that he could get right in Misty's face, and suddenly Merle's hand was there grabbing him by the shirt collar.

"She's my brother's girl," Merle said. "You know, the biker? One who just bought the Harley?" He tightened his grip, pushing Tony back so that he could stand up. Merle was not one of the guys left behind; his voice was deep, and he was at least as tall as I was, which was five nine. "You know, the one who slit a guy's nose because he didn't like the way he looked?" Again the whole class got quiet, faces white and eyes wide open. "My brother's in a club, and they look out for their own, you know?"

Perry Loomis stopped her doodling and stared at Merle with her mouth opened in surprise. There was no one more surprised than Misty, who now was grinning at Merle, patting his hand, winking, all to which he responded with only a slight smile and a nudge that was intended to turn her to the front of the room when our teacher finally came in, Mr. Radley still loitering outside the door.

"Sorry for the delay, class," she said, and without looking out closed the door right in Mr. Radley's face. Everyone was still stunned, Tony Bracey leaned back in his seat with a bewildered look of both fear and defeat. I could see his mouth dying to say "Greensboro" or "Alexandria," but he did not utter a peep. Misty turned and put a little folded-up note on Merle's desk, and he held it, passed it from hand to hand, and then put it in his pocket without even opening it. I imagined her saying something like "Thanks—I owe you one!" or "How will I ever repay you?" or "Merle Hucks, I love you." I could not really place what I was feeling right then except left out, and though I often glanced to the side to see what kind of drawing Merle was doing during class, I fought the urge that day and did not look at him once.

"Can you believe how he stood up for me?" Misty asked that afternoon as we walked from the bus stop. "I mean that's got to mean something, right?" She looked at me, earnestly searching my face until I responded with a shrug. "Oh, come on. He wouldn't have done that for just anybody," she said. "It means something."

Lately Misty had found meaning in everything; every little whistle of the wind meant something. It was *fate*, plain and simple, and it was out of our control, it was just part of a series of happenings like dominos, like her mother's death. Her mother's death was part of a much much bigger plan, and her little prayer about her coming home and never leaving again had nothing to do with it; it was all there, years, maybe centuries before, written in the stars. "I really do believe in predestination," she had told me many times, and much to Sally Jean's delight had begun going to the Presbyterian church, leaving me to the Methodists and my own supplying of "in the bed" to the hymn titles.

"Misty is searching," my mother had told me. "Some things are hard to understand." I wasn't sure if she meant that Misty's sudden interest in theology was hard to understand, or if she was speaking much more generally about all of us, how when in doubt, we search for answers.

"I mean," Misty continued. "Maybe Dexter Hucks does like me."

"Misty," I said, cringing at the thought of Dexter Hucks. "You don't even know him."

"But I know who he is," she said. "He rides by here, you know? And I do know R. Dubya." She laughed. "Hey, maybe that's who likes me." She went on and on, the same way my father might arrange and rearrange one of his twisted plots.

We stopped in front of Misty's house; Sally Jean was standing in the yard, stooping and standing, occasionally slipping some-thing into her pocket. When she saw us, she straightened up and acted like she wasn't doing a thing.

"She's picking up rocks," Misty whispered to me. "It drives her crazy to find one of Mama's little Japanese garden rocks, and now that everything's dead and she can see better, she's determined to get them all.

"What are you doing, Sally Jean?" Misty yelled, shifting her books to her other arm. "Picking up rocks?"

"Well, no, that's not why I came out here." Sally Jean looked flustered. "Occasionally I might see a rock and I pick it up, be-cause you know if Dean was to hit one with the mower it could be dangerous. It may not look like that much grass now"—she shook her head, pointed to the sparse brown patches—"but by summer I'm hoping to have this yard covered in a fine blanket of grass, and a rock hit by that mower would be a catatonic thing. Could break a window, put an eye out. That's why I just pick them up when I see them."

"Well, if it happens it happens," Misty said, and smiled in a way that seemed to make Sally Jean even more uneasy. "I mean, it's all out of our control, right?"

"Right." Sally Jean kept her hands in the pocket of her khaki overcoat, while Misty ran and put her books inside and then came back out to go over to my house.

"See you later, Sally Jean," Misty called cheerfully and Sally Jean stared after us, mouth open. As we walked up my driveway, I heard the plunk, plunk, plunk of rocks being dropped into the manhole. Her pockets were *full* of rocks.

It was dark by five o'clock when Misty and I went out on the sleeping porch to get my transistor. "Why is it out here anyway?" Misty asked. "It's too cold to sit out here." She flopped down in the rocking chair and propped her foot up on the railing. She was wearing lace-up boots with heavy treads, like what a mountain climber might wear, and bright red-and-yellow striped socks.

"Hey, look," she said suddenly, and sat up straight. I followed her hand as she pointed to Merle's house, and I focused on the water-pipe sounds coming from below, where my mother was in the kitchen.

"So?" I finally asked.

"Why, you can see right in their windows," she whispered. Then she slapped at me in the same way a cat might toy with a lizard. "Don't try and tell me that you don't ever look over there." She paused and crossed her heart with her hand to indicate a solemn swear. "If you do, you're a liar and will burn in hell."

"Shhh," I whispered, and pointed to the floor of the porch, though I knew there was no way my mother could hear us talking because the windows were all closed.

"All those times I've called, and your mama said you were sitting on the porch." Misty could mimic my mother to a tee, and she did it then with her shoulders thrown back and mouth sucked in. "You sit here and look at the Huckses' house. It's like *Rear Window*. You spy on your neighbors."

"No, I don't." I sat down in the glider and then followed her gaze, a bare bulb sharpening the walls of the Huckses' kitchen.

We both just sat, watching like a movie, and then Merle came out the back door and, in the yellow glow of the outside light, started moving around some old tires and other junk that was stacked back there. Dexter came up on his Harley and sat in the dark driveway gunning the engine.

"There he is," Misty whispered, ignoring my attempts to go inside. "He *is* kind of cute in a real rough way, isn't he? Sort of like a small Charles Bronson." I started to say "or Charles Manson" but bit my tongue. In a few minutes R. W. Quincy pulled up on a smaller motorcycle, and then the three of them were standing there. Then we saw a flare of light as Merle lit a cigarette.

I kept thinking of Merle coming to Misty's defense, so easily, not giving a damn what anyone might think, not giving a damn that one of them might sneak to one of the clean slick walls and write "Merle & Misty." All of a sudden I realized that Merle had changed, slowly, occasionally lapsing into his old ways, but nevertheless changed; I couldn't help but wonder when the softness had begun. Had there been some person, some teacher who pulled him close, an embrace of Wind Song or Tour Je Moi filling his head with hopes of a future other than that of his father? I wondered if it could be Mrs. Landell, the way she wrapped her arm around him that day in Mrs. Poole's kitchen. What had touched Merle that made him so different from Dexter or R. W. Quincy? Or did it just happen, all planned from the beginning of time like Misty chose to believe?

"What did that note say?" I asked suddenly, and Misty looked away from the dark yard, nudged me with her foot.

"What note?" she asked slyly, and I just looked at her, waited. "Oh, you must mean that note I passed to Merle Hucks."

"Yes." I watched Merle go back inside, the light go off, and in a few minutes, the engines revved and Dexter and R. W. rode away; we hadn't noticed before but there was a girl on the back of Dexter's bike, their bodies pressed together as they sped down the dirt road.

"Are you jealous that I wrote a note to Merle?" she asked, and I shook my head, shrugged. "Oh, it was nothing." She laughed and slapped at my arm again. "I wanted it to *look* like something, you know, to scare that old sourpuss Tony a little bit more." She rocked slowly, turned up the collar on her fake fur. She had taken Angela's advice and begun streaking her hair with summer blond and it really did look good, much less orange. "It just said 'Thanks for helping me.' You know, I really did need some help." It was quiet as she waited, and I knew I owed her something, an explanation, an apology.

"I'm sorry, Misty."

"It's okay. It's not your style." She laughed again. "But, I wouldn't have thought it was Merle's style either, would you? And do you think something's going on with Merle and Perry Loomis?"

"Why?" I was glad we were on the dark porch because I felt my face go hot with the mention of their names together. I had never told Misty about when I talked to Perry in the bathroom; I had tried to forget that it ever happened.

"I don't know. They look at each other an awful lot."

"Oh," I said, twisting the radio knob for the local station since it was too early to get Indiana. "I haven't noticed."

"Of course," she said, voice rising along with her thin, penciled eyebrows. "I see him look at you, too."

"No, he doesn't," I said, and she just smiled knowingly, stared over at the lit window. There was hope in her expression and I knew what would come next, what always came next. "You go for Merle, and I'll go for R. W. Quincy." I was surprised by her suddenly serious tone.

"Have you ever thought about *really* looking in somebody's window?" she asked, her voice a whisper. "You know like that time we tried to spy on Mrs. Poole?" We had many years earlier, on a dare, tiptoed onto Mrs. Poole's porch and peeked in until we saw her pass by the foyer in a nightgown. It was nothing, but we had never forgotten the fast rhythm of our hearts and the way we both grabbed at each other with sweaty palms and stifled giggles until we were safe in the darkness of the Rhodeses' carport. It was the same sensations we got when we carried out our dares in Whispering Pines: touch the gate, touch the tree, would you *dare* go as far as the caretaker's shed, as far as the Wilkins churchyard with its rusty iron fence. Misty had told several younger neighborhood kids that we had seen Mrs. Poole in some black lace underwear and no bra, a thought that horrified most.

That same night we had also rolled Mrs. Poole's yard in bright-pink toilet paper. We told Mo that some mean old boys must have done it, and she just nodded wide-eyed, asked question after question about wonder how many rolls it took to do such a good job, and wonder how on earth those boys had decided to pick pink toilet paper. We had all laughed about it, speculated on *who* those mean boys were and then opened Misty's bedroom door to find everything in there wrapped at least once in green toilet paper. "Wonder who did this?" Mo had asked, and gone back to the kitchen where she was preparing one of her made-up recipes, "Chop Gooey Olé" or pork chops smothered in melted Velveeta and jalapeño peppers, served on a bed of rice. "I cook by ear, by nose, and by tongue," Mo had said, and kissed Mr. Rhodes several times on the cheek and neck. It was so hard to believe that she was the same woman who had been unfaithful, that *that* Mo was the same woman Angela had described; it amazed me to think that something of that magnitude, one life and two lovers, could become as commonplace as juggling pork chops and Velveeta.

"Well?" Misty was asking, and I shook my head. I never told her how often I thought of her mother, how there were times when I felt so homesick, only to discover that what I was missing was Mo. Now just the thought of sneaking and spying, of being in that wide-open yard with the shadows and hedges sent a chill over me. I shook my head again, hoping the idea would pass from her mind.

"Let's sneak over there later," she whispered. "We'll wear black, and we'll sneak through the brush, climb that magnolia tree there at the far end of the cemetery." The magnolia was a dare we'd never made, a huge tree that grew right near the Wilkinses' graves.

"Well, what do you think?" Misty asked again. "It'll be the most exciting thing that's happened in a long time."

"No way," I said. "No."

"Think about it," she said, and stood to go. "You know I could get Dean's tent and sleeping bags, and we could sleep out in your yard. We haven't done that in ages."

"It's winter."

"But those sleeping bags are made for cold weather. Besides, no mosquitoes." She turned back to me. "And you know we could sort of let it slip out that we were camping, and maybe they'd come over, Merle and Dexter and R. W." I was panicked by the time Misty left to go home, all the while telling me to think about it.

"What are you two planning?" Mama asked as she watched Misty whispering in my ear.

"Your Christmas present, Mrs. Burns," Misty said, and then she bounded out of our house and across the street to her own, where in place of Mo's silver tree, Sally Jean had a real one, trunk cut and branches flocked with fake snow, all white lights and a big white star on top. It really was a beautiful tree and on their door was a cross-stitched sign, silver on navy, that simply said, "Peace on Earth." Clearly it was the best sign that Sally Jean had ever made.

Nineteen

uch to my relief, my mother said that it was way too cold to camp out in the yard, and soon Misty gave up on the idea. Instead we spent many of the nights over the holidays just wrapping packages, baking cookies, and listening to the radio out on the sleeping porch; from there we could see the blinking Christmas lights scattered about. I had to prove to her that it was the solitude, the peacefulness of the quiet nights, that led me out on the porch, the distant whoosh of the highway noise, the frozen branches brushing against the screens, rather than the glimpses into Merle Hucks's house.

It was after nine when Misty left the night of the twenty-third and I returned to the porch, where we had left the radio playing. The house next door to the Huckses' had lights of all colors, string after string, wrapped around the eaves of the roof

and every window and stick of a shrub. *Carnival* was the word
my mother and Mrs. Poole had batted back and forth. *Psychedelic*
was Misty's choice. They had a manger scene with life-size plastic
figures, a flood light fastened to the floor of the manger so that
the baby Jesus could be seen even from my spot on the porch, a
bright glow in the distance. Early in the evenings, the people put
their stereo speakers in the front windows and played Christmas
music—*Do you hear what I hear?*—and my mother responded that
she did and in fact she had heard all she wanted to hear. It was
times like that when my father called her *feisty* and offered her a
smoke, looked at her with genuine pride and love.

"And imagine what they must've spent on that plastic manger." She shook her head and sighed a sigh the magnitude of one
sighed for murder and pestilence. "They could've bought food
for a month."

Now, the house was silent but the lights still shone and Jesus
still glowed. It was odd that of all the houses I could see from
my spot, this was the one that did not leave me feeling empty. I
didn't know the people, had only seen them, a young couple with
two small children; I imagined the excitement that must course
through them each night when it was time to plug in the lights
and blast the music. I imagined that any parents who would go
to such lengths to proclaim Christmas joy must truly feel it with
every colored bulb that blinked and every chord of every carol.

I could see Merle, a brief glimpse as he passed in front of that
window; he was wearing the red flannel shirt that he had worn
to school the last day before vacation. Now strand by strand,
the lights of the carnival house were unplugged; it looked as if
the house were disappearing section by section as it gave in to
darkness and then there was only the glow of the baby Jesus, the
light softened by the blue blanket draped there. It seemed that,
instead of bringing quiet, the darkness was a signal for my parents
to begin as they had for several days, their voices mumbled like a
mouthful of marbles. Angela was planning to come for Christmas

after all; her romance was not working out as planned and she needed to be with *her family*. I had heard enough to know that it was the same old discussion. *The only time she comes around is when her life isn't working. Just once I wish there wasn't a catch. Just once I wish she would give me more than a day's notice.*

Now the bare bulb in Merle's house was the only light as I looked out over our backyard. There was just a sliver of a moon that night, a fairy tale moon like the pin Angela had given to my mother; it was too thin to give much light, so even after several minutes of concentrated staring, the shadows of the trees and the gates of the cemetery were hard to distinguish. My mother opened the door, her movement startling me.

"We're going to bed," she whispered. "I think you better come on in now. It's freezing."

"I'm coming," I told her. "But I might go downstairs and watch TV awhile."

"Don't sit up too late," she said, and stepped back inside. "We've got lots to do tomorrow." She paused. "Rumor has it we might be having company." I waited until I heard her bedroom door close, and then I went downstairs. The nightlight in the hallway was on so I didn't turn on any lamps, just went to the kitchen, where I could look and still see that bare bulb hanging. There were several motorcycles parked in the driveway, and I could see people passing back and forth in front of the window, the blacks and blues of their clothing, an occasional bit of red which I assigned to Merle. I sat on the kitchen counter, my feet in the sink, and got as close to the window as I could without causing it to fog over. The house was dark except for that one bulb.

The idea came suddenly, Misty's voice urging that we should sneak over and spy, sneak over and see what it looked like inside of that house. Sneak to the far end of the cemetery there near the Wilkins plot, climb the huge magnolia tree. If I had been watching myself in a movie, I would have said, *Don't do it, don't do it,* but

I acted without thinking, grabbed my jacket off the kitchen chair and tiptoed out onto the back porch, easing the door to behind me. Oliver was there in a second, weaving in and out between my legs and purring loudly. Everything seemed so loud, the squeak of my sneakers on the cement step and then the rustle of the dry grass. It was colder than I'd realized while sheltered on the porch with a blanket, but I didn't go back inside; my heart raced as I breathed the freezing air.

I was halfway across our yard before I even looked back. The sleeping porch was so dark that if my mother or father had been there, I wouldn't have been able to see them. Our yard had grown with the darkness, lengthening towards the bare bulb as I made my way through the shrubs along our drive and into the cemetery. Somehow the calming sense of peace, which I could conjure while in my bed or while looking at the tombstones from my window, disappeared and I was left with a sudden sense of panic, the same as when I crept through the gates that other night, the night Buddy was born. I moved quickly down the path, limbs brushing against my jacket. I never glanced to either side, but focused on my destination, faster and faster. I felt as if there could suddenly appear behind me something hideous and destructive. Everything looked different in the darkness; the trees were taller, the weeds higher, the monuments like a cold gray city in the distance; with every step, the weeds seemed to spring back with a rustling sound, pinpointing my every move and breath for whoever could be watching.

Once I got within reach of the tree, carefully stepping around and over the rolls of chicken wire and discarded planks, I crouched down. I heard the creak of a door, voices, and so I quickly crawled under the thick branches of the tree. The large waxy leaves shielded me from sight as I felt for the smooth trunk and as quietly as possible began to climb. When I was at a safe height, I stopped, my legs straddling a thick branch, my back against the trunk. If I pulled the branch above me to one side

I could see Merle's house, that bulb still shining; I could see a picture of a rooster, the kind fashioned from glued kernels of colored popcorn, hanging on the wall.

Again I heard voices, laughter. There were two people coming down the back steps and moving across the yard. They stopped near the clothesline, a concrete post, and again I heard whispers and laughter as the two pressed together, kissed. I leaned my head back against the trunk and looked straight up, the moon visible between two branches.

Somewhere there was a fire engine, the siren, loud and then faint, and there was movement beneath the clothesline; there was the sound of tires on pavement, a distant hum from the highway. I turned back to the yard and the rustling sounds. It was like I was paralyzed and couldn't turn away; now they were near the faint glow of the streetlight. I strained to get a better look and then I recognized my car coat, that faded blue quilted jacket, slick from wear, the white fur around the hood dingy, gray in the dim light. There was the flash of a cigarette lighter, and I saw Perry Loomis stretched out on the grass, her hair loose and falling over one shoulder as she beckoned to whoever was standing in the darkness. I held my breath, heart pounding. I focused on the window, the red oilcloth on the kitchen table, the dirty dishes stacked on the counter, empty plates and beer bottles. Then Merle was there, in the window, hands cupped up to his face as he peered out into the yard. I had expected to see him step from the darkness, but it was Dexter with Perry; he was rubbing his hand around her eyes, caressing her temples, pressing in so hard I could feel it. He stretched out on top of her and she laughed, locked her small white hands behind his neck. Her hands then moved up and down the back of his denim jacket, over the skull and crossbones painted there. "It's too cold out here," she said, and giggled, her voice just as I remembered it. "I mean it now, Dexter. Let's go inside."

I knew something was about to hit; I knew it. It was like seeing the headlights round the curve or hearing the loud roar of a freight train in the split second before a tornado touches down and inhales a portion of the world.

Out of nowhere, engines revved and three bikes came around the corner of the house, the bright white headlights scanning the yard like beacons. Merle was no longer in the window but at the back door. They cut the engines, leaving one headlight glaring. Perry sat up, her hand shielding the bright light, and then within seconds, R. W. Quincy was there, his large hands catching her ankles and pinning them down as if she were a trapped animal held for observation. Dexter had her arms and his slow caresses were now hard and binding as he held her. Her eyes were wide open, wide and staring, surprised to see R. W. there at her feet, surprised to see the other two who had just stepped up. They took their jackets off and tossed them to one side. "Dexter?" Perry screamed, and then she was struggling to sit up, her lips moving, face frozen in that glaring light. "Dexter, stop it."

It was as if Dexter didn't hear her; he didn't even look at her face, just motioned for one of the guys to hold her arms. Then he pulled a knife from his pocket, flipped out the blade and began circling her. Perry's face was stark white. Dexter had tossed off his jacket, and his wiry biceps flexed as he slapped the knife from hand to hand. I held my breath, looked at the house next door, the manger in their front yard dark. I heard the door slam shut, running footsteps in the leaves.

Then Merle was there, his eyes on Perry as Dexter unbuttoned her blouse to reveal a white lacy bra with the little pink rosebud in the center, the kind of bra designed to look pure and innocent.

"What's going on?" They all stopped and turned towards Merle, but his eyes were on Perry, and on the knife in Dexter's hand. He stepped into the bright light, fists clenched as he looked away from Perry and focused on his brother.

I could feel panic rising in Perry's chest as her stomach rose and fell faster and faster with her breath, her limbs thrashing to escape the holds. She turned her head to Dexter, and I knew that she was begging. "I'm cold," she said, her face turned my way, pale and distorted by fear and sobs. Merle lunged at Dexter, his fist raised. He was stopped by one of the other boys, who grabbed him around the neck and pinned his arm behind his back, pushing higher and higher as if he might break it. The blade of the knife caught the light as Dexter turned it from side to side. "Please. Please." Perry's hollow voice rose and then broke as he pressed the flat of the blade against her stomach. "You were begging please just a few minutes ago, too, weren't you? You wanted it until we had an audience, didn't you?" He moved the blade back and forth and she nodded. "Well, that's the whole purpose; just think of it as doing me a favor. I mean, I could be with somebody else right now, you know?" She was silent as he inched the blade under the pale pink rosebud, and in one swift motion lifted the knife, her bra severed as she lay naked and exposed.

"Leave her alone!" Merle's voice had the high shrill pitch of panic.

"Hey, if he ain't one of us"—the tall guy holding Perry's arms nodded towards Merle—"then get him out of here." He leaned down close, his hair falling onto her cheek as he ran his mouth up and down her neck. Dexter watched, his fist clenched, but he didn't say anything.

"Let her go, Dexter," Merle screamed, but his words were cut by the grip on his neck. He was thrown to the ground, and then I heard the punches and groans as the two rolled away from the light. "You're all crazy," Merle gasped, and pulled up on his hands and knees.

Dexter pressed the blade against Perry's stomach while the guy holding her arms ran his tongue along the curve of her breast. "Tell him"—Dexter's voice was shaking then—"tell my baby brother everything's okay, this is what you want." He rubbed his hand gently over her other breast and then up her neck to her mouth. He was whispering then, coaxing, I assumed, his mouth covering hers. "Tell him it's something I have to do, Perry," he said. "You don't want me doing this to somebody else, do you?"

"You're crazy, Dexter," Merle screamed, and got to his feet; he ran towards Perry again, only to be caught and held by the throat. "C'mon, R. W., don't let them do this. What's happened to you?" R. W. stood and came towards Merle, fist drawn back. I heard Merle clear his throat, struggle to spit towards R. W., and in that second, they slugged him, once in the face, three times in the stomach, and then they pushed him under the magnolia tree, limbs snapping as he fell; when he tried to get up, they kicked him again and again until there was silence below.

Dexter was on top of Perry then, the other boy still holding her down. He moved against her, the knife between them, and then he pushed up, his knees straddling her. I held my breath as I watched, though the ringing in my ears was so loud I felt dizzy. I was afraid to look below, at the quiet darkness where Merle had fallen. When Dexter rolled off her into the grass, R. W. stepped forward. The boy holding her arms leaned forward to cover her mouth with his own just as she started to scream.

I swallowed, stared upwards through the jungle of thick limbs, a height of a hundred years, the dim sky, thin moon; somewhere up there was the Christmas star. I focused my sight on only the limbs; if I had closed my eyes for a second, the dizziness would have caught up with me. I'm not sure how long I stayed that way, motionless, barely breathing, but it was long after they pulled Merle from beneath the tree, long after Perry had covered herself with my coat, *my* coat there on the frozen grass. It was long after the motorcycles had revved and sputtered and disappeared in the night. I could not shake the picture of Perry, her muffled screams as hands and mouths stifled and probed her, her body held and pinned, naked and helpless, an experiment, a specimen.

I must have clung there an hour after they left, and then I moved suddenly, urgently, down the tree and over and around the chicken wire and busted boards; I could not move fast enough, and I didn't even remember having acted at all until I was halfway across my yard and heard something rustling behind me. I looked towards Whispering Pines, and I thought I saw a red spark, the winking eye of an animal, or the glow of a cigarette. Again, it sparked and in that quick glow, I glimpsed a flash of dark red, blood red, maybe Merle's shirt there in the shadows of the cemetery. And again, I moved quickly, panicked, fearful that he would call my name, that he was like the watchman, the pimp who would give a signal—hoot owl cry or a rock against a window or his old cat call—that would send them all out into the yard, over the weeds and wire, through my yard, where they would dive, hands catching my ankles and pulling me down, catching me, flipping me over, pinning me as they traced my birthmark in that bright light; I could feel the cold silver blade of the knife daring me to cry for help, daring me to do anything other than give in to their gropes and slobbers.

I thought of the oddest thing in that moment. I thought of Mo Rhodes and the rainy day right after they moved in when she spread a quilt over the oil spots in their carport and then sat on it cross-legged with Misty and me. We played the old game *bear hunt*, our hands imitating all of the actions as we swam through the river, climbed a tall tree and then, spotting the bear, we began running faster and faster, hands clapping and slapping knees as we went faster and faster, back over the mountain, back down the tree and back through the river, faster and faster and faster, making us laugh so hard that Misty finally had to scream that we *please, please, please* take a break because she just couldn't take it any more. Mo Rhodes was stretched out on her back, her shapely legs up in the air doing a scissor kick while she held her stomach in laughter. "Stop making us laugh," Misty had screamed. "I've got to pee. Now no more laughing!"

"That'll be the day-ay-ay," Mo sang. That's what I was hearing over and over, Mo's voice, until I eased the door to and turned the lock. As I passed my parents' door, I paused to listen. Silence. I tiptoed up the stairs and moved slowly down the dark hall.

When I touched the cool glass doorknob of my room, it almost seemed like I'd never gone outside, that none of it had happened, that none of it was real. I tried to imagine how I could even begin to tell Misty what I had seen, how would I even describe it, or should I even try? Somehow it seemed that if I didn't tell it, didn't think it, that it could all go away, as if I'd never seen it, as if it had never happened.

I undressed in the darkness. The floor was cold to my bare feet, and I felt a sudden shiver down my spine as I stood naked a moment before pulling my flannel gown over my head and down around me. Now the fairy-tale moon had risen high above the cemetery. I knew as I stepped closer to the window that I would see him there, the same place as always. And this time I felt certain that he saw me, too. He knew I had been there, I was sure, and again I felt that deep empty drop of my stomach.

I tried to sleep, but every time I closed my eyes I saw Perry's eyes wide and frightened, her face frozen in silent terror; I saw the knife on her stomach, the snap of her bra, and those breasts that were the subject of all the adolescent boys' dreams of womanhood and sexiness, just those of a young girl, pale blue veins underlining pale white skin, breast bone as fragile as that of a chicken ripped and torn apart. I saw Mo Rhodes and the look of horror as she screamed out in that brief second, her hand reaching out for Buddy. I saw Merle begging his brother to stop, and I saw Misty clinging to the carport post and screaming for her mother to come back, her hair wild against the dark sky.

Finally, I went out on the sleeping porch. The air felt sharp as I breathed in. The light was still on, only now Merle's father's pickup truck was in the driveway, and I could see Mrs. Hucks bent over the sink, alone in the kitchen. I imagined she was washing that stack of dishes, crumbs and bones scraped in the trash; she was oblivious to how late it was or how her children had spent the evening as she wiped over the red oilcloth with a worn, grainy rag.

Within minutes, she turned out the light, and when my

eyes had time to adjust, the house became only another box-like shadow like all the others, identical in this light to the one housing baby Jesus. I was finally dozing, my head dropping forward, when I heard the rustling of weeds and looked up in time to see him moving over the chicken wire. He stopped and stood there a minute, the glow of his cigarette making the picture real, letting me know that I had not imagined it all. And then he was gone. When I went back inside, it was long after midnight; it was Christmas Eve.

Twenty

I woke in the morning with a start, and saw the blanket I had wrapped around me as I sat on the sleeping porch. It was all real. Suddenly everything else in my life seemed so minimal, just worthless worries. The memory of Perry's face sat on my chest like a rock. I got back under the covers, closed my eyes against the light at the window. I think I would have stayed there all day had my mother not been in the doorway calling for me to get up, she needed help, packages to wrap, food to prepare, gifts to deliver to neighbors and the rest home.

Every year she headed up the rest home project for her Junior League, and I hated going there most of all, delivering gifts and food to people who stared blankly from their wheelchairs, halls and doorways, these people at the very end of their lives, their food blended to the consistency of soup, their rooms smelling of urine, workers rummaging through their belongings when no one was looking, some perfume, some candy, a wedding band twisted and pulled over an aged swollen knuckle. *Yes, it's been there since my husband put it there in 1922.* Helpless, they were helpless, and yet this was now their home. The most frightening part was the realization that they *had* adapted, had gotten used to it all, had come to think of the smelly hallways as their homes and the people who stole from them, their families. I hated to think of what we could be reduced to when stripped of our own free will; it was scary to think of what we were capable of doing just to stay alive. It was horrible to even try and think what Perry must have felt when she saw them come for her, and there I sat, doing nothing about it, absolutely nothing.

"Katie, are you okay?" my mother asked over and over, her cool broad hand feeling my forehead. "I hope you don't get sick, honey. It's a holiday." I wanted to remind her how *dramatic* things happen on holidays, but the thought was not as funny as it would have been had I been safely shrouded in ignorance. She kept me busy all morning, loading and unloading our station wagon, and all the while I watched the cemetery and Merle's house for any movement that would send me running into my house to hide. There was a Christmas tree propped against the side of his house that I not seen the night before. I could see the tip top branches of the magnolia tree, the overgrown path I had taken, benign enough in the daylight.

"Katie, come see," my mother called, and I grabbed the last grocery bag and slammed the tailgate before she called attention to me there in the middle of the driveway. She met me in the doorway, a huge pink poinsettia in her arms. "Look what was delivered while we were gone," she said. "Read this." She thrust a note forward and I looked first to see the signature—Angela. *This is my formal apology for all the times I have let you down. You have been like a mother, a sister, a very dear friend and I hope that you will give me another chance.*

"That's what I needed to hear," she said. "It's her handwriting, too." She carefully placed the card beside the flower. "I mean, I am probably going to get a bill for that poinsettia, I know that, but she *did* write this." She was in an unusually good mood after that, though I couldn't help but be suspicious when my father returned from his *shopping* with nothing whatsoever to show for it.

"I don't know what you said *this* time," my mother told him when he came into the kitchen. "But you may have finally gotten through."

"I didn't say anything," he said, and sat down to wait for lunch, lit a cigarette. "Must have been an elf. Must be the Christmas spirit." I looked out the window to see Merle Hucks lifting the tree and carrying it around to the back door, his little sister running along beside him.

My mother worked twice as hard that day, making everything, decorations and food, look like something out of a magazine. She had searched all over Fulton in the crowded supermarkets for exotic fruits to dip and swirl in chocolate sauce. It was mid-afternoon when she headed out once more to the one store she hadn't visited in search of kiwis and mangos. I went outside, fully intending to go over to Misty's and unload the whole horrible story, but taking my time. She was going to be upset that Dexter and R. W. were no longer boyfriend choices, but more so that I had gone without her. She would say that I had betrayed her, or even if she didn't say it, would certainly think it. Or worse, she would say, *Why didn't you do something, Kate? Why did you just sit there and watch?* The phone rang, and though I yelled for my dad to pick it up, it kept ringing and ringing. Judy Garland's voice came from his study as I ran through the hall to answer.

"May I speak to Kate Burns?" It was a boy, the voice deep and slow. I took a deep breath, sat in the ornate Victorian chair, the *throne* we'd always called it, by the telephone table.

"This is she," I said, carefully choosing the pronoun my mother had spent years drilling into me, and then there was silence.

"I'm Kate," I added, fearing the worst, a prank call, a broken connection.

"This is Merle." Another pause. "You know, Hucks."

"Yes." I stared across the hall, where my mother had Blue Boy and Pinky hung side by side, an arrangement of pink silk flowers on the table below. "Hi."

"Hey. I was wondering if we could talk." He stopped again. There were background noises, pots clanging and what sounded like classical music, though I couldn't imagine that being true. I knew that he had seen me running across the yard; that's what he wanted to talk about. I used my other hand to hold the receiver steady. There *was* music in the background, Beethoven's 9th, *Joyful, Joyful We Adore Thee*.

"Okay," I whispered. "I think I know and I'm . . ."

"Not on the phone, though," he said hurriedly. "Hold on." He put the phone down and I could hear muffled voices, his hand over the mouthpiece, I was sure. "Look, you know the little house in the cemetery where the gardener keeps his junk?"

"Yes," I said, about to add *but*, the thought of being in the cemetery sending a rush over me.

"Be there in thirty minutes." Then the connection broke and I sat there just holding the receiver and listening to the buzz. Blue Boy and Pinky had always depressed me, and they had no different effect right then. I had to think through everything, how to get there without Misty or anyone else seeing me. And then there was the worst, what was he going to do with me when I got there. I imagined Merle waiting, Dexter and R. W. behind him, a knife in his open palm, slapping, slapping.

Like my mother, my father was also a bit out of his regular groove with the holiday and the knowledge that Angela was coming. He had already cracked open a bottle of brandy and was smoking great big smelly cigars like the ones Mr. Tom Clayton used to simultaneously smoke and chew until the two ends met. He had been working on a memory piece about Mr. Clayton and said that he wanted to use what I had told about the peeing Confederate statue. All of a sudden, he stopped Judy right in the middle of "What'll I Do?" and put on my mother's Bing Crosby record. *Have yourself a merry little Christmas.* He was in there singing along, wrapping paper rustling as he wrapped whatever surprises he *did* have stashed.

I called Misty to kill time and to make up a reason *why* I wasn't coming over, but she was in a rush, said that she'd have to call me later, that she had to do some shopping for her dad. "Sally Jean has her heart set on these really *eloquent* pajamas that are in the window of Ivey's," Misty whispered. "Just what we need, another speaker in the house."

It had been twenty minutes, so without saying anything to my father, and checking to make sure my mother had not just that minute pulled up, I went out the back door, looked back and forth—no Misty or Dean or Sally Jean. Then I ran into the cemetery. I got to the little house, no bigger than a child's playhouse, and waited. I had only ventured in this direction a couple of other times, once with Misty on one of our dares and once with my father when he came to rub an etching of a nearby headstone where the poor man had listed every single detail of his life. My father thought it was hilarious; my mother thought it was very sad.

Thick fuzzy moss covered the ground around the house; the vines were thicker, trees taller than when I'd been there before. I was looking around for that tombstone when I heard the bushes moving behind me. I turned suddenly and he was right there, not more than three feet away.

"Hey," he whispered. He leaned against the little house and slowly slid down until he was sitting, back pressed against it. He had a plastic bag with two wrapped gifts inside and he put it down beside him. "I know you saw last night." He looked up then, not a trace of the anger that I had expected to see. "I didn't have a whole lot to do under that tree except look *up*." His right eye and cheek were swollen and bruised. "Did you tell anybody?" I shook my head, leaned against a big pine tree, my palms pressed into the rough sticky bark.

"Good." He sighed, stretched his legs out. "Promise me you won't?" He stared, waiting for my answer. "Even Misty. I know you guys are best friends and I like her, she's okay. I just don't want anyone knowing."

"Okay." I slid down just as he had done and sat on the damp mossy ground. "I guess your brother would really be in big trouble if people found out." I looked off towards the sound of the highway, heard the whoosh of cars traveling north to south and south to north, all passing us by without a thought. "R. W., too."

"I couldn't care less about what happens to Dexter," he said, jaw clenched. "Or R. W. They can rot in hell for all I care."

"Oh." I felt my own face get hot with his anger, with my misunderstanding of what he meant.

"I just would rather nobody knows." He leaned forward, pulled his knees up, arms hugging them. "I mean, that's all Perry needs, right?" He stared at me again, watched as I sat braiding a piece of pine straw. "You know this gets out and every bastard in the school will be after her, people like that jerk-off Todd and his friend from Greensboro." He paused, teeth clenched again. "You know all those people you run around with. You know what they'd say and do."

I was stunned. The pine straw was motionless in my hand as I looked towards the highway. He was saying the same thing that Perry had said in the bathroom the year before; he was lumping me in with all of *them*, the group Misty and I had wanted to be a part of but had always remained on the fringe.

"They're not my friends," I said, and tossed the straw to the side. "And I won't tell, I promise." I stood to go, brushed off the seat of my jeans and was heading back to the path when he stood, too, jumped in front of me.

"Why *were* you in that tree?" he asked. I shrugged, looked

down first at my feet, tan Wallabies darkened by the damp ground, and then his, the same style Converse he had worn for years. "What were you expecting to see?" He bent down, trying to get me to look at him. "Thought maybe you'd see some fancy velvet drapes and wallpaper?" I shook my head. "What then? What were you looking for?" He stepped closer. "Did you see what you wanted to see?"

"No!" I looked up, swallowed hard to keep from crying.

"Why then?"

"I don't know." I shrugged again, looked away. "I guess I was curious."

"About what?" His plastic bag with his gifts was still on the ground, one of the tags visible. At first I thought it said *from* Merle, but now I saw that it was *to* him. *To Merle from the Landells.* That explained the classical music; he had called me from Mrs. Poole's house. "About what?" he asked again and stepped closer.

"You." I felt like it took forever to get the word out of my mouth, and then it fell solid and heavy. He stepped back, bent to pick up his bag, and then stood there, his breath visible as he stared out at the irregular pattern of granite. All the possibilities suddenly came rushing in. He could turn and run away without ever looking back, or he could clear his throat and spit on the mossy ground, or he could hold his sides and laugh and laugh. But he just stood there, the bag swinging as he rocked from side to side. "You were curious about me?" He looked at me, put his hand to his chest. In the distance I could hear the cars, could hear Christmas music and horns blowing. In less than two hours Angela would be in our house, turning the holiday into a holiday just by making it four instead of three of us sitting down to eat. He stepped closer, silently on the moss, and then suddenly leaned forward, his lips pressing mine for an awkward split second. Then there was a long pause as we both stared in the direction of the highway.

"Sorry, forgot you had a boyfriend," he finally said and stepped away, tilted his head in the direction of Misty's house.

"But I don't," I said and watched him kick the bottom of the shed door to loosen it. "Misty just likes to tell people that." I breathed in, smelling the woodsmoke and pine in the cold air. My hands were shaking so I stuck them in my pockets. "What you did for Misty the other day, the way you stood up for her was real nice," I said, and stepped towards him. "Except that now she thinks your brother is cute."

"She can do better than Dexter." He pulled on the rusty handle and the door swung open. "So can Perry." There was a softness in the way he said her name, and I couldn't help but wonder if *he* had ever been with her, in a different way, a tender way.

"I hope she's okay," I said as he squatted and peered into the dark shed where there was a rusty shovel and old black tarp.

"Says she is. I called her." He pushed the door to and stood, stared straight up into those thick pine branches. "She said she knew about it all, that she was *supposed* to act scared was all." He shook his head. "Says Dexter and her are gonna get married. He's giving her a pre-engagement ring for Christmas." He laughed sarcastically and looked at me then, shrugged a sigh of helplessness. "If he does, it's stolen."

"She *knew*?" I asked in disbelief, and he turned towards me.

"No, no way. She's lying," he said. "She's scared as hell of him." He reached out, fingers locking around my wrists, squeezing as he spoke. "She's not that kind of girl any more than *you* are," he said, squeezing still harder when he said *you*. "How would you feel if they had done that to *you*." He shook me with each word. "Think about it." I looked down when I felt the tears coming to my eyes. His knuckles were white as he squeezed me, my own fists clenched and pressing against his stomach. And then he released his grip, rubbed his open palms up and down my sleeves, barely touching. "I'm sorry," he said. "Really."

I wondered what we must look like. I saw an aerial view of

Merle reaching out stiffly to hug me, our heads pressing together as we rocked back and forth like in a slow dance. His wool plaid jacket was rough on my cheek, my mouth just an inch from his neck, the same neck that had once been wrapped in snakeskins and dirty rawhide-strung ratfinks. The house next door to his began cranking up the music, and though above us we could see patches of the afternoon sky, within the thickly wooded space where we stood it was like dusk. *Hark the herald angels sing*. In the distance horns were blowing as people drove home from work, and very soon the local radio station would begin announcing where Santa Claus had been spotted and his predicted arrival into the Fulton city limits. And late that night when I got into bed, I would think through the whole meeting, second by second, every single word and look and touch, and if Angela should creep into my room after midnight to tell her latest stories, then maybe I would surprise her, finally, with one of my own.

Twenty-one

Angela called at the time she was supposed to arrive to say that she was running late. "Oh, Kitty," she said, lots of background noise making it hard to hear all she said, "I'm so sorry that I can't get there for dinner, but something really important is going on. I can't wait to tell you all about it. I can't wait to see all of you. Wait a sec . . ." I heard her put the phone down, and then there were just muffled voices and music. Through the doorway I could see my mother in her green knit dress and matching pumps as she lit the red tapers in the center of the table; she was using her fine china, white with a gold band around the edge, and the Waterford crystal that she kept on the very top shelf of the china cabinet. She had put down her best linen tablecloth and the matching napkins, which she had some- where along the way learned to fold like swans. "I've always had a soft spot for swans," she had said many times. "They always remind me of the Public Gardens and growing up in Boston." It made me ache to watch her, knowing that in five minutes when I told her that Angela wouldn't make dinner, she would stiffen and bristle and say that she wasn't surprised. *Of course she can't make it. What kind of fool was I to think she would?*

"Kitty, I'm back." Angela laughed, her breath short and quick as if she'd just run around the block. "I'll be there around eleven, okay? It'll still be Christmas Eve, right?" She paused, waiting for me to say something.

"Please don't do this." Now I could see through the dining room and into the kitchen, where the big turkey, its legs crossed and tied, was golden brown in the roasting pan as my mother basted it again in butter and then left it on the top of the stove while she went back to her Waldorf salad. "Try to get here sooner. For dinner."

"Well." She paused. "You're afraid that Cleva will fly off the handle if I'm not there, is that it?" I didn't say anything. "Yeah, I see what you mean. Well"—her voice fell—"hold on." Again I could hear voices and music as I waited. "I'm on my way," she said. "I sure don't want the burden of you and Fred having a lousy Christmas." She paused. "See you soon," and then she hung up before I could say good-bye.

"Kate?" Mama was standing there, cheeks flushed with the heat of the kitchen. "Who is it? What's wrong?"

"Nothing." I hung up the phone.

"Angela isn't coming, is she?" She stood there, a red-and-green oven mitt covering her hand and arm like a cast, and stared around the room, past the flickering tapers and cut holly center-piece, as if she were disoriented and didn't know where to go or what to do.

"No, she is," I said, and followed her back into the kitchen. "She's just running a little late, that's all."

"Why the long face?" My father came in from the back porch, where he had said that Mama was, under no circumstances, to go. As a surprise he was going to have a greenhouse built for her and had built a little model of one to present to her on Christmas morning. He had borrowed tongue depressers from Sally Jean, who got them at the hospital, patiently glued the frame, and then wrapped it all in Saran Wrap; there was an African violet and a zebra plant from the florist inside. My mother had no idea what he was planning. "C'mon. It's Christmas Eve." He squeezed her hand. "Why did Theresa Poole throw the clock out the window?"

"Angela's running late." Mama sighed and went back to the sink. "That means she probably isn't coming at all."

"Yes, she is," I said. "She was leaving right that minute."

"We'll see." Mama was scooping the oyster dressing from the turkey and putting it in a big bowl. "I hope Sally Jean's meal turns out okay. She has Thomas's sister and husband visiting for the first time since . . ." Her voice fell off. My mother had stopped mentioning Mo, a loyalty to Sally Jean making her want to forget.

"I do, too." I went to sit on the counter by the sink where I could see Merle's house. I still could not believe what had happened that very afternoon; it made the blood rush to my head just to think about it, the way he had leaned in, his lips brushing mine. It was not even a second and yet, when I thought about it, it was like slow motion.

"Sally Jean is trying so hard. I hope they all have a real nice holiday. I hope the children got her something nice." Mama looked at me as if to pose a question, and I told her that Misty had gone shopping earlier.

"Today? She waited until today?" She shook her head and looked at my father as if to drive home a point. She was going to be surprised when she saw just how much thought he *had* put into her gift. I had gotten her some Wind Song cologne, which I gave her every Christmas, and a large tortoise-shell clip, since her hair had finally grown long enough that she could pull it back in her old style. I wasn't sure how much thought I had put into my gift either, considering I had gotten the idea of the clip from

"The Gift of the Magi," and was relieved I had not had to make any sort of sacrificial trade there at Belk-Hensdale.

Just the day before, Misty had found Mo's stocking carefully wrapped in tissue paper and placed on the end of her bed. "I guess Sally Jean wanted to get it out of the decoration box," Misty had said, and all I could think about was how the year before, Sally Jean must have found it and just left it there. Everything else was pulled from the box and then returned, with Mo's cotton quilted stocking still there on the bottom. "She made my dad a *new* stocking to match hers, a crocheted one." Misty made a face. "She said she'd make me and Dean crocheted ones, too, if we were interested."

"Santa Claus has lots of tricks up his sleeve." Daddy laughed, his hand patting his chest, as he pulled out the bottle of brandy he'd been *sipping* from all day. "You are never going to guess what you're getting, Cleva." He sat down at the table and lit a cigarette. "You're going to love it."

"You know what I'd really like?" She turned and I knew from the quick glance she gave his hand with the cigarette that she wanted to say *stop*, but then she changed her mind and I was relieved; what I really wanted was a happy, merry Christmas, though I really felt that nothing could dampen my holiday. When I felt the bits of tension, when I thought of Perry there on the ground, I forced my thoughts back around to Merle, the smoothness of his mouth, the softness of his voice. Before I left the cemetery, Merle had said that he would see me real soon, that he'd call me. Of all the times that I had thought through Angela's visits and days spent with Mo Rhodes, second by second, it was nothing compared to the careful dissection I had done of my meeting Merle in the cemetery; I had every millisecond memorized.

"Tell me what you'd like," he said. "You name it, Cleva. Anything within reason." He laughed a long deep Santa Claus imitation, his face red as he finished and took in a much needed breath.

"I'd like to have a very merry Christmas," she whispered, came and stood right behind his chair, lifted the cigarette from his hand and stubbed it in the ashtray, before massaging his shoulders. "I'd like," she whispered, "for you to go and get a physical, start the new year off with a good bill of health." She hugged him, her face right next to his, voice low and serene. "And I'd like for those people back on that street to turn off the damn music for five minutes. If I hear 'Frosty the Snowman' once more today, I am going to stick my head in the oven."

"I like it," he said. "Don't think much of the physical, but as for the merry Christmas, yes." He stood and walked over to her. "And, oh boy, do I like it when you're mean, Cleva." He muscled her under the mistletoe and kissed her right on the mouth, smudged that carefully applied lipstick all over her chin. "If Theresa Poole could see you now," he said. "And by the way, Mrs. Poole drew herself a picture of the nativity scene, and there at the back she drew a great big fat man. Well, Cleva Burns walked by and said, 'Why, Theresa, what lovely art you've done but now tell me, who's the fat guy there at the rear of the stable?' " He paused, jiggled Mama, who with cheeks flushed and eyes watery, smiled, mouthed, "Who?" He looked at me where I was still sitting on the counter in front of the window; in one glance I saw myself and then I could look beyond the darkness and see Merle's house. "Mrs. Theresa tilted up her nose and said, 'Why, Cleva, don't you know? Why, don't you know?' " He could do a wonderful Theresa Poole impersonation, and it had gotten better and better since he told this same joke every year. " 'That's Round John Virgin.' " My mother said the words with him, laughed. "Okay, so here's a better one." He stopped, swallowed hard, opened his mouth as if to belch but nothing happened. "Bad gas." He patted his chest.

"Fred."

"In the car. I bought some bad gas. Damn thing hopped all the way home like in that Gulf commercial—no knocks." He was in rare form, or maybe he was trying hard to do the same thing I was, to keep the holiday a holiday. "This traveling salesman stopped at Theresa Poole's house and asked if he could spend the night and she said yeah, but that she just had the one bed . . ."

"Fred?"

"Yes, dear?" He thumped his chest again and then swooped over and lifted the big roaster pan from her hands and ceremoniously carried it over to the counter. I watched her watching him, saw her look of fear that that big bird could slide from the pan and out into the hall.

We sat in the living room while waiting for Angela, just the tree lights on while we took turns shaking gifts and trying to guess what was inside. At the back of the tree was a big package for Angela "from Fred, Cleva and Kate"; it was the gift wrap they were using at Thalhimers, and it was my mother's handwriting on the card. Part of the time we just sat there, quietly, but it was comfortable; no Judy Garland, no fondue magazines, just the three of us in the darkened room. I sat on the floor near the tree, where I could see out the front window onto the porch. I pulled the lace panel curtains off to one side so I could see Angela as soon as she drove up. Except for the lights on Sally Jean's flocked tree, Misty's house was dark, but I could see them all moving about in the front yard. There was a flash, a lighter, and then there was Misty, a sparkler in each hand as she danced around the dark yard, another flash and then there was Dean standing completely still but his hand moving in a circle with the sparkler trailing. I watched them over and over, Sally Jean taking a turn as she twirled around and around in a circle and then draped her arm around Misty. To my surprise, it looked like Misty hugged her back.

"So how long should we give her?" Mama finally asked. The Rhodeses had exhausted their sparklers and gone inside, their dining room all lit up as they sat down to eat.

It was around nine when Angela arrived, and though Mama had fussed and reheated the dressing a couple of times, she looked genuinely relieved when she heard the loud engine of the Impala pull into the drive. We all three were in the doorway waiting when she walked up on the porch.

"Welcome," my mother said, and pushed past us to be the first to greet her. "Why, where is your coat?" She pulled Angela's crocheted shawl up higher so that it completely covered her shoulders. "Come on in and get warm." My father looked at me, one eyebrow raised suspiciously as we watched them. It reminded me of the scene in *Gone with the Wind* when Melanie goes to meet Scarlett at the entrance at Ashley's birthday party. Angela was wearing a red dress, too, smocked at the top with a low neckline, long puffy sleeves, and folds of the thin sheer material that hung in different lengths about six inches above her knees. She wore black suede boots and carried a matching bag.

"Wow, look at you," my father said, and gave her a quick hug. "You went all out."

"Well, I was invited to a party," she said, and turned to me, gave me a quick kiss. "That's where I was when I called you. I had a great time." She winked at me. "But I told them that I had to leave, that I couldn't wait to get here. Well, you know how hard it is to leave a place like that."

"Oh, yes, indeed I do," Mama said, and led the way into the dining room, while my father took Angela's keys and went to get everything from her trunk.

"I can't *wait* for y'all to open your gifts," Angela said. "There's no feeling quite like *knowing* that you've found the *perfect* gift for someone."

The dinner was beautiful, like a cover from one of my mother's magazines; she had candles burning all over the dining room, a pineapple centerpiece with oranges and apples pierced with cloves. With every dish passed, my mother beamed with the compliments, becoming more and more festive with each minute.

"Tell Angela the one about Round John Virgin," she said to my father, and then laughed uncontrollably when she realized she had given away the punch line.

"What have you been eating, Cleva?" he asked her. "I want seconds on whatever it is."

"Me, too," Angela added. "Do you remember that time you took me to Clemmonsville to see *Seven Brides for Seven Brothers?*" She was looking at my mother, who started laughing again, and then she turned to me. "Cleva took me to see that movie, and all of a sudden we got so tickled that we had to get up and leave because people were looking at us." I tried to picture the impossible, my mother and Angela sliding down in their chairs as they tried not to giggle.

"It all started because I said that I had never really cared for a Western," Mama said, with a straight face. "And especially not one where they suddenly burst into a song. Those great big men out building a barn—and all of a sudden the seven brothers were jumping logs and carrying on." She laughed, leaned forward on a propped elbow, face cupped in her hand. My father was staring at her and smiling, a cigarette burning in his hand. "Now for dessert," she said, but we all begged off until later.

"I need to leave for a little while," Angela said, looking at my mother as if to ask permission. "It's *real* important. You'll understand tomorrow."

"Sure, do what you need to do," my father said, but Angela waited to hear my mother say the same thing, and then she was gone, my father slipping out to finish his project on the back porch while I helped clean up in the kitchen.

"Don't blow out the candles," Mama said when we had cleared the table. She lit more candles in the kitchen and turned off the overhead light as well. "There's something so sad about going from candlelight to regular light," she said. "When you blow them out you should just let the room be dark."

"Cleva Burns, philosopher and chef extraordinaire," my father said as he slipped her Saran Wrap off the counter and carried it back outside. We washed the dishes by candlelight, and though I wanted to muse about Angela's errand, to ask questions about the two of them and their trip to the movies, I felt somehow that it was best just to leave it alone. From the blinking house below I heard "It Came upon a Midnight Clear," and it gave me a chill to think of the night before, the cold darkness of the cemetery, Perry on the ground. I concentrated on the fine gold band edging my mother's china, the way it glistened with suds in the glow of the candle. I concentrated on every flicker, every word of the carol, until I realized with surprise that my mother was singing along, her voice solid and clear.

It was almost two when I heard the floorboards in my bedroom creak, and when I opened my eyes Angela was there, already dressed in a long flimsy gown and robe. "Kitty? Kitty?" she whispered, gently shaking my arm. "Merry Christmas."

I felt disoriented, my first thought being the fear that I had dreamed myself into the cemetery with Merle and had never really been there at all.

"Oh, Kitty, it was the most wonderful night. Can I turn on the lamp?"

"Okay." I squeezed my eyes tightly so I could adjust slowly to the light, and when I opened them, there was Angela's hand, a diamond ring on her finger. I must have looked shocked and just sat there, blinking, mouth open.

"I'm getting married," she said, and hugged me close. Her gown was as thin as Mama's sheers in the dining room.

"Married?"

"Greg said that without me he had absolutely nothing in his life worth mentioning." She held her hand out, turning it from side to side as she admired the ring, her nails painted a deep burgundy, her thick hair pulled up loosely in a big leather clip. "I had a feeling tonight was the night." She laughed. Somehow in the midst of it all, being sleepy while she talked rapidly, I couldn't help but picture Angela and James Caan in the bridesmaid scene, and then it was Perry and Dexter, Perry and R. W., Mo and Gene Files, Merle and me. "So, that's something, isn't it, Kitty? The man actually got on his knees and begged my hand in marriage." She pranced around the room like a show horse, high steps and head tilted back, thin blue robe twirling around her legs. "He said that I was the most wonderful thing to ever happen to him, that he loved me madly and would forever." She stopped in the center of the room, hands clasped to her chest in excitement. "So tell me, Kitty. What's new with you?" She twirled once, ran her finger along my bookshelf and then sat at the foot of the bed, legs pulled up Indian style. Somehow, the story about Merle Hucks kissing me in the cemetery didn't sound like much after her spiel, so I decided to save it for a time that would do the afternoon justice.

"We're glad you're here," I said, and reached up to turn off the lamp, waiting to readjust to darkness.

"Now tell me truthfully"—she crept up beside me, making the springs creak—"did Cleva say anything about me getting here late?"

"No," I said. "She didn't."

"C'mon, Kitty, it's me you're talking to." She shook my shoulder and then just rubbed her hand up and down my back. "She probably sighed and said things like, *That Angela, you can't trust her.*" She leaned close to get my reaction, and once again I shook my head. "Well, if she did get mad, she won't be tomorrow when she sees my ring."

I tried to get back that aerial of view of Merle and me rocking back and forth beneath the trees, tried to hear his voice once again saying that he'd see me soon, but Angela kept talking and talking until I fell asleep, the last words I heard being "Me, a bride, isn't that just the craziest?"

The next morning my mother served coffee and cinnamon rolls in the living room while we opened presents. She wore a heavy green velour robe, the contrast making Angela's robe of the night before seem even flimsier. Fortunately, Angela was dressed for breakfast, in jeans and a Myrtle Beach sweatshirt, and she was still flashing her ring about. She had raved on and on about the robe we had given her, a nice thick flannel one in a pink and white stripe with matching long gown, but I knew from having seen what she wore the night before that it was not something she would have picked for herself.

She gave my parents a big pottery elephant that served no purpose other than to sit around and be an elephant. It reminded me of something Mo Rhodes would have had in her house, but I knew that my mother had had to bite the inside of her mouth to keep from gasping when she opened the box. She gave me a huge macramé purse, which I loved; unfortunately, my mother had also bought a purse, a neat navy canvas clutch, which paled in comparison. In short, we all tactfully lied a few times during the opening of the gifts. My mother really seemed to like her clip, but the most sincere look of joy came when she was presented with her greenhouse model, and was told that the *real* one was coming in the spring. And I wasn't surprised when Angela announced that she had a little something *extra* for my mother, and then emerged from the other room with the zebra plant and the African violet.

By late morning we began getting ready for the afternoon meal, while my father tuned in to the parade on TV and speculated as to whether or not a sniper could conceal himself under a big plastic flap and ride atop the huge Snoopy balloon. We had already invited Mrs. Poole for dinner, and I think now Mama was beginning to get a little nervous, knowing that Mrs. Poole would quiz Angela thoroughly throughout the day. Mrs. Poole had no sooner arrived but that Sally Jean and Misty came across the street with a big tin of cookies to say Merry Christmas. Misty was wearing a whole new outfit, new Levi's, new wool fishermanknit sweater, new leather boots. She even had tiny handblown glass earrings shaped like Coke bottles.

"Can you believe Sally Jean picked all this out?" she whispered incredulously. "I mean, the salesperson *must've* helped her, but still. Look." She pulled up the leg of her jeans so I could see the black leather boots. "But she *made* this." She thrust her arm out for me to feel the sweater. "Dean got one, too, only his is blue." Misty was talking as quickly as Angela had the night before, her face almost pretty with her hair put up the way she was wearing it. "I got two Jim Croce albums, and a set of electric rollers . . ." Misty's list went on and on while she looked at my things, mostly clothes, two pieces of blue Samsonite luggage. "Where are you going that you need a suitcase?" she asked, and laughed. We had always joked about how we carried our clothes back and forth across Wilkins Road in paper bags.

"Why, Sally Jean, what an unusual pin you're wearing," Mrs. Poole said, and I turned to see her lift Sally Jean's lapel, a big gold lizard with green glass eyes, pinned there. Everyone leaned close to look, and I noticed Misty's cheeks were flushed.

"Misty gave me this," she said. "I think he's beautiful."

"Well." Mrs. Poole nodded and turned away, commented on the suit my mother had picked out for herself, called attention as she always did to the fact that, though they were the same height, *she* was a *small* frame and my mother was at best a *medium* on the bone chart, probably a *large*. "Yes, a doctor would probably say you're a large."

"Aren't you excited about your greenhouse?" Sally Jean asked. "You know I got those tongue depressors for Fred. He asked me one day if I had anything he could use to build a model and I said, 'Well, no, I don't, but there are loads of things in a hospital that you could use,' and of course look at this. He did a fine job, didn't he?" She looked at Mrs. Poole, who looked up to the ceiling and then sat down and lit a Salem. She had been talking to Angela for a good thirty minutes and was just about ready to ask questions.

"Ferris Beach, you say? And did I hear Cleva say once that your mama died while birthing you?"

"The most exciting thing for me," Sally Jean announced, clapped her hands. "Well, you know how I've been trying and trying to get grass to grow and having such a time of it?"

"All those years of rocks probably ruined the soil," Mrs. Poole turned to say and then went right back to Angela. "And exactly what do you do?"

"Well, I want some grass in the worst way and so for my Christmas, Thomas has said that I can sodomize our yard."

"Well, I never," Mrs. Poole gasped and smoked her cigarette, sucked in hard.

"They're doing it in all the new subdivisions," she said, face and throat blushing.

"Well, good grief, Sally Jean," my father said. "Are you going to charge admission for this?"

"Fred Burns, you're a card, you know?" She looked at Mama. "Your Fred is something. It's no big deal anymore, Fred."

"Sodomizing a yard? No big deal?" he asked.

"No. They just bring the grass and roll it right out. Thomas tells me that they can even cut out around my trees and what not just like you might wall-to-wall carpet over a heating vent." She nodded assuredly, took a deep breath and then smiled at Mrs. Poole. "I'll have the greenest, thickest carpet of grass on this whole street." She thrust out her chin but with one stern look from Mrs. Poole began to crumble. "Well, that's what Thomas says anyway. You know my Thomas though, he does whatever it takes to make me happy."

"Yes, he was always that way," Mrs. Poole said, and then put her hand daintily to her mouth as if she hadn't meant to make reference to the time *before* Sally Jean.

"It'll look beautiful, Sally Jean," Mama said. "Can I get you some tea or coffee?"

"No, we just popped by to say hi." My father and I followed them to the door, with him reassuring Sally Jean how pretty her yard would be with grass. I was relieved that he didn't make any more mention of her sodomizing the yard. Even Misty hadn't commented, had only nodded right along with Sally Jean, who it seemed had racked up quite a few points with her Christmas shopping.

"I should've gotten her something other than that pin," Misty whispered. "How did I know she'd do all this for me?" My father and Sally Jean were at the steps when Misty spotted a gift all wrapped up beside our front door. "Hey, look." She picked it up, turned it sideways to read the card. "To Kate." She shook it just out of my reach. "Hey, who's it from, you guess?"

"I don't know." I reached and took it, stared at the neat print of my name.

"Well, open it," Misty screamed. "Let me see if that's Dean's writing." She studied the tag while I ripped off the paper and opened the box. If I had had a choice, I would have opened it privately, in my room, but I couldn't get away with that with Misty standing right there.

"Doesn't *look* like Dean's writing," she said; a car was pulling up and stopping in front of her house, but she was watching me lift the porcelain egg from its box. Violets were painted on the white egg, and it was all edged in gold. The top lifted and inside was a violet scented candle. "That's kind of pretty," Misty said, shaking her head. "Who else could it be?"

"I think it's from Merle," I whispered, reaching out to twist her arm in our signal of *graveyard talk*. "I wanted to tell you yesterday, but you had all those relatives over."

"What? Tell me what?" Misty's eyes were wild with excitement as she pushed me over to the far end of the porch away from Sally Jean and my father. "Have you talked to him?"

"Yeah." I stared out at the cemetery gates. "I was out here yesterday when he walked by, and we just sat and talked for a while." I rubbed my finger around the edge of the egg. "He really is nice."

"Haven't I been telling you that *forever*?" she asked. "You see, that flirting paid off, didn't it? Did he mention me? Did he mention his brother?"

"He said he thinks you're nice."

"And?" She reached up and twisted the tiny Coke bottle earring around and around.

"I found out that Dexter goes with Perry Loomis," I finally whispered. "They're pre-engaged."

"Oh." Her shoulders relaxed as she turned and watched the doors of the station wagon in her driveway open. "Great. Sally Jean's relatives," she said sarcastically and then breathed in, turned back to me. "Well, there's still R. W.," she said. "And now that you and Merle are together."

"I didn't say we're *together*."

"Well, you might as well be," she said, hope once again rising in her voice. "So you can fix me up with R. W." I cringed with the thought of R. W. Quincy, the way he walked towards Perry, hands fumbling with his belt.

"Misty?" Sally Jean was on the sidewalk, and I was relieved for the interruption until I could think of a way to get Misty's mind off R. W. I wanted so much to tell her the truth but every time I considered it, I thought of my promise to Merle. "C'mon, honey, our guests are here."

"Oh God." Misty twisted my arm. "See him." She pointed to a tall, gangly-looking guy who was stepping from the backseat of a big green station wagon. "He must be the guy who goes to Wake Forest. Sally Jean *said* he was cute and he *is*. How do I look?" She opened her eyes wide for my inspection, and I brushed a pale eyelash from her cheek. "Put R. W. on hold," she said and then was gone. Sally Jean waved as they crossed the street.

When I went inside, they were all standing and getting ready to go into the dining room; Mrs. Poole was now asking Angela about her education. I placed the egg up high on our mantel so it wouldn't get broken, but Mrs. Poole didn't miss a beat. "Now, where did that come from?" she asked.

"Well, Kitty," Mama said, "I thought Misty had already given you a gift."

"She had."

"Why, I bought one just like that the other day to go along with some things I had set aside for Gladys Hucks, you know." She pointed her thin arm to the back wall of our living room. "They live here right behind you. She does some sewing for me from time to time. Well, I guess I chose a popular item." She went to the mantel and turned the egg upside down to read the bottom. "Uh huh, 'Made in the USA,' just like the one I bought. You know, I don't buy Japanese things in memory of my Mr. Bo. This is exactly like what I bought." She shook the egg in her hand as she spoke. "I bought several. Make nice little gifts. Half-price table at Ivey's." Then she gasped, again as if she hadn't meant to slip, and placed the egg back on the mantel. "I hope Gladys likes hers. I mean, what do you buy for a poor soul who needs *everything*?"

"Something," my father said, looked at me and winked. "Now, who here knows what you get if you cross . . ." He faltered and then laughed when Mama gave him a sharp look.

"I told that boy to say it was from him and that little girl if he wanted. You know if he hadn't gotten anything for his mother." Mrs. Poole walked in front of me, and I wanted to stick my foot out and trip her like I never had before. "Now, what became of your father, Angela?"

"Excuse me," Mama interrupted. "Let's all say grace." Daddy prayed and I opened my eyes just long enough to glimpse Mama crossing herself, something I hadn't seen her do in a long time, her lips moving as she spoke a prayer all her own.

Before we even finished our pie, a horn blew in the driveway; when I went to look out, there was a bright red Mustang, a dark-haired man in the driver's seat. In a second Angela was right behind me and then out the front door, a constant cry of

"Greg, Greg, Greg," as she slid across the front seat and began kissing him.

"I hate to leave," she was saying to Mama and Daddy five minutes later. "And my, but Greg would love to come in but he's taking me to meet his family, and then we think we might go ahead and get married. It's okay if I leave my car here for a day or two, isn't it?" As Mrs. Poole watched, Angela hugged my father and then my mother, kissed both of my cheeks, and once again was gone with a promise of letters and phone calls and a couple of revs from the car's engine.

"Well, she doesn't linger, does she?" Mrs. Poole asked, and lit a Salem.

"No, she's always been the energetic type. Here today, gone tomorrow." Mama lifted her hands and made a twirling motion, like a tornado, and smiled. "That's our little Angela." She looked at Daddy, who nodded enthusiastically and then gave Mama a break by asking Mrs. Poole just what her problem was with blacks and whites going to the same school and did she really give a big donation back when George Wallace was running for president.

"Well, I did no such thing, Fred."

"You mean you didn't *vote* for George Wallace like everybody says you did."

"Voting is a private right, Fred, a private right of a U.S. citizen."

"Well, is it true that you are sponsoring a Japanese child here in the States?" He sat back and lit a cigar, laughed as her face got tighter and tighter. Mama was standing in the kitchen with a forlorn look on her face, a silver tray beautifully arranged with strawberries and kiwis that she had had to travel great distances and pay great prices to find, her fondue pot bubbling with chocolate, the semisweet kind just as Angela had requested.

Merle called late that afternoon and asked if I could walk and meet him in the same place. I could hear lots of loud talk and television noise in the background, and though Mama had invited several people from her garden club over to eat up all that fruit and said she needed my help, I begged off long enough to sneak into the cemetery. "Just for a walk," I had told her when she asked where I was going. It was one of those drizzly days where it never really rains hard, just mists steadily, making the day seem much longer, as if it had been late afternoon for hours.

"A walk in this weather?" Mrs. Poole had decided that rather than go home and sit alone she would just spend the time between dinner and the garden club gathering at my mother's kitchen table. I didn't answer her, just grabbed an umbrella out of the bucket by the back door and left, walking the long way around in case they were watching me. The house with the manger scene was quiet, no music, no lights, probably afraid that they'd short-circuit in the dampness. Angela had also given my father a stainless steel lighter, and when I approached him after lunch, saying that I needed a gift for someone I had forgotten, he held it out to me still wrapped in green tissue paper in the small white box.

"Is he a smoker?" he asked, one finger up to his lips as he breathed a long "Shhhhh." I nodded, and then he put the box in my hand, crossed his heart to keep my secret, and then shooed me away just as Judy began singing, *What'll I do when you are far away. . . .* He mouthed the words, a pencil in his hand as he drew an elaborate greenhouse that he could never afford to really build.

When I arrived, the door to the little shed was open. I bent down to look inside, and there he was, leaning against the wall, knees bent up as his feet pressed against the other side. Merle motioned for me to come inside and I did, sitting opposite him on an old blanket he had spread there. Water dripped from the low doorway.

Most of the time we just sat and listened to the other one fumbling for something to say, our knees touching.

"Thanks for my present," I said, all the while trying to blot

Mrs. Poole's sharp face and words from my mind. He shrugged a "you're welcome" and then I pulled out the lighter and waited for him to open it. Thank God, Angela hadn't had it monogrammed as most people would've done, or maybe it was a leftover gift from her as well, Greg quit smoking or never had.

"Thanks," he said, and rubbed his thumb downward to light it. We sat there and watched the flame until he said his thumb was scorched and let go. It seemed to have gotten a lot darker. We heard the streetlight in the far end of the cemetery buzz on. Mostly we talked about Christmas and food. He had gotten some clothes, some money, but didn't elaborate. He said his sister had gotten a doll that said the same three things over and over when you pulled her string and it was driving him crazy. He said Dexter did give Perry a pre-engagement ring.

"What about your mother?" I asked, trying to picture Gladys Hucks in my mind; I had only seen her at a distance, in the front of the pickup truck or bent over her kitchen sink.

"Old man gave her some old canisters or something like that," he said, smiling. "You know, like what you keep flour in." He squatted and awkwardly turned around so that he was sitting beside me, his hand warm as he reached out and took mine. "I gave her forty hours of hard labor. You know, like she can tell me what to do around the house and I have to do it." I squeezed his hand and waited, knowing that any second he was going to lean forward and kiss me. Just before I left, he said that he was wondering if I wanted to say that we were going together, like if people asked, would I mind if he said that I was his girlfriend.

"That's fine," I said in a very calm voice, my chest pounding twice as fast as Mrs. Poole could smoke or Angela could talk. "I'd like that." I backed out of the shed and, just before standing, watched him pull the lighter back from his jacket pocket and spark it. He said that he had always gone to the cemetery to sit; he said that in good weather he might sit on the great big rough gray tombstone near the gates, and I told him that I already knew that. "I know that you know," he said, and grinned.

It was the beginning of a routine; we met there every day, sometimes walking together from school and cutting in on the side street where Misty and I had spent so much time watching for parkers. "Better check the trees to see if anybody's watching *us*," Merle said one afternoon when I described all the time Misty and I had spent playing there, but the mention brought to mind that night with Perry, which was something we avoided discussing. She was absent a lot the first month after the holidays, and the rumors ranged from mononucleosis to pregnancy; Merle said she was just having a very hard time, no thanks to his lousy brother.

My mother often paused in the driveway or in an upstairs window to look over at the cemetery and see if she could see us. It was her belief that you should not be with a *boyfriend* in a place hidden from the public eye; it did not look nice. "Please invite this Merle *in*," she said over and over. "We hardly know him and certainly we should." She got that *stern yet sensitive* look which I'm sure she had employed as a school teacher when dealing with failing students. "Unless, of course, there's some *reason* you don't *want* us to meet him." She was still talking about Angela's quick exit at Christmas and how if she had truly found a winner to marry her this round, *then wouldn't she want people to meet him?* Mrs. Poole had offered ever since that day to have a bridal shower or a little engagement tea. "I mean this is Fred's niece, for crying out loud," she had said. "And a poor little orphan at that, though I never really heard what *did* happen to the father."

My mother was actually relieved when we got a postcard from Memphis, Elvis on the front, that announced she was married and on her honeymoon. "Why on earth did she go to Memphis for a honeymoon?" Mrs. Poole asked, and my mother, who had posed the same question the night before, repeated what my father had said. "I read just the other day that Memphis is the place to go for honeymoons this year." Sally Jean said that she had heard there was a foray of things to do, Graceland to name just one. "I guess *not* hearing from Angela means that all is well," my mother said one night, when there had been no letter or call to follow the postcard. "Our fair-weather friend. Though she could at least come get her car."

"I heard from her a week ago," my father said, pencil in hand as he doodled an elaborate building. "All is well." He looked up just as my mother was opening her mouth. "Really. All is well. She wanted to start paying us back some money, but I told her to take her time, get settled in good."

"You know, I used to spy on you and Misty some," Merle said one afternoon, a clear crisp day. It was after Valentine's Day because I was twirling the thin gold bracelet he had given me round and round my wrist while we sat on the rough gray stone facing my house. "I'd hide and watch you two twirling batons or singing songs up on your porch."

"Oh God." I felt my face go hot with the thought of the two of us out on my porch, arms locked as we mimicked Diana Ross and Marvin Gaye. "You couldn't *hear* us, could you?" He waited a long time before saying no, he couldn't hear us.

"Once I was out here. It was a couple of years ago." He stared down at my wrist, at the thin gold chain. "And you all of a sudden came running in through the gates. It was night, too." He sat waiting for me to explain. "It was like you were wild or something. You ran in and then right back out."

"I don't know why I did that." I shrugged, my heart beating faster with the thought of that night—the Rhodeses waiting to go to Hardees, my father's Al Jolson album playing. "Why did you spy?"

"I don't know either." He pointed up at our house, where the sheers in my window were pulled off to one side. "That's your room?" I nodded, and then we just sat there until my mother came to the far end of the porch to call me inside.

"Why can't you two sit in the house?" she asked one afternoon. "Or at least on the front porch." She was making baklava and held a thin piece of pastry in one hand. "Theresa keeps asking me what you all *do* out there."

"We just *talk*," I said.

"But why can't you just *talk* in the house?"

"Cleva," my father said and came into the room, "haven't you ever heard that old proverb about talking in the cemetery?"

"No."

"Well"——he turned and stared out at her greenhouse, which just that week had been completed——"it's good luck." He kept his back to us, and I imagined his expression, that same phony deadpan he used whenever he tried to lie. "Yes, it goes back to a legend associated with Mesopotamia. Seems the people believed that if you talked in a cemetery you would gain strength from the spirits."

"And how much is the tea in China *today*?"

"Ten cents a bag if it's Lipton, twenty for something better," he mumbled. "Get enough of that spirit strength and you become immortal. Yes, and still better than that, if you talk in a cemetery every single day after school, then your mother will be known as the most wonderful woman alive."

"Really," she said, and shook her head, looked with pride at her pan of baklava. "Well then, I'd be a fool to complain, wouldn't I?"

"Depends on the price of tea," he said, and came over, grabbed her around the hips; it was Jack Sprat and the Mrs. at their best. "Our whole life depends on the price of tea in China."

"I hope not," she said, and gently pushed him away. "That price is constantly changing."

Twenty-two

The night the Huckses' house burned down, everyone gathered in our backyard to watch. The small blue house was no longer visible, only the huge orange flames and dark black smoke that hung over the neighborhood like a fierce thundercloud. Merle had been at my house when it started, the two of us sitting on the front steps and shining a big flashlight onto the sidewalk, where Misty practiced her baton routine for the upcoming majorette tryouts. By the time the fire engines arrived, the flames had spread to the back of the house; Merle was there, screaming for his mother and Maybelline, but several men held him back, kept him from going closer. The pickup truck wasn't in the driveway, and he didn't know if his mother and sister were with his father or not. Dexter's motorcycle wasn't there either.

"I never thought I'd be thankful for that field of kudzu and all those old junky car parts," my mother said, and held onto my father's arm, her face yellow in the reflection that lit up the night sky. "But I sure am. It's at least slowed it down a little bit." Well, Lord forgive me when I whine, I wanted to say. But I just stood and watched Merle still standing at the edge of his yard, Perry Loomis suddenly beside him with her thick blond hair waving down her back, sparkling in the light of the fire. Mrs. Poole was standing beside Mama; she was fully dressed as if going to a social, and I noticed that Mama kept fidgeting with the collar of her green robe, wishing that she, too, had taken the time to dress for the fire.

"Is anybody in the house?" Mrs. Poole asked.

"Well, we know Merle is okay," my father said. "He was over here when it started."

"He's always over here lately, isn't he?" Mrs. Poole asked. "He seems like a nice boy but you might should watch it. You know they say the apple doesn't fall far." She turned and smiled a wry smile at me as if to say I didn't know anything. "Poor Gladys Hucks. You know, she is a simple, simple soul. Might've done it cooking."

"I'm surprised it didn't happen back at Christmas with all those lights and wires," Mama said. "I've always said it was going to happen."

"Well, thank goodness it didn't happen at Christmas," Mrs. Poole said. "Wouldn't that be sad to have your house burn down at Christmas?"

"Oh, yes," my father said and stepped over, hugged me up close as I watched Merle frozen there, the firemen still holding him back. "It's so much better that the house is burning now instead of at Christmas."

"Now, Fred," she began, but he turned to me before she could finish.

"Go on over there if you want," he said and nodded towards Merle. "I'm going to be right here."

"Okay," I said, but then hesitated again after taking several steps.

The ambulance came, and people stepped closer to the edge of the yard, hoping to be able to tell what was going on. "Old man Hucks probably passed out with a cigarette," one of the men said, and several others nodded.

"The boy smokes," Mrs. Poole said. "I've seen him. Marlboros, I believe." I knew that if she had a little umbrella over her and could sit those long crooked bones down that she'd have one herself. "There's just the three children living there now," she continued. "I took them a few canned goods back at Christmas, and Gladys told me how the boys had near about run her crazy. You know that oldest one is off somewhere and that one next in line is headed the same route. Then there's that one that has taken up here at your house and the little girl."

"Thanks for the live report," my father said, and stepped closer, pulling me with him.

"Fred," my mother said in a reprimanding tone. "Merle seems like a nice boy." She turned to Mrs. Poole. "He's polite."

"Yes, well, let's hope he doesn't take a turn." Mrs. Poole turned one way and then another to see who all had gathered.

"Could be it was an electrical fire," my father said. "Faulty wiring. All those houses down there are in bad need of repair."

"Not anymore," Mr. Rhodes said. "I just heard it's spread to that house next door, front of that house is gone. If they don't get it out soon, the whole stretch will go like a stack of paper."

"We do need rain in the worst way," Sally Jean said. Just that week, mid-March, they had come and sodded her yard and she had faithfully watered it every day for fear that it might die. In the distance, beyond the flames, I could see the baby Jesus family, father and mother and two children, as they watched all of their belongings disappear in the thick black cloud, years of collecting lights and ornaments and carols, gone in a flash of flame.

"Well, there's going to be plenty of work for me over the

next week or two," Mrs. Poole said. "We better start right now gathering up some clothes and food. I wonder if we might be able to rent out Brown's Econo Lodge again."

Merle was still talking to Perry, her hand clutching his arm; I kept waiting for him to turn around, but he never looked away from that house. A lot of the neighbors started getting restless and headed back home, asking others to call and let them know what happened. Finally I walked over and stood a couple of feet behind Merle. Perry was crying, a hand up to her face as she leaned into Merle, his arm draped around her back. A fireman was axing down the back door, beside which the kitchen window was a bright, blinding orange. I glanced up in our yard to where my parents stood and then back to the cemetery, where it was so odd to see the dogwoods in full bloom against the ugly black smoke and strange yellow sky. Something was going on in the front yard, where two more police cars had come down the road and screeched to a stop. I stepped right up beside Merle, reached and took hold of his hand. He squeezed back, fingers gripping mine, and took a step away from Perry, his arm dropping away from her. "Have you seen . . ." Before I could finish my thought, the pickup truck was rounding the corner, stopping when it was unable to pass the police cars gathered there, and we saw them, Merle's parents, the little girl in Mr. Hucks's arms, as they ran towards the house. "I gotta go." He turned to me. "They've got to let me go over there now." I heard his mother calling for him, and then he was gone, running along the edge of the yard, waving his arms and yelling back to her. I saw him get to her and then together the four of them stepped closer to the house. Perry and I were standing silently together, so close I could hear each labored breath and sniffle. "I hope Dexter's okay," I said, and she nodded, turned to me with a blank stare. "We're engaged," she said, and then walked in the same direction Merle had gone. I wanted to follow her, but I also felt that I didn't belong there right then. I heard a shrill scream like a siren, but then I realized it was Mrs. Hucks; I could see her in the strange light, kneeling forward, head in her hands, Mr. Hucks squatting beside her while Merle stood with his arms around his sister. Perry was right behind him, hands up to her face.

"Do you want me to walk over there with you?" Misty was there, still holding her baton, still wearing those old white go-go boots of Mo's that she used for practice. "I will if you want me to."

"No," I said. "Let's wait." Again I felt torn, wanting to go, but also feeling that I might see more than Merle would want me to see or want me to know. Now he had disappeared behind one of the fire engines with his parents, and Perry was left standing alone in the yard. The firemen were asking people to step back as they sprayed the whole field on the chance that there were any stray sparks.

"It's getting cold." Misty tugged on my arm. "Come on. We can watch from your house." I followed her back up through the yard, past my mother's gazebo, the greenhouse. Within the hour there were just sparse flames remaining, and the black cloud had lowered, leaving a fine mist of soot to cover our yard. It was hard to see, but as far as I could tell there was nothing left. My father and Mr. Rhodes walked over there with some other men, crossing the field and then disappearing around the fire engine and into the blackness. Misty and I had wanted to walk with them, but my father suggested we wait until they got back.

Mrs. Poole used our phone in the kitchen to call Brown's Econo Lodge out on 301 and reserve several rooms. Then she called the emergency number, asked for the police department and then asked for the officer's name, and then gave him his orders to go and pick up the homeless and carry them to Brown's, to tell them that somebody would be bringing around some clothes and food the next day.

"That's very nice of you, Theresa," Mama said, Sally Jean nodding, a mug of hot chocolate cupped in her hands.

"It's all a part of being who I am." Mrs. Poole sat down, propped a black patent pump on another chair, a position I'd certainly never seen from her, and lit a cigarette. "I sure hope the boy didn't start it," she said, blowing a stream of smoke upward.

"He didn't," I said. "He was right out there on the front porch." I felt my voice crack as it got louder, as I stood and pointed toward our front door.

"Might've left a cigarette, honey, that's all I meant." She smiled that wry smile again. "I mean everyone is not as careful as I am. Why, Mr. Bo was so careless about his cigars, and do you know what I did?" None of us responded. "I said, do you know what I did?"

"No." Mama shook her head, pulled the collar of her robe up around her chin as she stared at the empty stretch where homes had been, maybe saying a prayer of thankfulness that it was not us, maybe regretting her many wishes that those houses did not exist. Misty nudged me with the toe of her boot and crossed her eyes, stuck her tongue out the corner of her mouth as a gesture of Mrs. Poole's craziness.

"Well, every night I'd collect the ashtrays and I'd put them inside of my washing machine for the duration of the night."

"Hmmm." Mama was watching Daddy cross the yard now, her hand lifting to him, though he made no response. "Hmmm," I echoed her voice, wishing that I'd see Merle. Was he beyond that empty lot waiting to go to Brown's Econo Lodge, standing there with the other family, children shivering in the night air? I imagined him crouched and curled in the cemetery shed.

"Yessir, I put them in the washer because I knew they'd never start a fire there." She paused, lit another cigarette off the old one, another thing I'd never seen her do. "A refrigerator might work, too, dishwasher. I suspect any major appliance would work."

She kept right on talking even though Mama went to open the back door, me right behind her. "It's a real mess," Daddy said. A thin film of soot covered his face and shirt. His breath was quick and shallow, and Mama pulled him over to the table and urged him to sit. Mr. Rhodes followed, Sally Jean pulling him to the chair where she had been sitting and offering him her cup of hot chocolate.

"Did you see Merle?" I asked, causing everyone to look first at me and then at him. He nodded, propped his elbows on the table, face in his open palms.

"Did he say anything?" I waited for an answer, and he just shook his head. I knew that there was more, something had happened. It was just like when Mo died; we all knew and so were afraid to ask.

"That other boy's dead, though." His voice was hollow. "Damnedest thing. He was just sitting on that motorcycle on the porch. The man who lived in one of the other houses that burned said that they screamed for him to get off the porch, but he never even moved, just sat there with fire all around him."

"Oh God." Mama's hand was up to her face, a look of horror, but Mrs. Poole was as composed as if she'd just been issued a weather report, light rain.

"What about Gladys?" she asked, stubbed out her cigarette, reached for the pack, and then just held her hand there.

"She's fine," he said. "Nobody was home but that one boy."

"They're sure?" Mrs. Poole asked. "What about that worthless Beef?"

"He got home stock sober, or seemed sober. Wife and the little girl had been with him all evening." Daddy took a glass of water from Mama and drank it all the way down, making sooty fingerprints where he gripped the glass. "Said he'd been hunting work in Clemmonsville all day, and they'd stopped to eat supper on the way home. Broke down and cried like a baby when he saw that son of his off to the side and covered in a piece of canvas."

"About time," Mrs. Poole muttered, then sat up with a start, as if she'd been talking in her sleep.

"What did Gladys do?" Mama asked, and I realized we were

all charmed by the details, charmed by the voice in the same way that Mama had charmed Sally Jean all those times.

"She was in shock, I believe," he said. "She just sat there and shook like a leaf, the little girl clinging to her and screaming until Kate's friend came and picked the girl up and led his mama to the front seat of the truck."

"Did Merle see you?" I asked.

He nodded. "Yes, but I didn't go over where he was. There was another girl there, Perry I believe he called her." He paused, thinking. "She was all to pieces, and I saw him walking her down the street there when I was coming home."

"She was supposed to marry Merle's brother," I whispered. We asked more questions—Had those people gone to Brown's Econo? Did they know what started the fire?—but my father didn't know any of the answers. We just sat quietly, seeing no movement from the dark empty lots behind us. When the phone rang, we all jumped, and I ran into the front hall, grabbed up the receiver to hear Merle's voice.

"Hey, Kate." Misty followed and stood in the hall as I sank onto the edge of the throne chair. "Did your dad tell you?" He sounded far away. I could hear a baby crying in the background, and I assumed he was calling from Perry's house. I imagined her sitting there beside him the same way Misty was beside me.

"I'm so sorry," I said, and then listened, a long pause and a sigh.

"Yeah," he whispered. "Look, I gotta go." I could hear noise in the background, cries and whimpers, and before I could ask where he'd be, he had hung up, the dial tone buzzing loudly.

I didn't hear from Merle again that night, but we did have news that the families of the three homes destroyed were staying out on 301 as Mrs. Poole had provided. I imagined the four of them in one room, a phone on the old outdated desk but no privacy for him to call; how hard it would be for him to call me while his mother was curled on the bed, lips trembling uncontrollably.

The next morning we heard that the fire had been no accident but was set with old rags and gasoline, a can found under the Huckses' front porch, those other families just suffering the consequences of being in the wrong place at the wrong time. If the family next door had only lived three houses away, then the manger scene neatly wrapped in newspaper and tucked away for a year's keeping in their attic would have survived, as would have the baby toys and wedding pictures and family recipes scribbled in the familiar hand of someone long gone.

The most horrifying part of the story came out two days later; Dexter had not died *in* the fire, but before. *That* was why he had sat so stoically in the middle of the flames. Merle told me, many days later when we met in the shed, that he had gone with his parents to identify Dexter, there in the bright lights of the morgue where he had been declared dead on arrival. Though he was badly burned, on his throat was a hairline slit, blackened wine color, where a blade had sliced the pale white skin.

"Who did it?" My voice was a whisper as we sat side by side and stared straight ahead at the blank wall of the shed, our fingers locked tightly.

"Probably some old *club* member," he said. "Probably one of his *friends*." I didn't ask him anything else, just sat there, listening to the rise and fall of his breath, and trying to shake the picture from my mind.

"Where are you all going to live?" I asked Merle, turning towards him, feeling his breath warm on my cheek.

"I don't know." He shook his head, then playfully tied a piece of yarn around my finger and left it there, turning it around and around as if it might be a ring. "My dad says we might have to move. Says he was thinking about taking a job in Clemmonsville anyway. In the meantime, I guess we're in that old rotten motel."

It was not long after the fire when Mrs. Poole said that she felt she ought to buy a leg of lamb and smear a bit of the blood out on her storm door. "First Mo Rhodes, and then the fire. That child murdered, though he was mean as a snake, murdered nonetheless." She paused while in thought, her thin lips stretched in a straight tight line. "Seems like I'm forgetting something else bad that happened." She held up one finger. "Thomas Clayton died, though of course he didn't live on this street." She sat forward. "But his barber shop is not far. Just down there and around the corner. It's like a plague of some sort, isn't it? I believe it all started with the split-levels."

"Mr. Clayton was a sweet man," my mother said, to change the subject, and stared out at her greenhouse, where ferns covered the rafters. My father was at the edge of our yard with spade in hand planting canna lilies. He had said that they would bloom all summer, getting real tall like a fence to block out that blackened field and those cinderblock pilings like tombstones. "They're sort of Victorian, Cleva," he had explained when he came home with bags of the bulbs. "I know how you like Victorian things. You know those Victorians weren't so quiet and prim as you might think. Get them out of those long, cumbersome clothes and they were free spirits."

"I hear you," she said.

"Yes, they reminded me of you, these canna lilies." He grinned at her and then began plotting how he'd plant them. "I decided to go for the bright red ones. Come July they'll be six feet high."

"Thomas Clayton was all right," Mrs. Poole was saying, "though he could be hard to get along with." We both knew that Mrs. Poole had never quite gotten over the "Bo Poole School" comment.

"I thought he was a fine man," Mama said, and turned back to her orchid catalogue, causing Mrs. Poole to ask why on earth she would want to grow orchids, and why, why, *why* was she letting my father plant *canna lilies*. She spat the name as if it were poison, probably sorry that she had not thought of the fast tall hedge herself. My mother was watching him like a hawk, noting every time he stopped working and stood there mopping his flushed face. In her hand she held a letter addressed to him in Angela's tiny printed letters, the return address simply the Ferris Beach Post Office. The last time my father had talked to her, he had suggested to us that maybe all was not *perfect in paradise*, that he couldn't understand *how* she had the lousy luck and poor misfortune to keep winding up with men who changed like chameleons as soon as the marriage vows were spoken. "I guess they just learn they can take advantage of someone like Angela, you know, because she's so trusting and generous."

My mother opened her mouth, one eyebrow raised sharply, and then as if having a second thought, swallowed, spoke softly. "Do you think that maybe *she* fits into the pattern? Maybe the men don't change but are all just alike."

"What? You mean you think she *chooses* this?" he asked. "You think she *asks* for it? Only a fool would ask for such." And she just looked at him, eyebrows raised as if to say, *I rest my case*, but then again, with a change of heart, said, "I think I see what you're saying." I had seen my mother with several self-help books recently, and I knew it was a struggle for her to practice these bits of positive thinking. "What I'm hearing from you is that Angela is being taken advantage of. You're suggesting that Angela keeps giving people chance after chance and the benefit of every doubt there may be, and they all just keep slapping her down, poor thing."

"Yes," he said. "That's *exactly* what I'm saying."

Now she was watching as he knelt there in his clean white shirt and planted bulb after bulb. Mrs. Poole was tapping a cigarette on the edge of the table, still declaring her distaste for the flowers. "I *love* canna lilies," my mother finally said, a fierce expression on her face as she turned in her chair. "There's nothing on this earth that I love more than a big bed of bright red canna lilies."

"Well, I never knew you felt so strongly." Mrs. Poole lit her cigarette and breathed in, one eye twitching slightly, a tick she'd recently acquired to replace the memory she was beginning to lose. "Canna lilies, caladiums, it's nothing to get miffed over."

"And I *hate* caladiums," my mother said, folding the letter over in her hand. "I had some once and I *hated* the way I had to dig them up and store them year after year after year."

"Well, why did you replant them?" Mrs. Poole was asking. "There's no reason to get hostile, to berate a poor little plant just for growing when you're the one who planted it. You'll have to dig up those cannas just the same way."

"It's not always that easy," my mother said. "You can't always just dig up what bothers you. You dig it up here and it jumps up over there, doubling and tripling and spreading like a virus."

"Are we talking about the same thing, Cleva?" Mrs. Poole crushed out her cigarette and lit another. She had begun smoking only half of her cigarettes, convinced that the tar and bad stuff were in the second half. "I thought we were talking about canna lilies and caladiums."

My mother turned away from the window and looked at Mrs. Poole, studied her a full long minute before slipping Angela's letter under a magazine and saying, "I thought we were talking about kudzu and bamboo and wisteria and things that are hard to control, things that take over if you let them and choke everything in sight."

"Really?" Mrs. Poole sat forward, elbows on the table as she narrowed her eyes. "I think one of us got way off track."

Twenty-three

Much to everyone's relief, Misty made majorette try-outs that spring, and I spent many hours count-ing off marches as she practiced her routines. It seemed she had grown half a foot in the past year and now was much thinner, her legs long and shapely as she kicked and marched. Her hair was long and Sally Jean had taught her how to French-braid it; they had spent one evening streaking it with Sun-In, just as Angela had recommended almost two years be-fore. "Who would have thought?" she asked me so many times, a dreamy look on her face. "You with a steady boyfriend and me a majorette."

Now we were in my kitchen, with Misty stripped down to her underwear as I helped take her measurements so she could order her uniforms. "You should be ashamed to undress here in broad daylight," Mrs. Poole said, and shook her head. Mrs. Poole had begun spending more and more time at our house, and it was starting to get on my mother's nerves. "Why doesn't that step-mother of yours measure you?"

"Sally Jean has a job," Misty said, and turned to the side to thrust her chest toward Mrs. Poole. "Or she'd be glad to help me." Mrs. Poole settled back in her chair, one of my mother's prize needlepoint pillows crushed behind her back. Every day when Mrs. Poole left, my mother returned the pillow to the sun-porch and rearranged them all so that this particular one, most of it petit point which took my mother years to do, carefully hidden; then Mrs. Poole came back the next day and rooted through until she found it and carried it into the kitchen.

"Mrs. Burns," Misty said while I was measuring her hips, her voice very grown up and serious. "What do you think happens to somebody's body when he dies?"

"Oh my." Mama closed the cookbook she had been studying, voice stammering as she avoided any mention of Mo. "Well, let's see . . ."

"Ashes to ashes and dust to dust," Mrs. Poole said, and thumped her own ashes into the ashtray. I came very close to finishing our high school cheer, "Hate to beat you but we must, we must," but didn't when I saw how very serious Misty was.

"Well, these Mormon boys stopped by yesterday and I let them in," Misty continued.

"Hush," Mrs. Poole said and inhaled. "You had boys in while Sally Jean was at work?"

"Not *boys*," Misty said, and I made her take her hands from her waist so I could measure. "Mormons." She held her arms out so I could measure them. "We were talking and seeing what we agreed about and what we didn't and they said that they do not drink coffee, tea or soda or alcohol, or smoke, or do anything bad for them because they'll get their bodies back in the afterlife and want them to be in good shape."

"Well, I'd like to know if they're allowed to wear a color other than orange." Mrs. Poole ran her finger between the spokes of the Windsor chair beside her and then inspected to see if there was dust. "Any time I've ever seen them trying to sell a carnation in the Clemmonsville Mall, they're all covered in orange."

"They're not the Mormons," Misty said, sighed. "Anyway, if that's true then maybe it *is* true that the good die young, you know. They die young so that they have that good body for eternity."

"Doesn't sound very fair." I jerked her back around so I could recheck the measurements once more, hoping that the subject would change.

"And what about people who burn?" Misty asked, and everyone instinctively stared out at the blackened field; the kudzu was starting to reappear in sparse bits of green, starting to climb and twist around the cinderblock rubble. The Huckses' concrete clothesline posts still stood, a sagging line connecting the two.

"Well, Cleva feels that people go to an in-between place and wait, don't you, Cleva?" Mrs. Poole leaned forward and Mama just shook her head. "I thought you grew up a Catholic there in Boston, which has always puzzled me, seeing as how you have only one child."

"Maybe it takes two Catholics," I said, in an attempt to lighten the mood, and I realized I sounded amazingly like my father. Misty and I had long ago figured the Catholic angle when trying to find proof that I was not *really* my mother's child. Misty had told me that no *real* Catholic who *could* have children would stop with one; it's like Lay's potato chips, she had said and fallen out laughing on Mo's old purple bedspread.

"And the Mormons think there are lots of different parts of heaven, like neighborhoods," Misty was saying. "You know, like maybe our neighborhood would be for pretty good people and the new neighborhood over near E. A. Poe would be for *better* people and so on."

"This *used* to be the best," Mrs. Poole said. "And I bet if a vote was taken it still would be."

"Kind of defeats the idea of heaven, doesn't it?" I asked, immediately sorry since it was Mrs. Poole who wanted to latch right on to the discussion, saying it all depended on *whose* idea of heaven I meant.

Misty suggested that we take a little break, said she was tired of standing, her voice carrying over Mrs. Poole's as she continued giving reasons why our neighborhood was superior both on earth and in heaven. Misty went to our refrigerator and opened the door. "Maybe I misunderstood what the Mormons meant," Misty said. "That's what it *sounded* like to me, okay?" She reached in. *This*," she held out a bottle of Coke, "this is why I'm not a Mormon."

"So what are you?" Mrs. Poole asked, inching forward on her chair.

I watched Misty turn her head from side to side as if in thought before walking right up to Mrs. Poole. I was expecting her to use Jimmy Stewart's line from *Shenandoah* when he was asked if the boy was a Yankee or a Reb, and just give her last name, but instead she said, "I'm a majorette," and then she did a little turn, an imaginary baton doing a figure eight in front of her.

Tony Graves had asked Misty for a date just the Friday night before, and she told him that she was washing her hair, that she hated the thought that his breath could be trapped there in her telephone wire and please not to call again. She had also turned down Dean's old friend, Ronald, the one she had loved so madly the night Buddy was born. If R. W. Quincy's name ever surfaced, she made a horrible face as if on the verge of gagging. "Can you even believe I ever thought about liking such a loser?" she had asked. "I mean, isn't it incredible how much can *change* in just a few months, or in a few years really?" She had her eye on a friend of Dean's, a boy who would graduate that spring with Dean and the rest of the Class of 1974; he was going to Davidson in the fall. She had already been invited to a graduation party, and Sally Jean had promised that she could get any dress she wanted.

"I do not believe," Mrs. Poole was saying, voice loud and angry, "that I will have to spend forever with this arthritis the way that it's begun to take over my knees. Do you, Cleva?" Mama was at the window staring out over the yard. My father had become obsessed with gardening, more so than she'd ever been, and she monitored the time he spent out there, especially now that the days were dry and hot; the remainder of spring and the long summer stretched ahead of us like the Sahara. "I cannot believe that I will be stuck with this body for all of eternity and Mr. Bo Poole will have himself a nice fifty-four-year-old body. I do not believe that drug addicts who scream and holler and call it singing and kill themselves with too much medication in their veins can have a twenty-year-old body, and that I'm given this." I had never seen Mrs. Poole so upset, her face fire red, that one eye twitching.

My mother's voice was calm as she turned from the window. "We don't know what waits for us," she said, and paused. "I believe that *that* is a good thing."

"Well, I know what I *think*." Mrs. Poole's bottom lip trembled, and she looked away until she could toughen up.

"And no one can take that away from you, Theresa," my mother said, while Misty and I stared in amazement at the weak side of Theresa Poole.

"Whoever would've thought we'd *really* get there, Katie?" Misty asked me again late that afternoon as we sat on the front steps, the trees of the Samuel T. Saxon schoolyard within view. The main part of the school building was still standing. "You going with Merle Hucks and me a full-fledged majorette. I wish," she paused and I knew in that second what she was thinking, *I wish my mother could see us now*, "I wish that *we* could be like this forever. These youthful bodies. I wish—" She turned towards me as I anticipated the familiar, the wish that Mo was watching us, Mo looking just as she had looked the night of the fireworks, but then she elbowed me and laughed. "I wish Mrs. Poole would move. I wish she would have to spend eternity in a split-level." We laughed, still marvelling at Mrs. Poole and the way the whole neighborhood was talking about how she was beginning to *fail*.

There was a warm breeze, causing the leafy branches of the tall oak tree in Whispering Pines to move back and forth against the clear blue sky. It had been a long time since Misty and I had sat on that low-hanging limb, and I was about to suggest that we walk over when Sally Jean pulled up from work and asked Misty if she still wanted to go shopping for a new bathing suit. Mr. Rhodes had said that he'd never seen anything like it, that Misty and Sally Jean would buy *anything* if it was on a sale table. "You are two peas in a pod," he had said, and smiled proudly at the two of them with their arms full of shopping bags. "I don't buy anything that doesn't pass mustard," Sally Jean said. Now, Misty was off and running across Wilkins Road, greeting Sally Jean with a peck on the cheek as the two of them walked across the thick green carpet of grass to the front door. "See you later," Misty called to me, Sally Jean joining her with a wave. "I'm going to buy the green and purple Hang-Ten suit we saw in *Glamour*. What do you think?" I nodded, turning back to the tree and its tip-top branches; it had been there for hundreds of years.

E. A. Poe High was more of a greenhouse than my father could have ever hoped to construct, and all during the month of April when the air-conditioning system was broken and the heat was unbearable, we got to leave at noon. Willow Pond was not far from the old Samuel T. Saxon Building, and on many afternoons, after parting ways with Misty, who had majorette practice, that's where Merle and I walked; we usually carried a bag of stale bread or some popcorn to feed the ducks. My father had taken me there a lot when I was growing up, but we had stopped going after one particular trip when we witnessed a duck attack and kill a sea gull who was going after the same piece of bread. The scene kept him awake for nights after, and he still referred to the day as the Great Gull Massacre, refusing to take me back to the pond for that reason. "This from the man so interested in death and murder," my mother had said, gathering up some bread crumbs and bringing me herself.

Now it seemed that whole part of town was in a sad slow decline, as if it were the remains of a war zone, old homes stripped for their flooring or hoisted up and moved across town, leaving big empty spaces like craters. For years it had been my mother and Mrs. Poole's biggest fear, and now with the steady stripping away of Samuel T. Saxon the end seemed inevitably close. As much as they had complained about the row of little pastel houses where Merle had lived, the fire had left the property up for bidding, and very soon there was going to be an Exxon Station; *Close enough to hear folks drive over that bell, I bet*, Mrs. Poole had said countless times. My mother was already talking about a nice tall fence; my father, pencil in hand, was eager to draw a plan of her desires.

Merle's family was still living in the Econo Lodge, which he said made the high school feel cool and comfortable. His father had already started working in Clemmonsville, and as soon as he found a place to live and school got out, they'd be moving. "I'm gonna try to stay here, though," Merle said, and squeezed my hand. "I've got good reasons to *stay* here." He spoke the word as if there were serious doubts about his destination. "Of course, I've never been anywhere else, never been where people don't say, 'Oh yeah, you're a Hucks.' "

The last day that Merle and I walked to Willow Pond was in late May, summer vacation only two weeks away, so close we could all feel it, an energy that pulsed through the sterile halls of E. A. Poe. It was a Friday and neither of us carried books; we got a ride with Misty, who now had her driver's license and was forever borrowing Sally Jean's Toyota. She dropped us off in front of the stone soldier, and then we walked along the bumpy sidewalk, sometimes holding hands, always trying to stay in the shade of the huge oaks and elms growing there.

We stopped in front of Samuel T. Saxon; the main part of the building with the office and auditorium was all that remained. I could see the roof of my house in the distance, the top of the gates to Whispering Pines. I hesitated when Merle asked me to go in with him, partly because my parents had already told me a zillion times not to hang around there, but more so because there was a big NO TRESPASSING sign on the door. Still, I was easily persuaded that day, the sky a cloudless bright blue. "We shouldn't be doing this, you know," I whispered, while he looked around and then pulled open the big heavy door, just far enough for us to squat and slip under the heavy black chain.

"Forgive us our trespasses," he said, then laughed, and I suddenly thought of him gripping my wrists, begging my secrecy that day in Whispering Pines. The ancient flooring creaked with every step we took, and it was eerie to look in the old office, with the wavy pane of glass still in the door, and see it bare, a clutter of empty boxes stacked in one corner. "I sat in there often enough didn't I?"

"And you should have." I leaned in close. "Anybody who pees on the radiator."

"Never." He shook his head and then raked his fingers back through his straight hair, streaks of it already sun-bleached. "R. W. did it, but I never did." He said R. Double U just like the teachers had always tried to make us do. He laughed at first and then stopped almost suddenly. "Old Frankincense didn't turn out too good, or *well*, or whatever, did he?" I shook my head, wondering who corrected his English often enough that he had formed the habit of catching his own mistakes. "It's hard to believe that *that* R. W. who was my friend for so many years is the same R. W. who was in Dexter's club." He shook his head as if to rid the bad thoughts. Misty had spotted R. W. working at a gas station when Sally Jean had taken her way out in the country to practice driving.

"Yeah." I was uncomfortable in the school, jumped with every sound, but Merle just leaned back against the wall, traced his finger where someone had carved "B.G. loves J.M." in the door facing, and it seemed so amazing to me that there had been that moment when some junior high student took a pocket knife or nail file and formed those letters, probably jumping with every sound for fear of being caught, and yet it was so *important*, urgently so, that those initials be put there.

"What did you think of me when we were in school here?" he asked. "You know, like before we met in the cemetery that day, what did you think?"

"I don't know." I turned and peeked into the drafty old auditorium, those faded moss green velvet drapes still hanging there.

"Were you scared of me?" He was still leaning, rolling his head from side to side against the white plaster wall that had had to be washed down or painted every semester because of the pencil marks and names that ended up there. E. A. Poe had smooth cinderblock walls that were hard to write on.

"I guess," I said. "Maybe a little."

"Why?" He was wearing an emerald green shirt, with a tiny hole where it looked like there *had* been a logo that he or someone before him had ripped away. His eyes looked just as green as the shirt.

"I don't know," I said. His quizzing was making me uncomfortable; usually we just talked about school, or still easier, we just talked about how much we really liked each other.

"Well, at least you stopped hiding under your house when I walked by." He smiled and stepped closer, opening the door to the auditorium and propping it with a brick. The thick musty air escaped like from a tomb. "Do you remember that? And your dad came out there on the porch?"

"Yeah, I remember. I was afraid you were going to get my cat."

"And stuff a firecracker up him?" He shook his head, squeaked the toe of his sneaker along the old scuffed-up floor. "The bottom line is that you were scared of me because I was a Hucks." He pulled on my arm, gently twisted. "Right?"

"Yes." I looked at the wavy glass of the office door and further out the front window where the principal used to stand and watch us come up the big stone steps. The trees were thick and green; a breeze was blowing, and shadows swept like brooms across the dusty yellow ground. Merle cupped his hands and lit a cigarette, then lifted his eyebrows, motioned for me to enter the auditorium, and then he followed, hand on my elbow as if ushering me to my seat. The old hard wooden seats looked like a sea of initials, carved, Magic-Markered, chalked; now after all those years, these attempts of immortality would be ripped away and discarded.

"Now, what did happen to Cathy and John?" Merle asked, as if reading my mind, and pointed up to the high ceiling, where in spray-painted letters the names stood as if reigning over the room. "And better, how did they get up there?" He ran up the little side steps of the stage and stepped into the slat of sunlight that fell through the large windows. He stood there and turned around, his Levi's worn soft and pale blue, shirt tail hanging long in the back. It was cool in the old building, the heat rising way above us. "And now, I'd like to introduce Lily and the Holidays singing 'I'm Gonna Make You Love Me.' " He laughed loud, voice echoing in the empty room.

"Why did I ever let Misty talk me into that?" I asked, cringing at the thought of my standing up there and screeching out the background sounds.

"I thought it was good," he said. "Really." He walked and sat on the edge of the stage. "So this is what it looks like," he said. "This is what you saw from the stage."

"Where were you sitting?" I asked, and watched him push off with one hand and land with a thud. He kept walking up row by row, stopping and turning, examining the back of the chairs along the way. I followed about three feet behind him, still glancing out the windows for fear of someone finding us there.

"Here." He sat in the seat and ran his finger up and down the wooden handle of the arm, his own initials penciled there.

Backstage was a jumble of old ropes and boxes and in the midst of them all was a sleeping bag and bed pillow, a little Sterno stove and a paper bag with various cans. "Somebody's been living here," I whispered, ready to bolt from the dark damp building and out into the fresh air and sunlight.

"You sound like Goldilocks," he whispered, and tried to kiss me, but I pulled away, expecting someone to stumble in any second.

"Really, let's leave. Let's go to the pond."

"These are my things," he finally said. "I promise." He held up his hand. "I've stayed here a few nights." It gave me a chill to think of sleeping in this place.

"But why?" I felt behind me and eased down in the straight-back chair there. Merle had called me every single night at nine on the dot, and I had pictured him in the motel room, with two double beds and a bath and a table where you could eat, maybe even an extra little room like my parents and I had when we visited Boston. "And how did you call me?"

"That motel room is about the size of a closet and my mother is just so—" He paused. "She just goes over the same thing again and again, Dexter and what happened, my oldest brother and what happened, and then she looks at me like she's waiting for me to pull out a gun and shoot her or something." He stopped, breathed deeply. "I call you from Syke's Grocery," he said. "Pay phone. I spent one night over at the Landell's." I imagined him there, Maralee Landell's arm around his shoulder just as it had been that day in Mrs. Poole's kitchen when he talked about his mother being sick. He moved some boxes around and then sat down on the sleeping bag, stretched his legs out, bare ankles already tan.

"Does your mother know where you stay?" I asked, moving slowly from the chair onto the floor beside him, my arm pressing his.

"Look. It's not the same as you or Misty spending the night out, you know?" He laughed and began pulling cans from the bag, then absentmindedly placed them all back. "Do you know what my old man asked me?" The look on his face was the one I *had* been afraid of all those years, the one he gave the teachers or principal or Todd Bridger or anyone else who threatened him. I shook my head, leaned away as he jerked his arm away from mine and patted his chest. "The son of a bitch asked me if I killed Dexter." He patted his chest harder, voice louder. "Me, his son. Did I kill my brother?" He pulled the cans out again and then balled up the paper bag, threw it over some boxes, where it landed with a rustle. "I said, 'Who the hell are you, Adam? And she's Eve.'" He laughed sarcastically, leaned to the side and put his head against one of the boxes. "My mother doesn't ever say a word, not a solitary word other than to tell the stories over and over like a broken record. He says jump and she says how high, and Maybelline needs to be outside with other children instead of clinging to her skirts. I said, 'I'm taking Maybelline to the carnival,' and that's when Mama finally said something. Right. The mute stands up and says, 'I'm sorry, but Maybelline can't go with you.' That's all; she says 'can't' like it rhymes with paint, CAINT or Cain. She said, 'It's happened, a brother killing a brother, and

I've heard you fighting late at night. I've heard it.' And all the while Maybelline is standing there hugging that damned doll that Mrs. Poole dug up from some old give-away pile, and looking at me like I'm a monster, like I *had* killed Dexter."

He slumped onto the sleeping bag, hands locked behind his head, veins in his wrist bulging with the tension and tightness of his hands. I put my hand on his leg, but he jumped when I touched him. "I told my old man, I said, 'Well, it's easier this way, ain't, isn't it? Run me off so you don't have to be responsible.' And he got right in my face and told me that he'd heard me tell Dexter that he wasn't fit to live." His voice dropped off, very quiet as he drew in a deep breath, eyes closed. "And I did say that to Dexter. On Christmas Day, I told him that. My old man said, 'Maybe now you and that little blond whore can do as you please.'" He shook his head. "When Perry was standing there crying over Dexter, he asked her what did she care, there were plenty of guys who'd have her."

I thought of Perry then, that night, how ready she was to try and overlook what had happened to her just to hold on to Dexter and all the worthless hopes he was handing to her, how desperate she must have felt both then and the night of the fire when she saw that he was gone, her pipe dream of a future screeching to a halt. She had been absent much of the spring, and the days she was in school, she left class early, either sitting in the glassed room where the guidance counselor had his desk, or standing out on the curb until someone picked her up.

"It's the classic case of abuse," my mother had said not long before when Angela appeared at our door just to say hello, just to tell us how *wonderful* things were now that Greg had a job he liked and didn't feel so down on himself. She had a bruise on her thigh that showed briefly as she crossed her leg, tucked her skirt under. "I think it's a form of self-punishment," my mother continued. Psychology books from the local community college were stacked under her bedside table. "She could feel guilty just for being born."

"I told Perry on Christmas Day," Merle was saying. "I told her that Dexter was no good." I reached my hand to his face and that time he didn't jump, just pulled me close and then closer, pulled me on top of him like a blanket and then held on, his breath damp on my face, arms squeezing my back. "You know," he whispered, "I really think I *could* have killed Dexter. I hated him so much. Sometimes I hate all of them just because they're who they are and because they'll be that way forever."

"You couldn't have killed Dexter." There was a rip in the dusty old drapes and I could see through it into the empty auditorium; my cheek was pressed against his chest, my own breath falling in rhythm with his heartbeat.

"But Dexter could've killed somebody," he said. "And so what keeps me from being that way? Why should I believe I'm so different."

"Because you are," I whispered, and then just lay there, silent like the building.

When we left, the sun was no longer streaming through the auditorium windows, and the room looked dingy and shabby. We walked along quietly; I was torn between feeling frightened by all that Merle had said, the glimpse I'd been given inside his life, and the feelings I had had while lying there on top of him on the old sleeping bag. I had felt then that I could stay just like that, that the warmth I felt at that moment and the belief that what I was feeling was right, was enough to make me want to move there with him, to share the raggedy sleeping bag and to cook canned food on the little snap-together grill. I could hear some unknown voice issuing my ultimatum: Either you leave Merle alone OR you give up everything you have and move behind the auditorium of Samuel T. Saxon School, come and go like a thief. *That* day my decision was final, solid. On *that* afternoon I was prepared to do anything he wanted me to do; I was prepared for him to ask me anything as we walked along. But instead we walked silently, a new sensation between us with every look exchanged. When we got within view of the the pond, we walked faster, both eager to talk and break the awkward silence. The pond wasn't very big and like the rest of the area was in a sad slow decline; there was trash dumped on the side nearest the highway, but the wild ducks were still there.

The day my father had taken me, there were several gulls, whining and begging, swooping aggressively for the food; we had sat there, tossing bread piece by piece into the water, the gulls circling and crying in that high-pitched scream. My father threw a piece to one of the ducks, a white one whose blue eyes looked wild as it strained to bend its neck to eat. It moved slowly to one side as if it were blind in one eye or had no balance. The gulls and mallards were swooping and dipping, grabbing up the pieces before the white duck could get its long clumsy neck bent in the right position. My father told me to stay there on the bank as he inched closer to the pond, holding his hand toward that one duck. His shoes sank in the muck as he leaned forward and threw some bread right in front of it, but the gulls still stole every piece. He tried placing some on a log so it wouldn't have to crane its neck. Then suddenly the duck turned, beak open, and clamped down on one of the gulls; there were shrill screams and feathers spewing as the duck shook its stiff neck from side to side. Before I could get my legs moving, I heard myself screaming for it to stop, and then I backed up the hill, feet slipping as I grabbed the tall grass and pulled myself up, all the while begging my father to make them stop, the screams so shrill I felt I needed to cover my ears, and though I didn't *want* to see, I felt compelled to look. My father stood there holding a brick, his hand raised and moving forward as if to let go, and then again, and again, unable to let go, as the other birds fled from the scene, screams diminishing as the gull's neck went limp, as froth and feathers fell to the muddy bank, the duck's pale blue eyes still looking wild with hunger as it continued to shake its enemy, not yet aware that the enemy was dead.

"Sorry you saw that," my father said, then and many times after. "And I'm sorry I couldn't stop it all." He put his arm around me, put his other palm out to block my vision when I was tempted to look back.

"It was a bird," my mother said later, when neither my father nor I could eat the dinner she had just served. Later she repeated this to him when I was supposed to be asleep. "Fred," she said firmly. "Two birds. You saw two birds have a fight."

"But right now, somewhere, there is a person turning on another in that same crazy way," he said. "It was so frightening, Cleva. What could ever possess that kind of reaction?"

"I don't know, Fred," she said. "But I'm sure you'll put a whole lot of thought into it."

"Kate?" Merle's voice snapped me from my thoughts. Only a few mallards gathered for the bread, the male's head shimmering a brilliant emerald green. "What are you thinking about?"

"Your brother." I shrugged. "What happened to him." We sat there tossing the bread, his arm draped over my shoulder. When the bag was empty, I dumped the crumbs on the bank, and we walked back the same way we'd come; both of us carried our shoes, the old cracked sidewalks warm beneath our feet. He talked about everything *except* Dexter as we walked along. He talked about how he thought he could get his same job at the warehouse again, how the Landells had invited him to stay with them if he ever wanted. "You know, they don't have any children," he said, and bent to pick up a flat smooth rock. "There are lots of things I can do," he continued, his words designed to convince himself as well as me.

"We're home," I said when we got to Samuel T. Saxon and the

huge elm tree where the kids used to stand during lunch to be out of the sun. I looked behind me where the old wing of classrooms had been—the girls' bathroom where Misty and Lily had practiced their songs and where Perry had sat in the huge window —but it was only a pile of red brick and silver pipes.

"Looks like somebody had a war and forgot to tell us." He picked up part of a brick and hurled it over to a big pile of concrete and rusty cables. The few upstairs windows left in the main building were broken, neat jagged-edged holes where stones had sailed.

"Yeah." It was an incredible thought that as suddenly as anger and hunger could make an animal kill, as suddenly as an engine could fail or brakes go bad, a bomb could be dropped and leave nothing but a big mushroom cloud and a crater filled with rubble. I imagined a person stepping outside and catching a leaflet in the wind, a leaflet that said, *Your city will be obliterated unless your government surrenders*, and that night at dinner that person might have said, "How can I do anything about it? Who am I to tell the government what to do?"; and maybe he didn't believe it, or maybe he did, maybe he awoke in a cold sweat as he looked from his window and waited helplessly for obliteration to come. Maybe he lived in Japan, and maybe he sat with his child on his lap, wife there beside him, and waited, told them that he *wanted* to make it stop but he *couldn't*; he had no power. Everywhere, people were hidden and helpless and begging for it all to stop. *Dearest, Darling Kitty.*

"Kitty," he called in a singsong way, swinging my hand back and forth, telling me that if I didn't talk to him he would do the old famous cat call that had made me hide in bushes and under houses. "So, do you want to come into my home?" he asked, pulled my hand away from my cheek and held it as we walked across the dusty schoolyard. "You don't have to. I mean, I don't expect anything, you know, if that's what's got you so quiet." I focused on his features, the green eyes and pale hair, smooth skin and firm jaw, and in doing so was able to put everything else out of my mind. In the distance the sky was bright blue, shimmering in the afternoon light. I knew that I was going to follow him inside without even turning to see if a familiar car was passing or if someone we knew was walking past or spying from some window. I knew I was going to lie there with him on that sleeping bag and I was going to look through the slit in the drapes to that empty room, the windows there, beyond which the trees were lush and green. I was going to pretend that there was no day other than this one, no world beyond those trees; there was no future, no guarantee that I would turn sixteen, this was it.

Twenty-four

Much of my time that summer was spent swimming at the local pool with Misty, or sitting on my
front porch with Merle after he was through at
the warehouse. Several nights Merle and I walked to the movies,
both of us paying more attention to each other, our legs pressed
tightly together, my head on his shoulder as we sank down in
the cracked vinyl seats and enjoyed the cool darkness. Several
times my father offered his car to Merle so we could drive to
the movies; each time my mother stood there with an eyebrow
raised and breathed a sigh of relief when Merle shook his head.
His family had moved to a trailer park not far from Willow Pond
but his father said that as soon as Merle's mother could find work
in Clemmonsville they were moving; they'd probably move in
August. Merle still talked about staying, finding a place to live,
maybe with the Landells, but as the days passed there were more

and more doubts about his situation. "The worst that happens is I have to go with them," he told me one night as we sat on my steps. Across the street Sally Jean's yard was manicured to perfection. "It's not like we'd never see each other; it's just thirty miles from here."

Samuel T. Saxon was now completely stripped away, and Merle and I had stood to watch the huge bulldozer as it took over the old auditorium, the seats already uprooted and tossed aside. With the auditorium went our privacy, our chances to be completely alone, and we had to settle instead for late afternoons in Whispering Pines, his same old sleeping bag, which he now kept rolled up in the little shed, spread out under the low hanging branches, over pine needles thick on the ground. We would lie there, side by side, staring up through the trees, ready to jump at the slightest sound, a person on the path, my mother's voice calling my name from our porch. Some days we were reminded of Dexter and the night I spied from the tree; it was a thought that could turn our most innocent and inexperienced feelings into something ugly.

Misty had majorette practice every weekday morning in July, and rather than spend those hours at home, I decided to take my mother's advice and enroll in a typing course in summer school. The air-conditioning of E. A. Poe was finally fixed, and with the limited number of bodies present, I sometimes had to take a sweater in with me; Misty always laughed at my long jeans and long sleeves as she drove us to the high school in the ninety-degree heat. I typed things like *Now is the time for all good men to come to the aid of their country*, pausing occasionally to touch the keys that spelled Merle's name, while Misty marched up and down the football field, head thrown back to the full blinding sun, hips moving in rhythm to the band's latest accomplishment, "Bad, Bad, Leroy Brown."

It was late July, a Wednesday morning, when I was called

down to the office at E. A. Poe. It was not uncommon for me
to find Misty waiting there, her hair slicked back into a ponytail,
nose coated in zinc oxide as she swung her baton back and forth,
but that day I stepped from the stairwell to see the principal
standing there with Sally Jean, who was wearing her yard-work
clothes, purse looped over her freckled arm, eyes red and anxious as she searched the hallway. When she saw me, she lifted
her hand nervously and then began the slow walk towards me. It
was not hard to look into her eyes and figure out that something
very bad had happened, and I think I began feeling numb before
she ever even opened her mouth. She ushered me toward the big
front double doors. The heat hit us like a ton of bricks, like it had
hit my dad just an hour earlier as he stood on a ladder and, with
an electrical manual in one hand, tried to figure out how to hook
up a light and ceiling fan in my mother's greenhouse.

"Your mama told him he needed to rest after all that going up
and down the ladder," Sally Jean said, the air and radio coming
on full blast as soon as she cranked Mr. Rhodes's car, Ray Stevens
singing "The Streak." She reached quickly and turned it off. I
noticed that Misty was already in her car and following us, Sally
Jean glancing in the rearview mirror, and I knew that Sally Jean
had gone to Misty first with the news. "I'm so sorry, honey," she
said, and I think I could have handled those words from anyone
else on earth, but Sally Jean was so very honestly sincere that it
almost hurt me to look at her. "The rescue squad was right there,
less than five minutes." Her voice shook. "But they couldn't do
anything." I turned towards the window, the trees off to the side
a blur, as she patted my knee, the denim burning hot against my
skin. She kept her hand there, squeezing, those pale thin fingers
twitching with uncertainty.

Everything seemed in slow motion; we passed the little road-
side carnival that had been set up in a vacant lot for several
weeks, and it all looked so strange to me, the strung blinking

bulbs and two Ferris wheels, one big enough to let you view the whole high school in the distance, the other the kind with the little wire cages for children. There were bumper cars and a fun house like what I had expected and wanted from Ferris Beach all those years ago. Now the lights and the rides and the cotton-candy stand looked so garish, so tawdry. I could see tank-topped men swilling from cans wrapped in brown paper, their tattooed arms pushing levers.

Merle and I had been there just the week before, hugging and kissing in front of the crazy mirrors that made me short and fat like I had never been. We did everything we could to avoid discussing the end of the summer and his parents' plans to move. We threw softballs at bowling pins we were sure were glued to the table, and we tossed rings at crates filled with Coca-Colas, beanbags through the mouths of wooden cut-out figures, each time falling just shy of what it took to win a big stuffed panda, leaving instead with plastic beads and key chains shaped like little sneakers, or, my favorite, the old fashioned monkey on a stick like my father had once won for me. We bought paper cones of cotton candy, air-whipped pink sticky strands, and then we wandered over to the wild animal trailer where, much to our disgust, there was an old mangy bobcat who panted in the heat and didn't even go near his fly-covered food dish. There was a fox, no bigger than a pomeranian, pacing his glass box, nuzzling the corners each time in hopes of an escape, and there was one ape who sat in a cage not much taller than he was, his hand up to his forehead, fingers rubbing his eyes as if he had a headache. "Hey, you," Merle had said, and tapped on the glass; the ape looked up with large sad eyes, briefly, and then put his hand back as it had been, the nails of his fingers like those of a man, lines in the skin of his palm. The ape's big toe, opposable like a thumb, gripped the skin of a banana that had been dropped to him from a hole in the top of the cage.

• • •

Evolution, my dad had said, and laughed, the night he talked about wisdom teeth and beauty marks. I thought instantly, before my brain had time to connect as I sat beside Sally Jean, that I would run home and ask him what he thought of opposable toes; I could imagine the look on his face, his excitement that I had come to him with such a question, as he reared back in his ink-stained chair and lit a cigarette.

"This gives me the creeps," Merle had said, and turned away from the cage. "There's just something not right about looking at him." He took my hand and I followed him back out into the bright sunlight; he didn't even realize that the same thing he said could have easily applied to me the night I climbed the tree, curiosity leading me to look, the same curiosity that made people slow down and look at a wreck on the highway, that made photographers catch that single moment of despair, a bullet entering, a bullet exiting, a man suspended from electrical wires. "The stuff the Evening News is made of," my father had once said as he turned off the set, the piles of Vietnamese bodies fading from view.

Merle had said it was like the "Twilight Zone" episode where the man opens the drapes of his new home, which the people of the planet where he crashed have built for him, only to see people lined up and looking in. He runs to the door and it's fake; the windows have bars, and out front is a sign saying that he is in his natural habitat. It was all in the eyes, just as Mrs. Landell had said that time, but I could not imagine that look in my father's eyes; I could not imagine that his brain would suddenly stop, his heart, instantly like pulling a plug.

"Here we are, sweetheart." Again Sally Jean's voice made me ache. His car was in the driveway, window rolled down from

morning, when he had gone to buy *The New York Times*; he was
so excited that he was finally able to *buy* the paper in Fulton,
instead of having to wait for the Sunday edition that arrived a
week later in the mail. Mrs. Poole was holding our front door
open for Mrs. Edith Turner, who already had a dish of something
or another in her hand. Misty followed me in, her hand light on
my arm, her mouth trembling when she tried to say something
to me.

It was several hours and casseroles and phone calls later when
I asked my mother if anyone had called Angela, and she looked
up as if in a trance and shook her head no. Merle was over there
then; he was wearing a clean navy T-shirt, his hair still damp
from showering. He had brought a big pink geranium in a clay
pot, and though Mrs. Poole tried to take it from him, as did
Mrs. Edith Turner, the two of them vying for control of the front
door, he walked across the hall and into the living room and held
it out to my mother.

"Thank you," she said. "It's very pretty." And she just sat
there holding it until Edith Turner came and got it and took it
to the kitchen, where she was in charge of *arranging* all of the
arrangements.

"It's like a curse," Mrs. Poole was whispering to another neighbor. "The worst things have happened in this neighborhood—
adultery, murder, fire, and now this." She shook her head and
stared blankly at the floor, bent forward to pick up a piece of
lint. "It all started with integration, you know when we began
mixing with coloreds."

"Oh, now, really." Mrs. Landell had come in with her husband,
a pie pan in her hands. "You better cut that talk out, Theresa, or
we'll resign."

"Well, I don't mean *you* two," Mrs. Poole said, and laughed.
reached out to pat Maralee Landell's arm. "Why, I never think
of *you* as being colored."

I went into the hallway and looked in the front of the tele

phone directory where my father had penciled Angela's number, her name written in fancy curlicue letters he had doodled while standing in that very spot. Merle followed me, his face right next to mine as the distant phone rang and rang. Misty was in the foyer, her hand on Sally Jean's arm as she took in the all-too-familiar scene, neighbors gathered for a purpose but all avoiding the topic.

My father had picked out the headstone he wanted way back when he was so interested in epitaphs. A friend of his, Mr. Seymore Crane, made them and said he'd give him a good discount. The time the two of us had walked around Whispering Pines, he had apparently begun getting his own ideas of what he wanted and drawing them on paper as he always did. I had gone with him several years before to pick out his stone; I sat on a big cool slab of granite while he went in Mr. Crane's office to describe what he wanted. He had tried countless times to tell my mother about it and about how he had gotten a wonderful big corner lot out at the new cemetery; he said it was "within spitting distance of the statue of Jesus," but she did not want to hear it. Something about putting the words *spit* and *Jesus* into the same sentence made her resist still further. She had told him that she didn't want to discuss such, and the words *monument* and *grave* were never mentioned again until the morning after he died, when we went to the granite place to see the creation and to make arrangements for it to be carried to the cemetery. My father had been planning his own funeral for years, and though neither of us wanted to hear his plans, we both knew where he kept his envelope with all the details. It was in the top drawer of his desk, and along with the information about his tombstone, was the request that he have the song "His Eye Is on the Sparrow" and that this song was to be sung by Ethel Waters and no one else—he had it on a record—and if time permitted then by all means Bessie Smith's

"Graveyard Dream Blues" was to be played. Mama just shook her head from side to side and sighed.

"Okay, Seymore," she said when we drove out to see the monument. "I guess it's time for me to see this stone and talk about getting it moved." Seymore just shook his head like he might cry. I was already crying, and Mama started all over again when Seymore took us to the back and uncovered his piece of work. It was shaped like a great big boat with waves lapping at the front and a dove sitting up on the mast with something in its mouth, an olive branch, we presumed, like God's promise to Noah, but Seymore said no, he believed Mr. Fred meant for it to be a flag of some sort but it was hard to chisel it upright that way; arthritis often had his right arm aching if he held it up for too long.

On the base of the stone it said, "Break, break, break, at the foot of thy crags, O Sea! But the tender grace of a day that is dead will never come back to me," except that Seymore had misspelled and put *grave* instead of *grace* and *dad* instead of *day*.

"Just what is this supposed to mean?" Mama asked me, her eyes suddenly dry and wide.

"It's Tennyson," I told her, remembering from all the nights my father had sat and quoted poems aloud, over and over until I could guess who had written them.

"And how about this other?" she asked, and waved her hand toward the body of the ship where it had, "Alfred Tennyson Burns, a good husband and a good father, a good provider and a reasonable Christian, a mediocre singer, a good man with a love for nature and literature and an excellent mathematician who never did a damn thing with it—Born to Curtis Junior Burns and Mary Ray Burns in the town of Clayboro, county of Thompson, state of South Carolina on January 4, 1917, and went with light head and heavy heart to meet his maker on July 24, 1974."

"I just now finished the date," Seymore said, and shook his head. He looked sad but also was fishing for compliments on his work, so I told him how realistic the waves were as they hit against the boat.

"Break, break, break," he said and ran his dirty palm over the stone. "That's what the waves do, caught in the act of breaking."

"Why didn't he write a book?" my mother asked, and I could tell she was not far from breaking herself. Her eyes were now fixed on *her* side of the ship, the narrowed upward slant of the bow, where it said "Cleva O'Conner Burns, wife of Afred Tennyson Burns, May 11, 1924," and then there were some blanks and Seymore had already filled in the "19" on her death. Seymore saw her looking and explained that he had done the same thing on my father's, had it all measured out in advance so that when the time came he could fill it in at a moment's notice.

"And what if I decide to hang on until the year 2000?" she asked, with a look of indignation that caused Seymore to shuffle and stammer.

"Golly, now," he finally said. "I should've known better. Fred sure would've known better with his head for numbers." Seymore ran his fingers over the "19," forehead furrowed, mouth screwed to one side. I knew he was trying to figure out how he would turn that "19" into a "20" if he had to. "That's what happens when you try to put the cart ahead of the horse." He pulled a bandanna from his back pocket and wiped it over his face, blew his nose, shook his head from side to side. "It'll be hard, but I suspect I can make it work if need be." He looked at Mama and smiled. "And I won't charge you at all," he added, assuming that *he* would certainly be around for the turn of the century.

"It's obvious he *wasn't* thinking much of me," she said, waving her arm at her side of the ship. She started crying again after making Seymore *promise, vow, declare, and swear on the Bible* that he would not have that *monstrosity* delivered until after the funeral.

Seymore looked hurt but agreed before she could start explaining to him again why she did not like the monument, did not want the monument, but since it was in Fred's will she had no choice about it, at least for the time being, that she hoped it fell off the truck on the way to the cemetery. She was still mumbling all this when we were walking away, and I happened to turn back and see the other side of the ship: *Cleva, dear Cleva, mere words cannot express*. She rushed back to rub her finger up and over every letter of her name and then knelt there, face pressed against the stone, her neat cream-colored pumps and matching skirt covered in yellow dust. "Fred always said he'd give me the rest of the poem to go on that side but . . ." Mr. Crane stood there helplessly, raised his hands and shrugged as if to ask what he could do. I went and stood beside her, waited until she pulled herself up and dusted the front of her skirt.

I had my temporary permit—my birthday was only a little more than a week away—and was shocked when she handed me the key and said that I *had* to drive. "Wife of Lord Alfred," she said as we were driving down Seymore's bumpy dirt road to the main street, and I couldn't tell if she was going to laugh or cry. " 'Mere words cannot express'—well, he is absolutely right about that; there aren't many women who would have tolerated a man like Fred Burns with all his crazy ways and doodling, doodling on everything from the refrigerator to the arms of his chair, year in and year out, thinking up old rhymes and murders and numbers and nonsense." She wiped back the wisps of hair that hung around her face, her mascara smudged under her eyes. "It has not been the easiest life, I'll tell you that." Her eyebrows were raised like stiff circumflexes as she waited for my answer, my nod. "But, *goddamnit*," she screamed suddenly, beat her fists on the dash. I was so shocked that I almost ran a stoplight, causing the driver of the car crossing in front of us to slam on his brakes and blow his horn.

"Is that how they teach you to drive?" she screamed, shoulders shaking as she hunched forward, her forehead pressed into the dash. I sat until I got my own breath and then turned to her.

"Mama, Mama?" I put my hand on her back to try to get her to stop crying, to be that solid, never wavering person I was used to. "Please don't do this. Please?" I was crying then, too, the person behind us blowing for me to go. Mama rolled down her window and motioned for him to go around, then she straightened up in her seat, pulled a tissue from her purse. "Forgive me," she said. "I do not like to use the Lord's name that way. But I am going to miss that fool father of yours more than I can bear." She looked at me then, surprising me once again, her face grimacing as if she were going to burst into tears and then straightening. "I do hope Theresa Poole is not at our house when we get there," she said. "If she is I want you to tell her to go home. Fred was right when he said she was starting to get senile. Fred was just about always right, I guess." She sighed, shook her head. "Fred had one blind spot, that's all, that one blind spot." I knew she was referring to Angela, but I didn't say anything, just started driving again as she sat staring at her hands, at the wedding ring on the left hand and then, on the right one, the mother's ring. There I was, the only child, a chip of a stone harnessed in gold; that mother's ring had been all she'd talked about, all she wanted the Christmas when I was eight.

When I finally got Angela on the phone, she said that she would come as soon as possible, that her car had died and she'd have to find a way. She talked that fast way of hers—*What was Cleva thinking to make him work in such heat?* and *Why didn't you call me sooner?*—and then she paused, sobbed into the phone. "What am I going to do without Fred?" she kept asking me, as if I knew the answer, as if we weren't asking that same question.

She arrived at our house in a taxi the next day with just enough time to change her clothes before the funeral. She came in with

an overnight bag, a tissue held to her nose, sunglasses never removed, as she gave Mrs. Poole a brief nod and rushed upstairs
to the room where she had stayed before. Five minutes later, she
was back in the foyer with us, wearing a black jersey dress that hit
several inches above her knee and black leather platform sandals.
I saw Mrs. Edith Turner's mouth drop open, and my mother's
would have too if she had not been staring out into the yard
where the bright red canna lilies stood six feet tall, the large dark
leaves forming a thick hedge.

Angela sniffed and dabbed at her cheeks all the way to the
cemetery; my mother never even looked at her, just kept her
hands clasped neatly on top of her little black clutch as she stared
out the darkened glass of the funeral home limousine. "I've ridden in a limo before," Angela whispered to me. "But it was under
much happier circumstances." She drew in a sharp breath, voice
shaking, nostrils flaring as she tried to speak. "Fred was more
than an uncle to me." At this my mother turned slightly, gave
her a weak smile. "Fred was more like a brother. Or more like
a father." It was a sizzling day, not a cloud in the sky as people
stood there by the graveside and wiped the perspiration that
rolled down their faces and necks. Unlike Whispering Pines, the
new cemetery had been cleared in one big swoop and now they
were starting over with seedlings of trees here and there. It was
a barren stretch like a desert, straight gridlike marks dividing the
plots. I knew then why my father had wanted to add extra space
to Whispering Pines, to make a place for himself beneath the old
shade trees that leaned against our house.

Mr. Rhodes had brought an extra-long extension cord so he
could plug in a small record player in the outlet of the little office
of the cemetery. He had gone the day before to measure the
distance and now, Ethel Waters's voice, despite the bumps and
gristle of my father's old worn-out album, came through loud
and clear. *I sing because I'm happy. I sing because I'm free.* I glanced

in the distance and saw Merle leaning against a monument, awkward and stiff in a suit I'd never seen, maybe his father's, maybe
Mr. Landell's, a dark navy tie and jacket which he kept on in
spite of the heat. He held his hands in front of him, and of all
the people who were fanning and mopping their brows, Merle
never moved; it was as if he were frozen there. Overhead birds
were flying, and far away in the distance was a humming like
a lawn mower or an airplane. I felt my mother's hand on my
arm and realized that the song had ended, the prayer as well,
and now Mr. Rhodes was playing "Graveyard Dream Blues" just
as my father had requested. *Blues all around my head.* Mama was
pushing me forward, and I concentrated on everything except
the hole in front of us, and the pile of earth ready to fill it in.
Instead I thought of my father stretched out on the living room
rug. "C'mon Kitty," he teased. "All you gotta do is roll me up
and drag me down the hall."

That night my mother, Angela, and I picked over all the food
that had been brought; there was more food than the three of
us could ever possibly eat, and Mama in a tactful way had suggested that Angela take a lot of it *home* with her. I knew she
was trying to find out *when* Angela was leaving exactly and also
if she was still with her husband, but the plan didn't work and
Angela just nodded and said that she sure would. She was sitting
there, auburn hair parted down the middle and hanging to her
shoulders as she held a drumstick in one hand and a cigarette
in the other, a glass of my father's scotch in front of her. "You
know," she said, chin trembling all over again, "Fred was more
than an uncle to me." She paused thoughtfully, took a drag off
the cigarette, then put down the drumstick so she could sip her
drink.

The phone rang at nine-thirty just as Merle had said, and I
ran out into the hall to answer; I could hear voices in the background, his parents', a television. Oftentimes he just called to say
good night and that's what we did then, the comfortable silence

in the telephone line a promise that we'd see each other the next day when he finished at the warehouse. I forgot to thank him for coming to the funeral, to tell him that I saw him there, at the far edge of the crowd. "Good night," he said again, and I just sat there with the receiver pressed to my ear, the buzz making me feel numb. When I walked back to the doorway of the kitchen, I could hear Angela saying that same thing over and over. I just waited there in the darkness of the dining room, the furniture like dark shadows. I knew I could have felt my way over every inch of the room, so exact and precise was that room kept; the chair my father always sat in, a head chair with tooled mahogany arms, was against the wall on the far side of the china cabinet. I sat down in the darkness, watching and listening. "Fred was much more like a big brother to me. He was like the *father I never had*." My mother chimed in at the end with her, and Angela looked up suddenly, sharply. "Don't make fun of me, Cleva," she said. "I *loved* Freddie."

"I *loved Freddie*, too," Mama said, and began clearing the table. "And he *was* a lot more to you." Mama's voice got higher and faster just as it had in the car that same morning as we drove from Seymore's. "He was your guardian, and I'd say he did more than the average guardian angel."

"Money, right? We're talking money. Well, I have never taken a cent that I didn't deserve," she said. "Think what you want." Angela stood and drained her glass, placed it with a firm clink onto the lazy susan. "You promised to take care of me." She drew her thin robe tightly around her and faced my mother. "You were supposed to be like my mother, Cleva." She laughed and slapped her hand against the table. "That's what you told me one time, remember? 'Oh, Angela, I hope you can think of me like a mother.' " My mother's face flushed with her mimicry.

"And I tried my best," my mother said. "You're the one who never tried. And no, it's not all money. We had the money. It was feelings, our feelings, *my* feelings."

"Oh, I tried," Angela said. "But I tried for Freddie, not for you. You never gave me a chance. You criticized everything I ever did. From the first day I moved in with you, you were telling me what to do."

"Not everything." Mama sat down in a chair, propped her feet on another, ankles crossed. "You know that's not true, Angela. You also know that you weren't always honest with Fred. You took advantage of him."

"You wouldn't say that if he was alive."

"No, but now we don't have to pretend." My mother reached up and wiped her eyes, then kept her hands on her cheeks. "Kate?" she called, and I jumped with the sound of my name, backed out into the darkness of the foyer and answered her from there. "Come here a second, honey."

By the time I got back into the room, Angela was apologizing to my mother; she turned as I came through the door. "Oh, Katie," she said. "I've just been so terrible to your mother and here she's been so good to me. Why, I guess I'm just so racked with grief I just wasn't thinking."

"What happened?" I asked, and my mother opened her mouth but before she could speak Angela jumped in.

"It was all my fault," she said. "I hurt Cleva's feelings in the worst way. I told her how just over Christmas, Fred had asked me to try and help her get herself looking better, you know like we did that summer with her hair." Angela shook her head from side to side, patted my mother's stiff shoulder, ever stiffer with her touch. "But I guess I didn't say it very tactfully, did I?"

"No, you didn't," Mama said, and went back to wrapping pies and cakes in aluminum foil. "Now, Angela, I believe you said you prefer pie to cake so I'm going to choose a couple that are easy to travel with, maybe this pecan from Edith Turner." She wrapped the pie and then put it in a paper bag. "And this Dutch apple that Maralee Landell baked." There. She folded and wrapped the bag over the two pies and then handed it to Angela. "These should be easy to handle on the bus."

"The bus?" Angela's face went solemn. "I'll call Greg before I get back on the *bus*. That's why I was so late getting here, because *the bus* stops in every hole-in-the-road town."

"You're leaving?" I asked.

"Yes," Mama said. "I *begged* Angela to stay but she's got to get home. She'll be leaving tomorrow. You know she's got a man to take care of."

"Yes, and taking care of a man takes time and money."

They went on a few more blows, clearly sending little hidden meanings between them, every word intended to hit a target, some weakened and bruised area. "Maybe Katie would like to come visit me?" Angela asked, and again Mama's jaw clenched tightly. "You can come any time you want."

"Maybe she will," Mama said. "But you'll discover that when you put a child *with* a man, you *really* have a lot to take care of."

"Child? Why Katie's a young woman!" Angela put the pies on the table and lit a cigarette. "Before you know it, Katie will be having a baby. Won't that be nice? A grandbaby?"

I think my face would have flushed with that thought anyway, but when the two of them looked at me, I felt totally transparent; I felt they each had a private movie of Merle and me behind the auditorium stage that one day, that they knew my every wonderful sensation and thought, that they knew my every fear and doubt. I was relieved when the phone rang—Misty this time—and I was relieved when Angela breezed into the foyer, smiled, and blew me a kiss, and then turned up the stairs, leaving my mother alone in the kitchen.

"You doing okay?" Misty asked, and I could picture her on the bed, legs Indian style as she played with the phone cord, as she looked at the photo of Mo leaning against the old Chevrolet, the photo of the two of us on her bulletin board, our arms around each other as we smiled at her dad, Misty draped in purple carpet remnants and me in red leotards; while he was taking our picture, Mo Rhodes was in the kitchen cooking Tuna Surprise and filling the trick-or-treat bowl, and my father was across the street in his leather chair, smoke rings circling his head. "It'll take awhile before you feel right again," Misty was saying. "Just when you think you're okay, then it'll hit you again." She paused, her voice wavery, and I heard her moving, maybe curling on her side, pulling a blanket up around her. "I still have that happen sometimes, a dream or something like that."

"Are you okay?" I asked, feeling my own throat tightening, drying.

"Yeah," she whispered. "I'm sorry, Kate. I shouldn't be saying all this to *you*, but there's no one else, you know? I can't talk to my dad, and it would just hurt Sally Jean's feelings." She paused. "Dean can't stand to talk about my mother at all. I don't know, I guess it's easier for him not to."

I heard Mama coming through the dining room, heard the scuff of those same lavender bedroom shoes. "I just still can't believe he died," I whispered, knowing she was within earshot. I waited while my mother crossed the hall; she looked at me and then just lifted her hand as a goodnight, her eyes watery, that electrical manual in her hand. "I better go," I said, amazing myself with the cool calmness. "And you can always talk to me, Misty." She sniffed, apologized again. "Now we're talking *graveyard*, huh?" she asked, and forced a laugh.

When I closed my eyes that night, the thoughts that came to my mind were all of my father, his voice telling jokes or odd little bits of trivia about obscure inventors and scientists, people he said society had not properly received. For a second I spied him in darkness, the lid of his coffin closed tightly, airtight sealing to hold in all the secrets and thoughts that he had failed to tell me. His collar was buttoned tight, starched and buttoned, a Windsor knot in the necktie, tighter and tighter. I sat with a start, unable to breathe with the sensation of darkness closing in, air growing scarce, the panic that causes the best of swimmers to lose control and fight the one who has come to help, the panic that forces humans to riot and stampede, for air, for space, for freedom, the little and the weak shoved to the bottom, to the side, out of the way.

I could not stand to think of the question that Misty had asked in the kitchen the day I measured her for her uniforms; I could not stand to wonder whether or not our bodies are returned to us. The only way I could close my eyes again, was to *know*, to *believe*, that my father's body was mere skeleton in a Sunday suit and that *he* had risen above it all and at that very moment was a part of the world, a part of my world, the very air I breathed in relief as I opened my eyes to the familiar wallpaper, pink roses climbing the walls. Angela did not come into my room during the night and I was relieved. My prayer that night was to blot my mind of everything except thoughts of Merle, and somewhere within those to fall asleep; I saw Merle sitting on the rough granite stone, his hair blown by an approaching summer storm, or I saw him crouched in the little shed, Converse sneaker pressed against the wall, Merle in the auditorium of Samuel T. Saxon, sockless foot propped on the seat in front of him, Merle in the second grade with dried Kool-Aid in his dirty palm, a snakeskin wrapped around his neck, Merle behind the moss green drapes as he pulled me on top of him, his hands warm on my back.

Twenty-five

My mother was like a different person the next day; it was as if she had gotten up from her bed and made a vow to bend as far as she could possibly bend to make things right with Angela, or maybe she had made the promise the night before as she lay there alone, the sheets still smelling like my father; maybe she had promised *him* in some sort of silent prayer or thought or hope that he could hear her.

"I'm sorry I was so short with you yesterday," she said, and poured a cup of coffee, held the pot out towards Angela in question. "I just was not myself." She filled Angela's cup and then joined us at the table, where she had prepared a huge breakfast, the kind she only fixed on special occasions, with waffles and omelets and biscuits and ten different kinds of jam on the lazy susan. "You can understand that I was not myself?"

"Oh, Cleva," Angela started, her thin robe loose in the front. "It was just as much me."

I watched, expecting my mother to flinch with *shared* blame, perhaps *wanting* a full apology, but she just nodded in agreement.

"And," Angela said, right hand rubbing her temple, "mine was also liquor talking. Liquor has always made me feel mean." She laughed and nodded, looked at me. "Really, it's like Jekyl and Hyde or whatever."

"You're welcome to stay a few days." Mama sipped her coffee; all that food spread in front of us and no one had even taken a bite. "I don't know what your situation at home is, and . . ." She held up her hand in protest as Angela started to speak. "No, it's none of my business, I know that."

"Everything is really fine at home," she said. "If only Fred could have known just how fine it is." She speared a waffle and reached for the butter. "And I do need to be getting back. I'll call the bus station right after we finish."

"But last night the way you said that you'd call Greg before you rode the bus, well, that sounded—" Mama stopped short, sighed. "Forgive me, there I go again." She leaned back and took another sip of coffee, shook her head when I tried to pass her the waffles.

"Oh, I didn't mean for it to sound that way, no." Angela reached and turned the lazy susan, touching the lid of each jar as it passed. "I just meant he'd have to take off from work, and that's not such an easy thing."

"I see," Mama said. "Well, then I'll drive you home."

"Oh, no, Cleva, you have way too much to do. I wouldn't even think of it. No, no." Angela was sitting up straight now, shaking her head adamantly.

"I could drive," I offered. After weeks of waiting for my sixteenth birthday, I suddenly realized it was just ten days away. "You'd have to be with me." I looked at my mother and she nodded, but again Angela insisted that we forget that idea, that she would ride the bus, it was no big deal. *Why, it was even sort of relaxing just to sit on the bus and ride.* She was acting the same way Sally Jean used to act when caught picking up rocks, her pockets full as she denied that *that* was her reason for standing in the center of the yard.

Angela left that day with the promise that she would return for a meeting with the lawyer to discuss the will. "Fred wanted you to be there," Mama told her. "He wanted to make sure that you always had help if you needed it." We were at the bus station, me in the driver's seat, Angela with the back door open and one foot already on the pavement. It was raining, the asphalt steaming as the wipers squeaked and the motor idled. "But you know that, don't you?" Mama turned and looked at her, the rain blowing into the car, Angela's face damp and plain, no make-up. Angela nodded and then with the quick sound of a kiss, was racing up to the station, her suitcase in hand, as she pulled open the old screen door with the Pepsi advertisement rusting on it.

"I don't know why she wouldn't let us drive her," Mama said, and shook her head. "There's always a mystery, isn't there?" She shrugged and then we rode in silence. The rain was coming down so hard that when I pulled into our driveway we had to sit there until it slacked up. It was barely afternoon but the streetlights were on and in front of us the canna lilies swayed stiffly. "Yessir, I like 'em tall and healthy," he had said proudly just a few days before, pointing first to the lilies and then to my mother and then to me.

Merle's father had rented a house in Clemmonsville, and they were all set to move two weeks from Saturday. Merle and I were trying to ignore it, hoping that something or someone would intervene and change the plans. In the meantime the days were passing so quickly; my mother filled in every second of every day with an activity that could prevent her thinking of my father. "I just want to get through it," she told me. "We meet with the lawyer the end of next week, and then we'll get through it." She was reorganizing every cabinet and every closet and every drawer. A huge box in our living room marked for Goodwill was where she put his clothes, stacks of crisp white shirts, some ink-stained but most bleached like snow. I came in once to find her kneeling with one of the shirts pressed to her face, but with my presence, she straightened up quickly and went back to business as usual—though that weekend passed without her washing her bed sheets, a first in the history of her adult life.

Everyone made too much of my birthday, as if the over-indulgence could make us forget; even Mrs. Poole came bearing a twenty-five dollar gift certificate from Ivey's. "Sixteen is special," she said, smiled, and then added, "I do hope you'll buy something *nice*."

Misty and Sally Jean had a surprise party which included half of E. A. Poe High School. "You know, I've been dying to have a party anyway," Misty said. "And what better reason is there than your best friend's birthday?" The music blasted as people spilled from house to carport to backyard, where they had res-urrected Mo's old tiki torches and had them glowing in the four corners. I got more albums and charms and eye shadow than I had ever seen, and most of them didn't even have cards; they were from people I hardly knew, who handed them over, smiled, and said happy birthday. Misty had made up a whole list of songs that Sally Jean was supposed to play in sequence as I opened my gifts: "Sixteen Candles," "Only Sixteen," "You're Sixteen, You're Beautiful," and the Beatles' "Birthday."

"What about the regular song?" Sally Jean had asked and Misty answered her with a laugh and a sigh and an "Oh, Sally Jean," and then the two giggled, both talking faster than the speed of bullets. There were a lot of people there from Dean's class, people who I knew *of*, their faces filling the high school yearbook as Student Council officers and cheerleaders and best-all-around seniors. Many of them already seemed so adultlike as they stood there in their khakis and loafers, smoking cigarettes and talking about SAT scores and university courses. "I'll be taking pre-SAT, of course," I overheard Misty saying to the guy she had a crush on, her wooden earrings dangling with each word. She saw me watching her but never broke her stride for a second. "My step-mother quizzes me on vocabulary all the time." She glanced at me, eyebrows raised but not a smile cracked. "She has the most *incredible* vocabulary."

Merle and I ended up spending much of the party at the edge of the yard, in two webbed aluminum lawn chairs pulled as close together as we could get them, our hands clasped tightly as we watched the party from our dark corner as if it were a movie. I heard Misty calling for the "birthday girl" several times, but she got side-tracked in conversation or else she decided to leave us on our own. My mother had come briefly, to watch me blow out the candles on the huge cake she had made herself, to watch me open my gifts, but now she had gone back across the street, Merle and I watching as she went in, blazing a trail of lights through the house. Since my father died, she had stopped going around turning off unnecessary lights; instead she wanted more, constantly. She had bought a nightlight to plug into an outlet in the hall just outside her bedroom door.

"Do you even know all these people?" Merle asked, and I shook my head. Todd Bridger and some of the other boys from our class were standing around the food with several seniors. Dean Rhodes had his arm around a girl who was taller than I was, her hair similar to mine. Misty had told me that she was the salutatorian, but you'd never know it to talk to her, that she could even be funny sometimes. "Bet you'll be asked out by a bunch of them," he said, and squeezed my fingers. "As soon as I move . . ." His voice dropped off as he waited for me to deny what he was thinking. I was still hoping there was going to be a change in plans; I knew that if Merle hadn't been there with me, I would be moving through the party like Misty's shadow, Misty turning and pulling me up beside her, referring to me constantly as she had always done. I looked over where Misty was dancing, her hair twirling as her partner dipped her in rhythm with the Tams: *Be young, be foolish, but be happy.* Misty had told me that our summer project was to learn to shag like crazy, that that's all people did at college fraternity parties, Dean had told her all about it. "You know it's true," Merle said, and I turned suddenly, head shaking, no; no, it was not true. I couldn't think about Merle leaving; I couldn't think about my father.

"Here's your present." He handed me a small box carefully wrapped in gold paper, a white bow on top. It was a signet ring, my initials in fancy script, but when I tried to say thank you, everything caught up with me, and I ended up having to turn away and stare at my porch, the light over the door glowing, blurring as I tried not to cry. We just sat there until people started leaving, my name being called out with good-byes, called by people who were strangers to me. I was relieved when enough people had left that Merle and I could say good-bye as well. Misty and Sally Jean both hugged me, both oohed and aahed over my ring as they talked nonstop about the party. Mr. Rhodes went around picking up paper cups and drink cans and blowing out the tiki torches. It seemed I saw him linger in one corner of the yard, the little native face staring back, before he cupped his hand and blew out the light.

Merle and I sat on my front porch until midnight. The gates of Whispering Pines were like the entrance to a cave, the shrubs along our drive had grown so high. "You know, there still might be a way I can stay here," he said. "I'll talk to my dad again." He stared straight ahead, hands in the back pockets of his worn jeans as he leaned against the porch rail and stared at the gates. "If only . . ." He stopped, eyes focused in the direction of the magnolia tree, and then the hedge of canna lilies, behind which his old neighborhood was springing back in a row of convenience stores and service stations. And then we just stood there, our heads pressed together, as we rocked back and forth. When he left, I stayed out on the curb and watched until he disappeared in the direction of the trailer park. There was a slight breeze, warm and filled with the heavy scent of gardenias. As I was standing there, turning a slow circle, head tilted back to the sky, I saw the light go on in my father's study. Then, within minutes came Judy Garland's voice, the sound sending a chill over me, *what'll I do*, and suddenly I had the feeling that he was there in his ink-stained chair, pen and pad on his lap as he sang along, and all I had to do was run inside and find him.

I stopped in the doorway, heart pounding as I saw her there, staring at the record as it turned. On her lap she held his little obituary box, filled with the yellowed newsprint carefully cut during "Gunsmoke." I sighed and she turned as if snapping from a spell. "Have fun?" she asked, eyes puffy, a can of Schlitz neatly dressed out in a Coca-Cola skirt.

"I thought—" I took a step forward and then leaned against the open door, stared at the album cover there on the floor, a young Judy Garland with those sad brown eyes staring back at me.

"Oh, honey, I'm sorry." She was there then, face next to mine as she pulled me close. "I wasn't thinking you'd be home this early. I lost track of the time is all." She pointed to the box on the desk. "You know Fred would want his own write-up in the collection." She nodded with each word, smiled, and then turned away long enough to pull a balled-up Kleenex from her robe pocket and dab her eyes. "Maybe I should have waited for 'Gunsmoke' to come on, right?" She laughed, closed the box, and put it in the top desk drawer. "But Angela is coming on Friday and might spend the night. Who knows what all Fred had going on with the lawyer that I don't know about." She shrugged. "I mean, what do we do with all of his old mess, Katie?" she asked, with a bewildered look on her face that then softened to a smile. "I mean, I *can't* throw it away. Clothes, yes, because some poor soul can wear them and maybe get a new start in life; there are *plenty* of homeless, helpless, poor people, right?"

I nodded, ready to recite "Lord Forgive Me When I Whine" along with her, but she took a different path. "But these," she said, and opened another drawer, lifted a huge stack of loose papers, all covered in his sloppy little script. She held them to her chest. "Did you know that he has pages and pages about someone who cleans the beauty shop at night, puts a chemical in some hair dye?" She put the stack back in the drawer, her large hand patting it affectionately. "You see, there's this one woman who has her hair dyed regularly, and it's a strange shade of red, so strange that the killer knows this bottle of dye is *only* used on her." She shook her head. "It's a horrible story, and it doesn't work at all. I mean, wouldn't they suspect this man?" She took a sip of her skirted beer and motioned that we leave the room. I watched her turning off the stereo, turning out the light, and then closing the door behind us.

"Oh, by the way," she said as I turned to go up the stairs, "your father picked out a car for you a couple of weeks ago. It's not new, but it's in good shape." She patted my hand and then left hers there on top as I gripped the stair post. "Now, if you don't like it, I'm sure we can pick something else, really. Your father's taste was—" She stared down at her bedroom shoes, shook her head as if the sight of those shoes I had given her so long before mirrored her thought regarding my father's taste. "Your father bought you a used taxi, Mary Katherine." She said the words hastily, but firmly. "He had the meter removed and the plexiglass between the seats removed, and he had it painted dark green." She paused, took in a deep breath. "He thought you would enjoy a car big enough to carry around a lot of friends, so he asked that they leave the little pull-out stool. He said it was the safest car made, *built like a tank*. He was so thrilled when he found it, really, that's all I heard." Her hand tightened on my own. "You have to remember that there are a lot of teenagers who never have a car all their own, certainly no one in my generation did. I was not in favor of this decision, but your father insisted, so I want you to keep in mind how *lucky* you are." Her voice softened. "But if you don't want this car, well"—she squeezed even harder, took another sip of Schlitz—"I'll drive the Checker and you can drive the wagon. You sleep on it." She turned then and disappeared down the hall, stooping to turn on her nightlight, leaving her door open so she could see the yellow glow. "Happy birthday," I heard her call when I was halfway up the stairs, and I wished that she would ask me to come and get in her bed, to lie there in my father's spot as we talked; or I wished that she would appear in my doorway the way Angela had done so many times, to stretch out close to me and ask how I was feeling, to tuck in the covers the way Mo Rhodes used to do, to lean over and press her lips to my forehead, lips to my cheek. I wanted to ask her how she felt on my birthday, how she felt that moment when she first saw me; had she ever regretted it, ever regretted any second of her life? Had she been different when she was thirty-four years old and wanted Angela to love her, to think of her as a mother or even as a friend as the two giggled side by side in the movies? I woke throughout the night thinking that I felt her beside me— but nothing, a ghost of my own creation.

Twenty-six

Merle spent several late afternoons of that last week working in Mrs. Poole's yard, which meant we spent those afternoons together as I followed him around, helping prune bushes and rake the cut grass. "Your daughter is chasing him," I overheard Mrs. Poole say to my mother as they stood on the sidewalk; Sally Jean crossed the street to join them, while I waited for Merle to walk from the direction of the warehouse. Mrs. Poole was still mad that I had bought *boys'* Levi's with my gift certificate. "I'm paying that boy to work, not court."

"But he's moving soon," Sally Jean said, and then turned to my mother. "We have had such a time laughing over Fred buying that taxicab." She nudged my mother's arm. "It's a hoot. I think it's really—" She paused, taking her time. "It's *eccentric*." She nodded confidently with her choice of words. "And that's nice. What a wonderful man he was."

"I think it's"—Mrs. Poole leaned forward and then backed down as my mother stared at her—"not my style. I'm getting a new car as well."

Those afternoons when Merle took a break and waited for further instructions from Mrs. Poole, I sat with him either outside in her swing or inside on her sun porch. We talked about everything except his move by then, the avoidance of the subject and the suddenness of the passing days making our conversations stiffer than normal, our quick kisses as awkward and fumbling as they'd been in the beginning. We talked mostly about things that we'd like to do; he wanted to travel across the country, to see the Grand Canyon, giant redwoods, Old Faithful. I wanted to breed and raise Abyssinians and to drive an inconspicuous Toyota like everyone else in my class who had a car. Or better, I wanted the self-confidence to be able to drive the Checker without feeling like a large green monster. Merle wanted a car, period, no motorcycles ever, just the mention of which led us all the way back around to our beginning. I told him about Angela and how I had spent years wishing that she was my mother, that Misty and I had figured it out so many times, all the ways that it could have been true, all the reasons to believe it. "I guess I just wanted to have a secret," I said. "Something to make my life exciting and mysterious."

Merle shrugged, said he thought there were a lot of secrets better kept that way. "Like, don't you wish." We were sitting in the far sunny corner of Mrs. Poole's porch, beside a round table filled with geraniums. "Like, don't you wish you'd never been in the tree that night? Don't you wish that we'd just decided to start talking to one another one day at school or over here when I was working?" I nodded along; I didn't tell him that so many times I had wondered if that very event had somehow created our bond, that I had wondered if he would have even looked at me twice had I not witnessed it all.

He leaned closer to me. "Aren't you sorry that you saw what

happened that night?" My father used to say that information is only good if you plan to use it. Why should Misty's family be haunted by unnecessary knowledge? Why should anyone need to know who Angela's father was? Why put a secret door in a story if you're not going to open it? At the time I had interpreted the last question as an intimation that there *was* a secret door, a door soon to be opened. But would I have done anything with that information other than to tuck it away like a secret, the same way I tucked away Perry's cold stare and flat voice as she thrust that worn-out carcoat towards me—and the way I tucked away her look of horror as she lay pinned on the ground.

My mother was preoccupied for days on end as she went through my father's things; she was having a hard time sorting the important papers from his doodles. She made steady calls and visits to the lawyer. There was a determined look on her face, and I knew that she wanted everything neat and tidy before Angela arrived.

"I still can't believe you'd even want an outsider here," Mrs. Poole said. "When Mr. Bo died, I did not invite anyone to hear my business."

"Angela is family," my mother said, nodding as I entered the room where she had a stack of shoeboxes, each with a label neatly written in her handwriting. "Fred was her legal guardian until she turned twenty-one."

"Where *is* her daddy?" Mrs. Poole asked, and raised her eyebrows as if in an attempt to stop her twitch. "I never got all that straight."

"Her father"—my mother was speaking through clenched teeth, her Boston accent surfacing—"died in Korea." She looked at me in a way that commanded I pretend I had heard this story a million and one times.

"Oh, my," Mrs. Poole said. "I had no idea, I was beginning to think . . ." Her voice trailed off as she stared at the canna lilies and crumpled up an empty cigarette pack. "Well, at least she can take comfort that he died for a good cause and not of a rotten liver."

"Pardon?" Mama's eyebrows went straight up as she waited for an explanation for Mrs. Poole's slip of the tongue. *Bo Poole died of consumption, all right,* I could hear my father saying.

"Pardon?" Mrs. Poole repeated, realizing her slip. "I didn't say anything."

"You said something about a rotten liver," I said, and though my mother turned suddenly, face flushed, I knew she was glad I had pursued the subject.

"I said"——Mrs. Poole lit a cigarette and took a deep drag—— "I said I hope Maralee Landell never again cooks that old rotten liver and onions." She nodded emphatically. "I thought I'd die from it, which, as I was saying, would not be a very noble way to die like it is to die for your country." She thumped her ash, making little gray flecks land on the table. "Now, my Mr. Bo, well, he was one of the military's finest, you know."

"Just like Angela's father," my mother added, as Mrs. Poole stared back with her lips screwed up tight.

"I am *tired*," Mrs. Poole said fiercely. "Of people talking about Toyotas! They are of the Japanese and by the Japanese, and is *this* why Robert Manchester Poole risked his life in the Pacific? For better gas mileage?" She beat her fist on the table, and I watched my mother beginning to shake, first her shoulders and then her chest, hands pressed to her face before she suddenly let out a laugh like I hadn't seen in years, tears rolling down her cheeks as she begged Mrs. Poole to stop making her laugh so. "Give me a Lincoln!" Mrs. Poole said, clearly annoyed that my mother wasn't taking her seriously.

"Or give me death!" my mother screamed. She laughed for a solid five minutes, Mrs. Poole smoking like a dragon and shaking her head the whole while. When Mama finally pulled herself together, she apologized to Mrs. Poole. "I just don't know what crept over me," she said, eyes still glistening, her large hand on my arm.

"You need to make yourself an appointment, Cleva." Mrs. Poole nodded knowingly.

"That wasn't true, was it? About Angela's father?" I whispered later, as my mother was writing *old gradebooks and exams* on another shoebox, placing it on top of one that read, *Fred's ideas.* She stopped her writing, black Magic Marker held and bleeding onto the cardboard.

"No," she said, and shook her head. "You know all there is to know about Angela." She lifted her hand as if in a pledge. "At least you know what *I* know about Angela." She finished her writing and then put the cap on the marker. "Her mother got pregnant and *never* told who the father was."

"But there had to have been some *guess*." I found that I could not look her in the eye while discussing anything remotely related to sex and birth control, unlike Misty who would ask the dumbest questions just so we could hear Sally Jean's very *un*medical explanations.

"I think your father had two suspects, and I think he would have pursued it if his sister had lived." She pulled out another big box of papers and began sorting little scraps of paper. It seemed she was sorting by size, since she wasn't reading anything, wasn't wasting her time with unnecessary information. "But he always said that when she died, he and his mother decided *they* wanted Angela, and they didn't want anyone else staking any claims."

"Oh."

"Your father maintained that the poor girl was completely innocent." She shook her head, a little drawing of a turkey in a Pilgrim hat in her hand. "To hear him tell it, she was a virgin, and Angela a miracle of the flesh." Again I had to look away. "Now, why do you guess he drew all these turkeys?"

·   ·   ·

Angela arrived the following week on Thursday night, and as she and my mother prepared to go to the lawyer's office the next morning, I sat in the porch swing and watched Misty leaving for majorette practice. I had never been back to my typing class, though my mother had tried to convince me that the best thing you could do was have a busy, busy mind. Even at night when she finally sat down, she rifled through self-help type books as if on a quest. Oliver was stretched out on the far end of the porch, where already there was a hot patch of sunlight, his fur sparse and gray with age. He hardly moved anymore, just lay in the sun, tail barely moving.

Merle was moving the next day, and he had promised that he'd leave the warehouse as soon as he picked up his check; he was going to tell the Landells good-bye and to help Mr. Landell rearrange Mrs. Poole's living room as she had been requesting for weeks, but I could go with him. When we finished at Mrs. Poole's we were going to stop by Misty's and then walk to the duck pond; we might take the Checker and drive to the movies, maybe drive out in the country as the sun set over the wide flat fields. We were trying too hard to pretend that it was not his last day. "It's not like we're never going to see each other," we said daily, and though Misty kept telling me that I needed to *know* if we were going to date other people, I couldn't bring up the topic. "You can't go steady long distance, can you?" Misty had asked. "Or maybe you can now that you've got a car." We both stared over at my driveway, where it sat in all of its giant green glory.

When the porch was covered in bright hot sunlight, I moved inside where it was cool. I opened the door to my father's study, where the shades were drawn, and I turned on the small black and white TV he had on his desk. "I Love Lucy" was on, with Lucy now living in Connecticut, certain that her wedding ring is hidden somewhere in the mortar and brick of the new barbecue as she and Ethel sit up all night long dismantling it. "Aye yi yi,"

Ricky says when he finds the ruins. "Luuuuceeeee?" My mother called to say that she and Angela were still waiting and that I should plan something for my own lunch, if I went anywhere I should leave her a note. "It's probably going to take awhile," she said, lots of talk and noise in the background, while the music from "I Love Lucy" ran into "The Big Valley," Barbara Stanwyck reminding me of Stella Dallas, reminding me of Mo and Angela and my father and all the things that can possibly go wrong in your life in a flash of a split second. His clocks ticked all around me, one on the mantel, one on the desk, one on his radio, none with the same time. Being in the room was too much, too close, and I turned off the set and went back outside to the heat and the brightness. Merle would be there soon.

I stood and waited, the sidewalk hot as I slipped off my sandals. Sally Jean was watering her beautiful green grass, a big straw hat protecting her face and shoulders from the sun. Mrs. Poole's sprinklers were on, arcing and spraying mist in my direction, swishing. The absence of my father was more than I could stand, and somehow getting outside in the sunshine made it easier. It seemed that in every creak and settling of our house I heard his footsteps; the scent of cigar and pipe smoke in his study had been overwhelming, as if everything in there had permanently absorbed the smell. And maybe that's why my mother had kept the door closed. I heard Al Jolson and Judy Garland back to back without breaks, sometimes the two overlapping in the same way my father drew his intersecting circles and boxes, shaded his doodled designs. I saw Merle as soon as he rounded the corner way down the street and I concentrated on him, every step, right left right left, until he was close enough to see me, to lift his hand in a wave.

When Merle was only a block away, I began walking to meet him. Sally Jean paused to look up and wave to me as I passed. "Hey," he said, and caught my hand in his as I turned and walked back with him. Already I had begun practicing, writing letters to him in my head. "Come on in," he said when we had walked around to Mrs. Poole's back door and then into her quiet clean kitchen, where flowers and bowls were out as if a tea were in preparation. I had not been there since the C of C meeting when I had sat right at that very table with Merle. I followed him out into the hallway, the green carpet cushioning our steps, the whole house smelling of cloves and cinnamon and apples. I was looking at the portrait of Mr. Poole when Merle grabbed me suddenly and pulled me onto the wine velvet chaise, a piece of furniture my mother adored but said did *not* go with any other thing that Theresa Poole owned. My mother had tried to buy it a couple of times, and as a result, it had become Mrs. Poole's very *favorite* piece, the one she described to strangers in front of my mother as often as she could.

I pulled away from Merle, twisting to glimpse the door to the kitchen, but he held me tighter, his mouth on my cheek and neck. The house was completely silent, the ticks of the different clocks striking a new rhythm, the mantel and grandfather clocks not quite in sync. "Don't," I whispered. "They'll hear us."

"Who?" he called out loudly, and grinned. He smelled like the warehouse where he worked; it was just like the smell of my father's study. That sweet sharp scent of the warehouse was permanent; I loved the way in late summer our whole town was bathed in the heavy odor. I waited, expecting Mrs. Poole to come bursting into the room, but nothing. "Nobody is here," he said. "They called me at the warehouse to say that they had to drive to the Clemmonsville Mall and for me just to come in and wait." He spread his arms wide, as if to claim ownership to the house. "They said it would be after noon," he whispered, and then in a second was up and pulling me along with him.

"Mrs. Poole said it was okay?" I asked in disbelief, a little nervous to find myself completely alone with him, it had been so long.

"I guess." He shrugged. "She goes along with what the

Landells tell her usually. Remember that day we snuck in old Samuel T. Saxon?" he asked, and my heart raced as I followed him up the carpeted stairs, past Audubon prints in gold dustless frames placed every third step. The grandfather clock chimed once on the half hour, and I jumped with the sudden break of silence. I had never been upstairs at Mrs. Poole's, and now here I was. I knew that was her room off to the left, where I could see a crocheted canopy and a bay window. There was a frilly little vanity with a silver-framed picture of Mr. Bo Poole. It was so incongruous, the dainty table and the thought of Mrs. Poole sitting there, spreading her thin lips to apply that horrible shade of lipstick; there were so many pictures of Mr. Poole in the house it was like a shrine—saint with a rotten liver.

"C'mon." He pulled me along, his face and muscular arms already very tan. I followed, focusing on the back of his white T-shirt hanging out over his jeans, the film of yellow dust covering him. The whole upstairs smelled like roses, some kind of sachets or potpourri; it made me think of a doll I'd had once, a doll with bright red hair who was scented to smell like a rose and I had secretly named her Angela and hidden her for safety in the heating vent, not realizing that she was going to fall far below where I'd never be able to find her.

"This was Mr. Poole's room," he whispered, and then laughed, used his regular voice. "Mrs. Landell calls it the *man's man* room. She says that this is where he came to get away from *her*." There was a large desk, and leather-bound law books on a bookshelf. It *was* a real man's man sort of room, the head of a deer mounted on the wall, a marlin blue and shiny as it arched over the doorway. The drapes were also very masculine, a heavy brown linen that let in very little light. I peeked out and there in the bright light was Sally Jean going up and down the sidewalk with an edger. There in our driveway was Angela's old rusty Impala and *my* taxicab, but I could not see Whispering Pines; the front of our house, the corner with my room, blocked it from sight.

"I figure if he came here to get away from her"—Merle was

saying—"he must have used it a lot." I laughed, once again thinking of my father in *his* room. I could feel Merle right behind me, hear his breath as he also peered out the thin opening of the drapes. "Your mother's not home?" he asked, and I shook my head, jumped when I felt his hand on my waist. "Will she be home soon?" His face was pressed against mine, warm from the sun as we continued to stare straight ahead, Sally Jean coming and going within the narrow point of vision. I shook my head, took a deep breath. Merle was moving; in a few hours he would be helping his father empty their sparse belongings from trailer to truck, and then tomorrow they would be gone. There were no guarantees that I'd see him again, no guarantees that my mother and Angela would make it home from the lawyer's office, no guarantees that I'd wake up tomorrow or that I'd ever turn seventeen or that there was any kind of life waiting for me. I felt Merle's hand warm against my stomach as he slowly lifted my shirt. Mr. Poole came here for escape in the same way my father sank back in his ink-stained chair, Mrs. Poole into her teas and social chatter, my mother into her needlepoint and greenhouse and family trees. I was in my escape, there that very moment, and wasting the time thinking about it all. I turned to him then, urgent and panicked, more sure than ever before that there were no guarantees.

Awkwardly we fumbled and then within minutes we were on the cot just as we had been behind the stage. I could feel his heart beating as he pressed against me, as I stared up at the deer, the glass eyes so lifelike; the eyes were large and brown and passive, so unlike they really were at that last moment when paralyzed in fear, when Mr. Bo Poole raised his gun and fired, a shattering sound as the body collapsed in the silence of the trees. I gripped Merle's back, pressed in with my hands, his body lean and muscular. "I don't want to leave," he whispered, kissed me before I could even respond, and I closed my eyes against the deer and its moment of fear, the marlin as it leapt from the sea and twisted in the air, salt water glistening, and for that brief time I was able to forget about my father, his body closed in darkness, slowly disintegrating. I was able at that moment to push all thoughts outside the room, to close and lock the door, to concentrate instead on Merle and the words he whispered into my neck, his words in rhythm with his breath as we held onto each other, and then later, my head in the crook of his arm, hand on his chest, eyes begging to give in and close, to give in to the comfort of sleep. It was a moment of absolute peace, so peaceful that we did not bother to jump up and find our clothes, to close and lock the door, did not hear the next half hour chime, did not hear my mother's car in the driveway, her voice calling my name from the porch, Sally Jean offering my whereabouts; we did not hear the knock, the back door opening, did not hear until she called out, "Anyone home? Theresa?," and then it was too late, steps on the stairs and my mother appeared there in the doorway, my shirt in the center of Mr. Bo Poole's brown leather chair. I was fully awakened by her shock, coursing through me like an electrical current, and I sat with sheet pulled up to my chest to see her there, face drawn and white, hand to chest, mouth opened wide. Merle was asleep; his lips parted softly as he took that final sleepy breath before my mother's scream brought him bolting upright, helplessness washing over him as he leaned forward and put his face in his hands.

"I want you to get out. Right now, to get out." Her voice was high and shaky. "I can't take this. I can't." She was moving back and forth in that doorway as if being pulled from side to side. "I said, get out of that bed!"

"I will," I said. "I will as soon as you leave."

"Leave?" She stepped into the room, picked up my shirt with two fingers as if it were dirty and tossed it onto the end of the cot. "Leave? Why? So you can finish what you were doing?"

"Please." Merle had somehow gotten his jeans under the sheet and was pulling them on, then buttoning his shirt. "Mrs. Burns."

"I don't want to hear anything from you. Nothing." She rolled her head from side to side against the doorframe, tears seeping as she squeezed her eyes shut.

"Mother."

"Oh God," she said, and then took a slow step towards us. She grabbed me by the arm and pulled; my hand that had been clinging to Merle's there beneath the spread, was pried away as I crawled from the covers, tried to hide myself as I raced to my clothes. "Look at you," she said, and pointed to the mirror over by the window, and I glimpsed myself, lean and white; my body was so ugly there, a harsh contrast of my whiteness against the paneled walls, my hair loose from the barrettes, coarse and tangled, my cheek and neck splotched red like neon, raw like a burn. "Just look," she said, her voice breaking, and I hated her right then; all of the hatred that I had ever felt came rushing back in. I hated her for messing up one moment of peace I'd found.

"I don't want to ever see you again," she said to Merle before pushing me ahead of her. I turned and he was following slowly, hand held out as if he could grab and keep me there. I was trying to give him a sign, a look that would return the words he had whispered to me earlier but she wouldn't let me. Her hand was tight on my arm as we went down the carpeted stairs. The sunlight was so bright it blinded me, and I had to squint as we walked down the sidewalk, side by side but not a word spoken. Sally Jean was frozen there with her edger, somehow knowing not to call out to us, knowing that something awful was happening.

"I want you to go inside and take a shower," she said, shaking her head stiffly, her jaw clenched.

Angela stepped out onto the porch. My mother pushed me towards the front door. The sprinkler still arced and sprayed, the birds still sang, ivy swayed off the gates of Whispering Pines, Merle still stood in that window, the heavy drapes swung back, his hands clumsy against his sides, making him look so helpless, so much younger than he'd looked just minutes before. I reached my hand out but she pushed me into the dark foyer, and I was

hit suddenly with the smell of my father's cigarette smoke. He
was not there to settle this mess.

"Why, Cleva," I heard Angela say, her heels clicking through
the foyer. "You look so upset, and, Kitty, what's wrong? What
has happened?" I ran upstairs and into the bathroom; I locked
the door and ran water into the bathtub. The steam rose, then
disappeared in the breeze from the window. The bathroom window looked over the driveway, the cemetery, shaded by the huge
oaks there. I avoided looking in the mirror but got right into the
tub and just lay back and closed my eyes, hoping to erase all that
had happened. A shudder still came to me each time I pictured
my mother's face. *If only* I had heard her car in the driveway.
How easily I could have gotten up to go home, pulled Merle close
to say good-bye, and he would have peeked from the curtains
to watch me walking through the sunshine. I would have turned
and waved, a sign that we would meet again real soon. And I
would have gone into our house and, with a few deep breaths,
entered the kitchen to find my mother and Angela waiting. For
years Misty's wish had been: *If only my mother hadn't left on that
day, at that exact time.*

Twenty-seven

I was sitting in my room, staring out at Whispering Pines, when I heard a light rap at the door. I had seen Misty pull into her driveway an hour earlier and still had not called her though I expected to hear from her soon since she was waiting for me to stop by. I watched the trees swaying as the wind picked up with the sudden clouds; I braced myself, prepared for my mother's lecture, but instead I heard Angela. "Kitty?" she called. "Honey, I'm so sorry. Cleva told me what happened." She sat on my bed, her foot near the leg of my chair as I propped my elbows on the windowsill. "Believe you me, I know *exactly* how you feel. But you'll both get over it." She nudged me with her toe, the tone in her voice like I was a child who had just spilled a glass of milk.

"She *told you*?" I asked, suddenly feeling even more exposed, the thought of my mother putting the scene into words.

"Look." Angela reached and put a hand on my shoulder. "She's not the most understanding person, you know? And she certainly isn't with the times." She laughed a quick laugh, shook me, and then realizing she had failed to make me feel better, got serious again. "It wasn't the smartest thing you could have done, you know?" She shook her head. "It was more like something *I* would do." She put her arm around my shoulder and pulled me up close, her cheek pressed against mine. "You'll survive, Kitty."

The trees in the distance were bending, the sky getting darker. For a week we had had those afternoon rains like clockwork. I imagined Merle running towards the trailer park, hurdling tombstones as he had done that rainy day so long ago when I had sat on the sleeping porch and watched him; my mother was over at Mrs. Poole's tea and Mo Rhodes was showing off her purple shag carpet.

"I've got to be going, I guess," Angela said, her hand barely touching my hair. "Keep in touch. You know if you need to talk to somebody, I'm there." I nodded, listened as she stepped out into the hall and closed my door. I imagined my mother waiting at the bottom of the stairs, large hand clutching the railing. I couldn't stand the thought of facing her.

I rested my face on the windowsill, where the mist was slowly blowing in. The phone was ringing but I ignored it; I knew my mother would tell Misty that I'd call her back later. But what if the Landells had returned and were looking for Merle? Maybe he had stayed and waited for them as planned; maybe he had sat on the velvet chaise as if nothing had ever happened. Maybe now he was in the trailer, lifting cluttered pasteboard boxes from his mother's arms as his little sister hugged her knees and stared into the small TV set. Maybe he was on the phone, calling for me or calling to apologize to my mother, to make her understand. *Understand?* I could hear her asking. *How can I understand?* No wonder Angela left home; I envied her that freedom, the time she had run away and gotten married, the time she had said that the world could go to hell, she was doing as she pleased.

Now she was down in the driveway, her hair drenched and

stringy as she loaded some of the clothes boxes into the trunk of the Impala. "Greg is just about the same size as Fred," she had said that very morning at breakfast. She waved her hand toward the porch and then stood there with the car door open and looked up at my window. It was then that I knew I couldn't sit in that house another second; I opened the window and screamed out for her to please wait for me. "Please don't leave yet." I waited until she closed the door and headed back towards the porch, and then I grabbed one of my new suitcases and started wadding clothes and stuffing them inside. It was as easy as walking out.

It was quiet when I went downstairs. The two of them were standing in the dark foyer. The front door was open and there was a cool breeze, the fresh scent of rain as the pavement out front steamed. "There you are." Mama's eyes were red and puffy, more so even than they had been at the funeral. She stared at me and shook her head slowly; when she saw my suitcase, she turned away. "Where are you going?"

I ignored her and turned to Angela. "You're always inviting me to come see you," I said, and she, too, turned away, car keys clutched in her hand.

"Yes, but maybe this isn't the best—" Before she could finish, my mother began talking, fast and forcefully.

"Why not?" she asked. "This is the perfect time. You two can have a wonderful time comparing notes."

"Cleva," Angela said, and sighed. "I don't think it's a good time."

"So you don't want her to go, is that it?" Mama asked. "All talk and no action as always?" She thrust her hands in the pockets of her linen jacket; she was still all dressed up from the visit to the lawyer. "So tell her." She pointed to me. "Tell Kate that you don't want her to come. Tell her what a fair-weather friend you are."

"That's not *fair*," Angela said.

"What is?" my mother asked. "What I saw today wasn't fair.

Losing Fred is not fair. You running away from home was not fair." She held her hands up to her face briefly and then turned back straight as ever. "Why not go for broke?"

"I didn't run away from *home*." Angela spat the word as she narrowed her eyes. "That was *never* my home."

"So maybe that's how Kate feels, too," she said, and looked down at her beige pumps. "Maybe this isn't her home."

"Mother." I felt my voice crack and I focused on the lights in Misty's living room, on Sally Jean moving in front of the window with the vacuum cleaner.

"What, Mary Katherine?" she asked. "What can you say that will change anything?"

"Nothing," I said, once again feeling a hard wave of resentment; I was *not* going to feel guilty. Mr. Rhodes was coming in from work and surprised Sally Jean as he crept up behind her; they laughed as he hugged her close, as she held up the nozzle of the vacuum and shook it at him.

"That's what I thought," she said. "I guess I could say something to make it easier. I could say that I wish you weren't my daughter, that I'm ashamed of you, that I wish you had never been born?" She paced the foyer, hands clasped, wringing. "Or better." She turned quickly, hand to her chest. "I could say that I wish I had died in childbirth so that you could have taken your chances elsewhere." She waved a hand towards Angela. "That would make things easier."

"You can *say* anything," I told her, and picked up my suitcase, looked at Angela. "Are you going to let me come or not?"

"I knew I failed with Angela," Mama was saying. "But I had no idea that I had failed with you." She was crying then, face twisting as she tried to turn so we couldn't see. The rain had slowed to a drizzle, and the late afternoon sun came from behind a cloud like a bad joke, illuminating, highlighting the most horrible of moments before receding once again. "I loved your father, and when I look at you, both of you, I see our whole life together."

Her voice shook as she leaned against the doorframe of his office, forehead pressed against the closed door. "What do you expect from me? What do either of you expect?" She turned and ran down the hall to her room. I stood with my hand gripping the handle on the suitcase as I prepared for the slamming of her door, but instead she closed it quietly, making barely a sound.

"Well, I guess I've got myself a roommate," Angela finally said, and breathed out, jingled her keys. She looked anything but pleased as she walked onto the porch and let the screen door slam shut. Oliver was wet and huddled up under the swing; I wanted to stop and scoop him up in my arms, but Angela was already standing with the trunk open. Slowly I walked out and put my suitcase in, the gates of Whispering Pines to my back; I had the odd sensation that I was being watched, but when I looked over at my mother's window, the drapes were hanging perfectly still.

"Are you sure you know what you're doing?" Angela asked, and turned the ignition; it took three tries before she got the car cranked. I nodded and stared over at the gates of Whispering Pines, where rain was still dripping from the trees.

"You said you understood," I told her, and she nodded, lit a cigarette and then backed down the long drive. I was relieved that Misty was not outside to see me; I'd tell her the whole story later, when I had had time to think through it in my own way. When we got to the street that led to the trailer park, I asked Angela to turn and she did, driving slowly until I spotted Merle's father's truck, the back already loaded with boxes and lamps, an overstuffed armchair.

"So what are you going to do now?" she asked, and put the car in park, the loud engine idling. She turned on the radio and twisted the knob. I hadn't thought that far, yet. Somehow I had expected him to be there waiting by the side of the road. My hand was on the doorhandle as she fiddled, faint stations coming and going. His father came outside with an armload of clothes on hangers, and I was about to tell her to keep driving, but then there he was; he backed out the door, no shirt, and then turned with a big box clutched to his chest. He was down the one metal step and onto the concrete slab when he spotted Angela's Impala and set the box down.

"Go on," Angela said, finally stopping on a song by the Doobie Brothers. "Go talk to him."

His father was standing there staring at us, his white T-shirt damp and clinging to his broad chest. The mother was in the doorway with Maybelline. I rolled down the window as he walked over and bent down, forehead pressed against the top of the car. He eyed Angela and then looked at me, mouthed a "Hi."

"Go on," Angela said. "What am I supposed to do, sit here and act like I'm not listening?" Merle opened the door, and I followed him several yards from the car; we just stood there in the middle of the road, yellow mud caking our shoes. He caught hold of my hand, barely touching my fingertips.

"I'm sorry," he finally said, stared over at his father, who still had not moved from his spot. "I really am so sorry."

"It's okay." I shook my head. "You didn't do anything." I shrugged. "I mean you *did* but . . ." I felt my face flush and, instinctively, my hand went to my cheek. "It's okay." I avoided looking over at their trailer, ignored the gunning engine of the Impala. "I'm sorry we didn't get to do all the things we had planned."

"So we did something else." He gave a weak smile and then looked down, his toe rubbing a line through the mud. "Guess your mother really hates me now."

"Yeah, well, she hates a lot." I tilted my head toward Angela's car as she gunned the motor. "I'm going home with Angela for awhile." I shrugged. "I just can't stay there with my mother right now."

"I know what you mean." He glanced over at the trailer and then looked back at me, his eyes a deep emerald green. "Look, it's not like we'll never see each other. I mean, we don't have to say good-bye, right?"

"Right."

"You can drive over anytime; it's only thirty miles." He held my hands tighter now, stepped closer as Angela gunned the engine again. "And I can come visit anytime. The Landells have invited me."

"Hey, we don't have all day." Merle's father was standing there with his hands on his hips. "We gotta get this stuff covered in case it rains again."

Merle didn't even flinch, just leaned forward and kissed me quickly on the cheek. "I meant everything I said," he whispered, and I nodded. "I'm just sorry it had to happen that way."

"Hey, Merle, save it for after dark, okay? I mean it." His father was stacking the drawers of a chest on the tailgate. "You can carry on some other time." I avoided looking at his father as we walked back to the car. Angela put the car in drive, her foot on the brake, before I even closed the door.

"I'll call you," Merle said as we started moving. "I'll see you soon." He jogged beside us until Angela gave him a quick wave and turned onto the main road. I turned around in my seat and watched him there, his hand still lifted in a wave.

We rode silently until we were out of the city limits and on the long barren stretch of road that led to the beach. Paul McCartney's "Band on the Run" was coming and going in little bursts of static, and finally Angela gave up and turned it off. "Don't be so glum," she said, and patted the seat between us. "I mean, it's not like you're going to die without him. There will be another one to take his place in no time." She fiddled with her right hand, pulling a cigarette from her pack and holding it between her lips as she fumbled for a match. "And Cleva will simmer down. Give her a little time." She finally got the cigarette lit and took a deep drag.

"I don't want anyone to take his place," I said. "You make it sound like it didn't mean anything and it did."

"This is some serious déjà vu." She stared ahead at the straight flat road. "Yeah, I know it meant something. I remember when I was saying those exact same words." She inhaled deeply and then blew the smoke out her opened window. "I mean, I *do* understand what you're going through. Cleva and I went this same circle." She laughed, tossed her cigarette out the window. "Boy, did we ever. That's why *I* got married that time, so please, God, don't go and do that." I opened my mouth to speak but she continued. "Now, I know you think you're in *love*." Just the word in her mouth sounded like a disease; she tried the radio again, but all she got was the news so she turned it off. "But you'll live through it. Look at me."

I smelled the salty sea air before we ever crested the old draw-bridge. It was almost dark, but I could still see the water, dark and shimmering under the lights of the fishing pier, bright white bulbs strung on a wire. Angela turned on her headlights as we rode down the main road, small pastel cottages along the way, rope lines where towels and bathing suits whipped back and forth with the breeze.

"Does your apartment face the ocean?" I asked, breaking the long silence, and Angela laughed, patted me on the leg.

"It ain't the Waldorf," she said. "But there's a view." She laughed again. "I guarantee that you'll have a view." She turned off the main road and rode inland along the waterway where there were fishing boats lined up, huge nets thrown over their sides. She turned on a dirt road near the marina and parked in front of a blue cinderblock building. "I live upstairs," she said. "Some friends of mine live in the ground apartment." As I watched her bend in front of the side-view mirror and brush a fingertip over her eyelashes, it all came back to me: my mother's look of shock, the sick gnawing emptiness I felt.

I followed her up the metal staircase and waited on the landing as she fumbled with the lock. There was a laundromat across the street, a big CLOSED sign in the window. Angela switched on the yellow porch light. "Home, sweet home," she said, and pushed the swollen door forward, clicked on a dim overhead light. There were dishes in her sink, sparse furnishings with sandy, thread-bare upholstery, a floor-to-ceiling lamp with adjustable lights like some kind of insect; a square of lime green shag carpet covered the center of the floor.

"Now you'll sleep here in the guest boudoir," she said, and pointed to the cot in the corner, a bird dog print sheet dragging the gritty linoleum. She swung back the loud orange drapes just behind the cot. "And here's the view." She waved her hand and there I could see a streetlight, the laundromat, and the bait shop. "It's not *great*, but I'd say it beats the hell out of a cemetery."

She went into the bedroom and turned on the lamp. Her bed was unmade and clothes were piled over a straight-back chair. "Is this Greg?" I asked, and pointed to a snapshot wedged up in the corner of her mirror. She nodded. He was standing in front of the gates of Graceland. "What happened to y'all?"

"Nothing happened." She opened her suitcase and pulled out her thin nightgown, draped it over the foot of the bed. "He's still around. His job requires that he travel, is all." She stopped unpacking and stared at me. "We have not split up if that's what Cleva has been saying. Just wait, he'll be here tomorrow night." I stepped back into *my* room, not wanting to imagine tomorrow when the man in the photo would be there. The telephone was beside her bed, but I still wasn't ready to call Misty; by now she had probably been over to my house and my mother had told her everything that happened.

There was a small TV up on the kitchen counter, the antennae bound in aluminum foil. I was about to turn it on when Angela came out in her thin robe and went and stared into her empty refrigerator. "Do you mind eating eggs?" she asked, and I shook my head. "TV is broken," she continued.

"This wasn't your first time, was it?" she asked, and set a plate of scrambled eggs on the table. "Cleva wants to believe this was *it*, the great loss of virginity, but I told her not to get her hopes up." Angela held her cigarette in the corner of her mouth, blinked against the smoke as she reached for the loaf of bread on the counter. "What Cleva *really* wants to believe is that she got there in time. Virginity intact." She was waiting, eyebrows raised as she blew a stream of smoke, and I knew she was expecting an answer. "Well?" she asked, and I looked away from her, scooped some of the eggs onto my plate. "Look, I know you don't want to talk," Angela said, and sat down. "But just tell me that you *do* know something about birth control."

I didn't answer, just moved my food around, but she continued. "I asked Cleva if she had ever talked to you about whether or not you needed to be on the pill."

"What?" I stared at her. Neither she nor my mother deserved anything from me.

"Well?" she asked. "You do know something about birth control, don't you?"

"Do you?" I asked suddenly, and looked at her, her face frozen with a look of surprise. "You've been with enough people. Do you know what to do?"

"Well," she said, face flushed as she tossed her hair over her shoulder, "I believe someone is a little defensive. Look." She sat forward, elbows on the table. "The worst that happens is you weren't careful and you have to do something about it. It's not that hard; mistakes *can* be corrected." She pushed away her plate of eggs and lit a cigarette. "You just don't want to keep making them."

"Like you? How many mistakes have *you* made?" I asked, my voice shaking. "You are always so ready to talk about Mo Rhodes and her mistake, to say all those awful things about her, so how about *you*."

"Mo? We're gonna dig that poor woman up again?" She stood, swung back the orange drapes and stared out at the empty laundromat. "I told you about Mo. Mo did *not* practice birth control." She laughed. "Baby number three proved that."

"She was a good person."

"Believe what you want." She strolled around the room, one hand on her hip, the other with her cigarette held up near her mouth.

"She was," I said, suddenly determined. I wanted to *make* her take back everything she'd said about Mo. I wanted to twist her arm behind her back until she gave in and told me what I wanted to hear.

"Mo was a good person. Gene was a good person. They just couldn't stay out of each other's pants." She stopped and stared at me, tears in her eyes. "He was screwing Mo Rhodes for years, *years*, and everybody in a fifty-mile radius *knew* it, and all the while I thought——" She stopped suddenly, breath rapid, and there was no need for her to complete the thought. It fit into place as easily as a puzzle piece, a bit of information I could use. Her bitterness towards Mo crystalized, and though it didn't make what Mo did right, it somehow lightened the load of words Angela had handed me that other night when she talked about how pitiful Misty was with her *orange* hair.

"That's why you didn't like Mo," I said, and pushed my plate away as well. Whether I was right or not, I finally had a face for the man on the beach, Angela leaning into Gene Files, laughing there as my father and I walked up the dune.

"Oh, who cares?" she asked, and ground her cigarette in the sink, making a hiss as the ash hit a wet spot. "Think what you want to think. I'm not a bad person either, Kate."

"I didn't say you were." I waited, feeling her right behind me, so close I could hear her loud sighs. I wished I could stop all that was happening, had happened, and play through it all before I continued, but there was no stopping. "I used to think you were my mother," I said, and focused on the loud drapes, the lights of the pier in the distance. I heard her laughter, loud and then soft.

"Why would you have ever thought that?" she asked, frozen there beside me.

"You were such a secret, a mystery." I shrugged. "There were lots of possibilities." I avoided looking at her, even when she pulled out the chair across from me and sat down. "You left home when you were seventeen, and so the age was just right. I thought that maybe my parents couldn't have a child, and so they agreed to take me. That way they would have a child, and you could have your own life."

"Do you think you watch enough movies?" she asked. "Really. Why would you ever concoct such a crazy story?"

"I don't know," I said. "It didn't used to sound so crazy."

"That is the most ridiculous thing I ever heard." She shook her head and laughed again, lit another cigarette. "Though I can see why you'd be wishing for a new mother. Cleva would die for sure if she heard that one."

"It was *possible*," I said, throwing Misty's favorite word to her. "And I really *wanted* it to be true. I really wanted you to love me."

"Don't we all want to be loved?" She shook her head. "Don't you see?" She reached across the table, palms turned upwards. "I do love you, but that's *my* story. *My* life." She was patting her hand against her chest. "That was my mother, okay? That was my seventeen-year-old mother, only my story is easier, you see. My mother just died right then and there. I wanted a mother. I wanted a mother who loved *me*, okay? Obviously Cleva didn't fit the bill. You can see that, can't you, since she doesn't even fit it with her own flesh and blood." She stopped, took a deep breath, voice catching. "That's *my* story, okay? So come up with your *own* tragedy."

Her breath was rapid as she leaned back in her chair and studied me. I felt her gaze and instinctively held my hands up to my face, my wrists touching beneath my chin.

"What, a birthmark?" she asked. "Use some make-up, cover it up. It's not so easy just to walk in a door and say, *Love me. Somebody please love me.* Heaven knows, I've tried too many times. Your father loved me." She moved around the table and squatted by my chair. "He is the only person who ever really loved me. Be thankful you had him."

I didn't look at her; her hand was on my arm, squeezing, twisting the skin to make me look at her. "I'm sorry for what I just said." She let go, put her hand up to my cheek, but I jerked away. "We all want a fairy tale, Kitty," she whispered. "Nobody wants the truth. But sooner or later you learn that there are no fairy tales; there *is* no glamorous mother hidden on a faraway island, no prince on a white horse, no treasure chest full of jewels." She kissed me quickly on the top of the head. "That's the real story and the truth is that I'm sorry that's the truth."

"Me too," I said, and then Angela went in her room and closed the door, leaving me to the dirty dishes and stack of old magazines in the corner. I thumbed through a two-year-old *Glamour* as I tried not to think about anything. I heard Angela dial the phone several times, with each try slamming the receiver; finally she was talking, whispering. "Please don't wait until the weekend again," she said, and I imagined her on the rumpled bed, ankles crossed as she stared at the little photo in the corner of the mirror. With every whisper I imagined that she was talking about me, telling *my* story, recreating the scene that had nothing to do with her. I turned the pages, flipping past lipstick and nail polish, faster and faster as I tried not to think of my mother as she bent down in the dark hallway and turned on her nightlight. More than anything I wanted to be at Misty's, the two of us stretched out on her bed, as I told her the whole story. She would lean close to me as I talked. I willed myself into her room, surrounded myself with the picture of that room, the chewing gum chain, the picture of Mo. I wished more than ever to be there, to have Mo come in and stretch out at our feet. And even better, I wished to run out into the street and hear my father's music, to run inside and find him in his study. I wished that I could make my mother understand how she had misjudged me. I wished that I could go back and at least close the door to Mr. Poole's room, at least have that extra minute to wake and tell Merle. I thought about it all for most of the night, unable to sleep until the sky turned a light gray.

When I woke it was noon and Angela was gone, I assumed to the seafood place where she worked. I didn't give myself a second to change my mind, but went in and sat on her rumpled bed and dialed my number. It rang for what seemed forever, and I imagined my mother pacing the foyer, back and forth, back and forth in those bedroom slippers, her face set stubbornly as she refused to give me the satisfaction of an answer. I was about to hang up when she was there, out of breath, and I knew then that she had been outside; she had been as far as the canna lilies when the phone brought her running through the yard and onto the back porch. "Hello?" she called again.

"Please come get me." The words were barely out of my mouth before she said, *Yes, I will,* and hung up the phone.

Forty minutes later, I stood by the window and began waiting, trying to imagine what my mother must be thinking, all that she must be planning to say on the ride home. Angela's Impala was in the drive and I was wondering how she got to work, if she walked to work, when I heard her laugh and then saw her step out from the apartment below. I sat quickly, pulling the sheet around me as if I'd just gotten up; when she was halfway up the metal stairs, I opened one of the magazines that I had read cover to cover the night before and studied the flawless face of Cheryl Tiegs.

"I was wondering when you'd wake up," she said, and closed the door.

"I thought you were at work." I watched a woman going into the laundromat, a yellow sheet draped around her shoulders as she prodded her dirty-faced child into the cinderblock building.

"Not today," Angela said. She was wearing a bright yellow bathing suit top and a pair of white jeans. "So, what do you want to do? Go swimming? Play putt-putt?" She stepped closer. "My neighbor, Jake, might go with us. He's a *friend* of Greg's." She emphasized the word *friend* and then contined. "Did you bring a suit?"

"I'm going home," I said, without looking up from the Cover Girl ad. "I called Mama to come get me."

"Well, I'm not surprised," she said, and then just sat there for what seemed an eternity; she sighed as if she were going to say something, but instead shook her head and went to the bedroom. I watched through the open door as she pulled a straw bag from the closet and then began filling it with a beach towel and a bottle of Hawaiian Tropic, her radio and an old copy of *Cosmopolitan*. "I hope you don't mind if I don't spend my day waiting for Cleva's arrival," she said, and I shook my head.

"No." I didn't tell her that it had been an hour since I'd called. Within minutes, when Angela was preparing to make her exit, I saw the big green Checker round the corner and stop behind the Impala. My mother stepped from the car, her gardening shoes still on, and I knew that she had left immediately after hanging up the phone. She shielded her eyes and stared at the building. "She's here." I stood and put the magazine on top of the stack, shook and folded the sandy sheet.

"Must've flown," Angela said, with a look of surprise, and sat down at the kitchen table, glanced at her watch as if to speed up my leaving.

"Bye." I picked up my suitcase and opened the door. "Thanks."

"Any time," she said, and then I was out on the landing, my mother waiting beside the car. She did not move to hug or touch me as I put my suitcase in the big back seat, and neither of us spoke as she backed down the sandy drive. That child was standing in the doorway of the laundromat, her bare foot swinging back and forth as she studied her shadow. I saw Angela looking out her window, the drapes swung to one side, and then within seconds she was gone, the drapes closed. My mother was silent the whole way, her copy of *How to Be Your Own Best Friend* sticking up from her purse beside her on the seat.

"Misty has been worried about you," she said without looking at me when we turned the corner at Whispering Pines. "I told her you'd be over as soon as you could. I did *not* tell her anything else." She was staring out at the canna lilies and that empty field where the kudzu had grown by leaps and bounds. "Merle called as well," she said. "I took his number." When I turned to reach for her, to speak, she clutched her purse and opened the car door. "We're having Chef Boy Ardee pizza for dinner," she said, and stood up straight, slammed the door.

Twenty-eight

B y fall, when we had returned to E. A. Poe High and football season was well underway, with Misty high-stepping her way through each half-time performance, the canna lilies stood like a bed of corn stalks, brown and withered. After much deliberation, my mother asked Mr. Landell to come and dig them all up and to do with them whatever he pleased; she said that she didn't know that she could stand to set them out year after year and then watch them grow like a red-alert reminder of my father's death.

I spent my Friday nights that fall at the high school football games. Misty still depended on me to give my opinion of her twirling performance; *Did I throw it high enough? Did I look fat in the new uniform?* "You looked terrific," I told her on the way home every Friday night, which was the absolute truth; Sally Jean backed up my every appraisal.

Usually I sat through the games with a group of girls from my class, their conversations on everything *except* football, while my thoughts were occupied by the upcoming game in Clemmonsville and how Merle and I had made plans to meet. I had seen Perry Loomis at two of the games; both times she was sitting with a guy who had graduated three years before, a tall thin guy with glasses and a military haircut. Perry was in one of the high school work programs where she went to class in the mornings and then worked a clerical job in the afternoons. I had overheard her tell someone that she was going to try to graduate in summer school so she could go to business college at night, that she was sick and tired of high school.

The day of the Clemmonsville game, Misty somehow managed to get out of riding with the band, and instead, the two of us rode in Sally Jean's Toyota. "What are friends for?" she had asked and adjusted her skimpy little sequin suit, tossed her coat and baton into the backseat. She spent most of the ride talking about the difficulty of her latest routine, one which she herself had choreographed to go along with the band's playing of "Time in a Bottle"; she said that she was talking a lot to keep my mind off of getting nervous, that it must work because Sally Jean did it all the time. When we arrived, Merle was standing at the main entrance just as he had promised. He was wearing a new denim jacket and hightop sneakers. He said that his hair was wet because he had just showered in the locker room. Every day after school he worked out in the weight room. He was getting in shape to go out for the track team.

Misty was running late; she nudged Merle playfully in greeting and then waved to us as she ran out onto the field, where the band was crowded in the end zone. We spent the first few minutes just watching Misty and laughing about the day she had whistled when Merle walked by my house. Our conversation was slow and a little awkward but got easier once we were seated up in the bleachers, his hand clasping mine tightly as Misty marched out onto the field for the "Star Spangled Banner." We sat on the Clemmonsville side, and throughout the game, people passed and spoke to Merle, called him by name, referred to this or that thing that had happened in school or after school. Though he introduced me as his girlfriend from Fulton, I felt oddly out of place; our conversations seemed to revolve around all those days in the cemetery or at Samuel T. Saxon.

After the game, we sat on Misty's car and waited for her to emerge from the crowd. "I'll call you soon?" He said it as a question, and I nodded, leaned in close to him to say good-bye; we sat that way, his breath warm on my face, until I saw Misty running up, her baton pumping at her side like a marathon runner. "Okay, go ahead and say it," she said all out of breath. "I *almost* missed that catch there at the end of 'Time in a Bottle,' but I didn't." As we drove away, I saw Merle walk over and join a crowd of people standing at the front of the Clemmonsville High School, and I felt the thirty-mile ride along the interstate beginning to lengthen.

We got a card from Angela in November that said she and Greg were going to spend the holidays in New Mexico. *Why would you go there for Christmas?* my mother asked over and over, which was what I wanted to ask her about the trip she had planned for us. Every chance I got, I sang, "Oh, there's no place like home for the holidays," but she ignored me and continued planning our trip to Boston, where we would stay in a fancy hotel and have room service and do all sorts of fun things. She kept showing me brochures and maps, all of which I'd seen at least a dozen times before, each time her voice becoming more enthusiastic.

"It'll get better after this year," Misty told me, whispering because Sally Jean was in the kitchen all set up in front of her sewing machine; strands of red sequins covered the floor as she worked on the uniform Misty would wear in the Fulton Christmas parade. "Don't you remember how awful it was until that first Fourth of July had come and gone?" She sighed, all the while watching Sally Jean, who held straight pins between her lips. "It wasn't great after that, but it was a lot easier."

By Christmas vacation, the calls and letters to and from Merle were not nearly as frequent as they had been, and it seemed when we did speak, the pauses got longer and longer. That day in Mr. Poole's study seemed so far away, all clouded and blended with everything that had happened, sealed behind the drapes of Samuel T. Saxon, sealed like my father's vault. Merle had once said that it might be good for him to be some place where no one had heard of his family, where the very mention of his name didn't conjure an image, and it seemed he now had that, new friends and new teachers. He could have a wish come true, a new start, a second chance.

My mother never mentioned that day to me, and though we often talked our way around it, it seemed I could never get close enough to tell her I was sorry I had ever wished her away. That I *was* my mother's daughter, and that for every time she had misjudged me, I had also misjudged her. It was a breezy winter day when we drove out to put a poinsettia on my father's grave, that granite ship break, break, breaking. I held the flower upright while she packed dirt around it; she periodically stopped to look at the tombstone and shake her head. When we finished, she asked to drive and had just cranked the Checker, heat blowing from the vents at our feet, when out of the blue she started telling me how much she had loved Angela, how much she wished that Angela had never run away from home to get married. "You know she's a smart girl, smarter than you'd think," my mother said. "And she's very pretty. It's a shame she's *not* someone's mother."

"I never *really* meant," I started, but she reached and patted my hand, took hold of it as we sat there in front of the grave.

"I know that," she said. "I know a lot." She stared straight ahead, hair pulled back loosely on her neck. "I know that Fred is getting a good laugh if he sees us sitting here in the green monster looking at that ugly, ugly headstone."

"Is everything really okay?" I finally asked as she put the car in drive and we began moving.

"Oh, yes." She looked at me, dark eyes glistening. "It's copacetic."

We drove home in silence, past the Confederate statue, the large empty lot where Samuel T. Saxon had stood. "It's so hard without Fred, isn't it?" she asked, and I nodded. "But just you wait, Katie, this vacation will be good. I'll show you a statue to the *Union* dead," she said, and laughed. "I'll show you the Public Gardens and the Alcotts' house, the Alcotts' *graves*, for heaven's sakes. Let's see if their tombstones can compare."

"You really did love him, didn't you?" I asked when we were almost home. She waited a long minute before answering.

"You think I'd choose a life of grits and black-eyed peas and summers so hot I could have a damned heat stroke for nothing?"

"Does that mean you might want to move some day?" I thought then of Merle all settled in a new world, new friends, a new place, a second chance, but I also thought of all the things familiar in our life, Misty in her split-level, Mrs. Poole with her constant chatter, which more and more was directed at car dealerships, Honda, Toyota. In a way my mother and I *were* getting that second chance. And maybe Angela was looking for her new chance; maybe she had already found it. Maybe she was planning to appear one day on our front porch and surprise us with the order, the happiness of her life.

"Why, of course not," she said. "This is home." She turned the corner at Whispering Pines, and we drove past, the bare trees swaying. Somewhere in the distance I heard Christmas music, *Angels we have heard on high*. In spite of winter weather, Sally Jean's yard was still green, and as we got out of the car, I saw Misty out there practicing, her baton spinning, glinting silver in the bright clear light as she twisted and kicked. Sally Jean was standing in the living room window proudly watching this high-stepping girl she had grown to love; she was an answer to a prayer, a second chance. Misty tossed the baton high into the air, my mother and I watching as it spiraled against the bright blue sky and then fell neatly into her outstretched hand, a whole world of possibilities spinning around her.

TRUE LOVE

JENNIFER LOPEZ

PHOTOS BY ANA CARBALLOSA

Celebra
Published by the Penguin Group
Penguin Group (USA) LLC, 375 Hudson Street,
New York, New York 10014

USA | Canada | UK | Ireland | Australia | New Zealand | India | South Africa | China
penguin.com
A Penguin Random House Company

First published by Celebra,
a division of Penguin Group (USA) LLC

First Printing, November 2014

THE LIBRARY OF CONGRESS HAS CATALOGED THE HARDCOVER EDITION OF THIS TITLE AS FOLLOWS:
Lopez, Jennifer, 1970–
True love/by Jennifer Lopez.
p. cm.
ISBN 978-0-451-46868-0
1. Lopez, Jennifer, 1970– 2. Motion picture actors and actresses—United States—Biography.
3. Singers—United States—Biography. I. Title.
 PN2287.L634A3 2013
 791.4302'8092—dc23   2013027047
 [B]

Printed in the United States of America
10 9 8 7 6 5 4 3 2 1

Set in Bembo Std
Designed by Pauline Neuwirth

Owning our story can be hard but not nearly as difficult as spending our lives running from it. Embracing our vulnerabilities is risky but not nearly as dangerous as giving up on love and belonging and joy—the experiences that make us the most vulnerable. Only when we are brave enough to explore the darkness will we discover the infinite power of our light.

—Brené Brown, *The Gifts of Imperfection*

This book is dedicated to Max and Emme,
who saved me.

CONTENTS

PREFACE

IT'S OPENING NIGHT, the first show of my first ever world tour.

This was the first time we'd be doing the full show that we had been planning and working on for more than six months. I am in full costume, backstage with the usual cast of characters. I bend down to give Emme and Max a kiss before my mom walks them off to watch the opening of the show. This was going to be the first time they'd see their mommy perform in front of thousands and thousands of people. The last time I was on stage like this, they were in my belly.

As they walk away, Emme looks back and stops. I'm being buckled into the rig on a twelve-by-twelve-inch platform. The huge, full-feather train of my white skirt pours over the edges and it must seem to her like I'm standing in a cloud. She seems a little nervous, but excited. I'm nervous, but controlling my fear. I'm about to ascend sixty feet into the air. I know it's crazy, because the crew is watching with faces that say, *This is crazy!* I give the operator the thumbs-up; he gives me the thumbs-up in return . . . and up I go, disappearing into the rafters until I am perched behind a huge video wall, where nobody can see me.

Emme looks up, watching me rise and rise and rise . . . From my perspective, everybody looks like little ants on the floor. I take a deep breath and think about the past year, all the hard work and the hard lessons that have led to this moment.

If I let myself, I could go weak in the knees. But I don't. I hold strong as the band plays the dramatic intro while the opening movie plays on the screen. And when the video wall splits open, I'm standing there, a hundred feet above the audience, and the crowd goes wild. The spotlight hits me, and in my best old Hollywood voice I say: "HELLO, LOVERS."

In this book I'm going to take you on the physical and emotional journey of the year I went on the first world tour of my career. The year that changed my life.

When I started planning the tour, I knew it was going to be the anchor for a very personal show. What I didn't expect was how cathartic it would end up being for me. The process of building the tour and performing it each and every night for audiences around the world helped me get back to who I am—someone who sings, who dances, who expresses herself and connects with people through music.

So many times I wanted to abandon writing this book because I knew it would be a difficult process, delving into the past and reliving some of my darkest moments. Also, I didn't want to be misread. I didn't want anything to overshadow the magnificence of this great journey. This book is not a detailed account of any of my relationships, famous or not. This is not a "tell-all," so I hope that's not what you're looking for. But by the end, I think you'll agree, you'll have gotten so much more. This book is about a series of patterns that go back as early as my childhood. This book is about *my* path and what *I* learned. It's the story of

a transformative journey where I faced some of my greatest challenges, overcame some of my biggest fears, and emerged a stronger person than I've ever been. This is the story of how I discovered . . . the truest love of all.

My genuine intention and what I hope to accomplish with this book is that others can draw upon the experiences that changed the course of my life and find encouragement in the mantra that motivated the following pages:

You will live.

You will love.

You will *dance again* . . .

SETTING THE STAGE

I wake up in bed alone. The silence in my room reminds me of the emptiness in my heart. I failed at love—again. Except this time, it wasn't just me. I am haunted by the inescapable thought that I let down my beautiful babies, Max and Emme. I wanted so badly for things to have turned out differently.

As lonely as this bed feels, I can't bring myself to get out of it.

ROCK BOTTOM

HITTING ROCK BOTTOM

I remember the exact moment when everything changed. I was in the desert outside Los Angeles, getting ready for a photo shoot.

It was a beautiful day in July 2011, and Marc and I had just celebrated our seventh wedding anniversary. Anybody looking from the outside in would have thought my life was going great: I had a husband and two beautiful children, and my career was flying high. I was on *American Idol*, the number-one show on the planet, and my new single "On the Floor" had gone to number one all over the world. To top it off, *People* magazine had named me their very first Most Beautiful Woman in the World, a few months earlier. How could life get any better?

What people didn't know was that life really *wasn't* that good. My relationship was falling apart, and I was terrified.

And now here I was out in the desert, getting made up for a L'Oréal shoot. I had done hundreds of these before—you sit in the chair, get your hair and face made up, go out in front of the camera, and do your thing. But this day didn't feel like any other day.

As I sat there, my mind was racing. My heart was beating out of my chest, and I felt like I couldn't breathe . . . I became consumed with fear and anxiety. *What was happening to me?*

My mom, Guadalupe, who lives in New York and happened to be in town that week, came to the desert with me that day, and my dear manager, Benny Medina, was there too. As I found myself in a panic, I leaped from my chair and said, "Benny, something is happening! I feel like I'm going crazy."

In the end, the truth finds a way to surface, even if you don't want it to.

Benny, who has been through so much with me over the fifteen years we have worked together and been friends, took my hands.

"Hey, now, what's happening? What's going on?" he asked.

My mom rushed to my side, too, a look of concern on her face.

All I could say was, "I don't know. I don't feel right. I'm scared. I feel like I'm losing my mind."

He tried to calm me down, saying, "You're fine, Jennifer. You're good. Everything's okay." To him I looked completely calm. But I wasn't. It was one of those moments when you're so scared you can't even scream. It feels as if you're paralyzed.

We as human beings do this thing where we stuff down our feelings until they find a way to manifest themselves. We try to avoid them until there's no more room and they come bubbling up like a pot of boiling-hot water that overflows. And when it does, it burns, and it's scary. That's what was happening to me.

In a blur of fear and panic, I looked at Benny and my mother and blurted out the words: "I don't think I can be with Marc anymore." Then I burst into tears.

It was out.

The one thing I feared more than anything in the world. The one thing I had been trying for so long not to face. Deep down, I knew that nothing would ever be the same again.

I collapsed into their arms and began to sob. And like that pot of boiling-hot water, once it overflows, the pressure is released and it begins to cool down. All those crazy thoughts started to melt away because I had finally given voice to the real reason for my fear and panic. I knew what it meant to say those words out loud: It meant the end of my marriage. The end of our family. The end of the dream I had worked so hard to hold together.

And it meant more than that. It meant that once again I was going to be judged. I was going to be ridiculed, chastised, and mocked. I could already see the headlines: "Jennifer Lopez Headed for Divorce . . . Again!" Or, "The Woman Who Has Everything But Can't Get Love Right!" I was so scared to have another failure, to be scrutinized by the world, and to disappoint everyone . . . again.

But this time wasn't like any other time. It was worse. This divorce wouldn't affect just Marc and me. It would affect these two beautiful little souls we had brought into the world. I was devastated at the thought of hurting Max and Emme. I was afraid that I was about to ruin their lives, that someday they would resent me for not being able to keep this marriage together.

As I struggled with the idea of breaking up my family, I had to consider what was best for my kids in the long run, and I agonized over what would serve them best in life. I was pulled in both directions, which is why I had fought so hard against admitting the inevitable. I *couldn't* admit that this marriage was over. But in the end, the truth finds a way to surface, even if you don't want it to. That day in the desert, with my brain going wild trying to deny reality, I had finally hit rock bottom.

HOPE FOR A BETTER DAY

On Christmas day in 2010, seven months before that L'Oréal photo shoot, we had a house full of people. Marc was there, and Emme and Max, and Marc's other kids, Ryan and Cristian, Arianna and Alex, as well as our parents, siblings, and friends. It was the kind of Christmas gathering I'd always wanted to have: a big, sprawling affair with our family at the center of it.

The house was filled with food and gifts and laughter, and that afternoon, twenty-four of us sat down to a beautiful Christmas dinner. Things between Marc and me weren't perfect, of course—our marriage was never the kind to glide along peacefully. From the beginning, it was tumultuous, passionate, and explosive, but we also shared many fulfilling and joyful moments. I knew we had problems, but we loved each other and we were trying, and I wanted more than anything to have a family—*this* family. So I was willing to ignore whatever wasn't going well, for the greater good of preserving it.

I thought that Christmas was exactly what I wanted. I thought we were finally getting it right, that it was worth putting up with the difficulties because this was what life was about. Every marriage has its challenges, but it was about keeping that marriage together, having that family unit, and making the dream come true—whatever the cost. Part of that concept still holds true for me: Family is most important.

But the very next Christmas, twelve months later, I was waking up alone. The only people in the house were Max, Emme, and my cousin Tiana, who had come to keep me company. My mother and my sisters, Lynda and Leslie, had decided to stay in New York for the holidays, and they had asked me to come out, but I didn't want to go. I wanted to be in my own home, as empty as it now felt.

I cried a lot that Christmas, though I tried to let the tears flow only when the kids couldn't see me. There's nothing like the holidays to make you feel a loss, and I was really feeling it. But then my dad, David, came over for Christmas dinner, and Benny came and brought his mom. So with Emme, Max, and everyone else, we had a pretty full table—even if it wasn't as full as the one we had the year before.

What I will always remember about that Christmas is not the tears or the loneliness, but the toast that Benny gave.

Benny Medina is a legend in his own right. He's the original inspiration for the Fresh Prince of Bel-Air—a larger-than-life guy who always manages to make everyone around him feel special. He's also famous among his friends for his "Benny toasts." He loves to seize the moment, to raise his glass and offer up a story, a speech, or an affirmation. He works on them—you can sometimes see him typing out words on his phone right before he gets up to speak. So when Benny raises his glass, you know you're about to hear something special. And that dinner was no exception.

"A lot of changes have happened over this past year," he said. "There has been loss, and there has been gain. Look around you and remember that this family—the family that is sitting here with you—has always been here. And we will always be here."

I looked around the table at all these people I loved: my dad, my babies, Tiana, my cousins, my aunt, Benny.

"You make your choices in life, and these people right here," he said, "these people are the family that will get you through. They are your rock."

"You make your choices in life, and these people right here," he said, "these people are the family that will get you through. They are your rock."

As he spoke, I began to see that I did have people around me who supported and loved me unconditionally and had always been there. Families come in all shapes and sizes, and they don't have to fit the perfect dream ideal to make you happy. They are the people that support and love you by giving you strength when you need it the most.

As I looked around the table, it hit me; he was right. I felt the love. I felt that family. And I knew I was blessed.

I hoped that he was right about something else too. He said, "As painful as some of the past year's changes have been, they will ultimately lead to a better place. The adversity you come across in life may cause pain, but with pain comes growth and the opportunity to rise to the occasion as your strongest, best self."

There was nothing I needed more in that moment than the encouragement and the hope of a better day.

Benny's speech gave me that beautiful gift.

NEW DREAM

In my family, when I was growing up, divorce was not an option. My parents stayed together for thirty-three years, through thick and thin and everything in between. So when I married Marc, having already been through the disappointment of two divorces and a broken engagement, I wanted so much for our marriage to be "it." I was determined to make it last, no matter what. And once we had kids, I was even more determined. I was never going to give up on this love.

Tried to be someone I knew that I wasn't

I thought I could make myself happy with you

—"NEVER GONNA GIVE UP"

Marc was my guy, the one. The father of my children, the man I was going to grow old with. I believed that with all my heart . . . until I finally realized, in the months leading up to that day in the desert, that it wasn't meant to be. I wasn't listening to my own inner voice, and now my body and soul were physically telling me that I could no longer be there. I couldn't deny the truth anymore. I had to do something about it.

When I think back on it, years earlier I had reached a similar moment in my career. It was during a time when I was getting to do things that I had hardly let myself dream about when I was a little girl. Platinum albums, movie roles opposite Jack Nicholson, George Clooney, Sean Penn . . . I felt like I was doing it on my own terms, but actually, I wasn't.

I was mainly following the advice of managers, record executives, and stylists. They had the best of intentions, but because I wasn't also listening to myself, I ended up caring more and more about what they wanted and how I was perceived by the public and the media than what I knew was right for me as an artist. Instead of measuring my success and value by my own standards, I was measuring it by how others perceived me.

Because I was so used to being seen as that woman in the tabloids, the Hollywood diva, I forgot what it was like to be known as myself. It's vital to be in touch with who you are at your core and not to lose yourself in the hustle. I had always wanted to believe that my public image didn't affect my feelings of self-worth—but unfortunately, that wasn't always the case. If you keep hearing negative things about yourself, they start to seep into your consciousness and you start to feel like they're true. They cloud who you know you really are and you can lose yourself.

I was being painted in a way that wasn't me because I wasn't taking control of the situation. I was so wrapped up in keeping up with my schedule and giving people what they wanted that I neglected to ask myself what *I* wanted. I spent a lot of energy living up to those expectations and I lost my own sense of direction along the way.

When I first started my career, I always made my decisions on my own; I always knew what was best for me. I didn't have anyone telling me what to do or where to go. I followed my heart, followed my instincts, and listened to my gut. Because the truth is, nobody knows what's best for you better than you do. You have to really sit still and ask yourself: *What do I want? Does this feel right? What should I do?* I realized I had to go back and do what I had always done. Listening to my gut was just as important as listening to the advice of others, and only I knew what was best for me.

That's why now, whenever someone asks me, "What is the one piece of advice you would give an artist who is starting out and wants to do what you do?"

My answer is always: "Listen to yourself; listen to your gut. Because only you know what's right for you."

That's what being an artist is all about. Your power is in your individuality, in being exactly who you are. No two artists are alike, just like no two people are alike. That's why there is no competition in artistry. It's not about being the best or the biggest, the king or the queen. That notion is so ridiculous. That competition or comparison is actually the exact opposite of what being an artist is. As an artist, you should be in competition with only one person—yourself. You can't worry about what others are doing or saying. You have to keep that focus and stay true to who you are in order to be creative and make the best decisions.

As an artist, you should be in competition with only one person—yourself.

So when I came to a point where my relationship simply wasn't feeling right, I knew what I needed to do. If I turned down the noise from the rest of the world—critics, fans, friends, even family—and if I really listened to myself, what would I hear?

I had to ask myself that question. So just like I took control of my career in that crucial moment, now I needed to take control of my life.

"You make your choices in life," Benny had said in his toast. Now that my marriage was over and my life was going in a different direction than I'd thought, I had another choice to make, and this time I was determined to make it for myself. I began to ask: *What's next? What new dream am I going to build now?* In the days following that Christmas dinner, this was the question I kept coming back to. I simply couldn't ignore it.

CONQUERING THE WORLD

By January first, I had faced my worst fear: the breakup of our seemingly perfect family. Reality was setting in, and I needed to figure out how to make it all work. I was a single mom now: *How am I going to do this? Can I do this? Can I be their everything? Will I ever be able to fill that hole for them?*

Can just Mommy ever be enough? It was daunting and, at times, depressing to realize that I didn't always have the answers. It was even scarier to think that maybe I never would. But I couldn't stop to think about that now. I had to see it through. Even in my weakest moments, the moments when I doubted myself the most, my babies needed me. I had to be strong.

I don't know what it is about me, but for better or for worse, in the face of doubt or change, I get these crazy ideas—don't ask me why—that I should challenge myself beyond my normal limits and do something I've never done before. I guess, subconsciously, it's about distracting myself from the difficulty and pain of the moment. Example: After I had the kids—talk about a big change—I really felt like I'd lost my mojo. I was exhausted, out of shape, and I felt like a beached whale. So what did I do? I decided to do a triathlon! Now, understand, I had never done a triathlon before. I had run a 10K when I was twelve, but never anything close to a triathlon.

On the morning of the race, as I was standing there surrounded by a thousand paparazzi, about to jump into the ocean, I realized that this probably wasn't the best idea I ever had. All I could see was a buoy five hundred meters out, and the only thing blocking its view were the waves crashing toward me. The one prayer I kept saying over and over again was: "Please, God, I have two babies. Please let me survive this incredibly stupid thing I decided to do." But when the gun went off, I instinctually ran toward the ocean and jumped in. I faced my fear, and when I crossed that finish line, I felt invincible. I'd gotten my mojo back. I felt like I could do anything.

Now it was happening again. After a reflective Christmas and a New Year's I'd been trying to make the best of, it was one in the afternoon and I was lying in bed all by myself, staring at the ceiling. And then it hit me. One of those crazy ideas popped into my head. I picked up the phone to call Benny. The conversation went a little like this:

"Benny! I know what I want to do," I said.

"Yeah?" he responded.

And in a quiet, determined tone that Benny has come to know means I've had a revelation, I said: "I *have* to tour this year. That's what we have to do."

"Really?" said Benny. He paused for a moment. Benny had wanted

this for years. I awaited his response: "Okay . . . Let's do it," he finally said.

"Okay, then!" I said. "Let's do it."

"Okay cool . . ."

"Great! I'm excited," I said.

"I'm excited too," he said.

I hung up. End call.

What the hell had I done? Oh. My. God. What now?

PAAAAANIIIIIICCCCC!!!!

See? It was working! I was no longer focused on my sadness; my thoughts were somewhere else, on the colossal challenge I had put on myself of building my "new dream." Something that would take me through five continents, sixty-five cities, four hundred and sixty-two wardrobe changes, and five hundred thousand sequins (*I hoped*): my first ever world tour.

Despite what many people might think, I had never done a tour be-fore. And, on top of it all, I was about to do it as a single mom, with two kids in tow.

ACT ONE

BIG HOLLYWOOD

SET LIST

Intro: "Never Gonna Give Up"
———

"Get Right"
———

"Love Don't Cost a Thing"
———

"I'm Into You"
———

"Waiting for Tonight"
———

I was sad. I was heartbroken. I was scared.

But it was only through adversity that I found

my saving graces.

Sometimes they came from unexpected

sources—a song, a challenge, or a friend.

It was my responsibility to make the most of

them, apply them to my life, act on them, and

rise to the occasion.

NEVER GONNA GIVE UP

BECAUSE I HAD never done a solo tour before, I wanted to get it just right. I wanted to tell a story, to open myself up to people, to give them what they'd been waiting to see. I made my first record back in 1999, which meant that some people had been waiting thirteen years for me to come and do a show. I wanted to do all the hits for them; I wanted them to feel it had been worth the wait.

If I was going to do this, I'd have to work incredibly hard, and my goal was not only to grow as an artist, but also as a person. A part of me was petrified to take it on, as I knew there was a possibility that it might not turn out right. Yet part of me was so drawn by the fantasy of it. *What would I do creatively if I could do anything at all? What songs would I choose? How would I express myself as an artist?* And more important: *What was I going to wear? Who would make my costumes?* This could actually be a lot of fun! In designing the tour, I suddenly had this empty canvas that I could paint however I liked. But as with any blank canvas, facing it was both exciting and daunting. *Where do I begin? What do I want to say? What is my message?* I needed a concept to start with.

THE GIFT OF SONG

Right before my breakup, Enrique Iglesias called to say he wanted to do a duet with me. He sent me a song and we recorded it, but after he listened to it, he told me, "It's not a big enough hit. If you and I do a song together, it has to be a smash. I'm sending you another song."

He sent me a song called "Dance Again." By then, a couple of months had gone by and Marc and I had just split up. I was dying inside, feeling lonely and miserable and sad. I don't remember the song's exact original lyrics, but it had the chorus, "I want to dance . . . and love . . . and *dance again*." All I could think was, "Oh my God, that's what I want. I want to *dance and love and dance again* too."

I needed that song. I was at a moment in my life where I felt like I might not be happy ever again. That line expressed everything I was feeling.

I'm a dancer—that's who I am. I'm most happy and free and alive when I'm dancing. I wanted to get back to that feeling, that person. I wanted to feel happiness again. I wanted to feel love again. And that's what music does. Music is a declaration of what life is and what you want it to be.

And the sentiment of that song . . . was something I wanted to declare to the world.

This was *my* song.

Oops—record scratch.

Except it wasn't my song. It was Enrique's.

I said to Benny, "Enrique wants to do this as a duet, but I think it would work better if I did it alone. I can't just ask him to let me have it for my record, right?"

Benny said, "Well, *I* can. Let me talk to him." I don't know exactly what he said, but in the end, Enrique gave me the song.

As fate would have it, Enrique and I wound up doing the US leg of the tour together. I'll never forget opening night in New York. Enrique came up to me at the end of the show, after seeing people's response to "Dance Again." He looked me in the eyes and said, "Jennifer, you were right. That really *is* your song."

When Enrique gave me that song, he gave me a powerful gift. In some ways, every song is like that, because music is a gift in itself. When you listen to the right tune, and the lyrics express your soul's truest feelings, it lifts you up—it's a beautiful thing. I'd felt it as a young girl, listening to songs on the radio. And now, as an artist, to be able to make that music and sing it—sing it for myself, sing it for others—is one of my biggest blessings from God.

When you listen to the right tune, and the lyrics express your soul's truest feelings, it lifts you up—it's a beautiful thing.

I remember Puffy once saying to me while I was making my very first album, "Be careful what you sing, be careful what you record because it can define you." Music is very powerful. It goes out into the universe, and it takes on an energy; it becomes part of your story. That's why I would never record anything that's too negative or too depressing—because that's not what I want my life to be about. Music isn't just songs, it's your life as an artist. In many ways, you sing your future. I believed that and it always rang true with me. At this moment in my life, on a very visceral level, I wanted to dance again and I wanted to love again so I wanted to sing about it. I feel like every song I've recorded has been given to me in some way—every song has come to me at the right moment. And now, with Enrique's gift, I felt that way again.

Once I had the song, everything flowed from there. We named the new greatest hits record *Dance Again*, and when we released the single, it made it to the top ten in countries all over the world. Everything became about that message.

The Dance Again World Tour was born.

I wanted to *dance again* . . . and for the first time, I was about to do it all over the world.

JUMPING IN

The truth was, I had planned to do a world tour three or four times in the past. We'd do all the planning and get all the way to the stage where we were making the deals—and then I'd get a part in a movie. A tour you can move around, but when a movie comes up, it shoots when it shoots, and you're either in or you're out. So we would always say, "Okay, let's move the tour dates." And then somehow, even though we meant only to postpone, it always ended up falling apart. But because my records kept selling, even without the tours to support them, nobody seemed to mind that they weren't happening.

Many people seemed to doubt I could actually *do* a tour. Never having done one, I have to admit, I wasn't sure either. Would I have the stamina to be on the road so long? Could I really sing live and dance and do all those shows all those nights in a row? Would my voice hold up? Would it be too much for the kids?

Over the following weeks, I'd call Benny and say, "Listen, forget what I said. This isn't the right time." He'd try to calm me, and sometimes it worked and sometimes it didn't. We went back and forth, talking and thinking and weighing it all out. The tour was on; the tour was off. In my heart I knew I could do it, but my brain kept pulling me back.

As I considered the reality of doing this tour, I remembered a peculiar thing that had happened a decade earlier, when I was in Canada shooting the movie *Angel Eyes*. Everybody on set kept talking about this amazing psychic who lived in Toronto. I don't usually go for that kind of thing, but people kept saying how incredible this guy was. "You have to go see him! He'll read you like a book!" I was young and having fun, and so a couple of us decided, for the hell of it, to jump in the car and go see him.

I went with a girlfriend I've known since elementary school and who was working for me at the time. We found the psychic's place, and when I'd settled in for my reading, he looked at me and got very serious.

"Whenever you end up going on tour," he said, "it's going to be more than traveling around and doing shows. You're going to grow as a person."

This seemed like a strange thing for a psychic to latch onto, but then the guy actually started to get kind of emotional.

"I'm telling you," he said, "going on tour will change your life. It will change everything about you."

I looked at him and was shocked to see that he had tears in his eyes. It was so intense, so unexpected. So *weird*. And he wasn't finished.

"Spiritually," he said, "as a human being, it will take you to the next level."

Now, I don't know that I really believed in all of what he had to say, but I never forgot his words. And as I was going back and forth with Benny—I have to be honest—I found myself thinking about it. "Maybe if we do this, something really amazing *will* happen!" And after all the pain I'd been through, I wanted my old self back—strong me, happy me, dancing me. Maybe this tour was the answer.

So finally, when the clock had ticked down to our do-or-die moment, Benny stopped me and said, "They need to know right now, kiddo."

I was standing in my trailer about to go on live TV for *Idol*. I took a step back, took a deep breath, and said, "I'll do it."

A month later, we were in rehearsals.

Figuring it out what this is all
  about
when he came to me, when he comes
  to me
Gotta do what's best for me

—"NEVER GONNA GIVE UP"

I wanted the show to start like a scene out of an old Hollywood musical. I didn't want it to feel real; I wanted it to feel like a movie, like

people were watching the Ziegfeld Follies, with Rita Hayworth, or Ava Gardner, gliding across the stage.

On the walls of the den in my house, I have black-and-white photos of Hollywood stars from the thirties, forties, and fifties. When you look at those photos, you can imagine yourself right there with them, in a scene out of a classic movie. And I had. So that's how I wanted the opening of the show to feel. Something soft, beautiful, ethereal . . . something magical from another era.

I saw myself sitting at a desk, backstage in my dressing room, writing in a diary, dressed in a white gown, playing the role of the Hollywood star surrounded by dancing men in tuxedos and top hats. I wanted to make them feel like they were watching a dream . . .

As I was imagining this whole scene, I wondered what song I should be singing for it. I knew that "Dance Again" would be the final song, the get-on-your-feet encore, the final message I wanted everyone to take away from this show. But the first song is just as important, as it sets the stage for everything to come. *What should it be? What do I want this show to be about?* I turned to the person who had become my friend, my partner and collaborator for this show—Beau.

A FRESH PERSPECTIVE

I met Beau about a year earlier when I was doing the video shoot for "On the Floor." While we were in the editing process, I was watching clips with the choreographer, Frank Gatson, when I noticed one of the background dancers doing a really cool move.

"Wait," I said. "That's amazing. Let's put that in. Who is that?"

"That's Casper," said Frank, which is Beau's nickname. At the time, we had just lost one of our dancers and needed a replacement for an upcoming performance. So I said, "Let's bring that guy in. Let's hire him for the show."

Beau was pretty young at the time, but he had done choreography for Eminem and Beyoncé, had worked with artists like Michael Jackson and Pink, and had been on TV shows like *Jimmy Kimmel Live* and *Glee*.

Because I started as a dancer, I have always related to them. I get them, and they get me, and whenever I'm shooting a video or doing a show, I like hanging around them. It's a world I love and feel comfortable in. So right away, I felt a kinship with Beau. He and the other dancers saw me as strong and capable and determined again, and slowly, I was able to be strong and capable and determined. In the same way negative influences can bring you down, having positive people around can help lift you up.

We started as creative partners, but eventually we became good friends, truly valuing each other's opinions. So at the time, he was the natural choice to help me put the tour together.

We had already decided that we wanted to do a fifties musical-esque opening that felt dreamy and ethereal, with angelic voices singing some beautiful ballad. So we sat down and went through all the different songs from my albums, trying to figure out which one would intro the show.

"Maybe 'Secretly'?" I said, flipping through pages, looking at lyrics.

In the same way negative influences can bring you down, having positive people around can help lift you up.

"No," Beau said. "It has to be 'Never Gonna Give Up.' It's a perfect statement for you. Because that's who you are." He cued the song up, and we listened:

Now that I'm growing / Now that I'm knowing
Never gonna give up on / Never gonna give up on love . . .

"You're not about to give up on love, right?" he said. "People need to know that. Even though you went through this bad period, that's still how you feel."

He was right. So that's how we opened the show, with that sentiment. Yes, this big thing in my life went wrong, but I'm not gonna give up. I'm never giving up on love.

In the video that intro'd the show, I'm backstage in my flowing white dress, writing about love in my diary, singing about never giving up, about moving to that next chapter in life. *I don't want to hear no woulda coulda, maybe I shoulda . . . Never gonna give up on, never gonna give up on . . . loove looove loooove . . .*

And as the word "love" hangs in the air, I close my book, get up from my desk, and walk through the backstage of an old majestic theater . . . I fearlessly ascend a beautiful white staircase, and step by step, I begin my new journey.

Little did I know this tour would end up helping me reflect on the journey of my life, through my music, in a way that opened my eyes. I never expected it. I never thought, when we first started designing the show, that it would be such a life-changing experience.

When I reach the top of the stairs, the kabuki curtain drops on the real stage, revealing the first act of the show: Big Hollywood.

All of my dreams were coming true. Except for one.

Love proved elusive. But I kept trying. If I could make so many of my dreams come true, why not this?

BIG HOLLYWOOD

ART IMITATING LIFE

And here she is: the Jennifer Lopez that people have been waiting for. The woman in the sparkling gown, draped in jewelry, manicured, made up, glamorous . . . The diva rising up into the spotlight.

Because this is who I am, right? The person I've become over all those years in the public eye, the dancer who became an actress who became a singer . . . who became a star. This is the Jennifer Lopez everyone expects, so this is the person I want to give to the world. The Hollywood star, poised onstage in an arena of screaming fans.

> *Like a movie scene, in the sweetest*
> *dreams, I have pictured us*
> *together . . .*
>
> —"WAITING FOR TONIGHT"

This was the scenario I wanted to create in the Big Hollywood opening section of the Dance Again tour: the emergence of the star, with all the glamour and glitz. It was life imitating art imitating life, and I

wanted to give everyone the full Hollywood treatment exactly as it had happened to me . . .

Big Hollywood would feature the big hits—"Get Right," "Love Don't Cost a Thing," "I'm Into You," and "Waiting for Tonight." And the truth was, we had been waiting for tonight, all of us, for a very long time. Through nine albums, through thirteen years, through all the ups and downs. Through whatever fears I'd felt about putting on this show, we were finally here.

It's perfect, it's passion, it's setting me free
From all of my sadness, the tears that I've cried
I have spent all of my life, waiting for tonight . . .

—"WAITING FOR TONIGHT"

A DREAM TO DANCE

Ever since I was a little girl, there were two things that came naturally to me: dancing and running. I can't remember a time before I did these things, and from the moment I started, I've never stopped doing either one of them.

I never wanted to slow down. Moving fast, moving forward is a natural state of being for me. When I was in junior high school, my younger sister went to try out for the track team. I tagged along and ended up getting chosen for the team myself. From then on, I ran every race and tried to win every medal and trophy that I could. Just running and running and running.

I love the feeling it gives me. I get into a rhythm that puts me in this meditative state, a zone where I feel powerful, strong, healthy, and calm. There's a great line that Lil Wayne raps during "I'm Into You." He says: "Every finish line is the beginning of a new race." That's how I've always felt, my whole life. Always rushing and hurrying—never wanting to sit still. As I would later find out, that's a useful trait to have when you're building a career, but it's not so great in building relationships.

okay now I'm into you, like you never knew

I'm falling for ya baby, I need a parachute.

—"I'M INTO YOU"

I wasn't one of those people who had some master plan to get to where I am today. When I was a little girl, I didn't think, *I'm going to be a star!* I trained hard and worked hard and I liked to win. But I never thought it would lead to where it did—not that I ever stopped to think about it, of course. (Who had time? I was running!)

Now dancing, I started when I was fourteen, in the neighborhood community center at the Kips Bay Boys & Girls Club. As with running, I became obsessive about it. Dancing had a similar rhythm to it, and it felt natural to me. It made me feel good and I was good at it. I practiced until my legs and feet ached—I wanted to be the best at it that I could possibly be.

I put in long hours. That's what my parents taught me to do when you had big dreams. I followed their example of working hard, and I put everything I had into it. I'd go to classes and rehearsals early to warm up first, and I stayed later than everyone else, going over a tough move or getting in one more practice. All I knew during those long days was that I loved what I was doing and maybe, just maybe, I could do it forever.

SEARCHING FOR TRUE LOVE

Being a professional dancer was my dream and I worked hard toward reaching that goal. But from when I was very little, I would close my eyes in bed at night and imagine that perfect family, with children and a husband who loved me above all else.

Throughout my life, I've had a few serious relationships. Each relationship was different and each relationship had its issues. But there was one thing they all had in common: They all had a passionate intensity that I mistook, every time, for my happily ever after. In each relationship, I thought my childhood fairy tale was coming to life, and that was all that mattered to me at the time.

Reality is hard to see through the adrenaline rush of a new love. It's easy to project your hopes and dreams onto a relationship when it's new and exciting, but the truth is that it is only in knowing who you are at your core and staying true to yourself that you can possibly see the difference between passion and real love.

I was lucky—or unlucky—enough to be with men who were really intense about their feelings for me. They did some crazy things, and I mean *crazy things*. Like releasing hundreds of doves outside my window, buying me a Bentley (or two), giving me rare diamonds, throwing me giant parties, or sending me private jets to sweep me off somewhere. I'm talking about grand gestures of love, passion, or whatever you want to call it. And I loved it. It was intoxicating when it was happening.

When a man does something like that, it's easy to think, *Wow, look how much he loves me!* I believed that these gestures inevitably signified love. *He's giving me gifts that I could only dream of, or putting up posters telling me how special I am all along the street where I drive to work. Does it get any better than this? Nobody has ever loved anybody as much as this guy loves me.*

But passion is a pendulum that swings both ways. As beautiful as it can be, it can also get very intense. Yet, through thick and thin, I chose to stay in those relationships. Because how can you turn your back on a love so big, so amazing, so real? The problem is, it wasn't real love; it was passion. I just didn't know the difference yet.

Passion is a pendulum that swings both ways. As beautiful as it can be, it can also get very intense.

I found myself in relationships that ended in hurt no matter how much I tried. I was always focused on one thing. I always tried to be the perfect girlfriend, the perfect wife. I felt like I was doing my best, so why weren't things working out?

BECOMING SOMEONE ELSE

Throughout the turmoil in my personal life, and some heartbreaking disappointments in love, I continued to work hard in my career, putting all of my energy into new music and new movie projects. At some point along the way, I was no longer Jennifer from the Bronx, I was becoming Jennifer Lopez, the conglomerate. Now I was J.Lo "the brand."

Talk about running! I was in full stride. People were taking me seriously, as both an actress and a singer. I was living out my dreams, the dreams I had fallen asleep to while sharing a bed with my two sisters in our small Bronx apartment, exhausted after a day of dance classes. I was pouring my heart and soul into my career. I had honest intentions and I worked hard.

But there was still that other dream of a loving family, and unlike my career, where all the pieces were falling beautifully into place, love remained a puzzle that I couldn't find the right pieces for—the one thing I didn't seem able to figure out. I still wanted desperately to find "the one"—the man I'd settle down and spend my life with.

As I sat there envisioning the opening section for the first part of the tour, thinking about that time in my life, something happened. I was hit with the first of many realizations I was to have throughout the process of putting the show together: All that running I was doing in my career, I was doing in my relationships too. I had never stopped to take a look at that before.

I rushed into each relationship with optimism and hope, always thinking I'd found what I was looking for. And I was always disappointed when they ended, wondering what went wrong.

FOOLED BY LOVE

I think back to Lynda and Leslie and me, sandwiched together for all those years . . . I loved my sisters. I still do. I didn't mind a bit that we were all up in one another's space, even at night when we were sleeping.

But then, once my career took off and I was in the middle of the whirlwind of this Hollywood fairy tale, my life was so different. I was now staying in beautiful hotels and huge penthouse suites . . . Paradise, right? I was a grown-up now, out there on my own, traveling and seeing the world, and yet I couldn't stand sleeping by myself; I was always looking for another person to be with me. It wasn't that I *preferred* to be with someone else—the problem was, I hated not to be. You have to be okay on your own before you can have a healthy relationship with another person, but again, I didn't know that yet.

You have to be okay on your own before you can have a healthy relationship with another person.

I was never single for long, and whenever I got together with some-one, that was it—we were instantly inseparable, monogamous, together for the long haul. I never thought, *Well, let me take some time to see if I really want to be with this person. Do I even like him? Is he right for me?* I didn't see this behavior for what it was—an act of not really loving myself.

I'm about to sign you up, we can get right
Before the night is up, we can get
get right get right, we can get
right

—"GET RIGHT"

THE START OF MY FAIRY TALE

Sometimes love strikes when you're least expecting it. Marc came back into my life three days after I should have been at the altar saying "I do" to another man. With Marc, unlike my other relationships, I found common ground and similar dreams, instead of passion, at first. I thought I could build something real with him, something that would last.

It was the total opposite of the relationship I was coming out of. Be-ing a couple that was on the cover of every tabloid magazine for two years straight, hounded by the paparazzi and constantly judged—our relationship crumbled under the pressures of the media scrutiny that surrounded us. Ben Affleck and I called off our wedding, ending our very public relationship in suitably dramatic fashion just days before we were to walk down the aisle of a fairy-tale wedding we had planned for months. It was just the cover of a magazine or a headline to everyone else—today's joke, tomorrow's trash—but for me, when Ben and I split up at the moment when I thought we were committing to each other forever, it was my first real heartbreak, it felt like my heart had been torn out of my chest. And when the realization that I wasn't going to have the fairy tale family I wanted really set in, well, that was when I really started to fall apart. I was dealing with the emotional pain of all that buildup and letdown, the high hopes and excitement that ended in tears and frustration.

People do lots of things to anesthetize themselves in moments like these. Some people do drugs, some drink, and some go out and party. I get that, but I've never been one to do those things. No, my way of anesthetizing the pain was different. I sought out comfort in another person, tried to find someone who could make me feel loved and wanted in my loneliest hour.

And that was the moment when Marc reappeared in my life.

Marc and I had been friends for a number of years. We'd worked together on a few songs, and we'd sung a duet together for my first record, titled *"No Me Ames"* (ironically, "Don't Love Me" in Spanish). Right from the beginning, he never made it a secret that he liked me. He was warm and funny, a brilliant singer and artist who knew how to make me feel special. But the best thing about him, the thing that I loved the most, was that no matter what, he always knew how to make me laugh. I had always liked Marc, finding comfort in his humor and his easy way with people. He was confident and strong, he was so sure of everything, and at this moment, when I felt so lost, so broken and alone, there he was.

We thought that this was where everything was supposed to lead, that we were meant to end up together. All the heartache and pain of my recent breakup couldn't have been for nothing, could it? Maybe I had to go through the bad so I could end up with the person I was meant to be with all along.

After all, the first time I ever met Marc in 1998, backstage while he was performing on Broadway, his opening line to me had been: "One day you're going to be my wife." (True story.)

We make our own choices . . . and I chose to believe that Marc and I were meant to be together—that destiny was stepping in. In that mo-

ment, I needed to believe that; I needed to believe in something. The reality was, I didn't want to be alone—so when Marc was there, when he met me with his big smile, his heart on his sleeve, and his arms open wide, I was more than happy to let myself fall into them. I had always liked him, but now that he was coming to my rescue in my time of need, he was my knight in shining armor and I realized I loved him too. This had to be the start of my fairy tale.

And from there, it didn't take long for us to decide to get married.

Thinking back, maybe deep down I knew that this was a Band-Aid on the cut, that my wound hadn't been stitched or healed. But I pushed all that to the back of my mind. Because life takes unpredictable twists and turns, right? And you've just got to go with what you feel is best in the moment.

In that moment, Marc was the guy who swooped in and made me feel loved at my lowest point. I loved him for that, and I felt like I could love him forever. After all the turmoil, I felt like I had found my rock, the man whom I was going to spend the rest of my life with.

I think you need to take some

time

To show me that your love is true

—"LOVE DON'T COST A THING"

FINDING STRENGTH BEYOND YOUR LIMITS

When we first started doing rehearsals for the Dance Again tour, my body almost couldn't take it. Dancing all the time, working on all these different moves, different set pieces . . . Oh my God, I was so sore at

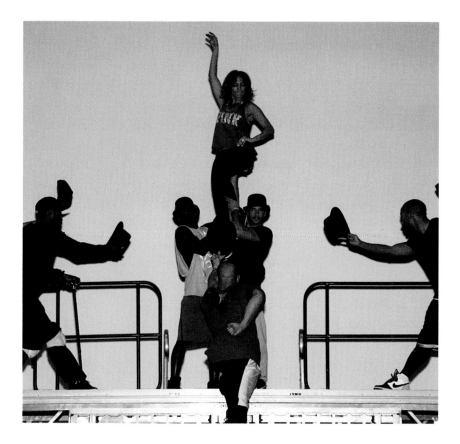

the end of each day. My muscles were tight, my whole body was aching, and I'd kneel on the floor in the shower and let the water beat down on my back.

I knew if I pushed through the pain, my body would get used to it. And soon I would get stronger, and feel better, and get to be in amazing shape. Because once you build up that strength and stamina, you end up feeling better than you ever could have imagined. By the end of a tour, you feel like you can jump over buildings. But to get to that point, first you have to push through the pain.

That's kind of how I approached my relationship with Marc. I never thought, *Maybe I rushed into this*, or *Maybe we're not the best people for each other. Maybe I made a mistake. Maybe we were too different.* I wouldn't let myself think that. I couldn't. Instead, I tried to convince myself that it was all going to work out fine if I could push through the rough spot.

I think of the days when the sun

used to set

On my empty heart all alone in my

bed

Tossing and turning, emotions

were strong

I knew I had to hold on

—"WAITING FOR TONIGHT"

Marc and I weren't the only ones who really wanted this marriage to work. Our fans were invested in it too. They wanted to see it last. Marrying Marc was like the happy ending, the twist in the story that turned me back in people's minds from J.Lo the Diva to Jennifer Lopez, married woman. "Bennifer" was gone, and now there was just Marc and Jennifer, the couple that was meant to be. I didn't want to give that up.

Because now I had lined up everything I needed for the perfect Big Hollywood life—the movies, the records, the glamour—and now the marriage that would really last forever, with the man who'd rescued me when I was lost.

During this whole period of my life, everything felt like a hurricane, and that's how I wanted the opening of the show to feel. It was exciting and moving and loud . . . and it was scary.

I knew people wanted to see the same dancing and choreography they'd seen in the videos for all these songs—so that's what we gave them, but with bigger arrangements, more dancers, a bigger stage, so it felt to the audience how it felt to me. We were taking something old and making it exciting and fresh. It was the perfect opening. Our eight male dancers started out in those classic tuxedos, with top hats and canes,

dancing like they'd stepped out of a Fred Astaire movie. But then, as we moved deeper into the set, the tone began to change.

Little by little, the hats came off, the jackets came off, and then the shirts came off too. We started to literally bare ourselves here. Now there were eight shirtless guys in bow ties and slacks, and the mood started changing. It was about to get . . . interesting.

That's when we go to what Ana—one of my best friends and the photographer for the Dance Again tour—called "the fainting transition" of the show: "Waiting for Tonight" accompanied by a beautiful, electrifying laser show. This was where things got very sexy and a little dangerous. All these elements combined created an intense atmosphere. Whenever we performed this part of the show, people started falling out left and right, fainting in front of the stage, right in front of me as I sang.

Every night, I would see them fall, and they'd be carried off and revived backstage. At first it freaked me out—Big Hollywood was out of control! And the funny thing is, that seemed right. Because that was how it had felt in real life . . .

ACT TWO

BACK TO THE BRONX

SET LIST

"Goin' In"

———

The BX medley: "I'm Real," "All I Have," "Feelin' So Good," "Ain't It Funny"

———

"Jenny from the Block"

———

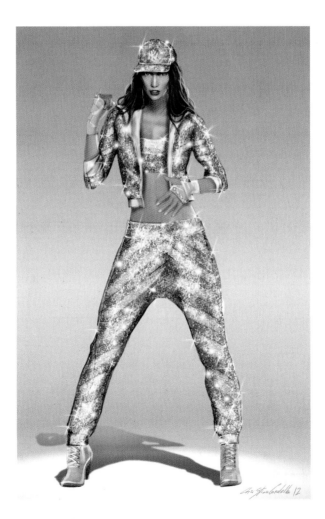

I lost some confidence. I almost lost my way.

I had to go home—to my roots, my
upbringing, my inspiration.

That's where I found the answer.

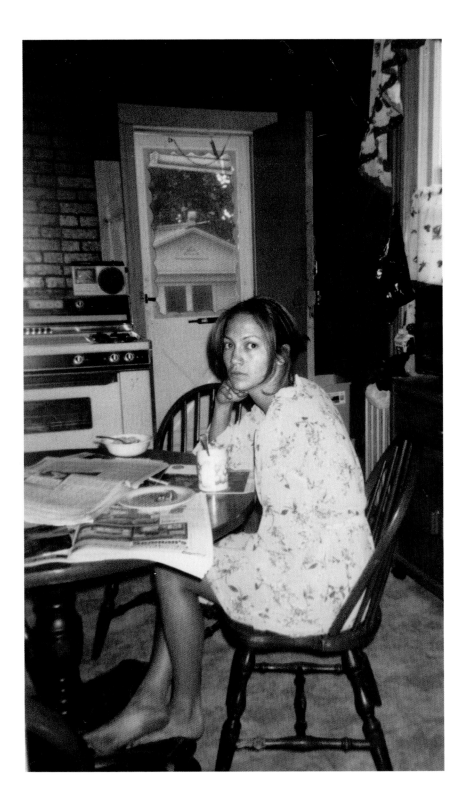

JENNY FROM THE BLOCK

REDISCOVERING DANCE

I had given the audience the big glamorous Hollywood-movie-star opening. That's how the world saw me. But where was I to go from there? To answer that question, I had to ask myself, *Who am I really?* I knew, but for the show, I had to revisit the place that inspired my passion: Castle Hill Avenue in the Bronx. That was my neighborhood, the place where I grew up hearing hip-hop, salsa, R&B, pop, and every other kind of beat, all while walking down the block. Our neighbors were so diverse—Puerto Ricans, Dominicans, African-Americans, Italians and Irish—and everybody was scraping and clawing, trying to get by.

My mom worked two jobs and my dad worked the night shift at Guardian Insurance. My sisters, Leslie and Lynda, and I shared a bed, and every morning we were bundled up and sent off to Catholic school. That was why my parents worked all those long hours, so they could pay for a good education and raise us right. I can still remember those days of walking to school at seven a.m., freezing in my little uniform skirt and kneesocks, the snow dusting the streets.

We used to dance and sing together, my sisters and I, putting on little shows in the living room. We did it because we loved it, because it was fun to act like we were on a stage somewhere. You could get so much material just walking down the street, seeing people and what they were wearing, and going into stores and listening to them talk. The Bronx was alive with sound and color and life, and I soaked it all up.

You could get so much material just walking down the street, seeing people and what they were wearing, and going into stores and listening to them talk. The Bronx was alive with sound and color and life, and we soaked it all up.

I grew up in the age of hip-hop, and I remember being in elementary school the first time I heard "Rapper's Delight" by the Sugarhill Gang. That song changed my world—I was like, "Play it again! Play it again! PLAY IT AGAIN!" I had never heard anything like it before, and it was so cool. It felt like the heartbeat of my upbringing, the soundtrack to my life. I always identified with that beat, the grit and the pulse of it.

Years later, I sang about those times in the song "Feelin' So Good," and the video took me right back to Castle Hill.

when I opened up my eyes
today
Felt the sun shining on my
face . . .

—"FEELIN' SO GOOD"

It was Big Pun and Fat Joe and me, all of us back in the Bronx, singing about the pleasures of everyday life there . . . simple pleasures like walking into the beauty parlor, picking up your check, and buying yourself something new to wear so you could go out with your friends and have fun. I remember those times, the feeling that endless possibility existed in even the smallest things.

Those were moments I'd think back to later on, whenever the hard times knocked me flat. Whenever I'd go through a breakup, when I'd feel like I was losing myself, I'd find myself thinking, *You need to get back to who you are.* And then I'd wonder, *Well, who am I?* Was there something missing from back in the days when I was that girl pounding the streets of New York, doing auditions and hoping for the big break?

Because that girl never worried about what the future was going to hold. I was always in the present, always knowing somehow that things were going to work out. Life was visceral; there was that Bronx mentality of taking each day as it comes. I'd get up and go to dance class, then go to an audition, meet up with friends, and then choreograph something for a little show we were going to do. It was about pressing forward every day. I was relentless, reaching, always reaching, trying to get that brass ring. Nothing was going to stop me.

There was a certain hustle I grew up with, a hustle that I learned from watching my parents. They showed me that you put your head down and work—you work for a living and then, when you're making a living, you still don't stop. That continues to be my mentality now. We don't stop working because we have money in the bank—we do what we do and we keep on doing it. That's the way I was raised.

You put your head down and work—you work for a living and then, when you're making a living, you still don't stop.

And that's what keeps me grounded. It's real life, people surviving, people working hard to support their families. There might be some who see me as this person who's been privileged forever. But my first record didn't come out until I was twenty-eight years old. So for more than half of my life, I was out there struggling like everyone else for a chance to make it.

That's what "Jenny from the Block" is all about. That's what I wanted to show people in the Back to the Bronx section of the show, the duality between Big Hollywood and life on Castle Hill. Because yes, there's a public image that I enjoy—I love dressing up. I love feeling glamorous. I love jewelry and beautiful things. But I'm still that little girl who's playing the part of a movie star, that same girl from the Bronx wearing big hoop earrings and listening to hip-hop.

FIGHTING THROUGH THE PAIN

There's a boxing ring set up at center stage. And I'm a boxer, walking out into the spotlight with my corner men, who hold the ropes for me as I step into the ring. I'm wearing loose-fitting pants, a bikini top, and a black cape with a hood over my head. I turn around so the crowd can see the word stenciled across my back: LOVE?

I shadowbox for a few seconds as the dancers, in boxing trunks, join me in the ring. And then I pull the hood off my head, an announcer booms, "The champ is *here*!" . . . and everybody goes nuts.

You think you know who I am? You think I'm just that sparkly, feathery, bejeweled woman you see on the screen? Well, think again. The music kicks up, and . . . I'm *Goin' In!*

Tonight feels like we can do
anything we like
Tonight feels like the best night of
my life
I'm goin' in . . .

—"GOIN' IN"

I wanted to follow up the Big Hollywood opening with the Back to the Bronx section, to show people who I really was, that girl with the New York fight in me—and I knew exactly who could make that happen. I had seen some clips from a New Zealand choreographer named Parris Goebel, and her stuff was so tough—girls dancing like guys, leaving it all on the floor, and everything infused with this amazing energy. She was perfect.

Parris was never formally trained—she taught herself to dance and went from there to choreography, creating a style she called "polyswagg." She and her crew were world-champion hip-hop dancers, but she had never been hired for a show the size of the Dance Again tour. No one out there was doing what she was doing, so we gave Parris her first shot, knowing that she'd create something completely different from anything else we had seen onstage. And she *killed it*.

Once again, the show became life imitating art, imitating life, because

we went in with this whole boxing thing—you're down but not out, and no matter what's happening in your life, you keep fighting.

After performing in music videos and some of the biggest award shows in the world, performing night after night in front of tens of thousands of people on a world tour—despite what I imagined—proved to be one of the most natural things that I had ever done. That stage felt like home. All the nerves went away, and much like with running and dancing, I had clarity and I was in the moment. And this Bronx section in particular became my own personal daily affirmation of how, when you fall down, you have to get back up.

I would hold out the microphone and ask the audience every night: "Do you know where I'm from?"

And they'd scream back: "The Bronx!"

Then I'd say, "That's right. I'm just a simple girl from the Bronx."

They would laugh at the irony of me standing there wearing a track-suit that was covered head-to-toe in sparkly Swarovski crystals. Anything but simple.

"Is that how you do it here in Sydney? When you fall down, you get back up?" I asked.

And the crowd would go crazy.

"That's how we do it where I'm from. Can I ask you a question? Do you all want to go back to the Bronx with me?" I'd scream.

The crowd would erupt with a thunderous roar. *Waaaahhhhhhhhhh.* It was one of the most beautiful, empowering, and electrifying moments of the show.

At this point, pretty much everyone in the world knew that I had recently gone through a divorce, and night after night they were helping me get back up again. Maybe I was helping them too.

The night I shouted this out to the fans in the Boston TD Garden arena, I put on my sparkly New York Yankees ball cap, like I did every night. And everybody started booing—of course! Die-hard Red Sox fans, what are you gonna do?

As they booed, I started laughing. And they all started cracking up too, and soon we were all laughing together. I shrugged my shoulders and said, "I got to wear it wherever I go, you know? I can't not be from New York today." I am who I am, no matter where life takes me.

No matter where I go
I know where I came from . . .

—"JENNY FROM THE BLOCK"

The stage is set, guys carrying boom boxes and hanging out on their bikes, girls wearing hot shorts sitting on beach chairs in front of chain-link fences, video content filled with graffiti and the six train running through the city . . . That's how we set the stage for this pulsating urban section of the show. No matter what city around the world we were visiting, at that moment everybody knew we were back in the Bronx.

Certain songs fell perfectly into this part of the show. "I'm Real," "Ain't It Funny," "Feelin' So Good," "Jenny from the Block"—they had become so much a part of my image, how people saw me, because that's how I saw myself. I always felt like I was this tough girl from the

streets who knew what was what and wouldn't take shit from anybody. The girl who had her head on straight and knew exactly what she wanted. Who would never let herself be treated like dirt, who would never lose herself in a relationship, who would never feel her whole world shaken by anyone . . .

Was I really still that girl?

I always thought so, but then I remembered a conversation from years ago, back in the beginning of my career. I was in a meeting with my agent and stepped out for a call with my boyfriend at the time. Through the glass door, my agent could see that I was arguing and pleading. She asked my assistant, "Does Jennifer have low self-esteem?" My assistant looked at her like she was crazy. Later, when my assistant told me she had said that, we couldn't stop laughing. Me? Low self-esteem? "That's so stupid!" I told her. But was it really? That agent saw something I didn't. She was a little bit older. Maybe she'd been through something like that herself, or maybe she'd seen it in others. Who knows what? All that mattered was, she knew it when she saw it in me.

ACCEPTING MY FATE

Now I know I'm not perfect, but I know I was a good girlfriend, a good wife. I tried my best. I always put up that old Bronx fight! I went to the mat for every relationship I was in. I asked myself the hard questions: How can *I* fix things? What can *I* do to make the other person happier? Or, How can *I* take care of their needs? I was asking myself all these questions—they seemed like the right questions—but for some reason it still didn't work out.

My life might have continued on like that forever, but then everything changed in 2008, when I had my beautiful babies, Emme and Max.

Marc and I had been trying to have kids ever since we got married. We never worried about birth control, figuring that nature would take its course and soon enough I would get pregnant. But the first few years of our marriage were kinda shaky, and with the stress of that, nothing happened. While at first it didn't seem like a big deal, later on I began to worry.

After three years of marriage, our relationship had settled down a bit, and my career was kind of in a lull. I'd released a record that wasn't my best one, and I hadn't done a movie in a while. It was this strange in-between time. All my focus was on my marriage, and it felt like the right time to have kids—but I wasn't getting pregnant. Marc already had three kids by two other women, so I began to think it was about me. *Maybe this isn't going to happen*, I thought.

Right as I started thinking that way, I had a conversation with my dad while he was visiting one Sunday afternoon. "Things are going pretty well with Marc and me," I told him. "And it's not like we haven't been trying to get pregnant. But it's not happening. I don't know. Maybe I'm not meant to have kids. I mean, I have this amazing career, wonderful friends, lots of extended family . . . Maybe that's asking for too much. I guess my life is going to be about other things—my work and career—rather than having kids," I told my dad.

And then he said something that was so simple and yet so profound that it stopped me in my tracks: "Well, why can't you have both?"

It sounded like such a practical question, but when my dad said it out loud, it was like the wall I had created for myself with my insecurities and feelings of unworthiness cracked open and the light came through. I was able to see that I deserved to have that blessing as much as anybody else. No matter what happened, I could do this.

Everything I'd been telling myself about having kids and having a career came out of the fear that I wasn't really worthy, that I didn't deserve it. That I already had so much. It came straight out of a lack of love for myself. But my dad put it so simply: *Why can't you?* And for the first time ever, I truly believed that I could.

The very next month, I got pregnant. It was almost as if I had to make the decision that it *could* happen before it did. But even when it did happen, I couldn't believe it. It took seven pregnancy tests before reality would set in. And then seven weeks later I found out I wasn't having only one baby but two. Twins! All I could do was laugh; all Marc could do was cry . . . tears of happiness.

Oh my God. I was *really* pregnant.

BECOMING A MOM IN FRONT OF THE WORLD

Six months into my pregnancy, I was scheduled to open the Movies Rock 2007 show, where Marc was also scheduled to perform. I was backstage with Marc as the show was about to begin. This was going to be my first real public appearance with my very pregnant belly, so I was a little nervous. As I walked out onstage, the first thing you saw was a gigantic belly draped in a white Versace dress, and people started clapping. They liked this Jennifer—the married woman, pregnant with twins, all safe and nice, rather than wild Jennifer, running around in clubs. It's funny—when you're single and out there doing your thing, people feel okay making you a target. But when you're somebody's wife, somebody's mom, then they back off a little bit on criticizing you. It was new for me and it was nice.

People kept clapping, and soon everyone was on their feet. I felt like it was the babies' first standing ovation, because people were clapping not only for me, but for the three of us! It was a very warm welcome to motherhood, and I was soaking it up. It felt like the first step toward redefining myself in the public eye as a mama. This was going to be the role of a lifetime.

TAKING A STAND

Any mom will tell you that becoming a mother is one of the most life-changing experiences you will have in life. My babies changed me in so many ways and even before they were born I started to notice the ways in which I started to see life differently.

There was one incident in particular that made me realize just how much they were changing me. When I was about six months pregnant, I was at an event and someone standing near me lit up a cigarette. Now, I've been around smokers my whole life and while it's not something I enjoy, cigarette smoke had never bothered me before.

But now I was pregnant. I didn't want to be inhaling the smoke, so I moved away from them. It was such a small thing, but it got me thinking: I've been around smokers before, but it never bothered me. I never even thought about the effect it had on me. But now someone lights up a cigarette and I don't hesitate a second to move as far away as possible because I'm worried it will affect my babies . . . Why did I never think about that for myself? Why were my health and well-being not important? I loved these babies so much. I didn't want anything to harm them in any way. Did I not hold myself in the same regard?

I realized that being pregnant, of course, wasn't only about me anymore; I had two other people to take care of. But in order to take care of them, I needed to take care of myself. In fact, I always needed to take care of myself, I had just never thought about it before!

This was a different Jennifer. Before, I might get frustrated at something someone had done but I'd swallow my feelings and move on. But now, because of the babies, I was thinking differently, and I was going to do what I thought was right for them, and for me. And I wasn't about to compromise.

It was a step, a tiny step, in the right direction. I was finally starting to behave in a way that was putting me and my twins first. It might seem like a small little thing, but this incident led to a big realization of how I was mistreating myself. That was the first of many ways in which my babies changed me, and there were more changes to come.

No matter how strong and self-confident I thought I was, I had ignored when things didn't feel right. In reality, I was accepting things I didn't want.

It was easy to blame other people for treating me in ways I didn't like, but now I was seeing that I was the one at fault. The only way you can be mistreated is by allowing yourself to be mistreated, and that was something I did over and over again. Somehow, I needed to find that glimmer of self-respect, buried deep inside, that would allow me to say: *I am never going to let that happen to me again.* I needed to learn how to stand up for myself in a different way, but I didn't know how.

So, here I was, that girl from the Bronx, fighting and fighting like I was supposed to . . . but who was I really fighting against?

"I'm still, I'm still Jenny from the block"

—"JENNY FROM THE BLOCK"

Back to the Bronx was one of the most popular moments in the show because it was nostalgic. It took people back to that old-school hip-hop feeling, back to that time when you felt like you knew everything, to that hip-hop cockiness that made you feel so powerful, like you could take over the world and nobody was going to get the best of you.

The only way you can be mistreated is by allowing yourself to be mistreated.

As energetic as that moment was onstage, while I was putting it all together, the realizations were coming fast and furious. Performing it every night was reminding me of so many past missteps but also of the essence of who I really was. I might have lost my way, but Jenny from the Block was still alive and well. She was still in there.

ACT THREE

FUNKY LOVE

SET LIST

"Hold It Don't Drop It"

———

"If You Had My Love"

———

The dawn of a new day.

I rekindled the feeling that I had something to offer to the world.

For the first time in a long time, I felt closer to myself.

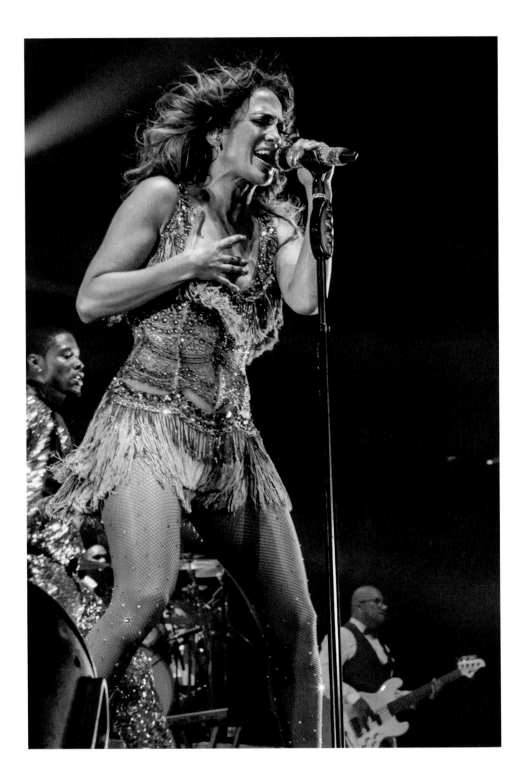

FUNKY LOVE

OBSESSED WITH LOVE

Over the years, love has been a constant theme in my music. I always knew this, but it was never clearer to me than when looking through my albums while putting the show together. I realized that over seven studio albums, I have more than sixty songs about love or with the word "love" in the title: "If You Had My Love," "Could This Be Love," "*No Me Ames*," "Love Don't Cost a Thing," "I Need Love," "I, Love," "Baby I Love U!" "Loving You," et cetera, et cetera, et cetera. Wow. Even I surprised myself on that one. I guess I really had a lot to say on the topic; I was really trying to figure this thing out.

So now, in the show, after having gone from Hollywood to the Bronx, the Funky Love section would get to the heart of who I was as an artist. Love has always been my message. Love in all its glory, the good and the bad—wanting to get it right, always wanting, always hoping, always fighting. It's about that passion that's so intoxicating, and it can be as healing as it can be destructive.

This is what my music has always been about: being in love. Love love love love love. So we decided to kick this section off with "Hold It Don't Drop It," a retro R&B–flavored song that ironically—or not so ironically—is about not wanting to leave or give up on somebody. I wanted it to be half James Brown, half Tina Turner. So for this section, Zuhair Murad, who created the costumes for the entire show, designed a short, fringy, electric-blue dress with a floor-length maribou cape. I came out shaking my hips and thrashing my hair as the band pounded out the soulful throwback. There were three male dancers in the most sparkly, sequined suits that you've ever seen. They were like the Pips, dancing funk-inspired choreography and killing it dead. I sang in my grittiest voice about how I wasn't going to leave, and it ended with the guys literally having to drag me off the stage, picking me up and throwing me over their shoulders as the band banged out the encore over and over until I finally gave up. It was metaphoric, I guess, for how reluctantly I would leave relationships, and never without a fight.

*Every time I try to run, something
keeps stopping me,
I try my best to turn around, but
your touch won't let me leave.*

—"HOLD IT DON'T DROP IT"

From there, we would slow it way down. We had to, after that. I'd say to the audience, "I know I get carried away with love sometimes. It ain't no secret. You guys want to talk about love? I have a lot of stories!"

They'd giggle. So would I. And that's how we took them into the first real intimate moment of the show, an acoustic version of "If You Had My Love."

"If You Had My Love" was my very first single from my very first album, a kind of defining song for me. I wanted to do it really pared down, so it would feel like a conversation—like I'm talking with the audience, sharing where I began and where I find myself now. The lyrics are all about the beginning of a new relationship and what I expect and what I want. And there's a little bit of fear in there too, a feeling of, *What will you do if I give you my heart?*

In the verses, I'm trying to lay down the rules, but the chorus expresses all of the fear that I feel . . .

> *If you had my love and I gave you all my trust,*
> *Would you comfort me?*

Love has always been my message. Love in all its glory, the good and the bad.

After finishing the song, I'd look out at everybody and say, "That was the very first song I ever sang about love . . ." And every single night as I said it, the feelings and weight of all my experiences were right there in that phrase. "A lot has happened since then." Again, we shared a laugh, because they knew what I was talking about . . . Because we've all been through it, right? I wanted to have that moment with them, to show that we've all been on this journey together. From the stage I could always see people nodding and smiling. They knew exactly what I meant the moment I said it.

It was my way of saying, *Yeah, I'm up here onstage, but I'm human. And this is one area that I can't seem to get right for some reason.* It's the moment in the show where I start to bare my soul.

What was amazing about doing that, night after night on the tour, was that every time I did it, I felt a little bit more forgiving of myself. There's something liberating about standing up in front of a crowd of people and saying, *I know that maybe I haven't made the best choices. Maybe things haven't always worked out. But I'm right here and I'm saying it. I'm not ashamed, and I'm still trying.* In doing that, I discovered that sometimes it helps to make yourself vulnerable. The people, the songs, and the show were helping me to learn to forgive myself and accept myself for who I was, mistakes and all. Little by little I was healing.

A NEW CHALLENGE

After the babies were born, as I embraced my strength and regained my sense of self, I began to look around and take stock of the rest of my life, including my career and my relationships. I was on the road toward trusting my instincts, following my own heart, and I was beginning to see things more clearly. Once all of the other aspects of my life were in order, those that weren't became impossible to ignore.

One of the areas of my life that fulfilled me during that time was being a judge on *American Idol*. It was a surprising safe haven during some very rocky times, and it profoundly changed my life.

When I first got the call to do *Idol*, it seemed like no one around me thought it was a good idea. A lot of things were in transition—Max and Emme were toddlers, my music and my acting were still in a lull, and I was concentrating on my family, traveling with Marc while he toured. It was a strange time, and I thought that doing *Idol* would be a new challenge, something different. Everyone around me seemed to think that doing a reality TV show would be some kind of comedown for me. For the most part, they urged me not to do it. But I disagreed.

"We're in a new era," I told them. "Television is the new radio. It's how people get music." For some reason, I knew it would be okay. I knew doing the show would bring other benefits too. I wanted to be home with Max and Emme, who were only two at the time, and working on *American Idol*, which shoots mostly in Los Angeles, would make that possible. I could make good money and stay put with my family. It seemed like it would be fun too. I really loved the show and believed that I had something to contribute to it. There were so many things about doing the show that I knew would be good. But I never imagined how much more, not only professionally but personally, *American Idol* would do for me.

When I was asked to do the show, I thought I was in a really good place. I was enjoying having a family and I loved being a mommy. This was so different from anything I'd done before. Would I really be up for this? *Come on!* I was a mom now. I could do anything! I had just birthed two human beings—from my belly!

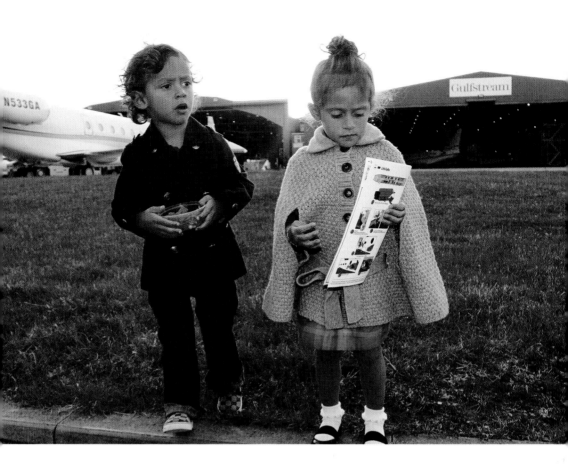

I remember that day so clearly. The day that Max and Emme were born. The first time I saw them, I was in the hospital, lying on that table, having my C-section, and my doctor shouted: "Baby number one on the left!"

I looked, and there was Emme, arms outstretched, legs shaking, a little purple creature screaming at the top of her lungs, "*Waaaaaaaa!*"

Then someone said, "Baby number two on the right!" I looked again and "*Waaaaaaaa!*"—another little purple creature, screaming even louder: That was my Max.

I reached out and pulled them to my chest, and all I remember was kissing them and saying, *I love you. I love you. I love you so much. I love you . . .* It was instinctual. It was pure. It was unconditional. *This* was love—a love I had never felt before. It empowered me in a way that I could have never imagined.

This was love—a love I had never felt before. It empowered me in a way that I could have never imagined.

Naturally, after I had children, my life became about them. Suddenly, there are these two little beings who are totally dependent on you, who literally can't live without you. It's so easy to lose yourself in that beautiful world when you have babies. It's magical and all encompassing.

So three years later, when the chance to do *Idol* came up, I welcomed the opportunity to reclaim some of my individuality. I needed to quiet all the voices in order to listen to my own, and to trust what I felt was right in order to make a decision. I followed my gut and jumped in.

When I first began working on the show—several months before it started airing—I fell in love with Steven Tyler, Randy Jackson, and Ryan Seacrest. They were all very different, but each one was so caring and generous—they all really looked out for me. They were like the brothers I never had. When I'd come onto the set, Steven would say, "Jennifer! You look gorgeous—what do you use on your face?" He always wanted to know what makeup I was using, what hair products. He made me laugh so much, always saying, "You know I'm only asking because I'm so *enamored* with you; I'm very *enamored* with you, Jennifer," with that wry smile on his face.

Steven was nothing like what you'd think. People think he's this skinny, crazy rocker, with that larger-than-life mouth and the wild clothes. But he's so deep, so soulful. When you look into his eyes, he's like a little wounded bird. He likes to lock eyes, in that un-self-conscious way of someone who loves to connect with people.

He'd look at me, and I'd see a little bit of sadness in those eyes, a little bit of pain in a way that made me know, *Yeah, that guy has lived*. He had a soulfulness; he was good a person. You could see it.

Those first few weeks, as we shot the auditions and met all these amazing young singers, who were fantastic, we got to know one another too. I loved working with the guys, and I felt good about what I was able to contribute.

When I saw the clips from those first audition shows, I thought they looked great. *Idol* had been slumping a little bit in the last couple of seasons, but if everything went well, twenty million people would be tuning in to watch us. How could things get any better?

STEPPING ONTO A BIG STAGE

It was the middle of the night, and Marc was asleep beside me in bed. I suddenly sat upright, my heart pounding. It was the night before my debut on the premiere of *American Idol*. I slipped out of bed and walked into the bathroom, and when I looked at myself in the mirror, I was as white as a ghost. All I could think was, *Oh shit. Twenty million people.* I was so nervous about the show airing the next day that I was completely freaking out.

I came back to bed and said, "Marc! Wake up!" He was in a deep sleep, so he kind of grunted and rolled over. I said, "Papi! Wake up! I'm scared!" I grabbed his shoulder and tried to shake him awake. "You gotta wake up!"

No matter what problems Marc and I had in our personal lives, we were always very in tune with each other when it came to work. When I was worried that my singing wasn't as strong as other things I was able to do, he helped me find my best singing voice. I really credit him with that, because he always encouraged me, giving me tips and telling me I could do it. And he always had a really smart take on things when it came to business—he was a wonderful partner in that sense. So, if anyone could talk me down from this ledge, it was him.

"Baby," I said, "I am freaking out."

"What's wrong?" he asked, his voice groggy with sleep.

"It's this whole *Idol* thing," I said. "It's so big! Twenty million people are going to be watching, and I've never done TV like this, without a script or lyrics or anything . . . It's only me out there, with the cameras and everybody watching!"

I felt like I'd be exposed, vulnerable—like I'd be running down the street with no clothes on. It's not that I was afraid of people seeing the real me. I knew who I was; I knew I was a good person. But this was new for me. When you're an actress, you're used to saying lines that someone has given you. You get to hide behind that mask. When you're a singer, you have a song. The notion of getting up in front of everyone and being yourself is really terrifying. If someone criticizes your acting, they're criticizing only one part of you. They don't know anything about who you really are or what's really important to you. If someone criticizes you on a show like *Idol*, though, they're criticizing *you*.

"Okay, okay," he said. "But that's not so bad. Think about how you'd feel if it failed. What if no one was watching . . . ? That would be so much worse, right?"

I thought about that for a second and then said, "Yeah, that would feel worse."

And with that, we both rolled over and went to sleep.

I had to laugh, because Marc was right. Did it make sense to be scared because the show was potentially a huge success? No . . . But it was really just that number—twenty million people—that threw me off. With television, people can flip through channels, and then suddenly they see you sitting on that judging panel—and now you're the one getting judged by every one of those people who've just happened to tune in. You're being scrutinized on a whole different level. And that was a really overwhelming thought.

But Marc knew exactly how to calm me down. He knew that what I feared more than any of those things was failure. "Listen, if the show failed, *then* you'd feel really shitty," he said, and he was right. Because I

know what it feels like to fail, to have something that you've worked really hard on, something that you care about, be judged a failure. Trust me, I have had that experience. And for me, there's no worse feeling than putting something out there that people don't respond to.

But when the show started airing, something wonderful happened. The very thing I was afraid of turned out to be the best thing ever: For the first time, people were seeing the real me—not the "me" fabricated by tabloids and magazines—and they liked what they saw.

BACK TO THE REAL ME

The truth about reality TV is that you can't hide who you are. When you're sitting up there on a panel, reacting to the performers you see in front of you, the camera catches everything. If you start laughing, if you shed tears, if you make a face—it's all right there for the world to see. When people started watching that season of *American Idol*, they were seeing something they weren't expecting to see. People were looking for a diva, but they found the mama instead.

Of all the good things I thought might come out of being on *Idol*, this one I hadn't expected—and it turned out to be the biggest, most important thing of all. It had been so long since I'd felt like just . . . Jennifer.

Before *Idol* started, I was hanging out with my friend Leah. She's my bestie, we have real love for each other, we connected instantly, from the first day we met. It doesn't matter what I say or how out there I think it is, she always gets it. We get each other. I remember saying to her, "I feel like I'm about to have a baby. Like, I'm pregnant and I'm pushing, and I'm feeling the pain, but it's not quite out yet. But there's this beautiful baby coming . . ." It was strange, but that's how I felt it at the time . . . like I was on the precipice of something amazing. I could feel it coming, even if I wasn't totally sure of what it was.

So many exciting things were starting to happen. People were loving the show. I had a new album coming out, and when "On the Floor," the first single, leaked right before *Idol* aired, it shot up the charts. It seemed like every day something great and new came along. I felt an amazing new energy in my life and career, the kind of energy I hadn't felt in a long time.

In so many ways, *Idol* was like a reinvention, a reintroduction into the public eye for me. I was finding my own voice, my own power again—I had something to say, and people were listening. It was the first time in a long time that I felt good about just being me. And the response to being

The truth about reality TV is that you can't hide who you are.

me, not only from Steven and Randy and Ryan and everyone at *Idol*, but also from the audience watching the show, was so warm and embracing that I felt protected and loved. It got me back in touch with myself.

That was a really big deal for me. It gave me back a little bit of the self-confidence I had lost over time, a little bit of the grounding I had been lacking since the Big Hollywood whirlwind took over my life. I hadn't even realized how much self-confidence I'd lost until it finally started coming back.

All of this happened gradually, over the course of that first *American Idol* season. It wasn't a "Eureka!" kind of moment—it was the slow realization that the parts of me that had been empty were starting to fill up again. Yet, as gradual as this all was, there was one surreal moment that crystallized it for me—one moment where I suddenly understood what *Idol* meant to people and what it was doing for me.

It happened during Oscar season, when the show had been on the air for about a month. I had been invited to a party celebrating one of the movies up for Best Picture, and so I got dressed up and went out to do that Hollywood thing. There are always lots of big stars at these parties—actors and directors and heads of studios, the people who make things happen in this town. I pretty much expected to blend in and have a good time, but when I walked into the party, people started swarming all around me, asking about *American Idol*.

It was unreal . . . People were coming up, saying things like, "Oh my God! I love you on that show!" And "Who do you think is going to win? Come on. Tell the truth!" And, "What's it really like behind the scenes? What's the scoop?" I couldn't believe that in this room full of the most successful, creative people in Hollywood, everyone wanted to talk about *Idol*. I mean, even Steven Spielberg came up to me to tell me about how he and his family all watch the show together. Steven Spielberg!

Wow. The power of TV.

At that moment, I realized how much people liked the show, how happy it made them feel, and how much it was changing the perception of who I was. People were saying they liked me, which made me realize how many years I'd spent thinking they didn't, and that affected how I felt about myself. That was the beginning of the beginning—the time

when I started to feel like myself again. I had found that taking risks, being true to myself, and making decisions with good intentions can exceed even my own expectations.

DEFINING MOMENTS

That February, things couldn't have been going better for me professionally: *People* magazine named me its first Most Beautiful Woman in the World. My record was number one, my video was number one, and I was on the number-one television show in America. I felt like I was on top of the world.

In the midst of all this excitement and outpouring of appreciation and love, the bubble was burst with three simple words: "I'm not happy." Marc was in the middle of venting to me about things between us that had been bothering him, and I was sitting there trying to figure out where he was going with it. Then he said it again: "I'm not happy. I'm here because we have a family, because we're trying to keep it together. But I'm not happy."

It was another moment where a crack appeared in yet another wall that I had built, and when the light came shining through, I immediately thought: *If you're not happy, then what am I?* I started crying. I really thought I had done everything I could to satisfy him in every way that I could—as a wife, as a partner, and as a mother to his children. But the truth was, I had never even stopped to think about whether *I* was happy.

It was like a light bulb finally turned on in my head: What sense did it make to keep suppressing my own feelings of what was missing in the relationship? How long did I need to keep trying to make someone happy who was telling me flat-out that he wasn't?

The floodgates were open, and the tears wouldn't stop. Marc tried to comfort me.

"Come on. Why are you crying so much?" he asked.

He now seemed completely fine—as if by getting it off his chest, everything was okay. To him it was some little argument, and now everything would go back to normal. I don't think he had any idea of the powerful effect those words had had on me; Pandora's box had been opened, and little did I know that, as much as I would try, there was no shutting it again.

In the time leading up to that conversation, I had been regaining my sense of confidence and self-esteem, first as a mother and then through my work. Through the kids, I had started to understand more about love and what it was to truly give love and receive it. I learned that there are certain things it's not okay to accept, and that was making me feel powerful and strong. But the thing is, in my relationship, I was still stuck in the same pattern I had been stuck in my entire life: My own happiness and sense of self-worth still depended on how happy *he* was. So when Marc stated so clearly that he wasn't happy, it broke me down completely.

For so many years I had managed to convince myself that if I worked at relationships hard enough, I could always fix everything, make things better. But now I was finally strong enough to identify not only that I couldn't, but that that wasn't the point. The point was that *my* happiness mattered too. I had reached a place where I looked at my personal life and said, *You know what? This is* not *okay.* No matter how great everything else was going in the rest of my life, this just wasn't. And I couldn't ignore it any longer.

When I woke up that morning, I never expected that such a simple conversation would lead to such an earth-shattering realization and the seismic shift it would bring upon my life.

ACT FOUR

QUÉ HICISTE

My hopes and dreams crumbled.

It was as if something had been destroyed,

something I'd worked so hard to build.

Something beautiful was breaking that I'd

once treasured.

But in its painful destruction, I found freedom.

QUÉ HICISTE

A POWERFUL MESSAGE

I'm wearing a flowing, fiery red dress while standing in front of the audience as the final notes of "If You Had My Love" play out, and I look out over everyone and say, "Sometimes love doesn't go right. And when it doesn't go right, I find that it helps to sing about it." Then the opening guitar notes of *"Qué Hiciste"* start.

Ayer los dos soñábamos con un mundo perfecto . . .
(Yesterday, we were dreaming a perfect world . . .)

—"QUÉ HICISTE"

"*Qué Hiciste*" was the first single off *Como Ama una Mujer*—my first and only Spanish-language album. And five years later, when we were putting together the Dance Again tour, I knew I had to include the song . . . with a very important message at the end.

Whenever it feels uncomfortable to tell the truth, that's often the most important time to tell it.

This song was very hard to choreograph, because we wanted to really portray what it was about—one partner mistreating the other and the physical and emotional toll of being in an abusive relationship. Liz Imperio, the brilliant choreographer who did some of the most powerful pieces in the show—the tone setters, including both the opening and closing numbers—set about trying to make the lyrics come alive.

As I stand onstage in my red dress, a screen above me shows all kinds of explosive, fiery imagery. Lower down on the stage are two couples—one to my left and one to my right—and they're dancing, but they're also acting out the kind of abusive behavior described in the song. Liz decided that she wanted to do a beautiful fusion of hip-hop and tango. I loved it; it was a brilliant idea. It was street-hard and it was passionate, which is exactly what the emotion of the song called for.

We wanted to portray the truth about abusive relationships, but not to paint men in a negative way, even though that's how most people picture abuse. What I wanted to say is that abuse has no bias. It's not gender specific; it's just never okay. So of the two couples on the stage, one was a man being abusive to a woman and the other was a woman being abusive to a man.

You can imagine how all that went over with the audiences during our shows in certain countries where women don't necessarily have the same rights as men. When I looked out over the crowds, I could see women crying, really feeling it. And I could see the men squirming uncomfortably at the suggestion of a woman abusing a man. In some of these traditionally macho cultures, our decision to portray a woman slapping, kicking, yelling at a man was playing it a little too close to the edge—but whenever it feels uncomfortable to tell the truth, that's often the most important time to tell it.

Pulling together this song was hard on everybody, especially Liz, who got very emotional while she was choreographing it. And I understood it—it was affecting me too. But the end result was beautiful and powerful and true. As I sang, the two couples kicked and slapped and fought, but as we reached the end of the song—"*Con tus manos derrumbaste nuestra casa*" ("With your own hands, you destroyed our home")—the man and woman who had been the aggressors exited the stage, as the woman and man who had been abused turn and walk away from them. They come to meet me in the middle of the stage, right where I was standing. I turn to look at one . . . and then the other . . . and as I step forward toward the audience, they fall in line behind me and disappear. I wanted everyone to see that these people were just like me . . . even that they *could be* me.

Now I'm standing there, facing the audience all by myself, the weight of the subject matter hanging heavy in the air, the message suddenly flashes up on the screen in huge letters: *Ámate*. Love Yourself.

CHANGE STARTS WITHIN OURSELVES

Putting *"Qué Hiciste"* in the show, with that message, had me contemplating my past. Once again, the show was helping me face my own truth. I've never gotten a black eye or a busted lip, but I've been in relationships where I have felt abused in one way or another: mentally, emotionally, verbally. I know what it feels like for your soul to be diminished by the way your loved one is treating you . . . maybe it's a push, a shove, or a nasty word that stays with you. The scars might not be visible, but they run just as deep.

It took me years to figure out that in that kind of relationship the intensity and the conflict are really coming from two people—your partner and yourself. Because every day that you don't walk out that door, every day you accept things in your partner *and* in yourself, is a day that you're saying it's okay. Ultimately, we can never change someone else's behavior—we can only change our own.

We can never change someone else's behavior—we can only change our own.

All I could do now was figure out my own part in it. Through putting the show together, I realized that what I was working through wasn't about any one relationship, issue, or person. It was about *anything* in my life that I wasn't okay with. Anything I wanted to change. And I was getting to a point where I understood that that change had to happen within me.

Se te olvídó que era el amor lo que

importaba,

y con tus manos derrumbaste

nuestra casa

(You forgot that love was what

mattered,

and with your own hands you

destroyed our home)

—"QUÉ HICISTE"

THE END OF AN ERA

It was now May, and ever since the "I'm not happy" conversation back in March, I was living with so many unanswered questions and conflicted emotions that we hadn't addressed. Now that I look back, maybe we were both deliberately avoiding it, yet I could feel that there was a wedge growing between us. But I loved my husband, and I loved my family. I wasn't ready to give up.

The *American Idol* finale was upon us, and Randy and Steven and I were supposed to do a big performance together. It was meant to be the culmination of this great, amazing season that had rejuvenated the show—but we couldn't get Steven to agree to any of the songs. We floated a bunch of ideas out there, but for this reason or that reason, it didn't work out.

I called Simon Fuller, *Idol*'s creator and producer, and said, "We have to make this happen! It's been such a great year!" He tried, but eventually it became obvious that it just wasn't going to happen. I was disappointed, because this finale was going to be *the* show—I mean, we had a whole roster of A-list artists who were going to perform: Tony Bennett, Lady Gaga, Beyoncé, Gladys Knight . . . It was an amazing lineup of talent and we were supposed to be at the center of it, the stars of the home team. But it just wasn't in the cards.

The next day, two days before the finale, Marc and I went down to the Hollywood Walk of Fame, where Simon Fuller was getting a star. There was a ceremony, and photographers and fans were there. I love Simon and I wanted to make an appearance to support him. As soon as he saw us, he came over and drew us both into a big hug.

"Listen," he said. "Whatever you want to do on the finale, we want you to do it. We want you to be happy." I knew he wasn't pleased that the song with Steven and Randy had fallen apart. And I loved that he wanted to make it right—which was really typical of how I'd been treated by everyone at *American Idol* for the whole season.

"Maybe you guys can do something together?" he suggested.

I looked at Marc and said, "Well, do you want to do something together?"

And although I felt vulnerable in that moment, I was hopeful that it was a chance for us to reconnect and bring us close again.

"Sure," he said. "We'd have to pull it together really fast, though."

"Just let us know what you need," said Simon. "Anything at all."

"Can you fly in my band?" Marc asked. This was not a small request—Marc performed with a full seventeen-piece salsa orchestra, and most of the musicians were based in Miami and New York.

"No problem," said Simon. "We'll make it happen." And he did.

Later on, when we were riding home in the car, I suggested to Marc:

"Since your band is coming, why don't we do one of your songs . . . How about '*Aguanile*'?"

I knew that *American Idol*'s mainstream audience would be blown away when they heard Marc sing this song even though it was in Spanish. I started to envision the performance.

"I can sing it with you," I said. "I can come in on the second verse, and we can do the chorus together . . ."

But Marc disagreed. In a very matter-of-fact way, he said, "You know, this is a guy's song," and suggested that maybe he should sing and I could maybe dance.

I wasn't sure about it but I reluctantly agreed. After all, I wanted this to be good for us. I was going to put all the love and all the power I had as an entertainer and a performer into doing it.

Right away I jumped into "producer" mode. "We need to get dancers, with feathers. It all has to look really chic, with no loud colors . . ." I wanted everything to be perfect. The show was in two days, we had no time to waste. We choreographed a beautiful, sexy dance for me to do, where I came in only after Marc had already sung the first half of the song.

On the night of the finale, the show was electric. It was amazing performance after amazing performance. Finally, it was our turn: Marc sang and was blowing the roof off the place. When I came onstage and danced around Marc as he raised his eyebrows, making the crowd laugh, the audience was on ten. The last part of the song got wild, as I had even gotten Sheila E. to do a percussion solo. The moment built and built, and as the trumpets blasted the last notes of the song, I posed next to Marc, my back to the audience, my hand on his chest—giving him the final moment in the spotlight. As the crowd erupted into screams and applause, we kissed, and I reached up to wipe away the red lipstick that had come off on his lips so he wouldn't look silly.

Marc was amazing, and it turned out great. But later I realized that performance should have been the culmination of an amazing year in my life and my career and for some reason it just wasn't.

It's true that sometimes, when you're trying so hard to make a relationship work, you can sacrifice things that are important to you. And that's exactly what I was doing.

When I look back, the finale feels like the end of an era. Marc and I were magic onstage, but that was the last time we would perform together as husband and wife.

ONE LAST TRY

The night after the finale, Marc and I were scheduled to fly with the kids to the Caribbean for a vacation. I had been feeling so anxious about things between us that I wanted to take some time away from everything, to talk and hopefully reconnect.

We talked a lot on that trip, and I remember saying to him, "Marc, you and I are the glue for this family. We have to be okay, because if we're not okay, the whole thing falls apart." I told him I wanted us to spend more time with the kids, to make our family more of a priority.

As I was saying these words, all I could think was, *I hope he gets what I'm trying to say.* In fairness to Marc, I'm not sure how he remembers all this—whether he saw this vacation as a potential turning point in our marriage or not.

Sometimes, when you're trying so hard to make a relationship work, you can sacrifice things that are important to you.

We both knew something was wrong, but I'm not sure Marc looked at things as being at the crisis point that I did, or maybe he did . . . The truth was, we were talking about the same problems we always had, but what he maybe didn't understand was that even though the problems were the same, *I* was changing.

Before, I would have accepted things as they were. I'd think, *Well, that's the way it is, so I have to deal with it.* But for the first time in years, instead of taking whatever was dished out, I thought, *This doesn't feel right, and that's not good for me and it's not good for the kids.* And although Marc understood, would anything change? Or would we go right back into the same old patterns?

I got my answers the very first week we were back—the week of our seventh anniversary.

On our return home, when the day of our anniversary came up, we were trying to put everything aside and enjoy the moment, but instead what transpired was another argument.

Here's the thing about kids: They don't do what you say; they do what you do.

However, like with so many things after the babies were born, this time was different. I realized I wasn't the same person anymore and I just didn't want to be fighting anymore, I didn't want Max and Emme to think that was normal. Because here's the thing about kids: They don't do what you say; they do what you do. They watch you. If you tell them not to drink, but you drink, they will too. If you tell them not to smoke, but you smoke, you can be damn sure they're going to pick up a cigarette. So if they hear you fight or argue all the time, they are going to think that's normal as well.

I wanted to feel good about the choices I was making for myself. I wanted to be able to stand in front of them and say, "I did the right thing"—not to be some broken person who stayed in a marriage for the wrong reasons. I had fought so hard to keep things together, but you can't fit a square peg in a round hole. In this moment, I realized that no matter how hard it would be, the best thing I could do was to walk away.

There is a love like no other. A love that requires no conditions. A love that can't be explained or learned.

It's a love that gives you a greater purpose. It's a love that can set the rest of your world aside.

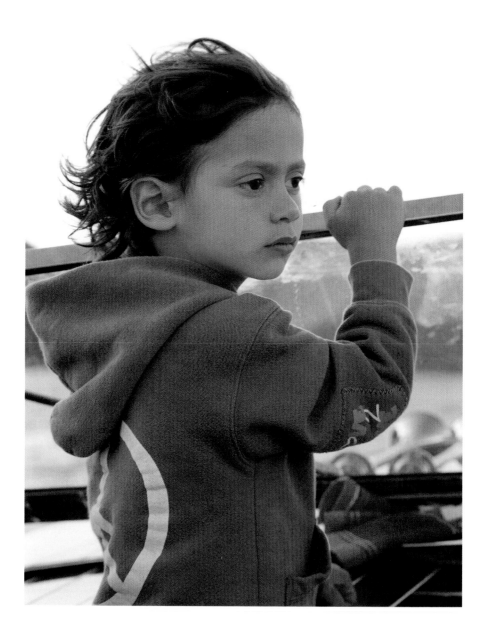

UNTIL IT BEATS NO MORE

WHEN YOU HAVE children, you feel love like you haven't felt before. The first time I held Emme and Max, when they were these tiny, helpless little babies, I felt such a pure feeling toward them. It wasn't traumatic, or tormented, or complicated. It was perfect and simple and true.

When I looked at my babies, I knew I never wanted to hurt them, or let anyone else hurt them. I couldn't stand the thought of it. There's a depth of feeling with my babies that surpasses anything I've ever felt before—a feeling that I'll do anything to make sure they're okay.

Romantic love is different from parental love, obviously, but it still has the same basic components. When I felt that pure love for Max and

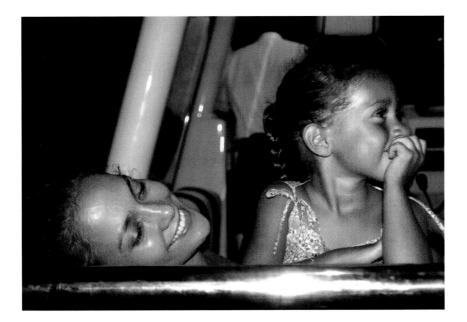

Emme, I started to understand that something was missing from the love I had received romantically. Too often, that love felt conditional, like I had to behave a certain way, or earn it somehow, to keep it. The Bible tells us that love is patient; love is kind . . . It is not self-seeking; it is not easily angered; it doesn't keep score . . . Unfortunately, too many of the relationships I'd been in didn't quite fit that description.

> *It's love and I have found it, feel the beat again, stronger than before I'm gonna give you my heart, until it beats no more*
>
> —"UNTIL IT BEATS NO MORE"

LEARNING TO TAKE CARE OF MYSELF

Shortly after our Caribbean vacation, I had to fly to Europe with my mom and the kids to continue promoting "On the Floor." Our first stop was Paris. My mom could take Max and Emme out anywhere—nobody knew who they were, so nobody messed with them. They spent their days exploring the city, hanging out in parks, enjoying the scenery. Paris has really lovely parks—it's one of my favorite things about the city. So, one day when the only thing on my schedule was a performance in the evening, I said to Emme and Max, "Okay, Mommy's coming with you to play in the park today!"

My mom and I packed some snacks in a bag, and we got ready to take the kids out.

"Do you want security to come with you?" Benny asked.

"No," I said. "I don't want a bunch of people—I just want to go out with Mom and the kids."

"I don't think that's a good idea," he said. "You're going to get mobbed."

I didn't want to have to take some big entourage to go to the park. Couldn't we just go and enjoy ourselves? I wanted to believe that no one would notice we were there, or if they did, that maybe they'd recognize that we just wanted to have a nice day with the kids and give us some space. But Benny wasn't having that, so I relented and had one of our security guys come with us.

We got to the park, and the kids were really excited when they saw there was a carousel. Mom and I put them on the ride, and they laughed and shouted as they went around—they were having so much fun, and it was like a balm to my soul to see my babies so happy. But as soon as we started to relax and have fun, a bunch of paparazzi appeared out of nowhere.

We tried to ignore the pack of men circling us and clicking their cameras, though it was pretty much impossible. Still, we tried to get on with our day, and when Emme and Max saw a little booth selling toys and candy, we walked over to have a look. I told them, "Okay, you can each pick one toy." Max picked a water gun. And when Emme saw what Max had chosen, she decided she wanted one too. So we filled them up

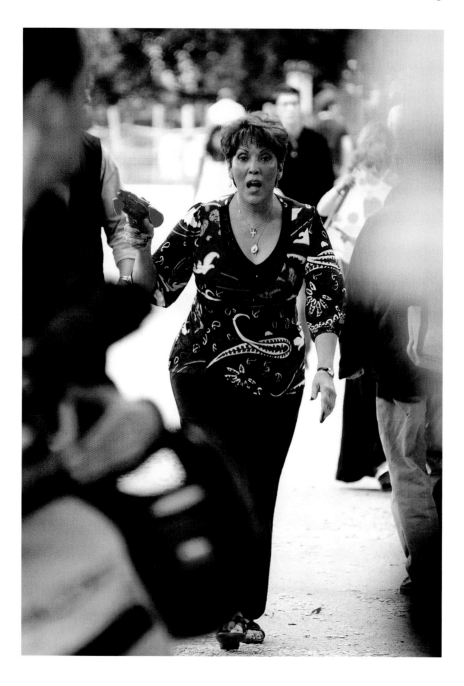

with water, and the kids started squirting each other and running around, laughing.

The photographers kept snapping away, and they kept getting closer and closer. The paparazzi in Paris aren't the most polite or respectful. I didn't like how close they were getting especially because I had the kids with me. So I said to my mom, "Hey, I dare you to wet those guys with a water gun."

She looked at me with her eyebrows raised. "You want me to squirt them?" she asked. "Because I'll do it!"

"Ah, never mind," I said. "You won't do it. I know you won't," I added, knowing, of course, that saying that was the one sure way to get her to do it.

"Give me that!" she said, and snatched a water pistol out of my hand, charging those photographers like a mama bear on a rampage. She'd had knee surgery a few weeks earlier, so she was still limping; but she took off after those guys, shooting water right at their cameras. The paparazzi seemed terrified of the crazy lady with the water pistol, and they all started to scatter, yelling and cursing in French. But my mom kept on limp-running at everyone, spraying water left and right.

I doubled over, laughing harder than I had in months. The one thing I love about my mom is that she makes me laugh like nobody else—it's like we're connected at the funny bone or something. Whenever I'm having a hard time, I want her there, because she says and does things that always make me feel better. And this was a much-needed break from all of the intense emotions I'd been dealing with during that time.

We're like any mom and daughter in that we have our ups and downs—times where we're super loving and times when we fight like crazy. But when I'm feeling down or vulnerable or alone, the one thing I know is that I want my mom there. I know she'll do anything to make sure I'm okay; she'll hug me, make jokes, and even sleep in my bed with me if I'm lonely. Whenever I need her, she's there. I hope that one day Max and Emme can say that about me with certainty. I will do anything and everything in my power to make it so.

Mom chased after those photographers that day because she always has my back, no matter what. Because there's something about a mother's love for her kids that transcends everything.

There's something about a mother's love for her kids that transcends everything.

During that time, the strength I got from being a mom carried me through one of the most difficult periods of my life. In planning the show, I felt that "Until It Beats No More" could be a key performance depicting a pivotal chapter in my story. I really wanted the audience to see, to understand that that kind of love—the love I feel for my children—is what I consider to be the purest love of all and the impact that it had on me.

At the very end of *"Qué Hiciste,"* the words *"Ámate"* and "Love Yourself" had flashed up onto the screen. And as the piano played the opening chords to "Until It Beats No More," I would say to the crowd: "There's all different types of love . . . but then there's real, true love. And in this life, I can honestly say, I have felt true love." And then a giant photo of Max and Emme filled the screen.

I was down for the count, feeling

like I've come to the end

Nothing really mattered, nothing

left for me to mend . . .

—"UNTIL IT BEATS NO MORE"

Throughout the whole song, photos and videos of Max and Emme, many of them taken by my dear friend Ana, flashed up on the screen—a collage of so many beautiful moments we've had together. I've never been one to parade my kids in front of audiences, but I felt really strongly about this part of the show. I wanted to show people the love that had changed me. The love that had shown me that life was to be celebrated, not just endured. My babies' love saved me, and I wanted to share that with the audience too.

Every time we did this song, the audience went crazy for it. One of the things that was so fantastic about the tour was that we had all kinds of people there—from dads and moms with their eight-year-old kids, to teenagers and girls in their twenties and thirties, to middle-aged couples, to grandparents. It was a family affair, seven to seventy. And all of them responded to this part of the show, which was all about family.

There were some shows where, because of local permits and noise ordinances, we had to cut a few songs to finish in our allotted time. Once or twice, I suggested maybe we could cut "Until It Beats No More." We already had two other ballads, and I figured people would prefer the more upbeat songs. But everybody—Benny, the band, the dancers, the crew—

all said, "No way!" People felt it was the most emotional part of the entire show. In many ways, it was the heart of the show—the whole reason I was doing it. And so it stayed in . . . every time.

I'm alive, I can breathe, I can feel,
I believe
And there ain't no doubt about it,
there ain't no doubt about it . . .
I'm in love.

—"UNTIL IT BEATS NO MORE"

SHARING COMFORT

In the middle of the tour, I had a very special moment with Max. I brought Emme and Max on the whole tour, as I couldn't stand the thought of us being separated for five months. Fortunately, the kids are great travelers, so we didn't have any problems—although there were some very long days and nights on the road.

One night, really late, we were flying into Turkey for the next show. Everybody on the plane was asleep, passed out. But Max was awake, and he was sitting on my lap, asking me the kind of questions that a four-year-old asks: *Will you always be my mommy? When are we going to see Daddy again? Will we always be together?*

I hugged him tight and whispered, "Listen. There's only one thing you need to know. Me, you, and Emme are always going to be together, no matter what, okay? No matter what."

Max looked up at me with his big brown eyes and said, "Okay." As if that was all he needed. I pulled the blanket up around his shoulders, and he relaxed into my arms. I'd never felt happier than in that moment, because I knew it was true.

ACT FIVE

LET'S GET LOUD

SET LIST

Video transition: "Baby I Love U!"

———

"Let's Get Loud"

———

"Papi"

———

"On the Floor"

———

I am grateful for the tough experiences in my life. They taught me some of my most valuable lessons. But I can't let the negative experiences haunt my memory and fuel regret.

It's time to extract the good from the bad and leave the rest behind.

I'm taking all the positives with me and I'm forging ahead.

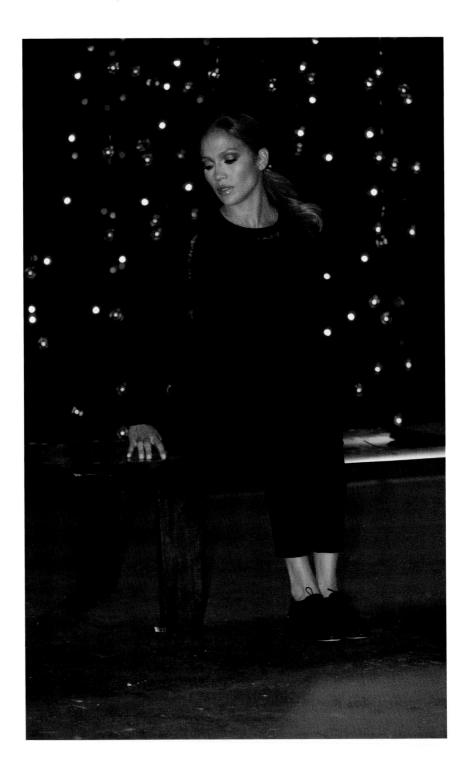

BABY I LOVE U!
(VIDEO TRANSITION)

AT THIS POINT in the show, there was what we call a video transition. We use these to do quick changes, but they can be so beautiful if done right and can really enhance the message of the show. Again, Parris Goebel choreographed it. It was based on a piece she had choreographed to Etta James, which I'd fallen in love with; the reason I'd hired her, actually. I asked her to do something similar to "Baby I Love U!," a song I had written many years before for my *This Is Me . . . Then* album. She thought it was a great idea. We wanted to show the blossoming of a new kind of romantic love. It was a beautiful, emotive piece, two people sitting side by side on a bench—together but independent of each other—meeting and discovering one another. It was loving but it wasn't needy; it was sweet and strong at the same time.

Creating this show and going through my songs and my life in this way was like holding up a mirror to myself. At this point in the show we had now established how people see me—Big Hollywood—how I see myself—the Bronx section—who I am as an artist and my message about love, and how motherhood had changed my entire perspective on love and how it wasn't what I thought it was. In fact, I was seeing romantic love in a whole new way. I still hadn't found the key to unlock the secret, but I was getting closer. I was in transition and this was the perfect transition piece, a perfect breather before the big finale.

. . .

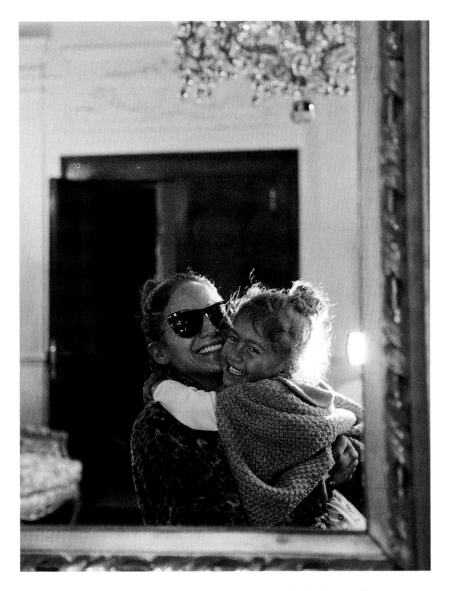

Boy I never thought I could feel the way I felt when I felt the way you were feeling me, baby.

—"BABY I LOVE U!"

*I*t was time to own up to myself.

Was I living the life I was supposed to live?

Were my relationships good for me?

Did I truly know myself?

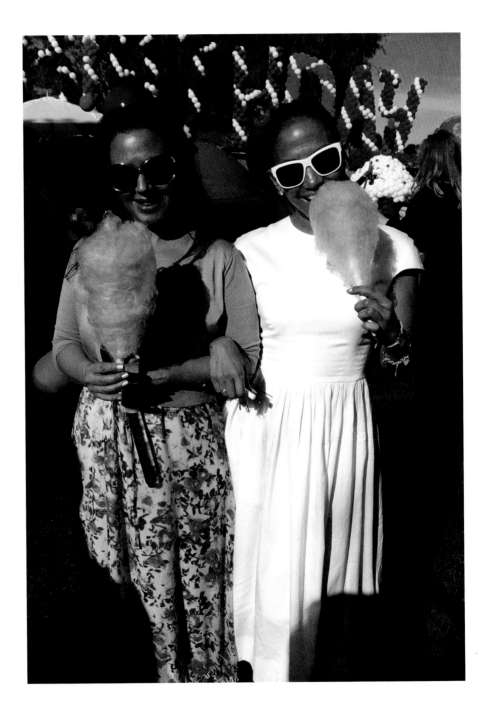

TURNING POINT

ACCEPTING HELP

In looking back at the crazy ride I'd been on with my past relationships, it was hard not to recognize that there was something I needed to examine. During my trip to promote "On the Floor" in Europe, between performances and interviews, I was desperately trying to figure things out. I called my friend Leah, I needed to talk. With everything that was happening . . . I told her I'd never felt so low in my life. She asked why.

"I feel like I'm doing things and accepting things I don't want to," I said. "Like, this is not how I want my life to be. I feel sick to my stomach." No matter how bad things had gotten in the past, this was a level of anxiety I had never dealt with before. I didn't know how to handle it.

"This is great!" Leah exclaimed.

Well, that was not the response I expected.

"What's that supposed to mean?" I asked her.

"You're hitting rock bottom," she said. "You know, Jennifer, you have to hit bottom before you can make a change, and it's finally happening."

I didn't say anything. Was she right? Was that what I was experiencing?

"Do you want help?" she asked me.

"Yes," I said. "I do." I had to find some way through all this, and I didn't know how to do it alone. I had to find the strength to make a change, but I didn't have that strength in me, and I didn't know where I could get it. And that was a very frightening, disorienting place to be. I felt helpless, and I felt scared.

Leah helped me hire a therapist, and during that period, while I worked really hard promoting "On the Floor," which was fast becoming the biggest-selling single of my career, I was working even harder behind the scenes—discussing, analyzing, doing exercises, everything I needed to do to understand the turns my life had taken.

I'm usually a pretty quick study, and hot off the realization that a change was necessary, I started recognizing my own patterns. One of the most important realizations I had was that the problems I was having with Marc weren't about him. They weren't about anyone else—they were about me. And there were *a lot* of problems. One, I discovered I had low self-esteem, which I had never really pictured myself as having. Two, I worked on learning what integrity meant, which would cause a massive change—but we'll get back to that later. And three, the biggest lightbulb that went off during those two weeks was that I realized I wasn't recognizing the value of my own love.

In analyzing, step by step, relationships that went as far back as high school, I noticed I had never stopped to consider just how special *my* love was. I never stopped to look at myself and say, *You know what? You're honest, you're generous, you're loving, and you're loyal . . . You deserve a love that is as pure and special and good as the one you are giving.* My love has value. I HAVE VALUE.

Hold on, back up. I have value? My love has value?

WOW.

Sometimes, especially as women, we don't feel comfortable giving ourselves that credit. We're selfless in the best ways. But that can be dangerous too. You need to feel comfortable with affirming the greatness of who you are as a partner, a wife, a mother, a person. You are great. What you have to offer is great. When you give your time, your love, your respect, you deserve respect in return. You deserve comfort, you deserve honesty, and you deserve to feel safe. That's what relationships are supposed to be about—a place where you feel good, right?

When you give your time,
your love, your respect,
you deserve respect
in return. You deserve
comfort, you deserve
honesty, and you
deserve to feel safe.

Okay, so now I'm thinking, keep the diamond rings, the Bentleys, the doves, the trips to Europe . . . Keep all of it! I can buy all those things myself. Give me your time, your honesty, your respect, kindness, patience, fidelity. Give me comfort when things are tough . . . Being me, being famous, doesn't mean I don't need those things like any other girl. It didn't matter if my partners were famous either, it was always the same scenario. I gave off the air of being self-sufficient and instead of expressing and demanding the right kind of love for myself, I always wanted to appear like I was fine, in fact, I thought I was fine—and so did they. But it wasn't true. Just because you're a strong girl doesn't mean you don't need to be loved and cared for like anybody else. And it doesn't matter where you sit in this world, poor or rich, famous or not, we all need to be loved in the right way. That's what matters. In discovering my own value, that's what I was finally realizing I deserved.

I remember a time when I was filming a movie and I had finished a really good take when I started experiencing some anxiety. I couldn't quite understand why I was feeling that way until later, when my acting coach, who was on the set with me, was able to quickly notice and diagnose the problem: "You're afraid of your own greatness," she said. At the time, I didn't know what the hell she was talking about, but now, thinking back, I understand what she meant. I had never really owned that feeling. I had never truly believed I was great at acting, or anything else for that matter. I never thought of myself in that way, I wasn't even aware enough to consider it. I never stopped to give myself credit, to say, "Jen, you're awesome; you're doing amazing." It never even occurred to me. I was always working and striving and going and running. I mean I knew I was doing okay. I knew I was a good person. But *great?* I was just trying to be as good as I could be.

Marianne Williamson has a wonderful quote that says:

> *Our deepest fear is not that we are inadequate. Our deepest fear is that we are powerful beyond measure. It is our light, not our darkness, that most frightens us . . . [But] as we let our own light shine, we unconsciously give other people the permission to do the same.*

I was finally recognizing a really unhealthy pattern that had entrapped me for so many years. I was always looking for the other person to tell me I was great so I could feel good about myself. I lived for that. I wanted their appreciation. Even worse, if they didn't give it to me, I tried even harder to prove to them that I was worthy. I would keep trying to fix things and make them better, searching for that validation. I always thought the reason it wasn't working had to be because *I* was doing something wrong. So no matter how I was treated, or what the other person did in our relationship, all I cared about was getting his approval. In fact, that would oftentimes become the glue that kept these relationships together.

Ultimately, the love I wasn't giving myself, I was trying to get from others.

Turn the music up to hear that
sound, let's get loud, let's get
loud
Ain't nobody gotta tell ya, what you
gotta do

—"LET'S GET LOUD"

The next day, just before Max and Emme and I were heading to the airport to return to LA, Ana came over to say good-bye. She had brought me something.

Ana likes to buy me books—loving self-help books to help me remember to take care of myself. (In fact, she was the one who gave me my first Louise Hay book.) She handed me one and said, "I bought you this book on meditation. You have a lot of emotions going on in your life right now, and this will help you learn how to move through them." And then she handed me something else: two little ceramic angels.

"This one is Max, and this one is Emme," she said. "When you're working, put them where you can see them, and remember you have two little angels in your life." I took them from her and nodded.

She had one other thing to tell me. "Pray for Marc," she said, "and teach the kids to pray for Marc. We need to pray for everybody, and you all need to heal."

Ana and I were sitting cross-legged on the bed, and I took her hands in mine, our eyes both filled with emotion, and I thought, *This is the beauty of friendship.* Your friends mourn your losses with you, because they experience them too. The truth is, no matter how lonely you might feel, you're never going through anything alone. Just as Benny would say in his toast that following Christmas, you can choose your family. Everyone who's a part of that family goes through your trials and difficulties with you.

Your friends mourn your losses with you, because they experience them too. The truth is, no matter how lonely you might feel, you're never going through anything alone.

And if you're lucky, as I am, those friends will always be ready and willing to throw you a dance party to remind you of that.

REALIGNING MY DREAMS

One of the hardest things about getting divorced is learning to let go of the dream. Because being in a marriage is all about planning the future, about hoping to spend your life with someone and trying to make that work. My dream had been to have this family forever, to grow old together and watch as our kids grew up and had children of their own. It was a beautiful dream, and it was so hard to let go of it when the time came. You end up thinking, *What do I do now?*

Funnily enough, Nancy Meyers gave me an answer. She's the writer and director of the movie *Something's Gotta Give*, starring Diane Keaton. The main character, Erica Barry, is a single woman in her fifties, with a beautiful home in the Hamptons and a grown daughter. Mom and daughter have a wonderful, close relationship, and even though she's single, Erica Barry seems to have a fantastic life.

I must have watched that movie ten times after the split. I'd be sitting there in my own nice house, dreaming about buying a nice house like Erica Barry's in the Hamptons and creating my own *Something's Gotta Give* dream life. Max and Emme would grow up to be amazing adults, and they'd come visit me, and I would end up being the kind of woman who's absolutely fine with sleeping in the middle of the bed all by myself. Thank God for Nancy Meyers, because that vision helped me get through some really tough nights.

Nancy Meyers helped me envision my dream life, but another woman helped me get through those tough weeks in real life: my mom.

My mother dropped everything and came to stay with me after everything happened. She was always there when I needed her, and the one thing I could count on was that she would always find a way to make me laugh. She's not as good at serious conversation, or the more intimate parts of a relationship, and that sometimes drives me crazy, but she will make you laugh until you pee your pants. In that way, she and Marc are a lot alike.

Mom was still staying with us at the house, helping out with Max and

Emme, when I had to fly to the Ukraine to do a show shortly after the divorce. With all the upheaval going on, and the long flights and quick turnaround, I decided it was better to leave the kids at home. I was going to be gone for only a couple of days, and I knew that doing such a long, fast trip would turn their systems upside down.

I asked my mom if she could help take care of the kids while I was gone. And right away, she said, "I don't want you to go by yourself. I'll come with you! Let Tiana take care of the babies." I frowned, and she said, "Come on . . . I've never been to the Ukraine! I want to go! I'm coming with you."

I remembered how nice it was to have her with me in Paris, when she expressed her maternal love by ambushing the paparazzi with a water gun, so I said, "Okay, Ma. Let's go together." And two days later, we were on a long flight to the Ukraine—my mom, me, Benny, and Benny's assistant.

Benny and I were sitting together in the back of the plane, talking about everything that had gone on in the last few weeks. I was still trying to sort things out from the divorce—from finances, to our home, to the kids, to all the projects that we had been working on together. Everything was so complicated, I was glad to have the long flight and a relaxed moment with Benny to talk it all through.

We were deep in our conversation when my mom suddenly limped down the aisle to our seats and said, "Jen, I feel funny."

"What's the matter?" I asked. She looked pale and kind of sweaty.

"I don't feel good," she said. "I think I'm gonna pass out." And then she did—plop! She fell right over in the aisle of the plane.

"Oh my God!" I shrieked. "Ma! Ma!" I turned to the front of the plane and said, "What happened? Did she take something?"

The assistant said, "She took a sleeping pill . . ." And of course, my mom was also still taking pain medications for her knees, having had a knee replacement not that long ago. The combination had knocked her out.

The flight crew brought an oxygen mask and tried to strap it on her face as she lay there, disoriented. I said, "Ma! What are you doing? You're supposed to be taking care of *me!*" She didn't respond, and her eyelids started fluttering. I leaned down closer to her face and said, "I swear to God, if you die right now, I will *kill you*. Do you hear me?"

And I started nervously laughing, convincing myself that everything would be fine because what else was I going to do? It was either laugh or completely fall apart.

The flight crew was discussing whether we'd need to make an emergency landing, but once my mother heard me threaten to kill her, she did exactly what I'd hoped: She started laughing.

"I'm sorry, baby," she said, still half in a stupor, chuckling weakly under her oxygen mask. We looked at each other and I shook my head. She ended up being okay, although she did have to get hooked up to an IV at a hospital after we landed. I had to tease her about being such a tremendous "help" to me on the trip. But the truth is, she was. Even when she was passing out and getting hooked up to IVs, I was so happy to have my mom with me, supporting me and keeping me laughing.

When I returned to the second season of *American Idol*, I was really happy to be back to my work family after such a difficult summer.

It was September when we started filming the auditions, and I can't remember which was our first city, but I do remember seeing Randy and Steven and Ryan and Nigel for the first time that day. We always had little sit-down planning sessions before doing the actual auditions— there was usually a big table, and food and coffee, and everyone would settle in and talk about that day's shooting.

I walked in and took a seat, and all the guys sat down. Everyone knew about the divorce by this time, of course, and right away they all started asking me, "How are you?" and "Are you doing okay?" I told them I was, and then somebody asked, "What happened? None of us expected this!"

It was true. Marc and I were great at masking the problems we'd had over the years and putting our best foot forward. I thought for a second, and then I said, "You know, it was a long time coming. We tried really hard to make it work." I didn't want to get into a whole lot of detail, but I tried to explain a little bit about what had happened.

And Steven in particular seemed to understand. I knew he had so much regret over his own divorce from his wife of many years, because whenever he'd speak about it, he'd get teary-eyed right away. He took my hand and squeezed it, and we didn't even have to say anything. Just looking into each other's eyes conveyed everything.

Then, as I looked around the table, each one of them was looking at me with such sweet concern.

"Marc was just my guy, you know?" I said, my voice cracking a little. "I thought he was my guy."

Nobody said a word, until Nigel finally said, in his lovely British accent, "Okay, darling. We don't have to talk about this anymore." He knew it was getting too deep, and we had to get in front of the cameras soon.

"Let's pull ourselves together," he said, clapping his hands. "We're ready to go, here." He left the table and went to the set, and we all followed him out.

I walked out onto the set like everything was fine, and we started doing the auditions—a normal day, as usual. I'm listening, laughing, being pensive, being emotional, just doing my thing, living the moment. Then I looked over to the side, where Nigel was sitting. Our eyes met, and he mouthed, "I love you." I mouthed back, "I love you too." He understood, and he appreciated the fact that I was there, doing my job, despite what I was going through.

That's always how it was on *American Idol*, because *these* were my guys too, the people who supported and appreciated and respected me. Doing that show felt like wrapping myself in a security blanket . . .

Which is, in some strange way, why it became so important for me to walk away from the show. In fact, doing that ended up feeling every bit as important as walking away from my marriage.

RISING TO THE CHALLENGE

I had just started the Dance Again tour when Benny told me I had to make a decision about doing a third season of *American Idol*.

Over the past year, I had undertaken two of the scariest things I'd ever done. The first was finally deciding to move on. The second was deciding to do the world tour. I had been so afraid of it all—afraid I would fail, afraid people would criticize me . . . I'd gone back and forth so many times with Benny when he was starting to make all the arrangements, because I couldn't convince myself it was worth all the risk.

And then I realized something. I realized that if I didn't believe in myself, nobody else would either. What was I so afraid of? What was the worst that could happen? Whatever it was, it couldn't be worse than simply being too scared to do anything at all. If I didn't do this tour, I'd probably regret it for the rest of my life. So I finally decided to make the leap, to choose to believe in myself.

We had been on the tour for only about a week when Benny said, "We have to talk about *Idol*." My second season had gone as well as my first one, and the producers wanted me to come back. It was so tempting, for all the same reasons I'd done it to begin with.

And yet . . . all the events of the past year had changed me in ways I was only beginning to understand. When you make hard decisions, when you follow your heart to places that terrify you, it's no longer possible to simply choose the easy path. My life was in transition, and it was a transition that I had chosen. I had to follow it through to the end.

So, when Benny asked me, "What do you want to do? What would make you happy?" I realized there was only one answer I could give. I loved being on *Idol*, but it was time to move on. It didn't make sense for me to spend a third year in a row sitting on a panel, judging other singers, especially if the main reason I was doing it was for the security of it.

The irony is, being on *American Idol* for two seasons was the very thing that gave me the strength to realize I needed to get back to doing the other things that I do. It was the spark that led me to value myself more, to respect myself as a person and as an artist. And now I had to use that newfound self-respect to put down the security blanket. I knew it was the right thing to do, but it was still so very hard.

We were on the tour, somewhere in Canada, when I called Ryan Seacrest to give him the news.

"Hey," I said, "I'm so grateful to all of you for everything, but I've decided I'm not coming back next year."

I was really emotional, and so was Ryan. He told me he wished I would stay, and I told him a part of me really wanted to, but right then I just couldn't.

"I feel like we're breaking up," he said.

"I do too," I told him. "This show has meant so much to me. Thank you, and I'm sorry." I barely managed to hang up the phone before I was overcome by emotion.

Benny put his arm around me and asked gently, "Are you okay?"

I said, "Yeah. It's just so hard to do." In some way, walking away from *Idol* felt tied to walking away from Marc—it felt like the final act in a play, the inevitable, emotional conclusion.

Benny understood.

"Being on the show gave you the strength to walk away from other things," he said. "It's like you're walking away from a whole period of your life."

Just a year earlier, it would have been really easy for me to decide to stay in both situations—my marriage and the show. There were plenty of reasons to stick with both, and the idea of leaving either one of them filled me with fear. Now I had confronted that fear head-on. I hadn't

When you make hard decisions, when you follow your heart to places that terrify you, it's no longer possible to simply choose the easy path.

allowed it to dominate my life and my decisions. As painful as it was at that moment, I knew that my life would ultimately be better for it, both personally and as an artist. And you know what they say, set something free, and if it comes back to you . . .

And the amazing thing was, it happened as I was beginning the Dance Again tour—the tour whose whole message was to live again, and love again, and *dance again*, to take chances and put yourself out there.

In choosing to leave *Idol*, I was putting that into action, really living it. Once the initial shock wore off, it felt like a weight had lifted off me. Like I'd been underwater, running out of breath, and finally dropped enough weight to float to the top . . . only to find that glorious moment when all of a sudden your head pokes through the water's surface, and there's air, and sunshine, and you can breathe again.

So, when I stood up on the stage in city after city and said to people, "You've got to love yourself," I really felt it. Because I was finally living it.

LET'S GET LOUD

"Turn up the lights!" I'd shout right after the end of "Let's Get Loud." "Let me get a look at everybody!" And no matter what city or country we were in, I loved to look out and see so many girls in the audience.

"I see a lot of beautiful ladies out here tonight!" I'd say. "All my girls came out! Let me hear you!" I'd point the microphone out to the audience, and the women would all scream.

In a lot of the places we performed, women don't have as much of a voice as the men do, so this part of the show was always one of my favorites. It was like a competition. The women would yell and stomp their feet, and then I'd call out, "Where my papis at?" And the men would let out a roar.

Back and forth I'd go—"Where my ladies . . . ? Papis, let me hear you!"—and I loved to hear how the ladies would let loose. The women were always louder than the men, and in their screams and shouts, I felt like they were shouting, *We're here. We're not afraid. And you are going to hear us!* Sometimes I'd go back and forth five or six times, talking to everybody, inviting them to let loose.

Then I'd say, "We did a lot of songs for the ladies tonight . . . And, ladies, even though you obviously won, let's do one song for the papis. But keep a close eye, because there's something extra special in here for you." And we'd launch into the song "Papi"—which seems like it would be for the guys, but really, it was for the ladies. At one point, the male dancers would take off their J.Lo tanks and throw them into the audience for the women to take home. A memento, from me to my girls, to remind them that we were in control that night. And then, for our last song of the night, an explosive finale— the biggest hit of them all: "On the Floor."

Dance the night away
Live your life and stay out on the floor!

—"ON THE FLOOR"

I started "On the Floor" singing a cappella in Spanish, a slowed-down version of the chorus: *"Llorando se fue y me dejó sola sin su amor . . ."* ("He left crying and

left me alone without his love . . .") It was kind of a callback to where this journey had all started, both literally and figuratively. Every night it reminded me of what I'd been through and how far I'd come during the last year. I had been so afraid to embark on this journey, yet here I was at the end of it, feeling stronger than ever. My voice had grown, I had grown. I had changed so much. I wasn't singing the way I did before—the fear was gone and I was better than I was when I started. I had found my voice; I had found myself. The journey was complete. I'd repeat the chorus line again, one more time, holding the last note as long as I could, echoing my newfound strength. The audience would yell in appreciation, and as soon as the first chords of "On the Floor" rang through the arena, all hell broke loose. We were all about to rip the roof off the place. A throne rose up from the floor, a moment for me to sit down (thank God—after two hours I had earned it!) while Pitbull's verse ripped through the speakers. Two of the dancers would bring me a black silk robe with a beautiful feathered boa collar as I walked down the stairs while singing the first verse of the song. By the time we hit the chorus again, all twenty thousand people were jumping up and down in unison, fists in the air, singing:

> *Laaa lalalalalala lalalalala la la laaaa*
> *Tonight we gonna be it on the floor . . .*

It was the perfect ending, a euphoric climax, a moment of true abandon where we were celebrating life to its fullest.

The crowd loved it. The show is over . . . but there's one more song to come, the encore, the song that brought the whole thing together . . .

ENCORE

My dream as an artist is to share my

experiences in a way that will touch people.

"Dance Again" allowed me to create

something beautiful from the ashes of

the pain.

This is my moment.

DANCE AGAIN

SEARCHING FOR THAT ONE LOVE

In October of 2011, just three months after Marc and I announced our separation, I was scheduled to do a one-hour show at the Mohegan Sun Casino in Connecticut, six months before the Dance Again tour even started. I didn't have anything pulled together—we had to create the show from scratch.

We were going to have to throw it together quickly. And once we had the whole thing figured out, there was still room for one more song. I decided I wanted to put in one of my new songs from the album I'd just released, *LOVE?*, one that people might not know that well, but that spoke to the situation everyone was still talking about—my divorce. I hadn't made very many appearances since our official announcement, so people were naturally curious: *How is she doing? Is she going to talk about it? Is she okay?* I decided I'd give them something to satisfy that curiosity.

The song, "One Love," from an album aptly titled *LOVE?*, was another song I had written—this time with the help of Anesha and Antea, two writers who contributed to the album greatly—it was about a woman's search for that one true love. When we wrote it, we made the verses very autobiographical, describing in detail some of my past relationships. It's a really intimate, personal song, and as we started working up the choreography, I decided, *What the hell. I might as well just lay it all out there.* So we worked up a staging of the song that would walk everybody through my life and past loves, one by one.

Is there one love, only once in a lifetime?
It's so hard to find, the perfect one to call mine.

—"ONE LOVE"

But the night of the show, I got cold feet.

"This is too much," I told Benny. "I feel too exposed putting all this out there right now. It's too soon." I told him I wanted to pull the song.

"Listen," he said. "You're the one who's always saying that being an artist is about baring your soul, about being introspective and making yourself vulnerable. So, if you feel vulnerable right now, then I guess we're doing it right."

"I know. I know," I said. "But I'm really uncomfortable doing this right now, okay?" Benny was firm, using all of my own arguments against me. He loved the number, and he loved the statement it was making. And as much as I didn't want to admit it, I knew he was right. All those beautiful words about what it means to be an artist were only words unless I followed through with them. So I did.

And this is how it all played out . . .

I was standing onstage, dressed in a white gown, and I sang the first verse of "One Love":

Took a shot with the bad boy from the block
Picked my love right from the start,
Mister Wrong, he plays his part.

To my right on the stage stood a man wearing sunglasses and a gray suit and a woman dressed in that famous green Versace gown—Puffy and me. Their images were projected on a giant screen above my head, so nobody could miss the point. I kept singing:

Back to the beginning, now round two,
Try my luck with something new
We danced until we said "I do,"
My luck is bad, no more us, too, no me and you

That was Cris and me, of course. To my left on the stage was a man with a shaved head, kneeling to propose to a woman. She had her hair in braids and was wearing a J.Lo shirt from the "Love Don't Cost a Thing" video, in which we'd famously danced together. Now the next verse:

It's take three, could there be a part for me?
Came and swept me off my feet
Went nowhere but kept the ring,
Once again, I'm lonely

And to my right, a tall, handsome actor with a woman wearing a mint-green dress, her hair pulled into a bun—just as I'd dressed to go to the Oscars with Ben in 2003 . . . And then finally:

Number four, you sang to me but I'm not sure
So worn out but loved you so
Made me wanna try once more
and I couldn't say no

To my left, a dashing man singing into a microphone while I danced around him in a short, sparkling dress—just as Marc and I had danced on the finale of *American Idol* only a few months earlier.

Is there one love?
Somebody that complements me
And makes me wanna never leave
Made just right for me
Is there one love, one love, one love, one love . . . ?

As the song came to an end, I had seen my four great love affairs flash before my eyes. I looked over at the dancers playing Marc and me, and the whole thing felt so surreal. I got stuck there looking at that image.

As I sang the final line—"Is there one love?"—I turned and faced the audience and I just stood there, still, looking out over them for a moment that seemed like an eternity . . . They were feeling everything I was feeling, and I was feeling them right back. We were sharing a real moment. It's one of those things that happens onstage when you truly connect with your audience.

I couldn't think of what to say. There were no words. All I could do was lift my hands and shrug my shoulders. At that moment, the place erupted. Their cheers transitioned from applause for the performance to a warm embrace of love. I could hear people screaming, "We love you, Jennifer!" and "Keep your head up!" and "It's gonna be okay!" I felt so emotional. Tears started welling up in my eyes. It was like they were telling me they understood that I was a girl, like any other girl, just trying to get it right. In that moment, I thought, *It doesn't matter what the tabloids print, or the picture other people want to paint—I can come onstage and show people who I really am.* It was a beautiful, powerful moment for me. For us.

Months later, when I was planning the world tour, I realized I could never perform that song again. It was a one-time thing, perfect for that moment in time, but it would never be as special as it was that night. That song was all about my past. It was over now, and I was looking toward the future.

BUILDING MYSELF BACK UP

In those first few months after the split, I certainly wasn't looking for anyone new—how could I? I had to get my shit together, to figure out why I'd been repeating the same pattern over and over every time I was with someone. I was sad, and hurt, and confused. But a part of me also felt stronger, like I had finally taken a step toward respecting myself. I lay low for a while, but when I started up again with projects that brought me back into the orbit of music and dancing, and we were in full pre-production of the tour, I began spending more time with Beau.

Throughout that whole fall and into the New Year, as we got more and more into the heart of the show, I started moving past the hurt, and believing there could be something after that, believing that I could *dance again.*

From the very beginning, whenever I would stumble, whenever I was unsure, Beau would say, "You got this. You can do it." But he took it even further, telling me, "You don't need me. You don't need Benny. You don't need your mom. You don't need Marc. You are always going to be fine."

And I realized that before, my relationships were always tinged with fear: *Is this going to last forever? Will he want to stay with me? Is this going to work?* But now, I don't worry about the future. My idea of forever has been shattered. Now, I just want to be happy. I want to be in the moment and learn to be happy.

LOVING THE JOURNEY

About three weeks before the end of the tour, all of us were feeling it. We still loved doing the show, but all of the travel, the hotel rooms, the time zone changes, and being away from home took its toll on everyone. Doing such a high-energy show, night after night after night, meant that everyone was feeling tired and rundown. And I knew that when the

tour was finally finished, I wouldn't miss all that packing and unpacking, bundling the kids up to get on buses and planes at three a.m., waking up and wondering what country we were in . . .

But then, one night in the dressing room just before I was supposed to go onstage, a thought popped into my head: *You are about to make so many people happy tonight.* Where had that thought come from? I had no idea, but it made my heart swell with joy. And I realized what I *was* going to miss when the tour was over.

When I decided to take on this tour, I was still at a low point from the divorce. I felt like things in my life had gone wrong, and doing this show was going to be my effort to make something go right—by using the experiences I'd had and choosing to learn from those difficult times rather than running from them.

My one job was to go out there and make people happy every night, to help them jump and dance and sing along, to make their lives a little bit better. What a blessing! For years, I had been afraid to do a big tour like this one, but by the end of it, I felt like it had healed me. My original intention had been to share this message with the world, this thing that I had learned about loving yourself and overcoming adversity. I wanted to put it out there: *You will live. You will love. You will dance again. Ámate. Love Yourself.* I never expected it, but I wound up living my own affirmation, every single night. Life is kind of awesome that way; when you put things out there, they end up coming back to you.

ON THE MEND

Doing all those shows, and being embraced by the crowds, was a cathartic process that helped me heal. Benny could see it too, so one day toward the end of the tour he made a suggestion that he knew I wouldn't have been able to consider even just a few weeks earlier.

The last days of the tour were upon us, we had been talking about what we could do to make the final performance, in Puerto Rico, really special. By that point, we would have done more than seventy-five shows, and we both wanted to go out with a bang.

"What do you think about having Marc come perform a song with you at that final show?" he asked.

For a moment, I was speechless. My mind flew in two different directions: The professional side of me knew that doing a performance with Marc, who's a legend in Puerto Rico, would be amazing. People would go crazy, especially if we kept it a secret until his actual appearance.

I thought about that, thought about whether doing this would be like giving the spotlight to Marc on that *American Idol* finale, letting him have a moment that might have been mine. Was I falling into the same old pattern that I had spent months pulling myself out of? Would inviting him to sing with me be a step backward?

By now I had learned to listen to myself. And when I got quiet and listened to my heart, I really didn't believe it was. Asking Marc to join me onstage wasn't about reverting to old habits. It was about showing the world—and proving to myself—that not only did we make it through the pain, but we came out the other side even stronger. We came out of it in a healthy way, and we were moving on as friends and as parents to our children. I really believed that making this offer to Marc was about moving forward, not backward.

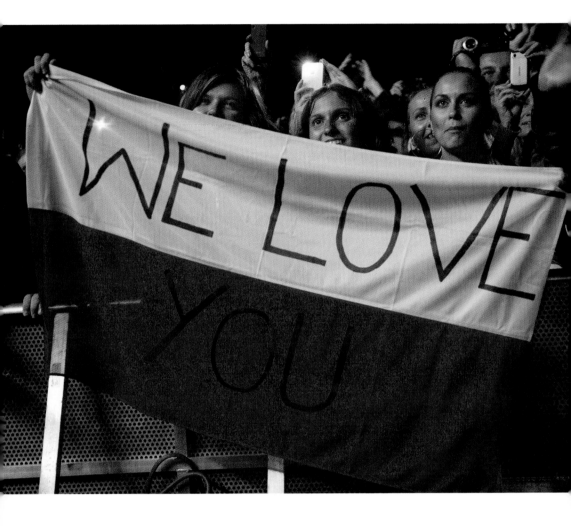

Life is kind of awesome that way. When you put things out there, they end up coming back to you.

I still had to call Marc. He's pretty picky about when he chooses to go onstage, and this performance would have that extra layer of prurient interest for people, so there was a good chance that he would immediately say no.

I called him up, and at first we talked about the kids for a little while. Then I said, "Listen, Benny had this idea for the last show of the tour . . ." I told him the last two shows were going to be in Puerto Rico, right before Christmas, and of course we needed to figure out when he was going to see the kids around Christmastime anyway . . . so . . . "I was thinking . . . it could be really beautiful . . . if . . . you came down . . . and did 'No Me Ames' with me in those last shows." Then we could figure out the holidays.

He didn't say anything, so I went on. "I think it would be amazing for the audience . . . I think they would love to see us together, knowing what we've been through, and that it could be a great message to everybody that we still support each other." I told him it had been a difficult time for me, and I knew it wasn't easy on him either, but that this could be good closure for us.

"Mm-hmm . . . okay," he said, and I could practically hear the wheels turning.

"We wouldn't announce that you were coming—it would be kind of a surprise for everybody," I said. "We'll make it really great."

He said, "Well, it's not a 'no,' but give me a day or two to think about it." I thought that was pretty reasonable, considering everything.

A few days later, he called back . . . It was a "Yes!" He would do it.

The day before the show, Marc flew down to Puerto Rico to rehearse with us. Marc had recorded *"No Me Ames"* with me on my first record, so we didn't need much rehearsal for the singing; we just needed to figure out the staging.

When Marc walked into the stage area, Max and Emme went running up to him, excited to see him. And a lot of the dancers made a point of coming to watch the sound check too, because they were big fans of Marc.

At one point, I looked over and saw Marc sitting on the floor with the kids. They were so happy to be with him; they were climbing all over him. At that moment, the band started playing the opening notes of *"No Me Ames,"* which was one of the first things Marc and I had ever done together, so we have a lot of memories associated with that song. The whole scene was so surreal. When those notes started floating out over the stage, I looked down at him, and he looked up at me and laughed.

"How the hell did all this happen?" he asked me. And I knew what he meant. He meant everything—all the crazy twists and turns our lives had taken since we first sang that song together. How did we end up recording this song all those years ago, and how did we not get together then? And then how did we wind up getting married years later, having kids, and then divorcing . . . and now how was he sitting here with our kids, looking up at me as this song played again? It was this lovely, bittersweet lifetime of moments, all summed up in that one question.

"I don't know," I said. And we laughed. But it was a heavy moment, and I think everyone there that day could feel it. The fact that we'd been through so much, I had invited him to come, and he was there to support me—it was a moment filled with every kind of emotion. Just like life is.

On the night of the show, I did something I rarely do—I decided to speak in Spanish to the crowd. I'm Puerto Rican, but I grew up in New York, so although I speak Spanish pretty well, it's not my first language. But I wanted to do it, to speak the language of the crowd, because I wanted this night to be magical for everyone:

"Estas son nuestras últimas actuaciones de the Dance Again tour. Esta gira ha sido un viaje increíble de música y amor. Y ha sido un honor y un placer terminarla aquí en Puerto Rico, donde hice mi primer concierto hace once años. Y como todos los grandes viajes de amor y música, incluso cuando se terminan, la música sigue..." ("These are our last performances of the Dance Again tour. This tour has been an amazing journey of music and love, and it has been an honor and a pleasure to end it here in Puerto Rico, where I did my first concert eleven years ago. And like all great journeys of love and music, even when the journey ends, the music goes on . . .")

With that, the band played the first few notes of *"No Me Ames,"* and I turned to face the back of the stage, where Marc was rising up slowly through the floor. As soon as his face was visible, the place erupted—the crowd went absolutely insane, everyone was screaming so much that the band actually had to stop playing. It was pandemonium, people yelling and crying and clapping . . . Marc took a little bow. And then we started the song.

Dime por qué lloras
De felicidad
Y por qué te ahogas,
Por la soledad
(Tell me why are you crying?
Because I'm happy
And why are you so choked up?
Because I'm lonely)

Singing with Marc felt like a perfect, beautiful closure to that part of my life. Things might not have worked out the way I had planned, but I was so proud of where we had come, especially after all that heartache. It was the perfect ending to those two years of turmoil and confusion and sadness, and ultimately, recovery. It was the perfect start to the rest of my life.

When we finished the song and ran offstage together, I had my arm around him, and as soon as we were in the back, he exclaimed, "That's what the fuck I'm *talking* about!" He was as happy and excited as I was. He gave me a big hug and said, "If you ever need anything . . ." His voice trailed off. We looked into each other's eyes.

"I know," I said.

He squeezed my hand, we both smiled . . . and off he went.

But the show wasn't over, of course. It was time for me to do a quick change and get out there, because now it was my time to *dance again*.

I WILL ALWAYS REMEMBER

The arena is completely dark. Suddenly, on the big screen above the stage, I appear like a black butterfly, with a black mask and the wind blowing through my hair. Quotes from different interviews I've done over the past year appear on the screen: *I still believe in love. It's still my biggest dream. You have to truly love yourself to be able to love another.* It's the encore of the show—the final song, the final message. I look out over the audience and say the words, "Always remember . . . You will live. You will love. You will *dance again*."

When I first thought of this mantra, I was doing the video for "Dance Again." I wanted people to really understand what the song meant to me. It was a declaration that I needed so much in my life at that moment, and that I know other people need in difficult moments of their own lives. I tried to think of the perfect line to put at the front of the video, a simple phrase that could help you get through any difficult moment . . . And then it came to me: I wasn't going to die, I was going to survive. Things were going to get better, I just had to hold on. I was going to live, I was going to love, and I was going to dance again . . . I just had to remember that.

And so that's what it was. After all, that was the theme that started it all. This is where we always wanted to end up. On that note.

My face disappears from the screen, replaced by the words: "*Ámate.* Love yourself."

The spotlight goes up on the stage, and I start to sing.

Only got just one life this I've learned, who cares what they're gonna say?
I wanna dance . . . and love . . . and dance . . . again.

Yes, I still believe in the fairy tale, but I want love in the right way. I want the kind of love that's truly possible only when you love yourself first. This is my favorite moment in the whole show—the moment when we get to the "Dance Again" chorus, where everybody in the whole place jumps up and down, waving their arms, singing at the top of their lungs, "I want to dance . . . and love . . . and dance . . . again!" At that moment, the elation in the arena is like a revival. It is transcendent.

In every city, every night we performed, this was the moment that made me feel it was all worth it. All the pain, all the regret, all the uncertainty had led to this, to sharing myself with all of these screaming, jumping, sweaty fans, all of us shouting this one big affirmation together.

And then, of course, when the dance break comes, the lights go low and art imitating life imitating art again . . . I'm dancing a sexy, fresh, totally revitalizing dance that reminds me, every time I do it, that life goes on and why I love to dance so much.

It's the perfect way to end the show—with a new beginning.

Love...

For me is a journey,

its not a destination.

I remain an
eternal optimist
about love

I want the fairytale,
its still my biggest dream.

You
must love yourself
to truly love another.

Always remember . . .

You will live. You will love.

You will *dance again*.

CONCLUSION

TRUE LOVE

IT WOULD BE easy to look back on those years leading up to the divorce and think, *Oh, this is a really sad story. That was so hard.* But I don't feel that way anymore. Now when I look back, I feel something completely different . . . pride. For so many years, when I was in situations that were bad for me, I was afraid to leave them. Then, somehow, I finally found that little speck of love inside myself that said, "Hey, you deserve better." And I actually did something about it, as scary as that was.

I'm proud that now I can make better choices for myself and for my kids. That finally, after forty years, I was able to understand what I was doing wrong. Proud that once I got okay with the fact that being just me was enough, I actually became a better version of myself—as a person and even as a performer. At first, I felt frustrated that it had taken me so long to figure it out. But then I ran across this quote from Charlie Chaplin:

> *As I began to love myself, I freed myself of anything that is no good for me—food, people, things, situations, and everything that drew me down and away from myself. At first I called this attitude a healthy egoism. Today I know it as* love of oneself.

That quote is from April 16, 1959—the day Charlie Chaplin turned seventy. So, I guess in some ways, I'm ahead of the game, right?

And yet . . . the truth is, I'm still a work in progress. I'm still learning. When you've been doing things a certain way for your whole life, you can't suddenly behave in a different way overnight. It takes time. You have to start practicing it, and little by little you keep practicing, and eventually it becomes second nature. We all second-guess ourselves, doubt our own instincts, and forget to love ourselves—especially women.

As women, we almost never give ourselves enough credit for what we're capable of, for what we endure and how giving we are. During the tour, I would look at all the amazing, beautiful women in the audience, and I wanted to pull them all into an embrace, to tell each one, *You're great. Trust yourself. Love yourself.* The emotion was overwhelming at times, especially in those countries where women aren't held in the same esteem as men. I wanted to open their hearts and pour the love right in.

Part of loving yourself is about forgiving yourself—which is something I've always struggled with. Being ambitious, being a perfectionist, means I've spent my life beating myself up for not being good enough, or for screwing something up. It took a long time, but I finally figured out that I wouldn't have half the instincts or insights I've had as an artist over the years if not for those screwups. It's the messy parts that make us human, so we should embrace them too —pat ourselves on the back for getting through them rather than being angry for having gotten into them in the first place. Because loving yourself is ultimately about self-acceptance, about embracing every part of who you are. And that's never just one thing. For example, when it comes to my music, I have never been about one thing: I can make a booty-bopping record that makes you want to dance all night and I can also create an emotional heartfelt ballad that makes you contemplate life and love in all its complexity. I've always been pop, but I've been hip-hop too, I've been R&B, I've been Latin, I've been ballads . . . and I feel very comfortable in every one of those places. Why limit myself? I realize that you have to be real, you have to be as honest as you can be and not worry about judgment or criticism. I have to accept all of that and I have to love all of that because that's what being a true artist is about: knowing yourself, accepting it all, and sharing it with others. And that's what I work on every day.

Even though I still have a ways to go, my family and friends tell me they can see the difference. Benny even jokes about it with me—if I disagree with him about something, or stand up for myself, he'll say, "Okay, okay, I get it. You're loving yourself!"

He teases me, but then he has moments where he'll say, "You know, Jennifer, you're like a different person now. You make different decisions; you don't stand for the injustices anymore." And he's right. I don't. I'm quicker to stand up for myself, to push back if someone is treating me in a way I

Sometimes you have to explore the darkness to get to the light and get back to who you are.

don't like. I've always pushed back if I see someone else being mistreated, but it took me decades to figure out how to push back for myself.

But as I've been reminded, a lot of people never figure it out at all. We all know someone who's had their hopes and dreams and belief in love destroyed because they couldn't figure out how to value themselves. "You did it," Benny says. "Even though it hurt so bad while you were doing it, you still did it."

My life now might not be how I always envisioned it, but that doesn't mean it isn't great. If it weren't for this tour, this time, these kids, that marriage, I would never be where I am today, which is the best place I've ever been in my life.

I found that same girl again. Sometimes you have to explore the darkness to get to the light and get back to who you are.

That's the whole message of the Dance Again tour, of course: We can survive anything, if we just keep on going.

This road of healing and rediscovery has been a long one, and it was much more difficult than anything I've ever done. It's taken me to some real emotional lows. But the view from the other side was worth the heartache.

Like Louise taught me, I keep dancing. I may not be getting all the steps right yet, but I'm dancing my heart out. I am the woman I've always wanted to be because for the first time I can truly say that yes, I love myself. That's the key. That's the greatest love of all, the one that matters most, the one that Max and Emme taught me all about.

That's TRUE LOVE.

ACKNOWLEDGMENTS

MUCH LIKE THE year I went on tour, writing this book has been another incredible journey—one that could have never happened without the love and support of so many people who have helped me along the way.

First off, I would like to thank my family: Mommy, Daddy, Leslie, and Lynda, thank you for supporting me all these years and for being the loving family you have always been. I could have never gotten to where I am without you and I love you so much. To my cousins Tania, Darci, and Tiana; and to my Titi Rose—thank you for being there every step of the way.

Thank you to Benny Medina, my manager and friend for over fifteen years who has been my partner in every new adventure I embark on and writing this book was no exception. Your wise words and comments made every page of this book even better and I am so grateful to have you in my life.

Thanks to Raymond Garcia, my publisher, for your dedication, enthusiasm, and unfaltering belief in this book, even when I had my doubts. Writing this book has been one of the most gratifying and enlightening experiences of my life, and I would have never done it if it hadn't been for you. Thanks to Andrea Montejo for your editorial support during our "booking" sessions and for helping me cut, paste, and rewrite until it felt just right. Thanks to everyone else at Penguin who helped make this book a reality: Jennifer Schuster for your editorial direction, Kim Suarez for photo editing, Matthias for the cover photo, Pauline Neuwirth for the beautiful interior design, and Anthony Ramondo for designing the cover.

Thank you to Marc Anthony, Leah, Elaine, Loren, Ana, Kevin, and all of my close friends for reading the first drafts of this book and giving me your precious feedback and comments. Thank you to my dear friend Ana Carballosa, to whom we owe the beautiful photos that truly bring this book to life.

Thanks to my personal team: Debbi Izzard, Day Ryan, my home team in LA and NY; my team at Nuyorican Productions, JLE, and the Medina Co.; Kevin Huvane and all of my agents at CAA; my attorneys; business partners; and of course to my loving fans . . . I appreciate you all.

And last, but not least, thanks to my beautiful babies, Max and Emme, for being the light of my life, the reason for everything I do, and for being exactly who you are. Mama loves you very much.

PERMISSIONS